An Animated Death in Burbank

An Animated Death in Burbank

MICHAEL JOENS

THOMAS DUNNE BOOKS
ST. MARTIN'S MINOTAUR
NEW YORK

THOMAS DUNNE BOOKS
An imprint of St. Martin's Press.

AN ANIMATED DEATH IN BURBANK. Copyright © 2004 by Michael Joens. All rights
reserved. Printed in the United States of America. No part of this book may be used
or reproduced in any manner whatsoever without written permission except in the
case of brief quotations embodied in critical articles or reviews. For information, address
St. Martin's Press, 175 Fifth Avenue, New York, N.Y. 10010.

www.minotaurbooks.com

Library of Congress Cataloging-in-Publication Data

Joens, Michael R.
    An animated death in Burbank : a detective Sandra Cameron mystery / Mike Joens.—
1st ed.
        p. cm.
    ISBN 0-312-30716-0
        1. Police—California—Los Angeles County—Fiction. 2. Burbank (Los Angeles
County, Calif.)—Fiction. 3. Policewomen—Fiction. 4. Cartoonists—Fiction. 5. Rich
people—Fiction. I. Title.

    PS3560.O246A85 2004
    813'.54—dc22

                                                                            2003058535

First Edition: January 2004

10   9   8   7   6   5   4   3   2   1

To my beautiful daughter, Shannon,
a river flowing with joy and blessing

Acknowledgments

My heartfelt thanks go to the following men and women for their valuable help in the making of this book: Deputy Sharon Falbisaner, Los Angeles County Sheriff's Department (retired); Detective Dixon "Bud" Tew, LAPD (retired); Detective Matthew Miranda, Burbank PD; Captain Joseph Valento, Burbank PD (retired); Captain John Nare, Burbank Fire Department; and Dr. Gary F. Hathaway, M.D. Any errors in police or EMT protocol or procedure are solely mine.

I would also like to thank my agent, Natasha Kern, for her investment of time, energy, insights, and moral support.

Many thanks to Marcia Markland and the kind folks at St. Martin's Press for believing in this work.

An Animated Death in Burbank

Chapter One

Detective Sergeant Tom Rigby of the Burbank Police Department pushed through the crowd of curious onlookers and showed his badge to one of the officers guarding the crime scene. The officer glanced at the badge and nodded perfunctorily as he held out his arm to restrain an eager gawker, whose nose was lifted to the possible scent of death.

Tom slipped under the yellow cordon tape and greeted his partner, Detective Dan Bolt, who had come down from the house to meet him. They started up the walkway to the tile-and-stucco bungalow tucked into the slope of the San Gabriels off Glen Oaks Boulevard. A light midmorning breeze carried with it the pungent scent of the junipers that provided a tangled screen along the property lines. Tom hated the smell of junipers.

Dan tossed a handful of beer nuts into his mouth. "Where've you been?" he asked.

"Busy. Stenton been here yet?"

"Left just."

"What've we got?"

"Good morning to you, too, Tommy." Dan flipped through his notebook, crunching on the beer nuts, a practice that annoyed Tom, but then, he was already annoyed this morning. He had reason to be. Dan read, "'Parker Stewart. White, male.' Neighbors describe him as a Hollywood type . . . throws wild parties. Quiet otherwise. Had a live-in for a while but she apparently moved out a couple of weeks ago."

"Any ID on the woman?"

"No. Wait'll you see this place, Tom. It's a regular Looney Tunes."

"Who called it in?"

"Latina woman. Didn't give a name. Made the call from a phone booth in Sunland at . . . Let's see. . . . Dispatch log puts it nine thirty-seven this morning." He tucked his notebook back into his coat pocket. "The FETs are dusting it. Probably got a million prints on it by now."

Tom looked at the house. "What do you make of it?"

"Suicide, likely. Twenty-five caliber through the noodle. Beretta Minx."

"What's that?"

"Beretta Minx," Dan repeated. "Lady's gun. Right through the noodle."

"Right."

"He was a doper, Tom. Found a dime bag of coke . . . all the fixings."

Tom thought about it a moment . . . took the score of front steps of the residence two at a time and entered the arched portico entrance of the small Spanish-style residence that probably dated back to the 1930s.

He paused in the foyer to sign in with the forensics officer. A sweep of his eyes took in the immediate surroundings: dining room and adjoining kitchen to his left; living room, hallway, and bedrooms off to his right. His eyes widened. The walls of the living room were covered with framed posters of cartoon characters, old heroes of the big screen like Daffy Duck, Porky Pig, Pinocchio. A horizontal celluloid featuring the characters of *Sleeping Beauty* hung over the sofa against the west wall. The other three walls were covered by floor-to-ceiling bookshelves, two crowded with all manner of toys and cartoon action figures dating back, Tom guessed, to the late 1920s. The third wall of shelves was stacked with art books and comic books. It seemed he had entered the fantasy world of some child. He smelled death.

Dan huffed through the doorway and stood beside him. "I told you it was Looney Tunes, Tom. You ever see anything like it?"

Tom noted the near-chaos of field evidence technicians in white lab coats moving from room to room, bagging, tagging, dusting, vacuuming, snapping photographs. "Anybody think to get shots of the carpet for footprints?"

Dan shrugged. "Sure. Look at all this stuff." He fed himself another handful of beer nuts. One fell to the floor. He picked it up, wiped it on his coat, and popped it into his mouth with a grin. "Five-second rule."

Tom shook his head. "Where's the dead man?"

"In the back room. That way." Dan pointed to the right. "The coroner is with the body now."

Tom and Dan crossed the living room and went down a narrow hallway. Black-and-white photos covered the walls. Landscapes. They squeezed past a couple of white lab coats, exchanging nods of greeting, turned left into a spacious back bedroom, and paused just inside the door.

"Over there, Tom." They walked across the room.

The dead man was a twisted wreck on the floor beside a large, L-shaped computer desk in the far left corner of the room. Phil Carlton was hunched over the corpse, like some white-coated vulture picking over a recent find. Balding, blue eyes, five-tenish, slight of build—the coroner, not the dead man.

The dead man lay on his right side, belly swollen out beneath an old tie-dyed T-shirt—legs twisted in the base workings of a swivel chair—right arm stretched behind the back, palm upward, fingers curled clawlike, the left arm thrust forward, as if the corpse were attempting to swim the sidestroke.

"There's a Kodak moment for you," Dan said, munching another handful of beer nuts.

Tom's gaze went to the dried scab of blood at the left temple, saw where the blood had leaked out of the tiny bullet hole, collected in the eye socket and nose bridge. "What've we got, Phil?"

The coroner, just slipping a bag over the dead left hand, looked up from his work. "Hey, Tom. Whaddaya know?"

Tom nodded, repeated the question.

Carlton grinned. "What we have here is a dead man."

Tom didn't laugh.

"Oh, you want specifics? Sure, Tom." Carlton stopped what he was doing, began a clinical recitation. "Potassium chlorate residue on the victim's left hand. Powder burns and tattooing on the skin of the left temple. Hairs scorched around the entry wound . . ."

Tom noted the diamond stud in the left earlobe, long red hair pulled back into a scraggly ponytail, as Carlton described in detail the probable route the bullet had taken into the brain.

". . . Pistol discharged at a very close range. An inch or two, maybe. All in all, it's got the makings of a suicide, I'd guess. That's off the record, of course."

Tom found himself staring at the ample buttocks of the dead man, showing over the faded blue jeans. He looked at the grisly face, right cheek and nose pressed into the carpet, lips pulled back from clenched teeth in a feral snarl. The visible left eye, half-shut, stared dully at the desk leg. Lovely. "Suicide, huh?"

Carlton finished bagging the hand and secured it with a rubber band. "It's consistent with the evidence so far. There's the probable culprit," he said, indicating a tiny nickel-plated automatic, bagged, on the desk next to the computer. The magazine had been extracted and bagged separately. Likewise the spent casing. Sitting next to the Mickey Mouse telephone on the desk return, the gun looked like another toy.

"Got it marked there," Dan said, indicating the adhesive tape on the carpet, about a yard from the victim's left hand.

"Any ID on the piece?"

"No. Low serial numbers. Pre-'68."

Tom grunted. In the wake of the assassinations of the Reverend Dr. Martin Luther King, Jr., and Senator Robert F. Kennedy, the Gun Control Act of 1968 had been passed, legislation that forced gun store owners to keep tighter records of handgun sales. Prior to the Gun Act, records of serial numbers were sketchy at best, sometimes ignored altogether. A pre-'68 meant that they would, most likely, be unable to connect the serial numbers of the Beretta with the gun's original owner. Tom looked from the Beretta back to the dark scab of blood at the temple. "No exit wound, you say?"

"No," Carlton said. "Bullet might've fragmented inside the skull cavity. Maybe used a hollow-point." He chuckled. "Did the job, though."

It certainly had. Tom looked at the dead man's left hand, as if seeing it for the first time. "Southpaw, huh?"

"It appears so, Tom." Carlton was fitting a baggie over the dead man's bare right foot. Tom noticed the dirty toenails. "Got a pretty fair callus on the inside middle finger," Carlton went on. "Nothing on the right hand."

Tom jotted in his notebook that the victim had apparently fired the weapon with his left hand, flipped the page, and began a sketch of the body. He was a lousy artist, but then, he wasn't entering any contests—*Draw Stiffy: Win an art scholarship!* "Where was the Beretta?"

"I told you," Dan said, indicating the tape. "You had your coffee yet, Tommy?"

Tom ignored the remark. "Guesses on the time of death?"

The coroner shrugged. "From the amount of rigor—more than twelve hours, less than thirty-six. Yesterday sometime. Maybe late in the afternoon, early evening. We'll tie it down later."

Tom wrote in his notebook: *Sunday afternoon. Late. March 31*— a date he'd remember for a long time.

"Got a cut on the inside lip," Carlton said, folding the lip back to better examine it. "Lower lip . . . left side. Looks like his tooth made the cut."

"Somebody pop him?" Tom asked.

Carlton examined the outer lip. "Might've. Happened a couple of days ago, by the look of it."

Tom turned to his partner. "He leave a note?"

"Check it out." Dan nudged the computer mouse with the end of his ballpoint pen and brought the computer out of its sleep mode. Across the monitor screen, in 36-point Helvetica Bold, were the words: THAT'S ALL, FOLKS!

Funny man. Funny dead man. Tom grunted. Arrayed across the desktop was a Macintosh computer with a Sony monitor, an Epson printer, scanner, fax machine, and the Mickey Mouse telephone.

He glanced around the room, a close copy of the one he had just come from. Covering the walls were framed cartoon posters of Daffy Duck, Bugs Bunny, Sylvester and Tweety, Batman, some Japanese robot monsters, a collage of others. Some were color prints; others were painted on celluloid sheets and mounted against painted backgrounds; others, old pencil drawings on paper, brown with age. More floor-to-ceiling bookshelves crammed with toys and cartoon action figures; more stacks of comic books. A gold Academy Award statuette stood on a little perch by itself. "I want those dusted."

"Already on it, Tom," Dan said.

An easy chair and lamp in the center of the room faced a 56-inch Panasonic high-definition television in the inside right corner as you came into the room. At the edge of a small, round coffee table in front of the chair was a 12- by 12-inch mirror, a dime bag of coke, opened, and a single-bladed razor. "Somebody taking care of that?" Tom asked.

"I'll get somebody on it," Dan said, and left the room.

"I'd like a toxicology report ASAP," Tom said to Carlton.

"You'll have it as soon as I have it."

Tom picked up a cellophane-encased piece of paper from the computer desk. On the paper was a pencil drawing of a heroic-looking rabbit in a spacesuit. At the bottom of the page were three holes: two $\frac{1}{2}$-inch–long rectangular holes, one on either side of a circular one, about the size of a small pea. He noted the number 5 in the lower left-hand corner of the page, above it was what looked like a chart of some kind, drawn in pencil: a single vertical line cut by four horizontal lines. There were additional numbers beside the horizontal lines of the chart—the numbers 1, 3, and 5 . . . 1 and 5 circled. Beneath the chart were the initials *P.S.* "What's this?"

"I think they found it in the scanner," Carlton said.

One of the FETs, a tall, rawboned man named Hal Peters, entered the room ahead of Dan. "It was flattened against the lid there when I opened it. Didn't see it at first. Vacuum suction held it, I guess. How're you doing, Tom?" he asked on his way over to the coke fixings.

Tom shrugged, lifted the scanner lid, a 14- by 20-inch rubber-lined surface, and looked at the drawing. He wasn't in the mood for chitchat. "Dead man was an artist of some kind, huh?"

"An animator," Dan said. "Check out the desk."

"I want the computer impounded," Tom said as he stepped over to the desk.

"You got it," Peters said.

The animator's desk was separated from the computer desk by a curtainless window open to the backyard. Late-morning light streamed into the room and threw a trapezoid of light over the dull blue carpet. Set into the desktop was a round, metal-framed disk, maybe two feet in diameter, with a rectangular piece of frosted glass, about 14-by-20, cut into the disk. A window. Adjustable metal bars, with white-painted calibration ticks on them, went across the top and bottom of the disk and framed the glass. There were $\frac{1}{4}$-inch–high metal pegs protruding from each bar, a round peg with horizontal pegs on either side.

"Animation disk," Dan said. "Animators draw on 'em—the glass part. A light turns on inside so you can see through your drawings."

Tom looked at him.

"My niece," Dan said. "She's taking classes at Cal Arts. She's pretty good, I hear. Must get it from my sister. I can't draw a straight line with a ruler."

Tom allowed a smile. Dan—a year his senior at thirty-four—had always reminded him of a load of stones piled up in a six foot heap. Today, a stone heap wearing an ill-fitting beige sports coat and dark brown trousers. Food stains on the paisley tie and pale yellow shirt. They had been partners on the force for three years; however, their friendship extended back to Burroughs High, where quarterback Rigby and offensive tackle Bolt had led the varsity squad to a division championship. Dan was solid, loyal. A wall of steel and guts between the enemy and himself.

"Pretty fancy rig, huh?" Dan said.

Tom followed his gaze to the desk. A stack of horizontal wood shelves, fourteen inches deep, a space of six inches between each shelf, ran about four feet over the middle section of the desk. They were empty, save a ream of blank hole-punched paper on the bottom shelf. A wooden tower, two feet high with swing-out trays, full of artist's tools, brushes, pencils, color markers, and erasers, stood to the left of the desk.

"That's a taboret," Dan said.

"Taboret, huh?" Tom had seen a setup like it at Disney World, when he and Carolyn visited her parents in Orlando, years ago. They had taken the animation tour, stood behind a glass window and watched animators at work on a Roger Rabbit cartoon. It had reminded him of a zoo, and he made a joke—"Animators in their habitat." Carolyn had laughed.

Tom looked out the bare window at the trees and shrubs on the hill that rose off the low brick retaining wall, beyond a swimming pool and spa. His mind made the calculation back over the weeks and days and finally the night they had made love on the boat. They had sailed to Catalina to celebrate their fifth wedding anniversary. It was one of those perfect Southern California nights, warm with just a hint of a cooling breeze that gently rocked the 42-foot sailboat against its moorings. Almost zero humidity. They'd eaten a meal of broiled red snapper and stir-fried vegetables and eased it down with a bottle of chilled Chablis. Then, as the lights and stars of Avalon danced a wild choreography over the harbor, they reconsummated their vows, then slipped over the edge of the boat into the cool water for a midnight swim. Tom felt an ache deep in his chest. That was the night. Had to be.

"What's eating you, Tommy?"

Tom looked at Dan then down at the drawing in his hand, at the three holes at the bottom. "Nothing," he said quietly. He placed the drawing over the animator's disk. They aligned perfectly with the three metal pegs. "This the only drawing they found?"

"The only one by the computer," Dan said. "Are you gonna tell me, or do I have to guess?"

"What's this number here?" Tom said, indicating the number 5 at the bottom corner of the drawing.

"Drawing number five, I guess."

"No other drawings?"

"None by the computer. There are stacks in the file cabinet." Dan opened one of the wooden files to the right of the desk, again using his ballpoint pen. He extracted a manila folder of drawings with a handkerchief and handed it to Tom. "What'd she do now?"

Tom ignored him, thumbed through the drawings: a coiled cartoon snake, striking and biting a bear on the rear end, each drawing advancing the action toward the bite and the comedic reaction of the bear.

"Pretty funny," Dan chuckled. He smoothed a hand over his ample stomach then pointed. "See, there. . . . Each of the drawings is numbered. Got to be some kind of animation sequence."

Each drawing was numbered like the one found in the scanner, and every few drawings there was the little chart of numbers off to the side. The initials *P.S.* were beneath each of the charts. *Parker Stewart,* Tom guessed. "No rabbits in space suits?"

Dan shrugged. "None in the file cabinet."

"We're finished with the preliminaries, Tom," Carlton said. "Anything you want to look at before we haul the body down to the icebox?"

Tom glanced at the dead man, the position of the body outlined with masking tape. Neat. Bullet hole through the noodle. *That's all, folks!* "No, you can have him, Phil."

Tom handed the folder back to his partner, took a single sheet of animation paper and went over to the scanner. He raised the lid and placed the paper flat on the glass surface, aligned the left edge and lower left corner against the edge of the scanner, then closed the lid. He waited a moment.

When he raised the lid the drawing was stuck to the rubber-lined underside of the lid. Tom wrinkled his forehead in thought. "Let's check out the other rooms, Dan."

Burbank Police Department. 4:30 P.M.

Tom sat at his desk brooding over photographs of the crime scene he'd just received from one of the photo-lab boys. He studied each of the rooms, the walls of cartoon characters . . . finally, the body of the deceased, Parker Stewart. They were mere photographs now. Whatever intimacy there had been at the scene was gone. It was like looking at proofs for a magazine spread.

Struggling to focus, he rubbed his eyes, glanced around the office he shared with Dan. The office was small, barely large enough to accommodate their desks, a far cry from the airy squad room of the old building on Olive and Third. Reminded him of an insurance office. The front edge of his desk abutted the front of Dan's desk, so that sitting in their chairs they faced each other. A real treat. The desks were pushed against the left wall as someone entered the office, Tom's first. Black-and-white photos and notes were pinned to a bulletin board on the opposite wall. Different case. Dan was poring over Stewart's records, his nose sweeping six inches above the desktop, bald spot showing on the top of his head. His "searchlight," he called it. He was munching beer nuts. Tom hated the smell. Beer nuts and death.

A glint of light caught Tom's eye to the left of his computer. Framed in silver, the happy couple smiled out at the world, a world full of hope and tomorrows full of hope. Full of love. He dropped the photographs of the crime scene on his desk, reached for the wedding picture and gazed at her face.

He felt dead inside, a cold emptiness in the hollow of his chest. Dead. That's what she had told him when she'd gotten back from her business trip. It was dead between them, and with the baby coming, how it had complicated things. He couldn't stop thinking about the baby. But he knew he couldn't allow himself that luxury. Not now. He was a cop. He had work to do. He looked at her face one more time, felt it stir in his breast—the ache—then nothing. Dead.

He shook his head, folded the black felt stand against the back of the silver frame, placed it in the bottom drawer of his desk, face-down, and closed the drawer. When he looked up, Dan was staring across the desks at him. They looked at each other for a moment. Partners. Best friends. Each had put his life on the line for the other more than once. But right now he wasn't in the mood for playing Guess What I'm Thinking, when Dan knew good and well what he was thinking. Cops who spent most of their waking hours together, as they had done, could tell what the other one was thinking before he even thought it. They were closer than most married couples. Maybe that's what did it. Maybe he'd sacrificed intimacy at home for his partner at work. Used it up. Maybe.

Dan was still staring at him.

"What?" Tom asked, knowing full well *"what."*

Dan shrugged his shoulders with a sad smile. *I'm with you, pal.* "Nothing," he said and went back to work.

Tom cleared his mind, picked up the crime-scene photos and looked at each one carefully. Something was there. He felt it. A story to be told. A clue. *What?* He forced himself to concentrate. He looked up at the sound of approaching footsteps.

Lieutenant Joe Stenton, a serious-faced black man built like a middle linebacker, strode into their office and tossed a sheaf of papers onto Tom's desk. Stenton was a fine-looking man—square jaw, short-cropped hair, broad shoulders, narrow waist, his dark eyes burning with the focused devotion to duty of one recently promoted. Wearing a pinstriped, white, long-sleeved shirt, navy silk tie with tiny white dots sprinkled over it, dark gray trousers, and shiny brown loafers with tassels, he might have looked like an up-and-comer out of a *Wall Street Journal* spread—except for the .357 Smith on his hip.

"Here are the officers' reports from the crime scene, fellahs," he said. "Been over them. Not much here."

"Did you hear that, *fellahs*?" Dan said. "It just goes to show you the brass knows what they're doing, promoting a mind like that. Why, we wouldn't've come to that conclusion in a million years."

Stenton shot Dan a look, then, seeing Dan's hands clasped behind his head, the wide grin, allowed a quick smile. "Okay, Dan." He looked at Tom, his game face on again. "Looks like a suicide to me, but see what you come up with."

"The voice of command," Dan said, still grinning. "Hey, Joe? Did anyone tell you you have shoulders a man could fall in love with?" He pulled up his shirtsleeve and showed his arm to Tom. "Look, I've got goosebumps."

Stenton shook his head, turned at the door, and looked back. "You're gonna go out and see the mother, right? Don't want her to hear it on the six o'clock news."

"Already took care of it," Dan said. "She's in a nursing home off San Fernando. Alzheimer's. Doesn't even know she has a son."

"No other family?"

Tom shook his head.

"Okay." Stenton walked down the hall toward his office.

Tom read through the reports. Joe was right. Not much to go on. According to the neighbors, Parker Stewart kept pretty much to himself, occasionally threw wild "Hollywood" parties—loud music, alcohol and drugs, people naked in the Jacuzzi. This bit of information came from the neighbor whose upstairs bedroom window overlooked Stewart's backyard.

A maid came in once a week: Latina. No name. One neighbor swore she came on Mondays, another on Tuesdays. Both women and men visited the deceased. Before he was deceased he was a popular guy. At least two of the neighbors questioned believed there was some shady business going on. Drug deals, they thought. There was nothing in the reports to indicate why Parker Stewart might have wanted to kill himself.

Dan blew out a low whistle. "I guess we can rule out bankruptcy as a motive." Dan had the dead man's financial statements spread out over his desktop. "Get a load of this, Tommy. Guy must've been worth half a million . . . maybe more."

"Who was his employer?"

"Let's see. . . ." Dan dug out several payroll stubs from a cardboard box. "Here we go—Empire Films. Toluca Lake. Gross, forty-eight hundred a week. Can you beat that?" He shook his head, opened the checkbook. "Here's something. Up till about three weeks ago, he deposited the net every week."

"Nothing after that?"

Dan thumbed forward in the checkbook. "Nope. Checks going out, nothing coming in."

"Any uncashed checks lying around?"

"None."

Tom thought about it. "Might be something. What kind of bills?"

"A couple here for the nursing home. Other than that, the usual. Utilities . . . phone . . . mortgage . . ." Dan looked up. "Six hundred and fifty bucks. Who has a mortgage of six hundred and fifty bucks? I pay eighteen hundred for a crummy three-bedroom fixer-upper."

"Chump change for a man of means like you."

" 'Man of means.' " Dan's "searchlight" was showing again. "Wait a minute, here's something. Every week he paid fifty bucks to a Maria Gonzales."

"Cleaning lady," Tom said. "Neighbors said a cleaning lady came in once a week."

"That would square with the Latina caller, wouldn't it?"

"Could. Any line on her?"

"Nope. You have his phone book?"

Tom tossed it onto Dan's desk.

Dan thumbed through it. "Here we go, Maria Gonzales." He dialed the number and waited. No one picked up.

He disconnected and dialed another number. "Hey, Martinez—Dan Bolt. . . . No I'm not calling for Dodgers tickets. You got any, though? How much? *Where?* You're nuts. Listen, Martinez, I need a cross-reference on a Maria Gonzales. No, I'm not kidding. . . . Maria Gonzales. Probably one of your cousins." He gave Martinez the number, hung up the phone, and looked at Tom. "What a crook. Wants twenty bucks for a couple of nose-bleeders."

Tom was looking down at photographs, struggling to concentrate. He felt Dan's eyes on him.

"Whatever it is, Tom, you can't keep it bottled up."

Tom ignored him. "Why would the cleaning lady call it in from outside the house and not give her name?"

"Beats me. What about the live-in? Maybe she was Mexican."

Tom consulted one of the officer's reports. Three eyewitnesses had described the live-in with equal authority as being around twenty-five, thirty-five, and fortyish. She stood anywhere from five foot four, to five foot eleven. Her hair was alternately mousy-blonde or auburn, cut short or medium-length. Hadn't been seen for about a week to a month. The only consistency was that she was white and probably a woman.

"That's a start," Dan said. "Anyone happen to catch a name?"

"No."

"Figures."

They thought about it for a few moments. "The cleaning lady made the call," Tom said.

"Okay, let's see how it flows."

"She comes in Monday around nine or so to clean the house. That squares with the report. She discovers her employer staring at the carpet, but instead of calling it in, she leaves. She's afraid of something. Her conscience gets the best of her, so she calls it in from a public phone."

"Without giving her name. Why?"

"Maybe she's an illegal," Tom said. "Maybe she's got a rap sheet. Who knows? Let's hear the tape again."

They listened to the 911 tape. The caller, a woman with a heavy Spanish accent, reported a dead man in Stewart's house, gave his name and address. Did not identify herself.

"Sounds pretty scared," Dan said.

Tom nodded. *Why?* He gathered up the photos, put them into a manila envelope, and stared across the room at an imaginary spot on the wall. After a while he said, "She killed him, Dan."

Dan looked at him. "What are you talking about? Who killed who?"

"Carolyn. She killed our baby. They said it was a boy." He opened his desk drawer and put the manila envelope inside. "She had him aborted. He was twelve weeks old."

Dan shook his head slowly. "Man, I'm sorry, Tom."

Chapter Two

Tom slept fitfully. When he awoke in the morning, he showered and shaved, then put on his faded blue jeans, striped oxford shirt and tie, combed his hair, and grabbed his sports coat. He locked the apartment behind him; he wished he could do the same with his feelings. The morning was bright and cloudless, maybe sixty-five degrees. The smell of star jasmine everywhere. He liked the smell of jasmine. April in Southern California. It helped.

Tom parked his Ford Bronco in the basement parking lot of the Burbank Police Department, walked the three flights up the back stairs, and down the wide, carpeted hallway toward the Bureau of Detectives.

Dan was sitting at his desk going over what appeared to be Parker Stewart's phone records when Tom entered the office. Two banana peels, an empty bag of beer nuts, Hostess Twinkie wrappers, and a cup of coffee cluttered Dan's desk. Breakfast. Tom hung his jacket up on the rack behind the door.

Dan looked at him. "Look what the cat's drug in."

Tom slid into his chair, opened the file drawer, and pulled out the folder on Parker Stewart. "Any word on the cleaning lady yet?"

"I've got Martinez working on it," Dan said. "He says a Ramirez family lives at the address of the phone number—claim they've never heard of a Maria Gonzales."

Tom glanced over the crime photos. "What else you got?"

Dan ran his finger down the list to the places he had yellow-highlighted. "Couple of numbers pulled some heavy traffic last week. Stewart made several calls to Empire Films, where he was employed."

Tom remembered. "What else?"

"A couple made to Panda Productions. Let's see. . . . Yeah, they're in Burbank. That new building up the street. I called earlier, got the duty guard. Only one there. Cartoonists have bankers' hours, I guess."

Lieutenant Stenton walked up the hall from his office, sporting his usual sartorial dapperness. "You have an appointment with the ME at ten o'clock," he said. "The Stewart case. Either of you fellahs catch the Channel Three news last night?"

Dan nodded.

Tom shook his head. "I was out on the boat."

"Take a look at this." Stenton tossed Tom a videocassette.

"What is it?"

Stenton grinned. "You were especially wooden."

Dan waited until Stenton was gone, looked at Tom. "You okay, Tommy? I mean about yesterday."

"Shut up."

"The boat help?"

"Some." Tom looked at the cassette. "Wooden, huh?"

Dan nodded. "A two-by-four."

Tom went over to the briefing room and turned on the VHS player. He popped the cassette into the slot, waited for the linkage mechanisms to lock and load, then hit PLAY. Moments later, he was treated to the tail end of a Dial soap commercial, then the ACN Channel 3 News ID faded up with the familiar station bumper. Anchorwoman Vickie Trumbo, a pretty brunette out of the Elizabeth Hurley mold, greeted the camera with a dazzling smile. "You may not know his face or remember his name, but you may well be one of his biggest fans," she began. A recent photo of Parker Stewart appeared in the upper right corner of the television screen.

"Creator of the hugely successful cartoon series *Buck and Wing,* and the hilarious, socially minded *Punching Judy,* Parker Stewart was found dead this morning in his Burbank home, where—according to sources—he had apparently taken his own life. Earlier today I was at the scene and spoke with Sergeant Rigby of the Burbank Police Department."

The scene changed abruptly to Tom in front of Stewart's house, Trumbo asking if he would give a statement concerning the case. The camera zoomed in on his face.

Tom fast-forwarded through the interview that he knew gave nothing of the details of the case, other than there was a possibility the deceased had taken his own life. Trumbo had asked him if there was any suspicion of foul play, hinting at murder. He replied that, so far, there was no evidence of any such thing.

He hit the PLAY button when he saw the scriggling images of the interview change back to the newsroom. "He was considered by many to be an artistic genius," Trumbo continued. "A man whose cartoon look at the world made us laugh, and while we were laughing he revealed a side of ourselves we perhaps didn't know existed. We go now to a short clip of an interview with Stewart made twenty-five years ago, after he won the Academy Award for one of his student films."

The footage was grainy and dark as the camera pushed into the room Tom immediately recognized as the one he'd been in the day before. "You might think you are entering the wonderland of a child," a voice—not unlike Rex Allen's of the old Disney nature films—began as the camera panned over shelves of toys and cartoon posters, finally settling on the gold Oscar statuette displayed on the animation desk beside the young animator. Stewart was thinner, had a full head of long hair pulled back into a ponytail. "But it is really the studio of Parker Stewart, the brilliant young animator who has just won the Academy Award for Best Animated Short Subject."

Drawing with his left hand, Tom noted.

The unseen interviewer asked, "May we come into your studio and watch what you do for a while, Mr. Stewart?"

The young Stewart turned to the camera and smiled. "Why not?" *It's your nickel,* he did not say. He glanced into the camera then resumed drawing on a small stack of drawings, hole-punched and secured by the metal pegbar at the base of the animation disk. Same desk.

"I see that you're working on a cartoon."

Stewart looked quickly at the interviewer as though he'd just said, *I hear the earth is round,* then resumed drawing. "It's just a little something," he said, a hint of irony in his voice.

"It must be wonderful to have such a creative mind. Such talent."

Stewart, seemingly oblivious, continued drawing.

"You work on several drawings at the same time," the interviewer observed. The camera pushed in on the drawings. "It seems a strange way to draw."

Stewart shrugged. "It helps to get a sense of the movement." He flipped several drawings he was holding between the fingers of his right hand, back and forth, studying the drawings as they rolled past his eyes. He added details to the top drawing, then flipped the lower drawings back and forth, again studying them. He added more detail to the drawing on top. "These are the extreme animation poses, or the keys. Later I'll add the inbees."

"Inbees?"

"In-betweens. The drawings that go *in between* the keys." Stewart chuckled. "To smooth out the action."

"It looks pretty smooth now."

"The eye is very forgiving," Stewart said. "It sees what isn't there, fills in the flow of action to give an illusion of motion." The camera cut in close over his shoulder to show Stewart's left hand flipping the drawings back and forth. In the scene a little girl in leotards and cape socked a bad guy on the nose. The drawings showed the windup and the punch, the crook flying up out of his pants and shoes.

"It's like a kinetoscope," the interviewer observed.

"Same principle."

The interviewer chuckled, a bit patronizingly. "Is this a scene from your next film?"

If it was, Stewart gave no indication as he continued drawing, flipping pages.

"For next year's Academy Award perhaps?" the interviewer added, a wink in his tone. The camera panned over to Oscar, gleaming in the sun, then back to the young animator.

Stewart shrugged. "Who knows?" Stewart was sick of the interviewer, Tom saw.

"Why so evasive?"

The camera pulled back to include the head and upper torso of the young animator, who turned to the camera and said, with a stick-it-in-your-ear grin, "If I told you about it, you might steal it, mightn't you?"

"Steal it?" The interviewer seemed incredulous. "Why would I want to steal it?"

"Look at all the [*word bleeped*] out there," Stewart said, his grin turning down at the corners. "Everybody copying everybody else's [*word bleeped*], waiting to see what [*word bleeped*] sells, then everybody running off carbon copies of the [*word bleeped*]." He laughed. "An original idea would die of loneliness in this town."

The interviewer chuckled nervously. "You're very passionate about it."

Stewart grunted. "Passionate?" Then with a wry smile he said, "It's all about ideas, isn't it? You got an idea and everybody's your pal." He grinned at the unseen interviewer, winked at the camera.

The film clip over, the scene returned to Vicky Trumbo who segued to other news. *Must* have been a slow news night, Tom thought; the death of a cartoon director decades past his prime wouldn't warrant the coverage otherwise.

Tom hit the OFF button, rewound the tape to the Stewart interview and viewed it again. There were fewer toys on the shelves, not quite as many framed cartoon posters. There was no computer desk, no computer, no scanner, no fax machine. In their place were an armchair, side table, and lamp with the Mickey Mouse telephone and a rack of magazines. He watched Stewart drawing at his desk, listened to his brief lesson on animation, listening for anything that might give insight into the personality and character of the man. The kid seemed self-assured, full of himself. Cocky. He was going to change the animation world. He did, to a degree, but that was back in the early 1980s, wasn't it?

Tom turned off the video player. A brilliant young animator, a meteoric rise to stardom, then a fall to relative obscurity. Motive for suicide? Sure. Motive for murder? Five hundred grand wasn't a bad start. He went back to his desk, got on the Internet and typed EMPIRE FILMS into his search-engine window.

● ●   ● ●

Tom slid into the passenger seat of the unmarked sedan and stared out the window. Dan headed north on the Harbor Freeway, out of Los Angeles into the San Fernando Valley. Dan was as quiet as Tom felt, though he had no idea if the reason was the same. They went under the series of old tunnels, took the connector ramp to the Golden State Freeway.

"What'd that give us?" Dan asked.

Tom continued staring out the window, the stench of formalin clinging to the insides of his nostrils. He hated the smell, formalin and death.

"Time of death, I suppose," Dan answered himself. "Confirms the suicide." He hit the accelerator, crossed three lanes of freeway traffic before settling in the second lane. "That cut in his mouth has me wondering, though. What do you make of that, Tommy?"

"Hmmm?"

"Somebody pops him the day before he offs himself. Curious, don't you think?"

"Best take Hollywood Way," Tom said. "Turn right on Riverside."

"I know how to get to Toluca Lake." Burbank was coming up on the east side of the freeway, the Verdugo Mountains, green after the winter rains, dark against the pale sky. "You hungry, Tommy?"

Tom was looking out the window at nothing, feeling a hunger in him that he could not define, did not want to define. "No."

Twenty minutes later they drove through Toluca Lake. A charming strip of restaurants and boutiques nestled against the foothills of the Santa Monica Mountains, it was a favorite lunching stop for industry people and tourists. Turning off Riverside, they drove past the old Bob's Big Boy then into the parking lot of Empire Films, three blocks ahead on the right.

"Always wanted to come here," Dan said, looking up at the ten-foot-high block letters spelling out the name EMPIRE FILMS. "Always loved cartoons. Ever since I was a kid."

Tom said nothing.

"I'm not kidding, Tommy. I'm what you might call a cartoon nut."

Tom looked at him levelly. *'Nuff said.*

The building was an old four-story brick-and-stucco with rows of small horizontal windows on each of the floors. It looked as if it had been built back in the 1930s; a building well past its prime, tired, worn out, and sad looking. It seemed out of place next to the more modern glass-and-steel edifices popping up here and everywhere in clusters of corporate arrogance.

Tom and Dan walked up cement steps worn smooth and rounded, past a lawn area to the left where young people sat talking and smoking in the shade of a mature elm. Tom and Dan went into the lobby, spacious and solid-feeling; despite its age. Tom asked the receptionist if Annabelle Lynch was in. Lynch, according to the studio's Web site, was the president of the company.

The girl smiled. "I'll see." She dialed a number, eyeballed Tom while listening to someone on the other end. She was maybe twenty, pleasant-looking in an artsy kind of way; defined by an assortment of face metal, black clothes, maroon lipstick and nails, and a hairdo that looked as if a chainsaw had been used to layer it.

She held her hand over the receiver. "Annabelle is very busy. Perhaps you can come back another time." She smiled, showing a diamond stud in her tooth.

Tom flashed his badge. "It's important that we see her."

The receptionist relayed this bit of news to the person on the other end of the line. "Yes, the police. They say it's important." She hung up the telephone. "Could you please take a seat? Someone will be down shortly." She smiled at Tom, the diamond catching a bit of light. "You're really a detective?"

"Him too." Tom thumbed at Dan.

She looked at Dan, looked back at Tom. "Is this about Parker Stewart?"

"Did you know him?"

She shook her head. "No. But I used to see him all the time—coming in to work, you know. He killed himself?"

Tom smiled.

He and Dan sat on the yellow vinyl couch facing the reception desk, their backs to Riverside Drive, heavy with post-lunchtime traffic. Stuffed orange and green vinyl armchairs with tables and lamps bracketed the couch, a bean-shaped coffee table, made of laminated wood, stood in the center of the arrangement. There were cigarette burns on the table's edge. Tom, Dan, and the receptionist were alone in the lobby, the latter reading a magazine beneath the counter of the large, semicircular desk that was probably considered "designy" thirty years ago. The place could stand a face lift. Tom picked up a copy of the *Daily Variety* and thumbed through it.

Dan stood and walked around the lobby, looking at the various framed cels of cartoon characters covering the walls that were painted in primary colors: red, yellow, blue. He was standing next to a life-sized wooden cutout of Earl Hollister, the founder of the company. It was an old photograph, blown up, and he was shaking hands with blowups of Tommy Tortoise and Sammy Snail, characters that, according to the research Tom had done on the Internet earlier, had put Empire Films on the map back in the early '60s. "Look at this place, Tom."

"What's that?" Tom was reading an article that gave a brief overview of the life and genius of Parker Stewart.

"Wait'll I tell my kid about this," Dan said. "Look, here's Tommy Tortoise." Dan looked at Tom, who could see the thought forming in Dan's mind. Dan looked back at the cartoon character, pointed at Tom, said, "Hey—!"

"Don't even go there." Tom resumed reading.

The article described how the 1970s had brought a dry spell to the animation industry. Warner Brothers had shut down its cartoon unit in the early 1960s, and after the death of Walt Disney in 1966, many wondered if the animation world could survive. The heady days of prime-time television cartoons, featuring the likes of Hanna-Barbera's *The Flintstones* and Empire's *Tommy Tortoise,* had degenerated into a morass of clones, each more disgustingly sappy and banal than the one before. Ad dollars, netting soft returns, went elsewhere. It was rumored that Disney might shut down its features department. Animation companies that had thrived over the past decade, shut their doors. Unemployment soared. Empire Films was edging toward Chapter 11, gasping for life.

Then a young animator named Parker Stewart descended from on high with a student film that sent a shock wave through the industry. Setting the standard for a new generation of animators with his *Punching Judy* series—an irreverent, in-your-face character drawn with a combination of "Disney classic" and modern graphics styles—Parker Stewart not only gave Empire Films new life, but rejuvenated the entire industry as well. With his keen eye for design, and a genius at storytelling, he was the one chosen by the

gods of animation to take on the mantle of Walt Disney—a wun-
derkind with a vision.

Now he was dead. The industry would miss him. Given the
shelf life of Hollywood celebrities, Tom was certain of that fact as
he tossed the trade paper on the table and looked across the lobby
as it filled with young people, laughing and talking loudly. They
were artists, Tom assumed, by their predominately black clothing,
and tattoos, shaved heads, or hair colored with florescent greens,
purples, oranges . . . some colors off the spectrum.

"Looney tunes," Dan said under his breath.

The artist in the lead swiped a badge through an electronic eye
beside the security door, a buzzer sounded, and they went chattering through the door. The receptionist looked across the lobby at
Tom. "May I get you anything? Coffee? Water? A soda?"

"You got any crackers?" Dan asked.

She shook her head. "Upstairs, maybe."

Tom looked at his watch.

Just then a man in his late twenties came through the security
door. He was about six feet tall, with short-cropped curly black
hair, jade green eyes; wearing designer blue jeans and a tight-fitting
black T-shirt with quarter sleeves that showed his muscles and
tanned arms. He looked like a Jack La Lanne poster boy. "Are you
the police?" he asked.

Tom and Dan stood.

The poster boy looked them over quickly, didn't offer his hand.
That was fine with Tom who felt an instant visceral dislike for the
man. "Miss Lynch can only give you a few minutes of her time,"
the poster boy said, with an edge of superiority. "She is very busy."

"We're busy, too," Tom said, smiled. "We should get along just
fine."

The man's eyes turned hostile. "May I see some identification?"

Tom flashed his badge. *See? Real tin.* "Shall we go?" he asked,
again smiling. "You are Miss Lynch's secretary?"

Poster boy's upper lip actually curled. "This way."

They went up four flights in a stairwell showing its age. There
were framed cartoon posters on each of the windowless landings,
one from *Punching Judy,* one of *Buck and Wing,* an assortment of
others. Stepping into the fourth-floor reception area they came to

a security desk. The guard sitting at the desk, an old black man with a kind face and short, curly white hair, looked up and smiled. "Hello, Eric."

"They'll need passes."

The guard reached into a drawer and pulled out two florescent orange passes that no doubt glowed in the dark, each encased in clear plastic and numbered. "You can just clip these onto your lapels." He smiled. "And if you gentlemen could please sign in here?" He pushed a clipboard toward them, and Tom and Dan signed their names and the time of their arrival.

"This place is tighter than Fort Knox," Dan said.

The poster boy led them down a wide linoleum-tiled hallway that was grimy and cracked in places, the walls covered with more framed cartoon cels, past offices and cubicles where artists worked at animation desks, some looking up as they passed, others remaining intent on what they were drawing. The end of the hallway opened into an alcove with couches and chairs of the same older style as in the first-floor lobby. Same primary colors on the walls. A desk stood next to double wood doors that, apparently, opened into the office of Annabelle Lynch. A desk sign read: ERIC GETZ. The desk was tidy—computer, IN/OUT trays, and day planner. No picture of girl- or boyfriend. It wasn't immediately clear which way the wind blew with Getz.

"Wait here," he said curtly, knocked on a closed door, then went into the room.

Tom and Dan exchanged looks. "I think he's precious, don't you?" Dan said.

"Just darling."

Getz appeared in the doorway and motioned them in.

Annabelle Lynch was the only woman in the office, which was large and airy despite small windows. She stood by a long formica-topped table against the left wall, talking with two young artists, drawings spread over the table—all of them talking over the noise of four television sets set abreast on a shelf opposite her desk. Wall-to-wall beige carpet, a bit worn in the middle, covered the floor.

"She'll just be a minute," Getz said, raising his voice. He indicated chocolate brown stuffed sofa and chairs to the right. "You can sit over there if you want."

Tom didn't want. He looked at the televisions, each set tuned to a different network, before making a quick scan of the room: a corner office with two windows in each of the south and west walls—the walls covered with cartoon cels and posters. A wall-length shelf crammed with art books, action figures and toys chronicling the history of Empire Films, statuettes, lunch boxes, and other toys and knickknacks and awards relating to the cartoon biz, ran along the east wall. An old faded green Moviola stood in the far corner next to a healthy-looking *ficus benjamina*. A stuffed, life-sized man-doll sat hunched over the Moviola, editing a length of film. Angled in the other corner, just beyond the drawing table, was Lynch's mahogany desk; on it a computer, and what appeared to be a half-eaten turkey-and-lettuce sandwich. The office looked like a clone of Parker Stewart's house; only it seemed older and more worn, perhaps. Tom looked over at his partner, who, eyeballing the office, was clearly in awe.

Cartoonland!

Their discussion apparently concluded, the artists gathered up their drawings. Frowning and talking to each other, they left the office.

"Edgier, guys! Edgier!" Annabelle Lynch called over the televisions after them. Tom heard in her voice the gravelly hardness of someone who drinks heavily, smokes cigarettes, or both. She looked over at Tom and Dan, her face visibly taking on a different mask. Corporate boss.

Tom guessed that she was probably in her early forties—steel-blue eyes, pale white skin that probably didn't see much sun, graying blonde hair she wore short and brushed back off her high forehead. Dressed in black slacks and a powder-blue cotton shirt with the sleeves rolled up to the elbows, she was a handsome, angular woman with a no-nonsense quality about her. Tough broad.

Lynch strode toward the men, her wide, tight-lipped mouth breaking into a smile. She extended her hand straight-armed, like a man, shook hands with Dan, two solid yanks; then, looking Tom in the eyes, shook his hand. Tom felt the strong grip of someone who was either very self-confident or doing well to hide her insecurity—certainly someone used to getting her own way. "Annabelle Lynch."

"Shall I leave the door open, Annabelle?" Getz asked.

"For now."

"Don't forget, you have a two-thirty with Mr. Park."

"Thank you, Eric," she said with a dismissive smile.

Getz shot a slanted glance at Tom and left the room.

Annabelle Lynch smiled again at Tom. Her smile was infectious, and Tom found himself smiling without meaning to. Dan was grinning like an idiot. "You're here about Parker?" she asked.

"That's right, Miss Lynch," Tom said, talking over the televisions.

"Annabelle. We're very informal around here, as you can see." She indicated the sofa. "Won't you have a seat? I've got a couple minutes before my next meeting."

"We'll stand," Tom said.

Dan agreed.

"Could Eric get you something to drink? Or a bagel?"

Dan's eyes widened like a dog panting for din-din.

"No, really, that's fine," Tom said for both of them. "We'll eat later."

"All right, then." She leaned back against her desk, beside a brass framed photo of herself with longer hair shaking hands with Earl Hollister, founder of the company; the photo showed that same straightforward determination in her eyes. Then, folding her arms across her chest, she said, "Now, what's this about Parker? He killed himself?"

"That's what we think," Dan said.

"What a tragedy. How'd he do it?"

"We're not at liberty to say."

"I see." She reached over and picked up the half-eaten sandwich. "Do you mind if I eat while we talk? I'm starving." She took a bite of sandwich and, chewing, said, "I knew you'd come."

"Why is that?" Tom asked.

"Because he worked here." She swallowed hard. "You'll want to know if I noticed a change in his behavior or anything like that, right? 'Was he depressed or melancholy?' "

"It would be helpful," Dan said.

"It's crazy," she said. She took another bite of sandwich; frowned. "This thing's dryer'n sand, Eric!" she called out the door. "Be a dear and get me a soda." She tossed the sandwich onto the desk.

"What kind?" Getz's voice fought over the four televisions.

"Anything. No, better make it a Coke. I need the jolt."

"Okay."

"You sure you boys don't want anything?"

"No thanks," Dan said, a note of regret in his tone.

Tom was looking at the television sets. "So I can be in four places at the same time," Lynch said. She reached over and pushed a button on a remote that muted the volumes. "There. How's that?"

For a moment the room felt of the emptiness of absolute quiet. A vacuum of soundlessness. Then, almost immediately, voices and laughter from the cubicles down the hall filtered through the open door.

"I didn't—" she said. Tom clearly noticed the whiskey-edged quality of her voice. "—notice a change in his behavior," she added. "Parker was Parker. He was mercurial as always."

"Mercurial?"

"Up, down, round and round. A circus waiting to happen."

"Did you know him well?" Dan asked.

"Everybody knew Parker, and nobody knew him. He was a very private person," she said, a shade of something crossing over her eyes. "Isn't it horrible?"

Tom nodded, wrote in his notebook.

"Did he have many friends?" Dan asked.

"Parker? Parker didn't have friends, he had associates—people to help him with his projects. He had touchers."

"Touchers?"

"Stewart was a genius," she said. "He was a creature of beauty . . . like a butterfly. People touched the magic dust on his wings until he couldn't fly any longer. Touchers."

Tom detected bitterness in her tone. "Did he have enemies?"

"Are you serious?" She threw her head back and laughed; the laugh, like a series of staccato barks, filled the room. "Who doesn't have enemies in this business? Ever hear of a temperamental artist? Try putting a couple hundred of them together under one roof."

Tom smiled. "Anyone in particular?"

"This is beginning to feel like an interrogation. Why do you ask?"

"Anyone in particular?" he repeated.

"Okay. I can see that you're the bad cop, and the pleasantly plump one here is the good cop—isn't that how you guys play it?"

Dan frowned.

Tom let his question stand. He could see her mind working behind the pale blue eyes. She could not hold his gaze.

"Anyone in particular? Not that I know of," she said, adjusting herself against the desk. "Like I said, Parker was very private. He didn't trust people." She pointed to Tom's notebook. "Am I going too fast for you?"

Tom continued writing. "Why do you suppose not?"

"That's just the way he was wired. He'd let you get just so close. . . ." She smiled, again looking out the window at the hills lush with trees. "With Parker, people were generally two-faced liars, or no-talent sycophants. The rest were fallible in one way or another. The line was the thing. He trusted only the line."

"'The line'?"

"The drawing. He trusted only what he could see on paper. The line was either true or false. You can see it right away. There's no hiding it. You can spot the fake. With most people the line is not so easy to see. Except in Parker. The line ran straight and true in him. The rest of us, well . . ."

"You sound like you knew him pretty well."

"No." She chuckled. "It's all very sad. I guess the line finally blurred for him."

"How do you mean?"

"I mean, why does anyone kill himself?"

Tom looked at Dan. Dan was looking at the half-eaten sandwich on the desk. "How did you find out about it?" Tom asked.

"About his death?"

"Yes."

She laughed; a sharp, barking release. "Do I have to answer that? Hell, it doesn't matter. I'll tell you anyway. I got a phone call last night from Charlie. . . . Charlie Doogan. One of my producers. That's D-O-O-G-A-N. He'd heard it on the news."

Tom wrote down the name. "I see. This Charlie Doogan—was he what you'd call 'an associate' of Stewart's? A 'toucher'?"

"Charlie?" She shook her head and chuckled. "No. I wouldn't say that."

Tom heard something in her voice. "What was their relationship, then?"

She smiled. "You'll have to ask Charlie about that."

"Is he here today?"

"I don't know." Getz came in with the Coke, handed it to her. "Eric, is Charlie Doogan here today?"

"I'll check."

Tom waited while she took a long pull.

"That's better," she said.

A black man with pierced eyebrows and a chain that went from his left nostril to his left earlobe, stuck his head into the room. "Sorry, Annabelle. You wanted to see my roughs before Mr. Park got here."

She looked at Tom. "Excuse me just a moment," she said, and set down the Coke on the desk. "Let's have a look."

The artist came into the room, spread several drawings over the long table adjacent to her desk. Annabelle Lynch looked at them quickly. "This one. Make it a little edgier, though. This one, too. These others . . ." She waved her hand. "The first two. Make them edgier. Remember our target audience."

The artist collected his drawings, and as he went through the door, a girl with black hair and magenta highlights came in holding two horizontal paintings. "Here are the background approaches, Annabelle. This is the traditional approach. Here's the digital. I kind of like the digital."

"I don't," Lynch said. "Too fake. Let's go with the other one."

"Okay. Hey, I'm real sorry about Parker," the girl said. She started to say something else, then saw there were others in the room.

"I am, too," Lynch said. She put her arm around the girl's shoulder, led her to the door, and said something to Getz. She closed the door behind her and walked back across the room. "I'm sorry. We're getting ready for MIP and it's pretty crazy around here."

"MIP?" Tom asked.

"MIP-TV." Again she leaned back against the desk and folded her arms across her chest. "Big convention in Cannes. Every studio and toy company in town is hustling to get their pitches ready. It's crazy around here, if you hadn't noticed. Last season it was superheroes. Next year it will be futuristic dinosaurs or two-headed chickens."

"What's 'in' this year?" Tom asked.

"That's the sixty-four-million–dollar question, isn't it?"

"How about outer space?"

She looked at him. "How about it?"

Tom removed Stewart's rabbit drawing from the manila folder, the drawing still encased in protective cellophane, and offered it to Lynch. She did not take it. "You wouldn't know anything about this drawing, would you?" Tom asked.

Tom watched her carefully as she studied the drawing. "It's Parker's, of course. But you knew that, didn't you?" Shrewd cookie.

Tom put the drawing back into the folder. "I understand he was fired a few weeks back."

"That's right. We had to let him go."

"Can you tell us why?"

"That's company business. We don't make it a policy of airing our dirty laundry in public."

"You consider Stewart 'dirty laundry'?"

Her expression narrowed. "That's not what I meant."

"I'm sorry. What did you mean?"

She stared at him.

"Routine questions, Miss Lynch. I would've thought Stewart might've been a permanent fixture around here, since he'd contributed so much to the company over the years."

"What's he done lately? Isn't that how it goes?"

"I wouldn't know," Tom said. "I'm paid by the city."

A smile broke at the corners of her thin-lipped mouth. "I'll tell you why I let Parker go," she said. "I let him go—bless his heart—because he couldn't stay on schedule or budget to save his life. I'd've hired him back, too, if he'd . . ." She looked out the window.

Tom noticed the hard lines of her face softening. "If he'd what?"

"What a stupid, stupid thing to do. Parker was a genius. Pure and unfettered. He just didn't know how to make it work for him." The hard lines of her face returned as she looked at Tom. "The rest is company business."

The intercom on her desk buzzed. She twisted back across the desk, one foot lifting off the floor for balance, and hit a speaker button.

"Mr. Park's here. Shall I tell him you'll be right out?" the voice of Getz asked.

"What did you find out about Charlie?" said Lynch.

"He's at an online session in Hollywood. Won't be back today."

"Thank you," she said, glancing at Tom to see if he'd heard. He had. She hit the switch and, straightening, said, "I'm really sorry, boys, but I'm going to have to cut this short. I don't know what more I can tell you, anyway."

"When was the last time you saw him?" Tom noticed a flicker of hesitation in her eyes.

She laughed. "This *is* an interrogation, isn't it?"

"A simple question."

She rolled down her shirtsleeves, buttoned them. "The last time I saw Parker I gave him his notice." She looked Tom in the eyes, all business now, "Three weeks ago. He stood right about where you're standing. I fired him. Happy?"

"That was the last time?"

"That's all she wrote, folks!" She went around her desk, picked up the remains of the sandwich and tossed it into a trash receptacle under the desk; took the black jacket off the back of her chair, and put it on. "I'm sorry, but I have an important meeting you're keeping me from."

She took a lint catcher from the top desk drawer, rolled it over her shoulders and sleeves, then returned it to the drawer and closed it. "Gentlemen."

She escorted them into the reception area where four Korean men and one Korean woman, in navy-blue business suits with briefcases, waited. They all commenced bowing and smiling.

"Sorry to keep you waiting, Mr. Park!" Annabelle Lynch said, stepping away from Tom and Dan to shake Mr. Park's hand.

The Korean woman translated to Park.

Park looked at Lynch, and smiled. "That's okay," he said.

Lynch put her hand on his shoulder, led him back through the door to her office. The others followed, smiling and nodding at Tom and Dan as they passed.

Eric Getz, eyeing Tom, came around his desk and gestured toward the hallway. "Allow me to show you down to the lobby. It's always best to make an appointment." Getz smiled.

"I'll remember that," Tom said. Then, as he turned to leave, he looked back into the office and, over the screen of shorter navy business suits, caught Annabelle looking at him.

Leaving the building, stepping out into the afternoon glare of the sun, Dan looked down at himself; grunted: "Pleasantly plump."

Tom grinned. "If the sweater fits . . ."

Dan ignored the remark, "Did you notice the way she looked at the drawing, Tommy?"

"I noticed."

● ●   ● ●

On his way home in the late afternoon, Tom stopped by the Stewart house for another look at the crime scene. He needed to see it alone; hoped the thirty-plus hours since he'd last been here would add a little clarity to his perspective. And right now he needed clarity. He pulled the Bronco over to the curb, parked, then slipped under the police cordon tape that, sagging now, crossed the entire length of the front yard. Bits of paper and debris scattered here and there gave the house and yard a neglected look. Forgotten, like the name and face of the world-changer that once lived here.

There was a heavy quiet inside the house, a stark contrast to yesterday morning when the circus was in town. Tom had the sense he had walked into a museum after-hours; that the ghosts in the place were watching from shadowy niches. He didn't believe in ghosts; he was a practical man: *Nothing but the facts, ma'am.* Still, walking through the house of the dead man, he felt sad, almost melancholy; feelings that were probably a mixture of Carolyn, the baby, and maybe the autopsy.

What'd that given him, anyway—the autopsy? *Probable suicide.* Had that, anyway. Time of death? Around five, Sunday afternoon. The cut lip was interesting. Someone pops Stewart on the mouth Saturday, maybe Friday, and Sunday afternoon he kills himself. *Yes, interesting.*

Tom went from room to room, allowing vague thoughts and impressions to move freely through his mind. Something would jell. Maybe. Maybe not. The key was to keep an open mind, stay alert for clues, listen to what the crime scene had to say. Listen, to the ghosts.

Tom walked into the hallway leading to the back bedrooms, stopped, and looked at the black-and-white landscape photographs along the wall. They reminded him of the works of Ansel Adams. It was good work. He turned on the hall lights, to better view them, noticed there were the penciled initials *P.S.* in the lower left-hand corner of each photo. Parker Stewart, he guessed. *Half Dome, Yosemite—P.S. Glacier Lake, Montana—P.S. Monument Valley, Utah—P.S.* Stewart was a signer. *I created it. My signature authenticates it. Mine. "If I told you about it, you might steal it, mightn't you?"* Isn't that what he'd said on the tape? Grin. Wink. Tom raised an eyebrow. Whatever else the guy may have been, he was an artist. Tom envied that in people. Didn't envy the people—they were usually kooks—but he envied the talent. He continued his sweep.

Everything else in the house was the same as he remembered it yesterday; even the intimacy of the crime scene was back now as he went into the room where Stewart had allegedly taken his life.

He walked over to the taped outline of the body. In his mind he could see the dead man lying on the floor to the right of the computer desk. Tom glanced over at the animation desk next to the window, saw young Stewart suffering through the interview, two decades ago. Tom glanced at the television in the corner, at the shelves of books and toys, at the tape marking the Beretta, at the computer desktop—fairly clean now that the computer, scanner, and fax machine had been removed by the forensics team. The lab boys would get to them when they could. Depended on the workload, like everything else in life. *Take a number, please.*

He sat down at the desk and faced the imaginary computer screen. The Mickey Mouse telephone, sitting on the desk return where it had been the day before, was just off his left arm, Mickey smiling broadly.

Weird.

Tom reconstructed a possible scenario in his mind. Stewart

scans the number 5 drawing into his computer. Just the number 5 drawing. Drawings 1 to 4 don't exist. Stewart goes to the coffee table and blows a couple liners. Maybe he blows the liners first, then scans in drawing number 5. Either way, he gets to feeling bad about something—really bad—so bad he comes back to the computer and types a suicide note.

Tom extended his fingers over the imaginary keyboard and typed, THAT'S ALL, FOLKS! then reached for the imaginary Beretta on the desktop where the technicians had found a trace of gun oil. Tom put the tip of his left index finger to his temple. "Bang!"

Tom looked down at the taped outline and saw how Stewart must have fallen, pictured himself falling, how the gun would land. *Okay. There's the Beretta, there's the body.* Then it occurred to him: Which came first? The Beretta, the coke, or the idea to kill himself? Did he type the suicide note first and then go get the gun? Not likely. The note seemed an afterthought—a wink at the camera. No, he would have got the idea, got the gun, blew the coke, then wrote the note.

Bang!

Maybe the Beretta had been sitting on the desktop the whole time. He gets the idea, blows the liners, writes the note.

Bang!

What about drawing number 5? How did number 5 figure? Maybe it didn't. Maybe it'd been sitting in the scanner for weeks. Tom hadn't thought of that. Maybe Stewart had tossed drawings 1 to 4 in the trash and missed number 5. Drawing number 5 was irrelevant, maybe. Maybe not. It sure had got a rise out of Lynch.

Tom sat there thinking. None of it made sense. Since when did suicide make any sense? He thought about the Beretta. A Beretta Minx. *Lady's gun.* Six-round magazine; four in the clip, one spent casing on the floor. Five. *Where's the sixth? That's easy; the magazine wasn't filled to capacity. Okay, then, what's eating you?* He made a mental note to ask the lab boys if they found any traces of gun oil on the computer keys. Check for fingerprints on the shells. He wondered if Martinez had got a line on the Gonzales woman yet. He wondered about many things. Nothing jelled.

He glanced once more around the room at the furniture, cartoon posters on the wall, shelves of toys and comic books, at the animation desk. He looked over at Oscar sitting on his perch. Something didn't feel right. Correction: Something felt very wrong. He could almost hear the ghosts laughing at him—death, the big chuckle. The grand hurrah. But then, he didn't believe in ghosts. Death, however, was a different matter. He took a deep breath, stood, and left the house, locking the door behind him.

Chapter Three

The dead girl stared up at her from the bottom of a bathtub full of water, lips parted slightly, showing the edges of her top and bottom teeth, as if uttering a word of protest. Strands of silvery blonde hair, fine and silky, lay still over the submerged young and very pretty face—partially obscured open blue eyes staring peekaboo-like through the hair. She was naked beneath a terrycloth bathrobe, arms floating a little above the hips; legs and feet slung over the side of the tub, scissorslike.

A camera flash flooded the face in white light for an instant. The eyes did not dilate. Another flash. And another. The light cooled into the incandescent ambience of the bathroom, the dead girl staring up at Detective Sergeant Sandy Cameron of the Los Angeles County Sheriff's Department.

She reminded Sandy of a water nymph, some ethereal sprite of Elizabethan literature. She did not seem dead. The legs were those of a dead person—gray, waxy—but did not seem to belong to the submerged girl who seemed somehow alive. Sandy half expected her to surface, take a giggling breath of air, then submerge again to continue her game. She did not surface. A single bubble of air escaped the girl's left nostril and rose to the surface as though to punctuate the horror.

Sandy was slightly shaken. It would pass in time, she knew, as the face fell away into a blurry haze.

Sandy imagined feeling the powerful flanks of Buster Brown with her legs as she bumped him into a lope, the wind in her face and hair as she came down through the rocks and oaks and manzanita to the place where she could sit and think without distraction. Her thinking place. She'd pack a lunch, sit looking out over the canyon, Buster Brown grazing contentedly in the sweet grasses that grew along the creekbed, the wild tart smell of sage cloying over her face. She'd think through the complexities and horrors of a case until the sun had set well behind a saddleback in the San Gabriels.

"The coroner should be here in a couple of minutes," Nick said.

The canyons were gone. Sandy was back in the Valencia townhouse bathroom of the dead girl, the damp smell of standing water filling her nostrils. She looked over at her partner standing in the doorway.

Nick Ivankovich was a big man, maybe 250 pounds, built low to the ground like a gorilla—long arms that ended in hands that could crush bones; thick, powerful neck and shoulders; a back that seemed a yard wide. He was wearing a brown double-knit sports coat, dark brown trousers and matching tie, white shirt with the top button unbuttoned, and the Windsor knot loosened on the tie. He frowned at his feet.

Sandy smiled as he stepped rather daintily back across the flooded bathroom floor. "Those your new shoes?"

"It don't matter," he said, looked at the dead girl. "Looks sorta like a doll, don't she? Like a doll locked in a glass case."

"Sort of." She glanced down at the hairbrush next to the sink, the dryer and beauty aids beneath the mirror that made the small bathroom seem larger.

Nick looked at her. "You okay?"

"I'm fine," she said. A transfer from NYPD, Nick had been her partner for five years and could read her like a book—her thoughts, moods. He was a good cop, smart, with plenty of street savvy. Good family man. Loyal on both fronts. She thought of him as a Tootsie Pop—hard as nails on the outside, soft and chewy on the inside. A grizzly bear with a heart of honey gold. Most importantly, she thought of him as a friend.

She looked at the dead girl, saw how the bathrobe had gotten caught in the overflow drain and clogged it. She leaned closer to inspect the underside of the calves where they pressed against the edge of the tub, noted purplish red bruises where blood had collected. She knew that this was the result of postmortem lividity, where the blood, without a beating heart to pump it, had settled into the lowest parts of the body. The feet were white, bloodless, toes as pale and delicate as sculptured porcelain. She touched the ball of one foot, pressed into it with her index finger, and left a mark whiter than the surrounding pale flesh. She wiggled the big toe. "Rigor's not gone through her yet."

"Whaddaya think, kid?" Nick asked, in flawless Brooklynese.

"I don't know. A few hours, maybe," she suggested, bending over and looking at the tap, then looking again at the right side of the dead girl's head—what she could see of it at this angle. "She might've hit her head on the tap."

Nick stepped over and looked. "Might've. How, though?"

"I don't know." A single marble step went around the base of the tub. "Maybe she was reaching to turn off the water, stepped up, and slipped on the marble. Marble's pretty slippery." Sandy felt her own feet, cold now, looked down at her low-heeled pumps that were soaked through. "What a mess." She was grateful she was wearing lightweight, washable clothes—cotton skirt, matching cream-colored blazer, an open-collar dusty-rose cotton blouse. "Who's with the boyfriend?"

"Cooligan," Nick said. "Crying like a baby."

"He getting his prints?"

"Yeah."

"Do you believe him?"

"I don't know. Something about him."

She grinned. "Women's intuition?"

He grunted.

"Lover's spat, maybe?" Sandy offered.

Nick shrugged his big shoulders. "Maybe."

"He pushes her; she falls and cracks her head against the tap and drowns."

"Assuming she drowned."

"Assuming she drowned," Sandy repeated.

"Then again, she might've just slipped, like you said."

"There are other possibilities, of course."

"Sure."

Sandy looked at the pretty face: the white, calm face that was strangely haunting, the look of wonder in bright blue eyes that would never see another day. "Twenty-eight, did you say?"

Nick looked at the girl's driver's license attached to his clipboard. "Twenty-eight."

Sandy shook her head. "We should probably remove the tap, don't you think?"

"Sure."

Sandy tiptoed out of the flooded bathroom—leaving the photographer behind, changing rolls of film—through the master bedroom, over soaked carpet, into the living room where Detective Bob Cooligan, a wiry-haired man with a slight hunch, sat at a dinette table fingerprinting Steven Weber. An L.A. county criminalist in the adjoining kitchen dusted an empty bottle of wine on the island; a half-filled glass sat by itself on the corner of the tile counter. A uniformed officer at the door admitted someone from the forensics team. It was getting busy.

Weber looked up at Sandy then down at the fingers of his right hand as Cooligan rolled the next digit over the inkpad, pressed it onto the prints card.

"My name is Detective Cameron," she said to the man. "How are you doing?"

Weber looked up at her, nodded absently, then looked back at what Cooligan was doing with his fingers. His eyes were red— he'd been crying.

Sandy pulled out a chair at the dinette and sat down. She handed Weber a tissue from her purse, a leather Brighton beautifully tooled with silver appointments, in which she kept the odds and ends of womanhood, as well as a .38-caliber Colt Detective Special. The piece was a present from her father upon her graduation from the Academy. Nothing fancy—2-inch blued barrel, Pachmeyer grips, six-round capacity revolver—a "wheel gun." The Department had issued her a .40-cal Beretta auto, but she didn't trust autos. Never had any jams with a wheel gun.

She set her purse on the table, her gold detective's shield clipped to the shoulder strap, facing Weber.

"Thanks," Weber said, accepting the tissue without looking at her. He glanced at the shield, looked back at his fingers.

Nick remained standing. Sandy could tell from his flat, dead-eyed expression that he didn't think much of the man who had discovered the body of Wendy Burgess. But then Nick wasn't exactly a touchy-feely kind of guy around possible homicide suspects. Given his druthers, he'd just as soon take the guy out back and use a little Russian charm on him. He cleared his throat.

"We have a few more questions, if you don't mind, Mr. Weber," Sandy said in a friendly voice.

"Sure."

"You understand we have to get everyone's prints. Even mine. Isn't that right?" she said to Cooligan.

"That's right."

Weber looked back at what Cooligan was doing with his fingers.

Sandy opened her purse and consulted her notebook. "Let's see. . . . You're thirty years old, correct?"

Weber nodded. He was a nice-looking man, in a boyish way. His dark hair was cropped short, greased up into sharp curling spikes, receding back from a stubborn point of growth that had once defined his forehead. His cologne smelled sweet, perfumey. He was very tan, the tan unnatural in its evenness, the kind of man who probably spent a great deal of time in front of the mirror, grinning and flexing his muscles as he splashed on too much cologne to hide his insecurity. This last bit of information she'd gotten from Nick.

"You live at one-five-seven-three-three Harding, Stevenson Ranch?" Sandy asked.

Weber nodded.

"You work at ACN?"

Weber nodded.

"The television network, correct?"

"That's right."

"What do you do there?"

"I'm a program executive."

"A program executive? You mean you help decide what shows ACN puts on the air?"

"Something like that."

"Big responsibility." She smiled at him. "And so young."

Cooligan started printing Weber's left hand.

"We're all around the same age there," Weber said, his gaze shifting back and forth from Sandy to Cooligan. "Network wants a young eye. Keep things on the cutting edge. You know . . . edgy."

"I see." Sandy wrote, *edgy.* She did not like the word. She did not like ACN, for that matter: too much sex and violence that catered to the more base elements of human nature. Nothing left to the imagination. She preferred the stations that showed the old classics; they had been made with a sense of decency and class. "I'd like to hear it from the top now, if you don't mind."

Weber shrugged. "Sure. Like I told—" He looked over at Nick. "Like I told that detective, I came over to see Wendy. Thought we'd maybe go out to a movie or something."

She smiled. "What was your relationship with her? Were you friends . . . or more than friends?"

"We were close."

"So you were dating?"

Weber nodded.

"How long had you been seeing her?" She watched his eyes. Blue. "These are just routine questions, you understand."

"I understand. I don't know. Six, seven months, maybe."

Cooligan finished fingerprinting, handed Weber a paper towel.

"Where did you meet her?"

"At work."

"Wendy worked at ACN, too, then?"

"She used to. She transferred to Panda Productions."

"Panda Productions is a film studio of some kind?" Sandy wrote down the name.

"An animation company in Burbank." He finished cleaning his fingers, handed the towel back to Cooligan. "It's owned by a Japanese conglomerate."

"I see. How long had she worked there?"

When Weber looked back at Sandy, his eyes came alive, as if seeing her for the first time. He blinked at her, stole a quick glance at her legs.

"How long had she been at Panda?" Sandy repeated, thinking it odd that a man who'd just lost his girlfriend would so quickly develop a roving eye. "Mr. Weber?"

"What's that? Panda? She left ACN after the first of the year."

"Did she know you were coming over here tonight?" Sandy noticed a flicker of wariness in his eyes.

"No. I just dropped in."

She made a mental note to check his phone records.

"You said you were going to the movies," Sandy said. "You're sure she didn't know you were coming over? Most girls like to know if they are going out for the evening. What if she'd made other plans?"

"I said maybe we'd go to a movie. If she'd made other plans it would've been tough luck for me."

"How'd you get in?" Nick asked.

"I already told you."

Nick's small dark eyes, shielded by a thick, bony Russian brow, gazed dully at the man, like some lizard eyeballing a juicy beetle. "And now you can tell my partner." He grinned.

Weber blinked a couple of times, looked back at Sandy. "The door was unlocked," he said, his eyes making a furtive sweep over her breasts beneath the lightweight cotton jacket.

"The door was unlocked?" Sandy asked.

"I rang the doorbell. No one answered. I was going to let myself in with my key . . . started to, in fact, but the door was open."

"You have a key?"

Weber indicated Cooligan, who was closing up the fingerprint works. "I gave it to him."

"So you let yourself into the apartment," she continued, watching him very carefully. "Then what?"

"When I opened the door I called out, but she didn't answer. I went into the bedroom, thinking she might be sleeping. I heard the water running, figured she was taking a bath and couldn't hear me. Then I noticed water pouring out of the bathroom."

"You could see water pouring out of the bathroom?"

"Not really see it," Weber corrected himself. "The carpet was soaked. Shoot, look at it." He jerked his head. "I knew something was wrong."

"Was the bathroom door open or closed?" Nick asked.

Weber continued looking at Sandy. "Closed. No, it was open."

"Which is it, open or closed?" Nick asked.

"Open," Weber said to Sandy. "The door was open. I thought it was pretty weird, Wendy leaving the water running—she's pretty conscientious about things. A neatnik. She didn't like things being out of place."

Sandy smiled. "What did you do next?"

"I went into the bathroom and saw her in the tub."

Just then the coroner's deputy arrived, carrying a black leather bag. He was directed by one of the uniformed officers into the bathroom.

Weber watched. "I can't believe she's dead," he said quietly.

Sandy gave him a moment. He seemed credible, and yet there was something about the guy that troubled her, gave her a sense of revulsion. Maybe it was his roving eye that hadn't stopped undressing her since he'd first noticed her. Maybe it was the cologne—over-compensating for something. Maybe it was too early to tell. "When you discovered Wendy in the bathtub, what did she look like?"

"Look like? What do you mean?"

"Was she sideways? Face up? Down?"

Weber shook his head. "She was like she is now . . . floating in the tub."

"Floating?"

Weber looked quickly at Nick, back at Sandy. "Well, not float-ing," he said, a bit flustered. "She was on the bottom. She was on the bottom, staring up at me. I thought she was playing a game at first but she didn't come up for air. I tickled her foot—it was cold. I waited for a while, and knew it wasn't a game." He began crying. "Oh God, I can't believe this is happening!"

"Just a few more questions," Sandy said. She waited while he blew his nose.

Nick shook his head in disgust, walked back into the bedroom. Weber watched him leave.

"What did you do then?" Sandy asked.

Weber was calm now. Outwardly, at least. "Do?" he said through the tissue. "I turned off the water."

"The water was running?"

"Yes. The place was flooded, like I told you."

"Then what?"

"I called nine-one-one."

Sandy consulted her notes. "That would've been around when?"

"I don't know—six-thirty, six forty-five. I didn't look at my watch."

The call had come in at 6:50. "Somewhere between six-thirty and seven, then."

"I guess so."

"Which phone did you use?"

"Phone? The one in the bedroom."

"You're sure."

"It was all so confusing. . . . Yes, I used the phone in the bedroom. I definitely used the phone in the bedroom."

"Almost finished here, Mr. Weber," Sandy said. "Are you all right?"

"I'm okay. I just can't get over this."

Sandy nodded. *Sure, take another look at my legs, that'll help.* "After you turned off the water, what did you do?"

"I came in here." He began pushing back the cuticles of his fingers with his thumbnail. Small neat hands, Sandy noticed. Nervous hands. The nails varnished. Her revulsion grew. She didn't trust men who varnished their nails. They were too self-centered, spent too much time in front of the mirror, which corroborated Nick's assessment of the man. Her mother would say he was vain. "What do you mean?" he asked.

"Did you *do* anything? Did you *touch* anything?"

"I don't know. I just came in here and sat down. Waited for you guys to show up."

"Is that your glass of wine on the counter?"

Weber looked. "No. It must be Wendy's."

"Did Wendy drink?"

"She wasn't a drunk, if that's what you mean. She drank socially, I suppose. Parties and stuff."

"I see." She wrote something down. "What can you tell us about her friends?"

"She didn't have many. Not at ACN, anyway."

Nick came back into the room, showed Sandy something in his notebook. Weber watched them closely, followed the notebook with his eyes as Nick returned it to his coat pocket.

"Perhaps she'd made some friends at her new job?" Sandy continued.

"I don't know about Panda," Weber said, shaking his head. "She was friendly."

"She was friendly, but she didn't have too many friends."

"She was kind of guarded," Weber clarified. "You know the type."

"Explain to me 'the type,'" Sandy asked.

"You know, outwardly friendly, inwardly standoffish."

"I see." *You mean she wouldn't put out.* "You said the two of you were close. What exactly does that mean?"

"We weren't engaged, if that's what you mean. We were just close."

"Was she free to see other men?"

He looked at her.

"She was a very pretty girl," Sandy said. "She'd gotten a job at another place; naturally, other men would take notice of her. Perhaps she had given one of them a key as well. We have to look at all the possibilities." She noticed the man's Adam's apple rise slowly, fall as he swallowed. "Mr. Weber?"

"Huh?"

"Was she free to see other men?"

He shrugged. "There weren't any chains, if that's what you mean." He continued working his cuticles.

"You obviously cared deeply for her," she continued. "It's natural you might be upset if other men started taking notice of her."

"Upset? Who said I was upset?" He looked at Nick, back at Sandy. "What's going on here?"

"We're asking you questions," Nick said. "Just a few questions, Mr. Weber. We would like a little information from you."

Nick took a step forward, nothing threatening; he just moved his bulk from one space to another, closer to the man. Sandy was sure Nick could pick him up and toss him across the room with little effort. Nick would find it pleasurable, no doubt. "There's a dead woman in the next room," he said. "We would like to know if she was seeing other men."

Weber looked at him, his eyes quick.

"Simple question, Mr. Weber. Would you like me to repeat it?"

"What's the big deal?" Weber looked at Sandy. "So she was seeing other men. What of it?"

"Anyone in particular?" Nick asked.

Weber shrugged.

"Name one," Nick said. "We'll start with him."

"A name, huh? Okay, I'll give you a name." Weber folded his small neat hands on the table. "Bill Pender," he said, his face narrowing coldly at the corners of his eyes and mouth. "She was seeing Bill Pender."

"P–E–N–D–E–R?" Sandy asked, writing.

"I don't know about any others, but she was definitely seeing Bill Pender."

"Who is Bill Pender?"

"The CEO at Panda. Used to head up programming at ACN. Wendy was his executive assistant." Weber chuckled sarcastically. "His *secretary,* I mean."

"When did she start seeing him?"

"I don't know, a month or so ago. I tried to tell Wendy he wasn't any good for her, but she wouldn't listen. Pender was her ticket."

"Maybe you didn't like this Pender," Nick suggested.

"Shoot, Pender was old enough to be her old man," Weber said, inspecting his nails.

"You get steamed about this new arrangement?"

Weber looked at him. "What do you mean, 'steamed'?"

"Let me try to clarify," Nick said evenly. "I mean, did you get *steamed* about it? Did you get steamed she was seeing this man who was old enough to be her father?"

Weber's mouth became small, petulant, like a spoiled child's. "No."

"You sure?"

"I'm sure."

"Not even a little bit steamed?"

"No."

Nick grunted. "I think I might get steamed if my girl was seeing another man. A little bit steamed, anyway."

"I told you, there were no chains between us."

A woman criminalist, on her way to the bathroom with a bucket and mop, gave Sandy a look that said: *Yeah, right. And I've got a bridge to sell.*

"What are you getting at?" Weber demanded, his eyes flashing warily. "Do you think I had something to do with this?"

" 'This'? You mean *this?*" Nick said, his accent very thick now as he gestured toward the bathroom. "The dead girl in the other room? Let me clarify the situation here, Mr. Weber. We are investigating a possible homicide. We would like to know what happened."

"How would I know what happened?" Weber looked frightened now; he took hold of the edge of the dinette, pushed slightly away from it. "I came over here to see Wendy, to talk. That's all. I never touched her."

"No one said you did," Nick said.

"You're trying to get me to say something."

"Just the truth, Mr. Weber."

"I said I would cooperate," Weber said to Sandy. "I didn't think I was going to get the third degree."

"This is only the second degree." Nick smiled. "We give the third degree at the station."

"Maybe I do want an attorney."

"Give him a call." Nick showed a wide grin. He looked over at the criminalist, a bald, bespectacled man dusting various items in the kitchen. "Say, Will, you dust the phone yet? We have a citizen who would like to call his attorney."

"It's yours, Nick."

He turned to Weber. "Go for it."

Weber looked at the phone, glared across the room, his mouth even smaller and more petulant, if that were possible.

"Okay," Sandy said. "We don't need to go down to the station. We can get everything we need right here, don't you think, Mr. Weber?"

He glared across the room, definitely a spoiled child.

"Mr. Weber?"

He would not look at her. "I'm just trying to cooperate. I called *you,* remember?"

"You did the right thing. We have just a couple more questions and you can go home."

Weber came back from his indignation in stages. "I didn't touch her," he said sullenly. He glanced contemptuously at Nick, looked at Sandy and, little by little, his shoulders, the tight corners of his eyes and mouth, relaxed.

"Is there anyone we can notify?" Sandy asked. "Parents? Siblings?"

He shook his head.

"Her parents are both dead?" Sandy asked.

He nodded.

"No brothers or sisters?"

"She never mentioned any." Weber shrugged. "No, I can't think of anyone." He looked at her, glanced at the shallow indentation of skin where the base of her throat and collarbone met, then pinched the bridge of his nose and began slowly massaging. "I'm pretty wiped out. Can I go now?"

Sandy looked at Cooligan. "I got what I needed," he said.

She looked at Nick. He shrugged his lower lip. "I think we have enough for right now," she said to Weber. "Oh . . . One more thing. What time did you get here tonight?"

Weber looked at her, the thumb and index finger coming away slowly from his nose. "I told you," he said, confused.

"You told us what time you made the phone call. What time did you actually get here?"

He seemed lost. "I don't know," he said, gesturing with his hands as if searching for an answer. "A little before I called nine-one-one, I guess. What time did I say I called? Sometime around six-thirty, wasn't it? Six forty-five?"

"Did you come here from work?" she asked. "From home? Where?"

"From work. Why?"

"Thank you, Mr. Weber. I think that will do for now."

He watched Sandy write in her notebook. "That's it? I'm done?"

"Unless you can think of anything else that might be helpful."

Weber shook his head, looked again at her notebook, stood. He was short, with thick, muscular thighs, disproportionate to his height. He nodded—a sad, confused expression on his face. He picked up his car keys from the table, then walked across the living room and out through the front door of the townhouse.

Sandy could smell his cologne long after he'd gone.

Nick grunted. "Kinda makes you wanna puke, don't he?"

She smiled wryly. "So, what do you really think?"

He shrugged his thick Russian brows. "You wanna know what I think, is that it?"

"Yeah, I wanna know what you think," Sandy said, mimicking his accent.

"Three-dollar bill, that's what I think." *Phony*—he didn't need to clarify. "How 'bout you?"

"I don't know yet." Sandy shook her head. "For someone who's just lost a girlfriend—"

Nick chuckled. "He wasn't lookin' at *my* legs."

"Funny man," Sandy said, rubbing her temples with the tips of her fingers. "So, what do we got?" She consulted her notes, looked at her watch. "He made the call at six-fifty. It's eight-fifteen now. Puts it pretty close to the coroner's 'two to four hours' since the time of death."

"If he got here after six-thirty like he said."

"I'll call ACN in the morning."

"Okay."

"What else did the coroner say?"

"Let's hear it from him."

The bathroom was mopped clean now, the water drained from the tub where the criminalist with a bridge to sell, a heavyset woman wearing scrubs, gloves, and hairnet, was busy removing the tap. The deputy coroner, a small, quiet man of Mexican descent with a sad face and delicate, beautiful hands, had the robe off the body and was carefully scraping each fingernail and placing the scrapings in small evidence bags. Jorge Ortega had been with the Coroner's Office a little over two years—a conscientious, thorough professional, whom Sandy found to be one of the best in the field.

"How's it going, Jorge?" she asked.

Ortega did not look up from his work; instead, he tilted his head in a kind of noncommittal shrug. "It goes."

Sandy watched what he was doing with an almost clinical dispassion. Whatever mystique or wonder there may have been earlier surrounding the dead girl, was now gone. Wendy Burgess was no longer a playful water sprite about to splash giggling out of the water; she was a corpse laid out on the bathroom floor, a liver probe protruding from her side. "Anything yet on the cause or manner of death?"

Ortega shook his head, glanced at the probe that resembled an oversized meat thermometer. "We won't know that until we take a look, downtown."

Sandy knew that the cause of death and the manner of death were two separate discussions—linked, certainly, but separate nonetheless. The "cause of death" had to do with the actual physical mechanism by which the body died: disease, gunshot wound to the head, loss of blood due to stab wounds, or whatever. In this case, the victim had apparently drowned as a result of blunt-force trauma to the head, either caused by the tap, or by some other instrument not at the scene.

The "manner of death," on the other hand, would establish whether the death occurred because of natural causes, accident, suicide, or homicide (justifiable or criminal). More often than not, a coroner worth his salt will establish both the cause and manner of death in short order. If the manner of death is ruled natural, accidental, self-inflicted, or if it is a justifiable homicide, then the case is closed and everyone skips merrily to the seashore. If it is ruled a criminal homicide (the unlawful taking of human life) or murder (add malice and forethought) then the *Who dunn it?* and *Why?* (if these are not obvious) are left for the detective to solve—a task that might take days or years, depending on the cleverness of the detective, or the cleverness of the killer. "Any guesses on the manner, Jorge?"

Again Ortega shrugged noncommittally. "Could've been accidental. Could've been deliberate." He tilted the girl's head tenderly toward Sandy, gently combed aside the hair to show where the right side of the cranium had likely struck the tap. "Did you see this?"

Sandy averted her eyes from the girl's unblinking stare, leaned forward to better see the head wound. "Oh, yes," she said. She leaned back and indicated the tap. "We need to take that with us."

"You got it." The criminalist placed it into a plastic bag, set it next to the girl's robe, also bagged.

"There is a bruise beneath the right eye," Ortega said quietly. "Did you notice?"

"No, I didn't." Sandy looked, saw a faded purplish area beneath the girl's right eye, on the raised portion of her cheekbone.

"It's an old wound." Ortega rubbed his thumb gently over the bruised area. "A few days . . . maybe a week. This poor girl."

"Yes," Sandy agreed.

Later, after two hours of paperwork at the Santa Clarita Sheriff's Station in Valencia, Sandy was beat. She'd been on her feet for sixteen hours, most of which had been spent cleaning up an earlier hit-and-run. Nick told her to go home, said he'd handle the background check on Weber and the victim, Wendy Burgess.

"Are you sure?"

"You spelled me last week. Go home, kid."

She did.

Chapter Four

It was just past eleven when Sandy unlocked the front door of her Sand Canyon home. She pressed on the light switch, and soft fans of yellow light fingered out of shell-shaped sconces up along the darkness of her living-room walls.

It was a modest, single-story contemporary-style house with dormers around the front elevation. It seemed larger with the high ceilings and open floor plan she had designed and her father had built for her in the early 1990s. It was an entertainer's dream. Double French doors along the back living-room wall opened onto a brick-and-flagstone patio, brick barbecue, and a pool and spa which, in daylight hours, had a panoramic view of the San Gabriels to the south and west. The sunsets would be magnificent from here, she'd said to her father as they sited the house, and they were: She loved her home.

She crossed the hardwood floor of the entryway into the kitchen, set her purse down on the granite counter, kicked off her shoes, bent over and massaged each of her feet, working her thumbs deep into the tired balls of her feet and the meaty parts of her toes. She removed her jacket, draped it over the back of the counter stool.

"Okay, where are you?" she called out into the quiet of the house.

No response.

"I know you're in here."

No response.

She had designed the kitchen to be the hub of the house so that standing at the in-counter sink she could see down the wide hallway to the bedrooms and office, look out over the counter into the large, open-beamed living room and talk with guests while she prepared the meal. That is, when she had guests over—which, her work schedule being so erratic, was rare. She barely had time for Buster Brown, her Quarter Horse gelding.

The cupboards were of whitewashed oak, the polished granite countertops were a rich forest-green with black veins swirling through them. Hardwood flooring covered the major passageways of the house, except for the bedrooms and living room, which were carpeted in a light rust color.

The flashing red dot of light by the telephone caught her eye. She ignored it, went over to the Sub-Zero and removed a pasta dish, left over from her date with Marvin this past Saturday night. No doubt the message was Mom calling to find out how it went. *Boy, was he a dud.* Sandy popped the dish into the microwave. At least he'd had good taste in food. She programmed the timer for two minutes.

Rhubarb appeared at her ankles, rubbed a welcome.

"There you are, Rhub," Sandy said, squatting and scratching behind the kitty's ears. "Did you miss me?"

Rhubarb, a riot of Halloween colors, flicked her bushy tail.

"It was a long day for me, too. Are you hungry?"

The cat meowed.

"Let's see what we can do about that."

She got out a small tin of kitty chow from the pantry and fixed Rhubarb's dinner. Tail flicking impatiently, the cat looked up, rubbing against Sandy's leg and meowing until Sandy set the bowl down next to the refrigerator. "There you go."

Rhubarb ate quickly, daintily, shook her head over a tasty morsel of tuna.

Sandy stood, noticed the little red light next to the phone still flashing. Again she ignored it. The microwave beeped a little tune.

She went over and removed a crystal wineglass from the cupboard rack, opened the freezer and scooped a few ice cubes into the glass. She poured a chardonnay over ice that cracked and settled in the glass, waited a few moments for it to chill, then stood leaning against the counter sipping the wine, feeling the light fruity liquid sliding refreshingly down through the worn stem of her body.

The microwave beeped again. "I'm coming."

She set the glass down on the counter, removed the pasta dish from the microwave, transferred it onto a clean plate and sprinkled a liberal amount of Parmesan cheese over it. She hit the PLAYBACK button on the voice recorder, went around the counter, sat down, and began to eat her much-belated dinner.

There was only one message. Her mother's voice, asking her when she was coming over for dinner. "Who knows, Mom?" Sandy shook her head, working the pasta with fork and spoon. And of course her mother did ask how it went with Marvin, the anthropology professor.

Sandy rolled her eyes and muttered her mother's incessant mantra: " 'If a woman isn't married by the time she's thirty, she has a greater chance of being struck by lightning than finding a husband.' " She grunted. "I'll take the bolt, thank you."

After eating, she took her glass of wine and stepped down into the living room, sat in the stuffed love seat by the huge stone-and-brick fireplace, retired after the short Southern California winter. A Crow war shield, bow, and quiver of arrows hung over the thick-beamed mantel. She reached over and turned on the table lamp, got up and turned on the CD player. By the time she was settled again, the silky voice of Sade was already pulsing a rhythm-and-bluesy sensuality into the quiet house. She drew her feet up into the love seat, glanced over at the small stack of books next to her Bible and journal, each with a bookmarker tonguing out. She was too tired to read, so she reached into the magazine rack beside the chair, found the latest *Western Horseman,* and flipped through it.

Her tastes in furnishings and wall coverings were eclectic— traditional, distressed, Southwestern. The room was designed for comfort. A tooled leather-and-silver show saddle stood on a rack in the corner beside a collection of silver belt buckles she'd won over the years and arranged in a wood-and-glass showcase. A silver bit and bridle looped from a wooden dowel beside the showcase. Paintings by Howard Terpning, Frank McCarthy, and Bev Doolittle hung at focal points in the room. A magnificent Civil War bronze sat on the coffee table in front of the sofa.

She took a sip of wine and, listening to the pulsing rhythms of the music, felt herself unwinding, slowly, steadily, the day uncoiling from her mind and muscles, work and the crime scene receding like a vapor going out and gone over the canyons. Even the face of the dead girl, gone. Especially the face of the dead girl. Shut out and gone.

Rhubarb appeared on her lap. "There you are, Rhub. Are we friends again?"

Rhubarb purred forgiveness, curled in a circle, and began licking her whiskers.

Sandy scratched her under the loose furry skin of the cat's neck. "You like that, don't you? Yes you do." Then, looking across the room at the Doolittle, she saw instead the face with its doll-like features, frozen in the rictus of death, the single bubble of air escaping the nose and rising, forever rising, it seemed, to the surface.

She shook the image from her mind, reached for her journal, opened it, and thought for a moment. *Dear Paul,* she wrote with a black-barrelled fountain pen. *It's been a couple of days since I've talked with you. It's been very hectic at work. Today especially. A young woman drowned in her tub. She was twenty-eight, pretty. We think it was an accident.* She set the journal down, shook her head. Dear God, what a waste.

A half-hour later she was undressed and in her bathrobe, padding barefoot over the terra-cotta tiles of the bathroom. She ran a bath. She braced her left hand on the tub rim, reached over with the other, felt the water, adjusted the taps.

She stood looking down at the beefy brass taps and spigot that goosenecked out over the tub. She looked out of her bathroom, but was seeing through the master bedroom of the dead girl's home the dinette and kitchen, the wineglass on the counter, and beyond, in line with the bathroom, the front door Steven Weber had said was unlocked.

She frowned. Who leaves the front door unlocked when they're about to take a bath? *Assuming the door was unlocked,* she corrected herself. *Assuming she was about to take a bath,* she corrected herself again. *Assuming a lot, aren't you, girl?*

"What else can I do at this stage?" she asked Rhubarb, who had come in and was curled on the bath towel draped over the steps.

Sandy selected an aromatic herbal bath oil. One of her friends had told her about aromatherapy, great for relaxation. She opened and sniffed the little vial—eucalyptus—sprinkled in a few drops, swirled her fingers through the hot water. She stood looking down at the tub filling with water, got up on the step, twisted her body into the position the girl had to have gotten into in order to fall the way she did.

"How in the world could she have done that?"

She was about to step into the tub when the telephone rang. She rolled her eyes, went into the toilet where she'd had the foresight to install a phone for just such occasions. It was Nick. She fended off his apology. "No, I wasn't in bed. No, I don't mind the interruption," she fibbed. "It's okay, Nick. What've you got?"

Nick told her.

"You're kidding! Two counts?" She listened. "The little creep. When are you bringing him in? All right, I'll be there at eight." She listened. "That's the bathtub running." Nick said something. "Never you mind. I'll see you in the morning."

Chapter Five

The Santa Clara was dry. Nothing but a trickle of runoff came through the sun-bleached stones of the riverbed that wound through the heart of the valley. The sky was a cloudless blue brilliance over the Santa Susanas in the north. There was always the wild smell of sage off the hills at this time of year, especially in the cool of the morning when Sandy drove down Soledad Canyon with the top down on her BMW Roadster. She wore a Dodgers baseball cap, bill forward like a ballplayer, a pair of sunglasses down over her eyes. She was listening to her favorite Shania Twain song on the CD.

The traffic was moderate for a Wednesday morning, mostly commuters heading toward the southbound Golden State Freeway that would take them into the San Fernando Valley. Sandy looked out over the river, upshifted into fifth for the long stretch past the old Saugus Speedway, saw the purple robina in bloom down the median, joggers and cyclists along the paseo. It was a beautiful morning—a shame that Wendy Burgess wasn't alive to see it.

Sandy turned into the parking lot of the Santa Clarita Sheriff's Station, parked in a little spot of shade next to Nick's brown Dodge. She removed her ball cap, felt her hair fall to her shoulders in a thick silky mass, brushed out the tangles, then put her cap back on, swung her legs out of the car, and headed into the station.

She found Nick talking with Lieutenant Ubersahl and two uniformed deputies in the Homicide bay. They were standing beside Nick's desk, laughing. One of them had made a joke, apparently.

When they saw her they stopped, all four men watching her. She knew the look well: *Woman on deck.*

She was wearing a faded pair of blue jeans, a blue-and-white–striped boat-necked T-shirt showing beneath a dusty-rose–colored linen jacket, and a pair of white crosstrainers. "Hello, boys," she said, placing her sunglasses in her shoulder purse.

Nick grinned. "Hey, kid."

The men were still smiling, but the joke had passed.

"Good morning, Nick—Lieutenant." She nodded at Lieutenant Ubersahl. "Frank, Tim." She greeted the deputies. She looked at Nick. "Did you get any sleep?"

"There's no rest for the weary."

"That's *'wicked,'* Nick. 'There's no rest for the wicked.'"

"You said it. We have an eleven-thirty at the cooler. I'm thinking of checking in."

"You'll wear yourself down," she said, and looked in through the open door of the interrogation room. "He in there?"

Lieutenant Peter Ubersahl—a square-jawed and brick-shouldered man with a Marine Corps high-and-tight—said, "He's on his way."

"A woman-beater, huh?"

Lieutenant Ubersahl indicated the two uniformed deputies.

Frank Dutton, a stocky man with a craggy, acne-scarred face, stepped forward and nodded. "We came in after our shift last night, saw Nick working on his jacket, and remembered the guy."

His partner nodded.

"Tim and I responded to a four-fifteen a week ago," Frank continued. "When we got there the place was a wreck. He roughed her up quite a bit."

"What address?" Sandy asked.

"On Oleander, same as last night," Tim Sturdevant, the taller and more slender of the two, said. "Her nose was bleeding, and he'd tagged her eye pretty good."

"Which eye?"

The deputies looked at each other. "The right eye, wasn't it, Frank?"

"Yeah, as I recall." He got out his notebook, thumbed back several pages. "Yeah, here it is. . . . Wendy Burgess. Sure thing, the right eye."

"That's what it says here," Nick said, leaning against his desk, reading the report.

That accounts for the bruise on Wendy Burgess's right cheek, Sandy thought. "Who called it in?" she asked.

"The next-door neighbor," Frank said. "He thought someone was going to get hurt."

"Someone did."

The deputies nodded thoughtfully.

"I was thinking we ought to question the neighbors again," Nick said, looking up from the report. "Maybe something got overlooked. You never know."

"Good idea," Sandy said, uncomfortable that she was trailing Nick in the details. She looked at the two deputies. "She didn't press charges?"

"When we got there, everything was quiet," Frank said. "She said everything was all right. There was nothing we could do."

"The little guy was crying and holding her," Tim said. "He told us to shove off. Never wanted to hit a guy so bad in all my life."

"It was the same guy as the other woman."

"What other woman?" Sandy asked.

Frank thumbed back through his notebook. "I don't remember her name. Too far back. I just remember it was a black woman . . . a real looker. Classy, you know."

"You bet," Tim added.

"I got it here," Nick said. "Chandra Tupelo. Canyon Country."

"That's her," Frank said. "Address on Flower Park. Real class act."

"That's her," Tim agreed.

"How did it go down?" Sandy asked.

"Same MO as with the Burgess woman," Frank said. "Lots of screaming and crashing around. Neighbor called it in, afraid someone was going to get killed. When we got there the jerk had calmed her down pretty good. He was blubbering."

"Any signs of battery?"

"Her mouth was bleeding. Right side. I remember thinking he'd connected with his left."

"Sweet man," Sandy said.

"We pulled her aside, asked if she wanted to press charges, but she wouldn't."

Sandy shook her head. "Most of them don't. Don't ask me. How long ago was it?"

"Oh, man. Five or six months, wouldn't you say, Tim?"

"About that. Nick?"

Nick was still reading through the reports. "November twenty-sixth," he said. "Pretty flowery report here, Frank."

Frank lit up. "You think so? I was taking a creative writing class at COC. What do you think?"

"You misspelled 'indubitably,' " Nick said showing him.

"Really?"

"What's *this* word?"

Frank looked. " 'Alacrity.' "

" 'We bounded to the door with alacrity'?"

Frank shrugged. "You know . . . 'enthusiastically.' "

Nick grunted.

"I already talked to him about it," Lieutenant Ubersahl said.

"Anything else on this guy?" Sandy asked, still a little behind in the count. "Anything that would stick?"

"No." Nick stood, looked across the room. "Here he comes now. Mr. Sunshine."

The Homicide room was bustling with activity. A tall, lean-muscled deputy negotiated desks, chairs, and bodies. The Kevlar vest beneath his uniform shirt gave him a false bulk, rather turtle-like in appearance. Behind him walked a very fat, gray-suited balding man, with wiry, unkempt gray hair that stuck out in clumps over the ears. *Lawyer.* He leaned forward as he walked, carried a briefcase, his free arm sawing as if he were in a hurry. Walking seemed a great exertion for him. Steven Weber was last in their winding parade. Black jeans and boots, a leather aviator's jacket with the collar up in back. Arnette sunglasses down over his eyes.

" 'Be still my beating heart,' " Nick said.

"No kidding." Frank pulled Nick aside. "You think 'alacrity' sounds too pedantic?"

Nick looked at him.

The deputy led the lawyer and Weber into the interrogation room.

"See what you can do," Lieutenant Ubersahl said to Nick and Sandy. "And, Nick, no unnecessary roughing of the passer."

Nick grinned. "Me? I'm hurt, Lieutenant."

Sandy stepped into the interrogation room ahead of Nick, took a seat across the long fold-out table from Weber and his attorney, who faced a one-way mirror on the left wall, adjacent to the door. Overhead florescent lights glared off bare white cinderblock walls. It wasn't a happy room. Nick set a small tape recorder in the center of the table, remained standing. Sandy felt his presence beside her, his imposing bulk. Intimidating. Nick was good for that.

Weber still wore his sunglasses. Different man than the one last night. Punk. His small, neat hands were palms down on the table, and he seemed to be studying his nails.

For just a moment Sandy saw in her mind the dead girl at the bottom of the tub, the look of wonder in her eyes, the slight discoloration of skin over her right cheekbone that had come from Weber's fist. When she looked back at Weber he was staring at her through the dark sunglasses, the faintest smile at the corners of his mouth. She felt a shudder of revulsion go through her, forced a smile, and said, "Good morning."

The fat attorney looked at her with open contempt, his eyes red-rimmed and rheumy—allergies, probably. He resembled a large toad. "I do not see that this meeting was necessary," he said, removing a handkerchief from his coat pocket and mopping the tiny beads of perspiration across his brow.

"We would like to ask Mr. Weber a few more questions," she said, still smiling.

Nick turned on the tape recorder.

The lawyer sneezed, blew his nose into the handkerchief, looked at the tape recorder. "No recorder."

"We like to use a recorder to ensure accurate testimony."

"No recorder."

"I would think he'd want to help us in any way possible," Nick said. "Since we're investigating the death of his girlfriend and all."

Weber glanced at the recorder, stared down at his fingers. "I got nothing to hide, Marty."

"Is my client a suspect of some kind?" Marty the Toad asked.

Sandy gestured noncommittally. "At this point Wendy Burgess's death appears to be accidental, Mr. . . . I'm sorry, I didn't get your name."

"Steiner. Marty Steiner." He produced a card from his brief-case, pushed it across the table with chubby fingertips.

Sandy let it lay there. "Mr. Steiner, your client is a valuable resource to us. We just need to fill in a couple of blanks from last night to round out the picture here. Then Mr. Weber is free to go."

"My client has come in voluntarily. He is free to go now."

"That is correct. But like my partner said, I would think he'd want to help us in any way possible, since we're investigating the death of his girlfriend."

The lawyer eyeballed everyone in the room.

"I got nothing to hide, Marty," Weber repeated.

The toad grunted, adjusted himself in the metal chair that seemed too small for his enormous bulk. "My client is a very busy man."

"I'm sure he is," Sandy said. *Spends his time beating up women.* "We apologize for any inconvenience. If we get straight to it, we can wrap this up *tout de suite*."

"Toot-sweet," Nick echoed.

The lawyer looked at the detectives speculatively. "Okay. Hum a few bars and we'll see how this goes."

Nick stated the date and the names of those present in the room, for the recorder. He started to ask a question, but Steiner cut him off with a raised hand. "Not you—her. We'll answer questions from the lady."

Nick shrugged his big shoulders. "All right. Detective Cameron."

The toad looked at her dully.

"Very good," she said, consulting her notebook. "Mr. Weber, you said last night that you started seeing Wendy Burgess at ACN. How long ago was that?"

Weber looked at his lawyer. Steiner nodded, folded the hand-kerchief, again mopped his brow.

"Six or seven months ago," Weber said, not looking at her. "I already told you."

"Yes, you did. And as you mentioned last night, you and Wendy were close."

Weber shrugged. "You could say that."

"You also mentioned that Wendy had started seeing a Bill Pender about a month ago. Could you tell us a little more about him, please?"

Weber glanced at her, looked back at his hands. "What do you want to know? He's a jerk." He looked quickly at the tape recorder, as if just noticing it, straightened himself in his chair. "A first-class *jerk,*" he repeated, for the benefit of the absent Bill Pender, Sandy guessed.

"I see."

"Why do you say that?" Nick interposed. Weber looked at him. "Because he was dating your girlfriend, or for some other reason?"

The lawyer sneezed and blew his nose, shaking his head. Weber did not answer the question.

Sandy smiled. "I take it Pender left ACN before Wendy made the transfer?"

Weber shook his head. "No, they left at the same time. Pender took her with him."

"That's interesting. So her transfer must've been in the works before that."

"I guess so."

"You don't know?"

He shook his head.

"You were dating and she made no mention of her leaving?" Sandy adjusted her ball cap. "I find that hard to believe."

Weber shrugged.

Sandy and Nick exchanged dubious glances. Sandy asked, "What did you think of that? . . . I mean, Wendy leaving with Pender?" She could see his eyes move behind the shades. "Were you happy for her? I assume it was a promotion."

Weber hooked an arm over the back of his chair. "So she said."

"But you disagreed?"

The toad cleared his throat.

"Wendy wanted to get into production," Weber said, ignoring him. "Don't ask me why. She was always hanging around the production types when they'd come over to pitch shows."

"Any in particular?"

He shrugged, checked his nails as if the answer was written on them. "Annabelle, mostly."

"Annabelle?"

"Annabelle Lynch. She's the president at Empire—heads up the animation wing of production there."

"That would be Empire Films?" Sandy asked, writing it down. She had watched the old Tommy Tortoises, years ago, and had liked them. She didn't like their newer ones, however. They weren't funny. "Annabelle Lynch, huh?"

"Yeah, that's right. Wendy used to think the sun rose and set on her. A real sharp cookie." He looked at his watch. On his right wrist, Sandy noticed.

"Any other 'production types' come to mind?"

Weber continued looking at his nails. "Charlie Doogan." He looked at her, smiled. "He's a drunk, lives in Malibu. Wendy liked talking to the dude for some reason. Guess she felt sorry for him."

"I see." Sandy wrote it down, consulted her notes. "You said last night Bill Pender was her 'ticket.' Why is that?"

Weber's mouth again became small and petulant, reminding Sandy of a recalcitrant schoolboy.

"Mr. Weber?"

"How should I know?" he said. "The guy's loaded. He has a big house up on Mulholland. What do broads want, anyway? You tell me." He laughed.

Sandy looked at him steadily. *I can tell you what* this *broad would like to do right now.* "How would you describe their relationship?"

Weber did not answer.

"Were they just dating, or were they getting serious?"

"He told her he loved her. Isn't that all it takes with broads? 'I love you, babe, why don't you come to MIP with me? We'll make some contacts together.'"

"MIP?"

"MIP-TV. Big media convention in Cannes. You ever been to Cannes?" He chuckled. "She'd make contacts, all right. Listen, I know the guy. Bill Pender had one thing in mind, and it wasn't Wendy's mind. She was his flavor-of-the-month. She just couldn't see it."

"So you went over to her house to explain it to her."

"That's right."

The high-pitched whine of the tape recorder punctuated the

silence that fell upon the room. Weber looked at her, looked quickly at the tape recorder. Sandy saw a flicker of light in his eyes behind the sunglasses, and knew she'd trapped him. "Last night you said you'd gone over to her house to maybe go out to a movie," she said, flipping back a page in her notebook. "Now you're telling us you went over there to talk her out of going to Cannes with Bill Pender."

Weber unhooked his arms from the chair, put his hands on the table.

"Which is it, Mr. Weber?"

The toad moved, blew his nose again. "My client has been very helpful," he said working each nostril, "but I'm afraid it's getting late."

The interrogation was over.

Sandy put both hands on the table, leaned toward Weber. "She wouldn't listen, would she, Mr. Weber? Did that upset you?"

The toad was mopping the beads of sweat that had collected along his thick upper lip. "I thought so," Steiner said, folding then placing the soggy handkerchief into his briefcase. "Let's go."

Nick stepped forward and shrugged. "What's the matter, Mr. Weber, you didn't hear the question, maybe?"

"Let's go," the toad repeated.

Weber would not look at Nick.

Nick grinned coldly. "You like to get a little rough with your ladies, do you, sonny-boy?"

Weber and his lawyer stood. "Don't answer him," Steiner said, picking up his briefcase.

Nick opened the door. "Frank, Tim." Frank Dutton and Tim Sturdevant, who had been observing the interrogation through the one-way mirror, stepped into the room. "Is this the guy?"

"That's him," Frank said.

"Yep," his partner agreed. "That's the woman-beater."

"My client was not charged with anything," Steiner said.

"Who said he had been?" Nick said. He turned off the tape recorder, smiled at Weber and Steiner. "Gentlemen," he said, indicating the door.

Steiner started toward the door, turned back. "Don't call us in here again. There will be no more fishing expeditions."

As Weber, easily a half-head shorter than Sandy, passed in front of her, she said, "Mind your head in the doorway."

He stopped and glowered at her.

"Whatever you're thinking, I wouldn't try it on me," she said. "Some of us broads fight back."

"Let's go," Steiner called back into the room.

Weber chuckled contemptuously as he left.

Sandy felt Nick's eyes on her. She turned, saw the corners of his mouth turned up in a wry smile. "What?" she said. Then: "I don't like bullies. Especially bullies who beat up women."

"I can see that."

Sandy went to her desk, sat down, and dialed Chandra Tupelo's number. She wanted another woman's perspective—a live one. Someone named Havers picked up. There was no Chandra Tupelo at that number any longer. Sandy repeated the number. Havers said that was his number now. He'd just gotten it and was getting annoyed by all the calls for Chandra Tupelo.

"What kind of calls?" Sandy asked, after identifying herself as a police officer. "Were they from women or men?"

"Both," Havers said gruffly, and hung up.

She thought about it for a minute, looked across the aisle at Nick. Nick was talking to someone on the phone, looking at the picture of his wife Mary and five kids on his desk. Nick was Roman Catholic.

She stood. "You want a cup of coffee?" she asked. He shook his head.

She walked across the Homicide bay to the break room, pretended not to notice as a few heads turned in her direction. She smelled something burning by the sink—a smoldering scab at the bottom of the coffeepot. She frowned, made another pot, and bought a granola bar from the vending machine. She sat down at a table, waited while the coffee brewed. A candy wrapper, newspaper, and empty coffee cup cluttered the table. She picked up the newspaper, thumbed through it. Yesterday's. She set the paper down, picked it up again when a headline on the back page caught her attention.

The article beneath was a biographical sketch of animation director Parker Stewart, his life and accomplishments, and indicated his death probably had been by his own hand. Sandy perked up. The lead investigator was Sergeant Thomas Rigby of the Burbank Police Department. She set the paper down and looked across the room, thinking. After a while she stood, poured a cup, and walked back to her desk.

Nick was on the phone talking to the neighbor who had called in the 415 on Weber and Burgess a week ago. "Yes ma'am," he said politely. "Thank you, ma'am. Call me if anything occurs to you. Yes, ma'am, you've been very helpful." He hung up the telephone with a grunting sigh. "Well, that's that."

"No luck?"

"Zip. Zero. *Nada.*"

She handed him the newspaper. "Did you hear about this Parker Stewart suicide on Sunday?"

Nick glanced over the article. "Who's Parker Stewart?"

"An animation director. Lives in Burbank. Kind of interesting, don't you think?"

"What's kind of interesting?"

"Two people in the animation industry turn up dead within forty-eight hours of each other."

Nick set the paper down, looked at his watch. "Man, I hate going downtown at this hour. That four-oh-five is murder. You ready to do it?"

"You don't find that curious?"

He looked at her. "You think there's a connection?"

"I find it interesting."

"And curious. Did this Stewart fellow end up in a bathtub blowing bubbles?"

"He shot himself in the head, apparently."

"Well, there you go. Case closed. You ready?"

"Just a second, I want to make a call." She flipped through her directory. "Do you know the number for the Burbank PD?"

"You're serious."

"Never mind, I got it." She dialed the number and waited.

"Burbank Police Department, Sergeant Haskins."

"Could you put me through to Sergeant Rigby, please? That's right. This is Sergeant Cameron from LASO." She waited, frowned. Voicemail. "Sergeant Rigby, this is Sergeant Cameron of Santa

Clarita Sheriff's office. I read an article in yesterday's newspaper regarding your investigation into the death of Parker Stewart. My partner and I are investigating a possible homicide involving someone in the animation business as well. I think we should compare notes." She left her number, hung up the phone.

Nick was still looking at her. "You *are* serious."

"I've got the hot flashes about this, Nick." She stood, picked up her purse.

"God speak to you or something?"

"Very funny."

Nick shrugged his arms into his sports coat. "Why doesn't God ever talk to me?"

She smiled. "Maybe you don't listen."

Nick shook his head. "This Sergeant Rigby any relation to Eleanor?"

On their way out of the station, Sandy asked Senior Deputy Judy Nesbitt, a middle-aged woman with a tight perm and fierce blue eyes, to try and locate the whereabouts of a Chandra Tupelo. "The number we have on her is old," she said. "I'd start with Canyon Country. That was her last known address."

"You got it, Sandy."

Chapter Six

"Did she have sex?"

"She wasn't a virgin, if that's what you mean."

"You know what I mean."

"You mean, did she have sex prior to drowning?"

"Come on, Del, quit horsing around."

"Specificity, my dear. Specificity."

The body of Wendy Burgess was laid out on the table, the Y-section made, the organs and bowels removed and weighed and the contents of the stomach examined. At this stage of an autopsy the body always reminded Sandy of a dugout canoe. "Did she have sex on the night she drowned?"

"No. She hadn't had food, either," Dr. Delbert O'Connell said through his protective mask. He was a thin man, fiftyish, with long, spidery fingers; his eyes quick and sharp-edged like a ferret's. "Give us a hand, Lonny."

The coroner's assistant, a tall black man with a shaved head, steadied the head while the pathologist made the incision from one ear across the top of the scalp to the other ear. He pulled back the skin flap and periosteum, as if peeling the skin off a grape. The exposed skull gleamed a dull oyster white, except for a two-inch area just behind the left temple, where there was a dark clotted mass—the result of blunt force trauma. Del gently wiped this area clean with a sponge, revealing a crushed depression in the skull, then, picking up the bathroom tap, fit it neatly into the depression.

"A perfect fit," O'Connell said. "See?"

Nick and Sandy stepped closer to the table, bent over, and looked. "And you think slipping and falling could have provided enough force to do that?" Sandy asked.

"Might she have been pushed?" O'Connell said. "By the estranged boyfriend, perhaps?"

Sandy nodded.

"It's possible, of course. However, more than likely she slipped and fell, cracked her head against this little devil, and drowned." He set the tap on the table. "She was quite drunk." He shrugged. "Occam's razor."

Sandy thought about it. *Occam's razor: "All things being equal, the simplest explanation is probably the correct one."* "How drunk?"

"Point–one-three."

Nick whistled.

"Can you tell us anything about that bruise on her cheek?" Sandy asked.

"I was noticing that," O'Connell said as he moved around the table. He angled the head to one side, with none of the tenderness Jorge Ortega had shown the previous night. "My guess is it's about a week old."

"A week to the day," Sandy said thoughtfully. "Point–one-three, huh?"

"The amount of alcohol in her liver suggests she had been drinking steadily for several hours. Someone who drinks alone like that is either a lush or is fighting off demons."

"Assuming she *was* alone," Sandy said, looking down at what once had been a very pretty woman. For reasons Sandy could only describe as a hunch, the simplest explanation for how Wendy Burgess had drowned in her bathtub did not quite cut it with her—Occam's razor or not.

● ●   ● ●

Tom Rigby looked down at Stewart's impounded computer. "So, you're saying the dead man typed it, Fitz?"

"That's the funny part, Tom." Detective Robert Fitzgerald, a thirty-something Irish welterweight, had short-cropped red hair, and round, sad, poet's eyes that seemed to Tom always to be contemplating some great injustice. He also had a knack with computers. "He typed it, all right. Using his right hand, though."

"That's quite a feat for a dead man," Dan Bolt said as he joined them, chuckling at his pun. He was eating a Snickers bar.

Tom cocked his head. "What do you mean?" he asked Fitz.

Fitz took them around the corner into his office. "Look here, boys." He indicated the keyboard of his computer. "Can either of you two type?"

Dan shook his head in feigned disgust. "Can either of us *type?*" He tossed the candy wrapper into the trash, sat down at the computer. "You want me to type your resignation, maybe?"

Fitz rolled his big sad eyes. "Type 'That's all, folks!' "

Dan wiggled his fingers over the keyboard, began typing out the letters.

"See what I mean?" Fitz said. "The letters T, A, F, S, and the exclamation point—especially the exclamation point—are usually made by the fingers on the left hand."

"Okay," Dan said, verifying it with his own fingers. "What if he couldn't type? What if he used the old search-and-destroy method?" He demonstrated with his right index finger.

"You said he was left-handed, didn't you?"

"Yeah."

"And he didn't use only his index finger. He used his index and middle fingers haphazardly, middle finger here, index finger there. Didn't use his third finger or his pinkie at all—not to type out the note."

Tom frowned. "But you found them on other keys?"

"That's right. All eight digits, thumbs on the space bar. Just not for typing out the note. I thought it was pretty weird."

Tom thought about it a moment. "Any other prints?"

"Not on the keyboard. Plenty of prints in the house, though. The FETs are still cataloging them."

"How about the gun?"

"Victim's prints all over it. Just his. Checked the bullets in the magazine and the spent casing. Same."

"Gun oil on the keys?"

"Clean." Fitz walked over to a long bench where there were other forensics paraphernalia the field evidence technicians had gathered.

"Here's something else." Fitz held up a petri dish with grains of sand in it. "The sand vacuumed up from the carpet around the computer desk. There's no sand like it anywhere else in the house, only around the desk. We got dirt samples from the dead man's toenails. No match. Doesn't match anything we got from the garden, either."

"What is it, beach sand or something?" Dan asked.

"Don't know yet. We're sending it to LASO."

"That sand could've been there for weeks."

Fitz smiled at Dan as if humoring an imbecile. "You said he had a cleaning lady, right?"

"So the legend goes," Tom said.

"Well, that's it for now," Fitz said. "I just thought it was curious about the keyboard."

"It is. You do any snooping inside yet?"

"First the outside, then the inside. I'll install some file-recovery software in a day or so. Maybe sooner. I'll try."

"Thanks, Fitz. Let us know what develops."

Fitz looked at Tom almost mournfully, sighed deeply, and went back to Stewart's computer.

Tom and Dan headed back to their office, met Lieutenant Joe Stenton in the hall. Stenton handed Tom a manila folder. "Just read the ME's report."

Tom opened the folder and glanced through the report. The medical examiner had officially ruled Stewart's death a suicide. "What do you want us to do with it?" Tom asked, handing the folder to Dan.

"You've got a pretty full caseload, right?"

"Sure."

"Prioritize." Stenton clutched his stomach.

"What's the matter, Joe?" Dan asked. "You're looking paler than usual."

"Very funny."

"He's right, Joe," Tom said seriously. "You might be coming down with something. You look white as a sheet."

"Don't mention sheets around Joe, Tom," Dan said. "That's very insensitive of you. Not to mention politically incorrect."

"Shut up, Dan," Stenton said, gingerly kneading his stomach.

"Okay, Joe. Say, does it feel like you've got hamsters crawling around in your guts?"

Stenton went back down the hall, holding his stomach.

Tom noticed the message light blinking on his phone, sat down at his desk, hit the MESSAGE button, and listened. He hung up the phone. "You ever hear of a Detective Cameron from LASO?"

Dan shook his head.

"A woman?"

"Sorry, Tommy."

"The name rings a bell."

"Friend of Carolyn's, maybe?"

"No. She says she's working on a case that may be connected to ours." Tom dialed Detective Cameron's number and got her voicemail. He left his name and number, the time he'd called, and hung up.

"She got a nice voice, Tommy?"

Tom shrugged.

"You got to watch those nice voices," Dan said. "I've known some real train wrecks with voices that could start fights."

Tom ignored the remark, dialed Empire Films's number, got the receptionist with the face metal, and asked for Charlie Doogan. She put him on hold. He waited, rap music playing. He hated "rap music," an oxymoron if he'd ever heard one. He looked across the desks at Dan. "Train wrecks, huh?"

"Five kinds of ugly."

The receptionist came back on the line, said Doogan wasn't in. He was working at home today. She sounded bored.

"Where's 'home'?" Tom asked.

"I'm sorry, but we can't give out that kind of information."

Tom identified himself. The receptionist remembered him, put him on hold. More rap music. Tom held the phone away from his ear. A minute later the girl came back on the line, a smile in her voice as she gave Tom the address; followed it by saying she dated a guy once who'd wanted to be a cop. Tom said that was nice, thanked her for the address, then hung up the phone. He stood.

"Where're we headed?" Dan asked.

"Just me, partner. I've got some business that needs tending, then I'll head out to Malibu. Charlie Doogan."

"What business?"

"Some leftover goodies from the divorce. Legal crap. I won't get out to Malibu till late in the afternoon." Tom put on his jacket.

"You mind riding herd on the John Doe prints? Lot of unaccounted traffic in that house."

"Sure. You ain't buyin' the suicide?"

"I don't know. Something screwy about it." Tom looked down at the phone.

Dan grinned. "Train wreck, Tommy."

"Shut up."

Tom left the office, stopped at Detective José Martinez's office down the hall. Martinez reminded Tom of a pit bull. Short, compactly built, tough as nails in a fight. Grew up in an East L.A. barrio. "Let us know if you hear anything on the Gonzales woman, okay?"

"Okay, Tom."

"The minute you hear, okay?"

"I said I would, didn't I?"

Tom went down the back stairs two flights to the basement, slid into the driver's seat of his Bronco. He left the garage, feeling a knot of dread in his stomach as he turned left onto Orange Grove, then headed crosstown to meet with Carolyn's attorney.

Chapter Seven

The name PANDA PRODUCTIONS and the black-and-white panda bear logo stretched across the top of the building in bold, backlit lettering, three feet high, so that it could be clearly seen from the Golden State Freeway, day or night. The twelve-story glass-and-steel edifice was a modern marvel located in the heart of the Burbank entertainment district, one of the recent efforts by the city planners to give the city a face-lift and to lure media moguls from Hollywood. It appeared to be working; aside from live-action studios, cartoon studios were springing up all over town—Nickelodeon, Dic, Cartoon Network. Nowadays you couldn't trip and fall without landing on an industry type.

Sandy and Nick waited in the sprawling penthouse lobby. Nick said he didn't like industry types, eyeballing a steady stream of same breezing in and out of the bank of elevators. Called them "fruits and nuts—L.A. is full of them."

Sandy smiled wryly. "Half the town is from New York, Nick. That why you moved out here? To be near some of your homeboys?"

Nick grunted.

Ten minutes later a girl in a red miniskirt and white blouse came out, spotted Sandy and Nick standing next to a potted fern, and said brusquely, "The party isn't until Thursday. You're a day early."

"Party?"

"Yes. You're with security, right? For the party?"

"We're police detectives." Sandy presented her badge. "Different party."

The girl's head bobbled slightly. Sandy saw in her dark green eyes that shade of curiosity and distrust of authority with which many people greeted agents of the law. "What—?"

"We wish to speak to Mr. Pender."

"Bill?" A pretty redhead, her hair cut short and teased up into a sassy swirl that spiked down over her pale forehead. A sprinkling of freckles went over the bridge of her pointy nose. "May I ask what about?"

"It's private."

The redhead glanced at Nick, back at Sandy, made a quick, woman-to-woman appraisal. It wasn't pretty. "Really."

"Really." Mexican standoff. Sandy wasn't budging.

The redhead looked at the balding, bulb-headed guard behind the huge entryway desk, as if to enlist his help, glanced at her watch, looked back at Sandy. She seemed caught in a situation she was not prepared to handle. Didn't surprise Sandy a bit. "All right, then," she finally said, glanced at her watch again. "I suppose it will be all right. This way, please. I'll see if Mr. Pender can fit you in."

Good answer, Sandy did not say. "Thank you," she said, smiling as pleasantly as she could.

"I hope Bill isn't in any kind of trouble."

She and Nick exchanged looks, then followed the girl down the hall. The carpet was a plush mauve, with coordinated wall coverings. The furnishings in sitting areas off the hall were upscale. There were offices along the right, names on little plaques. As they passed by open doors, Sandy saw people in business suits or dresses, standard in corporate offices for large firms. No one remotely resembled an industry type.

On the left there were cubicles, a racial hybrid of young men and women, working on computers mostly, everyone dressed nicely. Soft, up-tempo music piped in through invisible speakers. There were plants, small trees, paintings, and statuary everywhere. Nothing like Sandy had imagined a cartoon studio would look like. "You *do* make cartoons here, right?" she asked the redhead. "Where are the artists?"

"The artists? On the second floor, mostly," the redhead said coolly. "Most of our shows are co-productions. The work is done overseas mostly, so we don't need many artists."

"I see."

The redhead was trim, about five-five in her spiky heels. She walked pertly, with economy of movement, except for the parts of her anatomy that jiggled. Sandy placed her in the Little Miss Efficiency pigeonhole. "How many floors does Panda occupy?" Sandy asked.

"The top ten."

"What do you use the other nine for?"

"Recording, post-production, legal. We're a full-service house."

"Just the one floor for artists?"

"That's all they need."

By her condescending tone Sandy imagined the second floor was crammed wall-to-wall with cages. They rounded a corner and made their way along a similar hallway.

Nick appraised the landscapes and foxhunts on the walls. "My uncle was an artist," he said. "Painted billboards."

The redhead quickened her pace. "That's nice."

Nick turned to Sandy. "All over Queens. Big ones."

Sandy smiled.

They came into an open area where there were three young women at desks, typing. A plant custodian was tending a healthy looking *dieffenbachia* on one of the side tables in the waiting alcove, opposite large oak doors. "My name is Sharon O'Neill," their escort said, indicating upholstered chairs and sofa along the wall to their right. "You may wait here."

Sandy smiled cordially and elected to remain standing.

O'Neill disappeared behind the oak doors. Sandy looked across the room and found the typists looking at her from their desks. One was a pretty black girl, one a pretty Latina, the third a pretty Asian. *Concubines,* came to Sandy's mind. Babes-in-waiting. The air was thick with a mixture of perfumes. They resumed typing.

Sandy looked to the right of Pender's office, saw an empty, low-walled cubicle with a large desk and return. WENDY BURGESS, EXECUTIVE ASSISTANT, was embossed on the horizontal plaque by the opening of the cubicle.

She stepped over to the cubicle and peeked over the low wall. Against the wall behind the desk was a bookshelf with books and plant arrangements, knickknacks, everything neatly arranged.

Framed in silver on the desk was a photograph of Wendy in a bikini, her arms wrapped around a handsome, black-haired man with a great tan. He was perhaps in his mid-forties, trim and healthy-looking. They were aboard a sailing yacht of some kind, the man at the large chrome wheel. Sandy saw clearly in Wendy's smile the answer to the question she had put to Weber concerning Wendy's relationship with Bill Pender—assuming the man in the photo *was* Bill Pender.

Sharon O'Neill stepped out of Pender's office, saw Sandy by Wendy's office, and her eyes narrowed with disapproval. "Mr. Pender will be just a moment."

The way Sharon said it made it clear to Sandy she had not been given liberty to snoop around the office. "Thank you," she said. She returned and stood next to Nick, who—hands folded behind his back—was admiring the three concubines.

The sound of voices intruded, grew steadily louder, then the doors opened and three men stepped out of the office into the waiting area. The first two were young—artists, Sandy presumed, by their trendy, noncorporate apparel. Lesser mortals. The third, standing between them, dominated them in height and stature. The man in the photograph: Bill Pender.

The room felt immediately charged with the high wattage of his personality. The three concubines looked up from their work and smiled adoringly at him.

He was wearing a pair of off-white linen slacks, Armani loafers, a light-turquoise polo shirt that showed off his muscular physique. With a confident jawline, intense blue eyes set wide and deep, and a dark, golden tan, he was strikingly handsome.

"This is good stuff, Bill," one of the artists said to him.

"I need the designs by Friday," Pender said. "Remember, I want different approaches for MIP."

One of the artists held up a drawing of a voluptuous girl in a space suit, with fox ears and tail, the only evidence in the building, so far, that they were in a cartoon studio.

"Keep it sexy," Pender said.

"No problem," one said, and the two of them left the office.

O'Neill gestured to Sandy and Nick. "Here are the police, Bill."

Pender turned his attention to them. His gaze went from Nick to Sandy and, glancing over her body as though it was his for the taking, he flashed perfect white teeth. "My name is Bill Pender," he said in a rich baritone. "Aren't you lovely."

Sandy, taken aback, felt the heat rise to her cheeks. Before she could utter a response, O'Neill stepped forward, touched his arm, and said, "Bill, she's with the police."

"Oh?" He put out his arms toward Sandy in mock surrender, his wrists touching. "Arrest me, I'm yours." He smiled. The concubines giggled. Then, without missing a beat, he looked over at the empty cubicle and said, "Still no word from Wendy? I need the results from the focus group."

O'Neill shook her head. "I called twice. No one answered."

Sandy cleared her throat. "Actually, we're here to talk with you about Wendy."

He looked at her, the smile returning to his face. "Yes?"

Sandy glanced at O'Neill, back at Pender.

His expression changed. "Is something wrong? She's not in any kind of trouble, I hope."

"I'm afraid we have bad news. Ms. Burgess is dead."

There was a collective gasp from the concubines. O'Neill's hands rose to her face. "No!"

Bill Pender looked at Sandy as though it had to be a joke of some kind. Apparently reading her eyes, the color drained momentarily from his face. It was like a brownout, a dimming of light and energy in the room that affected his face, his carriage, his voice. "Wendy . . . dead?"

"That's right," Nick said, with a shrug of his shoulders. "She died last night."

Pender seemed visibly ill.

"Perhaps you should sit down, Mr. Pender," Sandy said.

"Yes." He slumped down into a chair beside Wendy's cubicle, arms resting Lincoln-like on the padded armrests. He stared across the room. "How?" He found Sandy's face, her eyes. "Was it an accident or something?"

"We think so. She drowned in her bathtub."

"Her bathtub?"

Nick said, "She apparently slipped and hit her head against the tap."

Pender stared at him blankly, then looked back at Sandy. "You're serious."

"I'm afraid so."

"My word! Last night?"

Sharon O'Neill and the three concubines sitting at their desks were staring at Pender, dumbfounded.

"I suppose I should cancel the party," he said, to a vague point about two feet in front of his nose. "Sharon?"

O'Neill stepped forward. "I'll take care of it, Bill."

"Perhaps we can go somewhere a little more private," Sandy suggested. "In your office, perhaps?"

"What? Oh, yes, of course." He stood, glanced at the cubicle to the right of his office door. "Wendy, dead. I can't believe it."

"Can I get you anything, Bill?" O'Neill touched his arm.

"No thanks, Sharon." Then: "Maybe a glass of water."

Sandy followed Pender into the large corner office. The one wall of solid glass, shuttered now against the bright afternoon light, drew her attention. She caught glimpses of the mountains, roofs, and treetops through the horizontal slats. The adjacent wall was dominated by a state-of-the-art entertainment center with multiple screens. As Pender stepped to the desk in the center of the room, Sandy glanced around the room. While the walls were otherwise bare, they were hung with a few photographs—no cartoons—mostly of Pender with movie and television stars, civic leaders, a congressman or two. Nick pulled the door shut behind him, gave the office a quick once-over, then raised an eyebrow at Sandy, which, if translated, meant, *Willya get a loada* this *joint!*

Sandy agreed. Opulent—from technology to picture frames, from the plushness of the gray carpet under her feet to the subtle scent she recognized as bergamot. She could only guess what had been spent on just that essential oil. Extravagant.

Pender had picked up a silver framed photograph from his desk, stood visibly slumped as he stared at it. Finally, still holding the photograph, he walked around behind the desk—all chrome and glass and angles—and gestured for Sandy and Nick to be seated in the black leather chairs in front of the desk. He sat, too, stared down at the photograph. His chair, also black leather, tall and sleek, was positioned behind the desk in the center of the room so that he could comfortably swivel to face the windowed wall, the entertainment center, the entry, and what appeared to be a conference room through open double doors on the fourth wall.

Sandy had studied his physical reactions and facial expressions. He was either a very good actor, or he was indeed grief-stricken. Sandy knew it could be either one.

"She drowned in her bathtub, you say?" he said, his voice a mere echo of its former resonance.

"Yes."

"Isn't that odd? In her bathtub."

"She had been drinking heavily."

"Drinking?"

"Yes," Nick said. "Quite a bit."

Pender looked at each of them with obvious incredulity. "Wendy never drank."

Sandy followed his gaze into the adjoining conference room, which was similar in decor—foxhunts and landscapes on the walls, bronze sconces, green plants and ornamental trees softening its corporate edge.

"She'd drink a little at parties, but only to be sociable," he said, his voice halting, uncertain now. "She never got drunk."

"Her blood alcohol level was point–one–three." Sandy gave him a moment, then asked, "Mr. Pender, can you think of any reason Wendy would be drinking so heavily?"

"No, I can't."

"There was nothing that happened yesterday that might have upset her?"

He shook his head. "Nothing I can think of." Again he looked down at the photograph in his hands, the shock still evident in his features. "I just can't believe it. Wendy . . . She was so young."

"And beautiful," Sandy added.

Pender looked at her. "Yes . . . Yes, she was."

Pender's solemn declaration was followed by a moment of silence. Only the four world clocks over the double doors could be heard ticking their overlapping cadences.

There was a soft knock on the door, and O'Neill stepped into the room with an eight-ounce bottle of Perrier, a glass tumbler filled with ice cubes, and a twist of lime. Her face was streaked from crying, her eyes red. She poured the Perrier into the tumbler, the ice tinkling, placed a cocktail napkin beneath it, and offered it to Pender. He set the photograph down on the desk, took the tumbler with his right hand. O'Neill stood looking at him. "Are you all right, Bill?"

"I'm okay."

Her hand rose in an obviously aborted gesture—as if some compelling thought had died—then fell helplessly to her side. "I'm sorry, Bill. Really."

"It's all right, Sharon. Thank you."

"I can't believe it. . . . Wendy, dead." She started crying again and Pender stood, put his arms around her, and gave her a hug.

"Oh, this is horrible," she sobbed. "Are you sure you're all right?"

"I'll be fine." He let go of her.

She dabbed her nose with a tissue. "I'd better get to work. With MIP and everything."

"That's right, MIP," he said, a glimmer of light coming to his eyes, his shoulders squaring, some color and vitality returning to his face. "Best get to it."

O'Neill looked at Sandy and Nick, smiled, and as she turned to leave, said, "I can track down the focus-test results, if you want, Bill."

He brightened, electric-blue eyes snapping to life. "Would you? We must have them."

"I'll get right on it. Don't forget your videoconference at four."

"Thank you, Sharon. . . . Sharon—?"

She looked at him.

"About the party. Just trim the fat a bit. You know, get rid of some of the also-rans. We can't just cancel. I don't think Wendy would have wanted us to."

This brought a renewed wash of tears. The pretty redhead wiped at her eyes. "I'll make up a new list and show it to you."

"There's a dear. Be sure to include Chandra."

O'Neill's eyes flickered. "Who? Oh, right—Wendy's friend."

"I would like to see her. I miss her." Pender smiled. "Her number should be in Wendy's Rolodex."

O'Neill bit her lower lip. "I still can't believe it."

Sandy and Nick exchanged looks as the redhead jiggled across the room. Nick stood and followed her. *Fruits and nuts,* he didn't say, but Sandy knew Nick was thinking it. He closed the door behind him, leaving Sandy and Pender alone in the office.

She smiled at him; he smiled at her. A handsome man, a beautiful woman. The world clocks ticked onward.

"Would you like something to drink?" Pender asked.

"No, thank you." She set her purse down on the floor. Sunlight coming through the blinds made patterns over the desk and floor, ran up the ornate wainscoting of the wall. "You have a beautiful office."

"Thank you." Pender walked around the desk, sat down in the chair where Nick had been sitting, crossed his long, elegant legs, and smiled appraisingly at her. "Beauty reflects beauty, don't you think?"

She looked at him, not certain how he'd meant it. She smiled, took her notebook from her purse. "Mr. Pender—"

"Call me Bill." As he settled back into his chair, confident, masculine, she could see the pectoral muscles jumping beneath his shirt, the ripple of tendons in his forearms as he raised his glass. "Everyone calls me Bill." He smiled before taking a sip of his drink.

"Bill," she said. "I'm sorry to trouble you at this upsetting time, but I must ask you a few questions."

"Yes, of course, Ms. ———? Mrs. ———?"

"Detective Cameron."

"Detective Cameron. A real policewoman. Do you like what you do?" he asked, the slightest edge of condescension in his baritone.

"Yes, I do."

"Someone with your looks—"

"—needs a steady paycheck. Mr. Pender . . ."

He leaned forward, touched her hand, and she felt something go out of her, as though he had fed on her. "Bill," he reminded her.

"Yes, of course, Bill."

Whatever brownout of power there had been in his personality, she could almost feel her scalp tingle from the electricity that again charged the air.

She crossed her legs and, supporting her notebook against her knee, clicked her ballpoint pen. "I understand Wendy was your executive assistant. How long had she been with the company?"

He shrugged his shoulders, took a sip of Perrier. "Since the first of the year. Why?"

"These are just routine questions, Mr. Pender."

"Bill," he corrected.

"Yes." She turned the page in her notebook. "Forgive me for seeming to pry, but—"

"Go right ahead. 'Shoot'—as they say in the movies."

"I couldn't help but notice your reaction to Wendy's death. It's clear there was more than a working relationship between you."

"You mean, were we romantically involved?"

She nodded.

He thought about it a moment. "We were close, very close. Let's leave it at that."

"When was the last time you saw her?"

"Wendy?" He picked up the tumbler, took a sip of Perrier, gently rattled the ice. "Yesterday afternoon. Why?"

"Can you be more specific?"

"Four o'clock, maybe. She went home early, said she wasn't feeling well."

Sandy looked up from her notes. "You said earlier she didn't seem upset about anything."

He made a point with his left index finger. "I didn't say she was upset. I said she wasn't feeling well. She'd been working hard with the focus-testing. It takes it out of you."

"Can you define 'not feeling well'? Was it physical? emotional? stress, perhaps?"

He smiled wanly. "I learned a long time ago never to ask a woman what's ailing her."

"Wise man. Did you talk with her before she left work yesterday?"

"Of course we talked."

"About work?"

He thought about it. "I might've asked her about the focus tests. Yes, I did. She said that they would be in sometime this morning. Then she told me she was going home because she didn't feel well."

"I see. These focus tests have something to do with the upcoming conference in Cannes, I take it."

His blue eyes sparkled beneath the deep-set brows. "You know about MIP?"

"A little."

He took another sip of Perrier, again rattling the ice in the tumbler. "Yes—to answer your question. They give us our demographics. Our target audience. If an idea tests high with, say, boys ages six to twelve, we market it accordingly. If it tests low, we scrap it or retool it. Or if it tested better with girls—ditto. Everything is based on audience response, you see."

Sandy frowned.

"Something wrong?"

She looked at him. "It just seems a bit like putting your finger in the wind."

"How do you mean?"

"I mean, whichever cultural wind is blowing at the time, you chase it."

"That's one way of looking at it."

"What if a good idea didn't test well and a bad one did?"

"There are no bad ideas or good ideas," Pender said matter-of-factly. "There are ideas that make money and ideas that don't."

"A 'bad idea' might make money, then."

"There you go."

"Based on the focus group."

"That's where we start, yes." He took one last sip of his drink and set the empty tumbler down in front of him. "A successful franchise can net hundreds of millions. We can't just leave potential revenue like that to some one person's conviction that he's got a winner."

"Not even yours?"

"Not even mine."

Sandy raised her eyebrows. "No room for the visionaries, then—the Michelangelos . . . the Walt Disneys?"

"They're dead. We live in a different world now."

How true. "No room for someone like Parker Stewart, then?" Sandy watched to gauge Pender's reaction. There was none.

"I suppose not. I was sorry to hear about that."

"You knew him?"

"Everybody knew him." He picked a piece of lint off his trousers.

"I'm sorry, I got a bit off the track." She smiled apologetically. "It's all very interesting."

He smiled.

She looked at her notes. "Panda is a Japanese entity?"

"That's right. Our parent company is in Tokyo. We have offices in New York and London also."

"Like your wall clocks."

"Like my wall clocks," he said, without looking at them.

"Because of your background at the network, they've put you in charge of the production wing to see whether you could make a go of it?"

"You've been reading up on us."

"What if it doesn't fly?"

"It will."

"You seem confident. Got a shoo-in at MIP?"

A curious shadow played over his features. The smile held.

"Okay, new question." She flipped the page in her notebook. "What would happen if someone—say, one of your employees— was disgruntled with the company and wanted to take an idea over to a rival company?"

"What are you driving at?"

She shook her head. "It's just hypothetical. Corporate espionage. I'm sure you've heard of it happening in a business where there are hundreds of millions to be made."

"There are no disgruntled employees here," Pender said emphatically. "At least not in the inner circle of people who are involved with R and D. We screen people tightly before they gain access to anything of importance. Why do you ask?"

"Parent-company directive?"

"That's right. Panda treats its people very well. Why . . .?"

"I suppose the security around here is pretty tight. To prevent leaks and such."

He did not answer at first. "Most studios have security," he said finally. "What's this got to do with—?"

"And Wendy came through the filter with flying colors."

Again she watched to see his reaction. No response. "She'd only been with the company—what?—three months, and already she was going with you to MIP."

"Who told you that?"

"I'm sorry." She looked up from her notes. "She *wasn't* going with you?"

He glanced at his wristwatch, looked up at the four clocks as though to verify the watch's accuracy. "Listen. . . ." He stood, walked across the office, took the two oak steps that ascended into the adjoining conference room, and walked around the long table that stood in the middle of the room. "MIP is a Chinese fire drill. Wendy is . . . *was*"—he corrected, looking back at her over his shoulder—"very bright and extremely well organized. People liked her. That goes a long way in this business."

"Do you know of anyone who *didn't* like her?"

"What kind of question is that? Do you think—?"

"I don't think anything. I'm just trying to construct a background, a profile. Can you think of anyone?"

He opened the mahogany cabinets facing the table, revealing a large television monitor. "Everybody liked her. She was a sensitive person who cared deeply about people." He shook his head. "No, I can't think of anyone who didn't like her."

She stood, followed him into the conference room. Pender was busy attaching a cable leading from a telecommunications device to the back of the monitor.

"Still, she came far in this company in a very short period of time." Sandy left the thought hanging.

"Like I said, she was very well organized. I reward intelligence, skill, and hard work. Background or no background, I really don't see how these questions have anything to do with anything."

"Mr. Pender, a young woman, who drinks only occasionally, leaves work early—apparently not feeling well—goes home and proceeds to get roaring drunk by herself, then ends up drowning in her bathtub. I would like to know why."

Pender was looking over at her, his expression thoughtful. "I would, too." He went back to attaching the cable. "I have a video-conference in five minutes. I'm sorry, but I'm afraid I'll have to cut this short."

"Just one more question: What is your opinion of Steven Weber?"

Pender stopped what he was doing and looked at her. "Steven?" He grunted contemptuously. "The next time I see him I'm going to pop him in the mouth."

"Really?"

"I'm sure you know why, since you asked the question. If Wendy was upset by anyone, it'd be that runt."

"Had he upset her lately?"

"Lately? *Constantly.* He kept harassing her on the phone, going over to her town-house, begging her not to leave him. He was obsessed with her. Last week . . ." Pender's eyes filled with anger. "Did you know he hit her?"

Sandy nodded.

"She came to work with a shiner. Said it was an accident, or something. You know, the old 'I fell into a doorknob' business. But I knew it was Weber. I wanted to pound the crap out of him. I will, too, next time I see him."

"How did you know it was Weber?"

"The little runt couldn't take no for an answer, that's how. He wouldn't leave her alone."

"Did he call Wendy at work yesterday?"

"I have no idea. He's sick. I told her to press charges but she wouldn't. . . . There we go," he said, finished with the cable. He picked up the remote, pointed it at the machine, clicked it. The speakers buzzed as the monitor became a large blue screen, a single eye of electric light. "Why all the questions about Weber? Do you think he had something to do with her death?"

She closed her notebook. "I think that should do, for now."

"He's a sick man, Detective. He should be locked up. Anything more I can do to help, you let me know."

"You have been very helpful, Mr. Pender."

He smiled. "Bill—remember?"

She nodded. "Bill."

He rechecked his watch, and she felt the mood in the room change, become solemn again, as if an invisible curtain had fallen then risen again to begin the next act.

"It was a pleasure to meet you," he said, taking her hand. Then, bringing his other hand up, he held hers firmly but tenderly in a double clasp and gazed thoughtfully at her. "This has been a terrible shock. It hasn't hit me fully that she's gone." Sandy saw a hidden pain somewhere deep in his blue eyes, a mist appearing, then disappearing.

"You're trembling," Pender said, releasing his grip.

"Yes. It's a bit chilly in here," she said, rubbing her arms, again feeling as though something had gone out of her.

He smiled warmly at her. "Right now I have work to do. That's a blessing, I suppose. I know that, later tonight, once the merry-go-round has stopped spinning, it'll hit me. She was a wonderful girl. I'll miss her."

Sandy nodded, looked quickly to her left, startled by the sudden sound of movement and voices. She saw in the television monitor a room, not very different from the one in which she was standing, with several Japanese men in business suits entering and taking their seats around a large conference table.

"The horses are lining up at the gate," he said.

"Thank you for your time."

Pender removed a business card from his wallet and handed it to her. "Here are my numbers, in case you have any more questions. You can reach me on the cell phone anytime, day or night."

"Thank you." She walked over to where she had been sitting, picked up her purse, placed her notebook inside it. She turned back and said, "I do have one question before I leave."

"Yes?"

"Who will go with you now?"

"Go *where* with me?"

"To MIP. Any replacement in mind?"

A flash of teeth, a charming smile. "Obviously I haven't thought about it."

"Of course." She slipped the card into her purse. "If I have any further questions I'll be sure to give you a call."

"Do, please."

As Sandy entered the waiting area, she felt relieved to be away from the charismatic CEO of Panda Productions. Nick was just concluding his interview with the concubines.

"What did you find out?" she asked him as they were getting into their vehicle and pulling out of the parking garage underground.

Nick raised his eyebrows. "Not much. Wendy may have been a little tense and distracted, but so was everyone else in the place, with that MIP business going on. What a racket."

"No visitors or anything?"

"None that came to her office. It was a busy day, apparently, so no one was paying much attention."

"Any calls from Weber?"

"If there were, no one knew of them." He shrugged. "O'Neill did say that Wendy wasn't feeling well and went home early."

"That jibes with Pender's story. Anything else?"

"Just that the two of them went to the gym every night after work. Last night Wendy passed. No reason given. O'Neill thought it was maybe her 'time of the month.'"

"We know from the autopsy that that wasn't the case."

Nick looked at her. "What's next, kid? Empire Films?"

"You got it. Annabelle Lynch."

As Nick turned down Orange Grove, Sandy saw the Burbank police station. "Wait a sec, Nick, pull in here first. I want to talk with Sergeant Rigby."

"Another hot flash?"

"Just pull over, wise guy."

Chapter Eight

Tom stepped onto the stoop of the tiny, shingle-sided bungalow, rang the doorbell, and waited. He felt lousy. He didn't know which was worse, the smell of formalin or the smell of lawyers. It was a toss-up. A couple hours on the boat would wash the smell from his nostrils. At least *he* was clean of it—if "clean" was the right word for it. Carolyn made more money than he did, so there wasn't any alimony to pay. She'd got everything she wanted—house, Volvo, cash settlement. Tom got to keep the boat and the TV. Her lawyer said that he should consider himself lucky: "At least there's no child support." Tom almost decked him. He should have.

He looked out over Malibu Beach at the sun, still high overhead, beginning its dying descent into the Pacific Ocean. The air was cool for the beginning of April, but there were still a few sunbathers on the beach. There were also a few gray-haired men in the water on longboards, sitting off the point like a pride of old sea lions. He felt like joining them.

Tom glanced down at his feet. The stoop upon which he was standing was made of sawn railroad ties bolted together. There were weeds coming up through the ties and through the sand all around the base of the bungalow. Made it seem as if the house were squatting in a nest. Behind him, a narrow flight of wooden stairs ran from Pacific Coast Highway down to the beach. He ran the toe of his shoe over the sand.

He was about to ring the doorbell a second time, when the door opened. Tom was greeted by the truculent glare of a white-haired man in his midfifties, two days' growth of white stubble covering his lower face, and a cigarette hanging off his thick bottom lip. He was a big man, about five-eleven or so, maybe 250 pounds. Big shoulders and arms. He was wearing a faded Hawaiian shirt, opened in front. A massive swell of belly ballooned over a pair of denim cutoffs. The man's belly button—about a mile deep—was aimed at Tom's kneecaps.

"Charles Doogan?" Tom asked.

The man stared unblinking at him for a moment, his eyes nearly colorless except for the red rims that were either from sleep-deprivation or alcohol. "I ain't buyin' today," he said brusquely.

Tom put his hand out and caught the door as it swung toward his face. "I ain't sellin'."

"What the hell—!"

Tom produced his badge. "I'm Detective Rigby with the Burbank Police Department."

Doogan eyed the badge, grunted. "What do you want?" he asked, his thick fingers opening and closing slowly. "A bit out of your bailiwick, don't you think?"

"You don't mind answering a few questions, do you?"

"What about?"

"May I come in?"

"What about?" Doogan repeated.

"I'm investigating the death of Parker Stewart."

"This is the day for it." He started to close the door. Tom caught it. Doogan looked at him, squared off, and for a moment Tom thought it might come to blows. Hoped it would; give him a chance to work out some of the lawyer. "I didn't kill him," Doogan said.

"No one said you did."

"I already talked to that other detective."

"What other detective?"

"The broad. You just missed her."

Tom felt a flash of anger.

"A police woman was here?"

"A detective something or other."

Tom figured it was Det. Cameron nosing into his case. "She was asking you about Stewart?"

"She got around to it. She led off with something about some stiff named Wendy Burgess. Asked if I knew her."

"Who?"

"Forget it."

"We can talk here, or we can go inside," Tom said. "It'll only take a few minutes."

Doogan looked at his watch. "I'll give you five." He turned abruptly and padded barefoot back into the bungalow, leaving the door open. Tom stepped inside.

The bungalow was a single open room, the kitchen to the left, and, to the right, through a span of horizontal picture windows, a view that took in a good stretch of beach and ocean. A telescope pointed at the old pier. An easel and paints were set up in the corner. Reed mats covered a parquet-tiled floor. A bamboo-framed sofa stood against the wall. The middle cushion, the one in which Doogan obviously spent much of his time, was sunken. Over the sofa were hung some paintings of beach scenes, a fishing boat, a nude. There was a photograph of a girl on the side table next to a stack of *Daily Variety*s and *Hollywood Reporter*s. The placed reeked of cigarettes, beer, and cheap cologne; even so, the bit of sea air that eddied through the room kept Tom from being asphyxiated.

Doogan went to the refrigerator and pawed out a bottle of Coors Light. There were several empties on the counter. He came back into the room, twisted the cap off, and sat down in the sunken middle cushion of the sofa.

Tom remained standing. "Nice place."

Doogan grunted. "I work at home for the privacy."

Spread out over a bamboo coffee table, the table pulled up close to the sofa, was a cartoon storyboard, a script, and a stop-watch. Doogan picked up the stopwatch, leaned forward to better view the storyboard, clicked the starter button. Clicked again and looked at the time, wrote it down under the drawing in the board. Right hand. Tom guessed he was writing the timing for each scene. He'd seen them do it at Disney World—"slugging the board," they called it. Every scene, every bit of action or dialogue, took a certain amount of time. It was the director's job to pre-edit the film, cut the excess before it ever got animated. Save a ton of dough.

Tom glanced at the photo of the girl—seventeen or eighteen, he guessed. "Pretty girl."

Looking down at the storyboard, making a correction, Doogan gave no indication he had heard Tom.

"She a relative of yours?"

"My daughter," Doogan said, not looking at the photo or at Tom.

"Pretty," Tom repeated.

"She's dead."

Tom looked again at the photo.

Doogan shook his head. "You're here about my little run-in with Parker Stewart last week."

"That's right."

"It was a professional disagreement."

"Do you always threaten people you have professional disagreements with?"

"Is that what you heard?" Doogan clicked the starter button, turned the page in the storyboard, looking at the drawings, clicked the button again.

"Witnesses say it got pretty heated."

Doogan shrugged, wrote down the time on the storyboard. "I didn't kill him."

"Okay, so you didn't kill him. He did the job for you. Got any ideas why?"

Doogan looked up at him, his eyes as tired and mean as an old, worn-out bull's. "He had a rare moment of conscience and decided to do the world a favor?"

"I can see you're overwhelmed with grief."

Doogan laughed, a smoker's rattle. The ash from his cigarette fell to the floor. He started coughing, still laughing. "Oh, yeah . . . *overwhelmed*. That's a good one." He flicked what was left of his ash into the ashtray. "No, I guess I'm not too broken-up about Parker Stewart killing himself. The world is a better place with that scumbag dead." He took a sip of beer, wiped his mouth with a deft flick of his index finger. "He did everyone a favor."

"You think losing his job might've put him over the edge?"

"If it did, the next time I see Annabelle Lynch I'm gonna kiss her feet."

"I take it you two weren't on the best of terms."

"I hated him."

"Enough to kill him?"

Doogan chuckled.

"What was it between you two?" Tom asked.

"That's my business."

Tom tossed a copy of the *Daily Variety* onto the storyboard in front of Doogan. Doogan glanced at it, batted it aside. "Maybe you didn't like what he said about you in the trades," Tom said.

"Everybody's entitled to his opinion. You think I had a motive or something, is that it? Is that what you're angling at?" He grunted. "You cops."

Tom watched him take a sip of beer, noting he held the bottle daintily for a big man; noted also that he had a Band-Aid across the knuckles of his right hand.

"You didn't read the article very closely," Doogan said, wiping his mouth. "I was given *his* job. *He* had a motive to kill *me*. You ever think of that one, Sherlock?"

"Why was he fired?"

"Oooh, now, there's an angle for you."

"Do you know, or don't you?"

"Sure I know. He had the mistaken idea that because his name was Parker Stewart he didn't need to stay on budget or make deadlines. Imagine that! 'Pick up your pink slip on the way out, please.' " Doogan chuckled, started to cough, but caught it in time. He sipped his beer and cleared his throat. "And he had the gall to call me a 'dinosaur.' "

"Among other things."

Doogan took a long pull on his cigarette, squinting at Tom through the smoke. "Let me tell you a little something about dinosaurs, Sherlock." He cupped his hand to catch an ash. "Stewart was the dinosaur. He couldn't change with the times. Now he's extinct."

"How do you mean?"

"I mean, the business changed, and he couldn't change with it." Doogan again dropped the ash into the ashtray, sat back in the sofa. "Used to be, studios were run by artists. People coming up through the ranks were made heads of departments, even studios."

"Like Hanna-Barbera?"

"Clever boy. It was a different ball game back then."

"How so?"

"The network would pay a studio a license fee for a show, and the studio would go away and produce it with minimal network involvement. The artist with a good idea was king. It's all changed now."

Doogan finished his beer, got up and went into the kitchen, set his empty on the counter with the others. He opened the refrigerator, grabbed another Coors Light. "Back in the late 'seventies, early 'eighties," he said as he walked over and sat back down on the sofa, "'show' content—at least on the made-for-syndication series— became toy-driven. Thank *Star Wars* for that."

"*Star Wars?*"

"Action figures. Toy sales went through the roof." Doogan eyed Tom as he wrote in his notebook. "All the big toy companies suddenly wanted to get into the animation business. Rather than toys being ancillary to good cartoons, cartoons were showcases for toys; they became nothing more than half-hour–long toy commercials. Toy companies made a killing."

He took a long pull of the beer, and Tom saw that Doogan had overstepped some delicate balance of timing. "Networks, hurting from the bite the syndies were taking out of their ratings and market shares, wanted a piece of the pie," Doogan continued, now slightly slurring his words. "But they couldn't *own* shows; they could only license them from the studios, for maybe a two-year domestic run. The networks could only make their money from ad dollars. Afterward, the studios could take their shows and syndicate them internationally, making a haul in the ancillary markets."

"Neat deal for the studios," Tom said.

"No kidding. You could own a piece of it in those days." Doogan looked out the span of windows. Tom followed his gaze to a pelican gliding low over the shore break. "Then everything hit the fan," Doogan continued. "With the advent of cable, the market expanded. Network ratings and market shares splintered even more; ad dollars decreased; and so did license fees. The networks lobbied Congress and cried foul. The result—deregulation."

"Deregulation?"

"Death knell for the artist: the little guy with an idea—God love 'im."

Doogan took another lengthy pull of beer, and Tom watched the color rush into his throat and cheeks. Doogan sat back in the sofa, his face suddenly expansive, his belly button now aimed at the ceiling like a trench mortar. Whatever initial surliness the man had displayed against the world in general—cops in particular—alcohol seemed to have taken care of it now.

"It's all about ideas," Tom said.

"You bet." Doogan drew on his cigarette, left it dangling on his lip. "Now that the networks could own a percentage of the shows they broadcast, they weren't about to give any of it to the lousy artist. Little studios either went out of business or were bought up by bigger ones now being run by the suits. 'New school' in session."

" 'New school'?"

"Lousy broads runnin' everything." Ash fell onto Doogan's chest; he brushed it off. "Most of your key positions run by broads. . . . Used to be receptionists . . . production assistants. Heads of studios now. None of them are artists. Wouldn't know a good story if it bit 'em on the butt. But they sure know how to network, don't they? Let me tell you, can *they* network!"

Tom let him talk.

Doogan took another healthy pull of the beer. Some of it ran out of the corner of his mouth and down through the stubble on his chin. "Everything's so stinking inbred and market-driven now. Everything designed by a lousy committee. No one can take a crap anymore without some lousy focus group telling you which way the wind's blowin'."

He scratched the white hairs on his chest, clearly peeved. "New school. The whole industry, shot to hell."

He drained the bottle, looked at it in the light. He labored up off the sofa, slopped into the kitchen, and got another. "Hey, you want one of these?"

"Sure."

Doogan handed him a bottle. "They let you boys drink on duty?"

"I was off-duty an hour ago."

Doogan got out another bottle and opened it. "Cheers," he said, then disappeared around the corner. Through the opening Tom could see a bedroom to the left and knew, based on the general layout and vintage of the place, that there was probably a second bedroom to the right, separated by a bathroom.

Tom heard Doogan in the bathroom.

"Co-production is the thing nowadays," Doogan said over what he was doing. "Toy companies partnering with the networks, partnering with the big studios, partnering with the international syndies. Any entertainment is a by-product. An accident, really."

Tom sipped his beer, looked at the photo of Doogan's daughter. There was something about her face that struck a chord. He'd seen her before. He looked at the nude; if it wasn't the daughter, it was her sister or her mother. He made a closer comparison. Probably her mother. A close likeness, except for the hair color and the shape of the jaw. It was a good piece, reminded him of a Gauguin painting. He heard a toilet flush.

Doogan came back into the room zipping up his fly, and sat down again in the sunken cushion of the sofa. "It's all about vertical integration now," he said, his eyes glassy. "Big studios like Disney and Warner buying up the networks, controlling the whole shootin' match. You see it happening now with ACN and Panda. Vertical integration. Bill Pender wants to be the next Rupert Murdoch."

"Who's Bill Pender?"

"CEO of Panda. Used to head up ACN. The broad asked about him, too. Good-lookin' broad," he added. "Great legs—"

"What about Pender?"

"He's a suit . . . a sharkskin suit. Sharks like Pender are eating up the animation business."

"Death of the artist."

"You bet."

"You're still working."

Doogan took a swallow, sighting at Tom over the bottle. "That's because I don't give a rip anymore. Get check, cash check."

"What about the Internet?"

"Webisodes? No money in it yet. Maybe five years, there'll be money, but not now."

"What if someone wasn't in it for the money? What if someone just wanted to get his ideas out into the public? Do an end run on the suits?"

Doogan looked at him curiously.

Tom set his beer down on the coffee table, removed drawing number 5 from the manila folder, and showed it to Doogan. "Ever see this drawing before?"

"It's Stewart's."

"You've seen it before, then?"

"I didn't say that."

"You can tell just by looking at it?"

"That's right. The guy may've been a scumbag, but no one ever said he couldn't draw."

"So, you've never seen this drawing before."

Doogan tapped another ash into the ashtray. "How many times do you want me to tell you?" he said, renewed surliness coming through in a darkening scowl.

"Ever been to his house?"

Tom caught an edge of wariness in Doogan's eyes. "No," he said. "No, I haven't." He looked at his watch, stabbed out his cigarette in the already-full ashtray. "Your time's up. I have a storyboard to slug."

"One last question: Where were you between five and six o'clock last Sunday afternoon?"

Doogan chuckled as he reached for another cigarette. He lit it with a silver Zippo, blew a cloud of smoke into the smoky room. "I was where I always am on Sunday afternoons."

"Where is that?"

"None of your damned business."

"I can make it my business."

Doogan's eyes became cold and deadly. "You do that, Sherlock.

There's the door. Don't let it hit you on the way out." He picked up the stopwatch, looked at the next drawing on the storyboard, and hit the starter button.

Tom stood looking down at him. He didn't like drunks, especially drunks with an ax to grind. He picked up his beer, went over to the kitchen, and poured the remaining contents into the sink.

"Just set it there," Doogan growled.

"I'll just take it with me as a souvenir." Tom tossed a nickel onto the table. "Here's for the deposit." Tom crossed the room and exited.

Stepping onto the stoop, Tom took in a breath of clean sea air. The smell of the ocean grounded Tom, gave him clarity. Perspective. He looked at the angle of the sun, figured he could get a couple hours of sailing in yet. Had to.

He took a small envelope out of his coat pocket, bent down, and picked up and poured a handful of sand into it. As he started up the steps toward the highway, he looked back into the bungalow through the kitchen window, saw Doogan sitting on the edge of the sofa, holding the photograph of his daughter. Tom shook his head, continued up the steps.

Tom opened the door of his Bronco and slid into the driver's seat. He placed the beer bottle with Doogan's prints on it into one of the evidence bags he kept in the glove box, and put in a call to Dan at the station. There was no word yet from the Gonzales woman, Dan told him; she'd probably hightailed it back to Mexico. The forensics boys had cataloged a dozen sets of fingerprints from Stewart's house. Got a partial on the phone booth that matched, putting the Latina caller inside the crime scene. "Run a make on Doogan," Tom told him.

"Already did. No wants or warrants." Dan added that a Detective Sandy Cameron from LASO had stopped by to talk about the Stewart case. He had filled her in on some generalities, no real specifics. She gave him the highlights of her case, said she thought the two deaths were more than coincidental.

"Talk about your train wrecks, Tommy! Had all the guys here running into walls."

Tom said nothing.

"You didn't see her?" Dan asked. "She said she was heading out there."

"I didn't see her."

"You must've just missed her then." Dan whistled. "A real train wreck," Tommy.

Chapter Nine

He remembered Carolyn coming up from belowdecks, carrying a plate of jumbo shrimp with one hand and holding two bottles of St. Pauli Girl with the other, the bottles beaded cold from the icebox. She wore a lightweight yellow windbreaker over her new bathing suit, and—as she came toward him, her long legs, tanned from the sun—he remembered the spread of her toes as they gripped the teak deck. The boat was on a close reach, and she steadied herself against the tilt.

"I brought you a beer," she'd said, pleased with her sea legs, as was he.

"I'm going to miss you," he said. He took the beers until she sat down, then gave one back to her. They touched bottles.

"It'll only be for a couple of weeks."

"Yes—but Hawaii. Why do they have to do these things in Hawaii? Couldn't they have found a place here?"

"Jealous."

"You bet." Tom looked at her. "You're not taking that bathing suit, I hope."

"Why? Do you think I'm beginning to show?"

"You show plenty."

"That's not what I mean, silly." She combed his hair with her fingers, purred, "Do you like?"

He grinned at her. "I like."

"After dinner." She smiled. "Aren't these shrimp delicious?"

"I don't think I can wait until after dinner."

Afterward, they lay in bed and talked about the baby, traded names until they'd agreed on two: Emily, if it was a girl; Hudson, if a boy.

Tom felt the sails luffing. Back on the boat; all that behind him now. Some of it, at any rate. He made a steering correction. The bow swung slightly to leeward, air filling the sails with a snap of canvas. He could feel the 42-foot Downeaster pull through the water as he steered a course for the mouth of the harbor, the sun a shimmering gold coin on the horizon to starboard. She had left him the week she got back. No explanation. Just: "I don't love you anymore. I don't think we should waste our lives, do you?"

"Is it another man?"

"No," she had said. But, of course, it had been.

The channel was crowded with boats. Tom lowered his sails and started the motor. He'd always kidded his sailing buddies who lowered their sails inside the breakwater—real sailors sail in. But he was through with sailing for the day. He was through with a lot of things. At least he'd got to keep the boat. That was something. Motoring up the channel—past boats bobbing to gentle swells, masts rocking, keeping time with the rhythm of the sea, a sea as old as time itself—Tom saw his slip, angled the bow to port, then cut her in sharply to starboard to make the slip.

A leggy blonde wearing a Dodgers baseball cap watched from the dock. "Ahoy there!" she called. "Isn't that what you sailors say?"

Tom didn't know what to make of her. She wore a pair of faded jeans, a striped T-shirt, and a light-colored jacket. Then, when he saw how pretty she was, he knew at once, and he felt something come up cold inside his chest.

"Detective Rigby?" She waved.

He put the boat into reverse, throttled the motor to cut the speed, throttled it again. Feeling the swell of his wake lifting the boat, he killed the motor and let the boat coast forward neatly into the slip.

"I was told I might find you here," she said as he tossed two lines off the port side of the boat onto the dock, one fore and one aft. "We've been playing phone tag."

He threw over the fenders, swung himself off the boat, and caught the bow before it nosed up to the dock.

"I'm Detective Cameron." She smiled.

"That's nice." He tied off the bow on the deck cleat, hurried back along the dock to the stern. "You're in the way," he said, passing in front of her.

She stepped back. "Sorry. Your partner told me you were coming out here," she said, her voice a little less *"Ahoy there, matey!"* "I've been waiting here for a couple hours. I must've just missed you."

Tom pulled in the boat to hold against the fenders, tied off the stern with a cleat hitch, then stepped back onto the boat.

"Pretty boat," she said. "Do you need any help?"

He went below without a word. Through a port window he could see the bottoms of her legs. She wasn't going anywhere. He shook his head, opened the closet, and got out the nylon boom sleeve. He climbed topside, could see Cameron out of the corner of his eye, her hands on her hips. Didn't look at her.

"I'd like to talk to you about your case," she said. "I think there might be a connection between yours and mine."

He began tying down the mainsail to the boom.

"Can I come aboard so we can talk?"

"No."

"Why not?"

"Don't want you to."

She stiffened. "Okay, Tarzan, what's eating you?"

Tom ignored her. He finished tying down the mainsail, picked up the boom sleeve, spread it over the boom, and began fastening it shut.

"I think there may be a connection between the deaths of Wendy Burgess and Parker Stewart."

He stopped what he was doing and looked at her. "You got any evidence?"

"I'm working on it."

"You got nothing."

She looked away at a seagull in flight, looked back at him. "You're about the friendliest guy I've met today."

"I don't like people walking through my cases."

"Who's walking through your case?"

"You are." Tom coiled the lines, stowed the seat pillows below, then came back up, closed the hatch, and locked it. He poured the water from the cooler over the side, then carried it off the boat and set it down on the deck.

"Can we go somewhere and talk?" she asked.

Tom looked his boat over, saw that everything was in order, then picked up the cooler and started up the dock.

"Did you hear me?" she asked.

"I heard."

Sandy followed him. "I think it's rather odd that two people in the same business—a *small* business, I might add—turn up dead within forty-eight hours of each other. . . . People who knew each other."

Tom opened the back of his Bronco, set the cooler in the cargo area, then shut the door. "You know for a fact they knew each other?"

"I know they'd probably met."

"Oh, 'they'd *probably* met'! 'Did you hear that, members of the jury?' I wonder what the odds of that were?"

"Stewart pitched a show at ACN while she was an employee there."

Tom looked at her. "Who told you that?"

"Charlie Doogan. Animation director for Empire Films. Annabelle Lynch told me he'd had a fight with Stewart, so I checked it out. I find it interesting."

Tom thought about it. "How long ago was the pitch?"

"About six months."

"Six months. Talk about your coincidences!" Tom shook his head as he opened his car door and slid into the seat. He started the engine, looked out the window at her. "Like I said, you got nothing."

"So, just forget about it, right?"

He put the Ford into gear. "I'm working on a suicide. From what I hear, yours is an accident. Unless you got something more concrete than that they *probably* met six months ago, stay out of my case."

She glared at him. "Do you always carry that chip around on your shoulder, or did you just forget to eat your Wheaties this morning?" She started across the parking lot toward a steel-blue BMW Roadster.

He watched her walk away, shook his head. *Way to go. Why don't you take it out on the world?* He put the vehicle in PARK, called out the window: "Six months is a long time."

She continued walking.

"Was Doogan at the pitch?"

No response.

"All right," Tom said. "It's interesting. I'll give you that."

She stopped, stood with her back to him. "Aren't you generous."

"What was Stewart's pitch?"

She looked back at him. "I don't know. Look, Detective, I didn't mean to pee in your sandbox, okay? It won't happen again." She started to leave.

"Wait a minute."

She stopped.

Tom tapped the top of the steering wheel with both hands. "I'm a first-class jerk when I don't eat my Wheaties."

She turned, folded her arms across her chest. "Nice of you to admit to it."

"A little crazy, too."

She tapped her foot, appraising him. Finally, the hard lines of her face softened into a smile and she started forward. " 'We all go a little mad sometimes.' " She quoted Norman Bates in *Psycho*.

Tom watched her. Dan certainly had been right about her looks. Shoulder-length blonde hair, bright—maybe hazel—eyes, light olive complexion. Probably had a touch of Latin in her ancestry. But, seeing the way she carried herself, the way she seemed to glide over the pavement with unaffected grace, he saw she was something more than a looker. She had a natural beauty that wasn't learned, and it didn't come out of a tube. He managed a smile as she came up to his car door, extended his hand through the window. "Truce?"

She shook his hand. Long, cool fingers. "Forget it. I'm just looking for some answers, Detective."

Aren't we all? Tom did not say.

"Can we go somewhere and talk?" she asked.

Tom looked at her, felt the old ache in his chest. No—now was not a good time; he wanted to be alone. Alone, he could bury it. "Sorry," he said, averting his eyes from her gaze. Definitely hazel. I can't. Tomorrow okay?"

She stood looking at him, her eyes probing for the lie. "Okay. I'll call you tomorrow, then." She stepped back from his car.

Tom put the Bronco in gear.

"By the way, I don't believe in coincidences," she said. "Acts of men and acts of God, yes. But coincidences . . .?"

They both smiled. A beautiful woman; a lonely, confused, angry man. "I've gotta go," he said. "Tomorrow, then. I'll call you."

She waved.

Tom pulled away. Looking into his rearview mirror, he saw her standing in the parking lot watching him, her hair glowing in the last light of the day. He thought about turning the vehicle around, going back and taking her someplace to eat, someplace to talk, maybe get some of it off his chest. He certainly needed to.

He kept driving.

Chapter Ten

A search into the unlisteds by Judy Nesbitt had turned up Chandra Tupelo's phone number, and Sandy dialed it. She waited for four rings.

"Hi, you've reached Chandra. Please leave a message at the tone."

Sandy gave her name, cell-phone number, said she would like to talk with her as soon as possible. She hung up the phone, typed in her police access code, then typed the woman's name into her computer. She took a sip of coffee, stared at a layer of dust in a neglected corner of her desktop while waiting for the information to download. She wondered if there was something metaphoric about her life in that. She also wondered where she'd seen the photo of the girl in Charlie Doogan's house. Still waiting, she reread the note Nick had left on her desk: *You'll never meet Mr. Right if you never get away from the office.*

She raised an eyebrow, wiped away the dust with the palm of her hand. *Mr. Right is a myth.*

She was thirty-two, a spinster by Victorian standards, with no Cupid's arrows in sight. She had gotten close to a couple of men over the years, but nothing she considered a serious relationship. The first man was a well-known horse trainer she had met at one of his clinics. He was a good trainer but, as she discovered quite by accident one night, he had other love interests, so she had broken it off. The second man she'd met at church—a decent, moral, upright man—but their interests were miles apart. She had a passion for horses; his was dirt bikes. They had drifted down separate paths. No one since.

The photograph of an attractive black woman downloaded onto her screen, along with her particulars: olive eyes, brown hair, five feet eight, thirty-one years old. Chandra Tupelo lived off McBean in Valencia. Sandy knew the area, very upscale. Unlisted phone number. Marital status: single. Sandy wondered if Steven Weber had anything to do with the relocation and unlisted number. She hit the PRINT keys, waited while the printer did its work.

She was about to turn off her computer and head home when, on a whim, she typed the name DETECTIVE SERGEANT THOMAS RIGBY, BURBANK PD into the search window. Moments later, the photo downloading onto her computer screen showed a ruggedly handsome man. Not GQ-pretty. More a man's man. Blue eyes, brown hair, six-two, thirty-three years of age. He lived off GlenOaks Boulevard in Burbank. Marital status: divorce pending. Sandy raised an eyebrow.

He had entered the Burbank Police Department; served as a patrolman until 1997, when he received the Medal of Valor, for heroism in the line of duty. He had taken two 9-millimeter slugs in his chest, rescuing a mother and two child hostages from a drug bust gone bad. Later, after a six-month convalescence, he was back on the streets as a detective sergeant.

Quite a record; only blemish, the divorce. How pending? Why? No clues in his record. Her curiosity was aroused. Cops had an inordinately high divorce rate, she knew. Job stress. Walking through the sewers of human society every day, it was difficult not to track it home.

She looked at his eyes. Blue—the same color as her Roadster—set with the proud intensity of someone who had the world by the tail. Quite a contrast to the man she'd met at the marina earlier. She remembered the look on his face. It was there; a clue. She had seen it in a fleeting glimpse, like some mischievous ghost that vanishes when you turn quickly to it. Pain. Whatever else had played in the lines of his face, there was pain. Suddenly, compassion for him bloomed in her chest. Perhaps it was her maternal instincts; perhaps it had been a very long day. Yeah, that must be it. She wrote down his phone number, collected her things, and left the station.

● ●   ● ●

Rhubarb attacked her when she opened her front door. "I'm sorry, Rhub," she said, scratching the back of the cat's head. "What? You think I've been putting in too many hours? Well, we'll have to see about that, won't we?"

Rhubarb rubbed against her leg, mewing plaintively.

Sandy poured a glass of white zin, went over and sat down in her favorite chair, kicked off her shoes, and wiggled her toes free of the stress and the heat of the day. She needed to relax, unwind, to luxuriate in the quiet solitude of her home. Her refuge against the world. She looked across her living room, took in the whole of the room that in many ways defined who she was—the tooled saddle, the silver buckles in the glass case, the Western paintings, the earthy solidity of her furniture, her mother and father smiling at her from the mantel.

The ceaseless ticking of the grandfather clock against the wall echoed some unutterable lament, and drew from her a deep sigh. She picked up the *TV Guide*, saw that *To Catch a Thief* was playing—one of her favorite movies. That would do it. Cary Grant and Grace Kelly. The cloud of melancholy lifted, a breath of anticipation stirred. But when she turned on the television she found it had been preempted.

She turned off the television. Chasing a myriad of troubling thoughts from her mind, she sat thinking about nothing until a needling thought wormed its way to the front of her mind. *Should I?* She looked at her watch. Not too late. She stood, went over to the telephone, and dialed the number. One ring . . . two rings . . .

"Hello?"

Sandy perked up. "Is this Chandra Tupelo?"

"Yes. Who is this?"

Sandy set her glass of wine down on the counter. "My name is Detective Cameron. I left a message on your phone earlier."

"I was just about to listen to my messages," the woman said. "Is this about Parker?"

"Actually, no."

"I came home as soon as I heard."

"Came home?"

"Yes, I was gone on . . . vacation. I guess that's what you'd call it. . . . He killed himself?" Even not knowing the woman's normal tone of voice, it sounded strained now to Sandy: a voice edged with pain. Northeastern accent—New York, probably. "It doesn't make sense."

"No, it doesn't." Sandy opened a drawer in the counter, pulled out a pad of paper and pen, wrote across the top: *Phone interview— Chandra Tupelo*. She wrote down the date and time.

"Why would he do it?"

"I don't know," Sandy said. "Actually, Ms. Tupelo, I'm calling about Wendy Burgess. I'm told you were friends."

There was a moment of silence. " ' Were'?"

"You haven't heard."

"Heard *what*? What's happened to Wendy?"

"She's dead, I'm afraid." Sandy heard an intake of wind, a gasp, on the other end of the line. "Ms. Tupelo, are you all right?"

"What? No. Yes. Give me a moment."

"Take your time," Sandy said. "I'm sorry about this."

"Was it an accident? A crash?"

"She drowned in her bathtub."

"Her bathtub? Dear God, what's happening? Parker kills himself, and Wendy . . . What? Drowns in her bathtub? How do you do that?"

"She apparently slipped as she was getting into the tub and hit her head against the tap."

"How bizarre."

"Yes."

"I can't believe it. . . . Wendy. When did it happen?"

"Last night," Sandy said, suddenly feeling as if it had been a year since she was looking down at the submerged face of the dead girl. "The two of you were close?"

"We were friends. Not close. We didn't socialize or anything. We went out a couple of times after work. She'd come to me for advice. Big-sister stuff. She was naive."

"Naive?"

"Do people do that? Slip in their tubs?"

"It happens."

"Well, it must. . . . I mean . . ."

"You said she was naive."

"She was terribly naive. A child in many respects."

"How so?"

Chandra grunted. "Her choice of men, for one."

"Men like Steven Weber, perhaps?"

"So, you know about him," Chandra said, contempt edging the pain out of her voice. "Isn't he something?"

Yes, isn't he? "I understand the two of you dated awhile."

Sandy heard her take a sip of something, heard the glass clink on a hard surface. A wood table, perhaps. "Guilty as charged."

"What can you tell me about him?"

"Easy. . . . Little man, big ego."

"There must have been some attraction."

"There was," Chandra said, her voice stronger now. "He was handsome. A bit on the short side, but I didn't care about that. He was friendly, charming, did little things for me. You know—flowers, notes, little presents, opened doors. The perfect gentleman. I thought to myself, 'Hey, he ain't so bad, for a white boy.'"

Sandy smiled.

"We dated for several weeks," Chandra said. "Had a great time. Then one night he asked me to marry him." She laughed. "*That* set me back on my heels. I told him we ought to slow down a bit, and that's when I began to see another side of him. The demons showed their fangs."

"Demons?"

"My momma used to tell me there really were demons in the world. I believe a few of them set up shop in that boy."

Sandy perked. "Can you be more specific?"

"He's very controlling. It came out in little ways—the way I did my hair, how I did my nails, the clothes I wore. He wanted me to be somebody else, one of those Stepford women, or something. That wasn't for me, honey."

"So you broke it off?"

"Eight months ago now. September."

Sandy wrote it down. "Is that why he hit you?"

"So you know about that, too? No, that little present didn't come till later."

"How much later?"

"A couple of months or so."

Sandy thought about it. "That seems odd. Why a couple of months?"

"It gets a little confusing." Chandra took another sip of her drink. "Not long after I broke up with Steven I got a call from Wendy, asking me if I would mind if she went out with him. I guess he'd been making passes at her." She laughed. "So, what else is new? I told her it was fine by me. Believe me, honey, I was relieved. I thought about warning her about his ways but—hey—none of my business. I didn't hear any more about it until after the party."

"Party?"

"There was a party for Bill Pender . . . a big blowout back in November. Panda and ACN were merging, you see. Bill was leaving his post as Head of Programming to take the helm at Panda, and the network threw a bash. Everyone from Panda and the network was there, hobnobbing—department heads down to secretaries and runners. It was something."

"What's this got to do with Steven hitting you?"

Chandra chuckled. "I told you it was confusing. That night—the night of the party—Bill asked Wendy to come to Panda with him. Apart from being beautiful, Wendy was a sharp cookie—naive but sharp, know what I mean? She knew the ins and outs of the network and had a savvy sense of production. She called me the next day, asking me what she ought to do. I told her that she was a big girl and ought to follow her heart. She left."

"And Steven blamed you."

"That's right. He figured I poisoned Wendy's mind against him. Came over to my house one night and knocked me around. He was a crazy man—called me every name in the book. Tore my place up pretty good, too."

"Why didn't you press charges?"

"I don't know. He cried like a baby. I felt sorry for him, I suppose. Steven is the kind of boy you feel sorry for. Like I said, he's got demons. He's terribly insecure about his height."

Sandy glanced at her notes. "From what I've read about you, you're a tall woman. Five-eight. So was Wendy."

"Go figure. I'm no psychologist, but maybe it makes him feel in control—you know, like he can dominate tall women or something."

Sandy frowned. *Yeah, then cut them down to size.* "Did you know that he hit Wendy a week ago?"

"No . . . No, I didn't," Chandra said quietly. There was a long pause.

"Ms. Tupelo?"

"I should've pressed charges."

Yes, you should have. Sandy started a new page of notes. "Is Steven's hitting you why you left ACN?"

Chandra made a deprecating noise in her throat. "I decided to leave long before his little game of tag. No, the main reason I left is that I had high expectations for children's programming. I thought I could make a difference, really make a mark. You know—fun, quality entertainment that makes kids laugh? Boy did I roll craps with that one."

"How do you mean?"

"The way things were going, everything was either too violent, or too full of psychobabble. Definitely too toy-driven. Heaven forbid we should entertain children to entertain them. What a concept that would be, huh? When Bill passed on Parker's idea, it was the last straw. I decided to pack it in."

"I'd like to hear about Parker's idea . . . his pitch."

"Oh, you'd have to see it. Me telling you about it over the phone wouldn't do it justice. 'It's all in the line,' as he would say." She paused. "I'll tell you this much: It was funny and it had heart. Lots of heart—something Bill Pender wouldn't understand if it landed on his head."

"You sound bitter toward him."

"Does it show?"

"A little. Were you—?"

"—*lovers?*" She laughed. "No way. Billy-boy worked his charms on me once but I showed him the gate."

Sandy smiled. "Was Wendy at the pitch?"

"No, it was just Bill and me. Wendy would've had no reason to be there. She was in Business Affairs."

Sandy wrote it down. "To your knowledge, did she and Parker ever meet?"

"They might have. Who knows?" Chandra paused. "Wait a minute. Now that I think of it, they might've met. Parker may've signed a nondisclosure form."

"A nondisclosure form?"

"The network usually won't look at any proposals without one. It protects them. The network may have a property already in development, then in comes a studio with a pitch that's similar. Happens all the time. Without the nondisclosure, the studio or artist could claim that the network stole their idea."

"And Wendy's department would've handled this?"

"Yes." She grunted. "I still can't believe it. Parker's idea was pure genius . . . a breath of fresh air. Good old Bill waved it off like a bad smell."

"But wasn't he leaving?"

"Didn't matter. The whole industry was going that way. Bill was just leading the charge. He thought Parker's idea was too soft, too old-school. 'Not edgy enough,' was how he put it. It's like someone telling Mozart his music wasn't up-tempo enough for them." Her voice cracked, and Sandy heard the pain return in her voice. "Parker was a sensitive man. . . . He took it pretty hard."

Sandy weighed this last comment against the "the scum of the earth" description she'd gotten earlier from Charlie Doogan. Clearly there was a disparity in people's perceptions of Stewart. "I can tell you were close," she said.

"Close?" Chandra cleared her throat of emotion, laughed quietly. "I guess you could say we were close. I'm carrying his baby."

Sandy recoiled. "I'm sorry," she said. And when other words failed her she said again, "I'm very sorry."

"That's all right." Chandra was quiet for several moments. "I have his baby growing in me. That's something. That's something, isn't it?"

"Yes, it is," Sandy agreed, not wishing to enter into a moral discussion. This was a potential homicide investigation. "Did Parker know about the baby?"

"No. I just found out myself. That's why I went away, to think things through. I didn't want Parker to feel trapped."

"Can you think of any reason why he'd want to take his life?"

"No."

"Pender passing on his idea?"

"That was the past. Parker lived in the present—" She choked. "Oh God. Maybe if he'd known about the baby he wouldn't have—" She broke down. "I'm sorry. It's only just now hitting me."

"That's all right, take your time." Sandy let her cry. "Tell me when you're able to talk."

Sandy heard her blow her nose. "I'm okay."

"You're sure?"

"I need to talk it out. You're the first person I've talked to about it since I heard it on the news."

"I'm sorry you had to find out that way."

"I'm all right now," Chandra said, took a sip of her drink. "I must be careful not to drink too much with the baby. I'm going to keep her."

"'Her'?"

"I got a feeling it's going to be a girl. A little princess."

Sandy was truly happy for her and told her so.

"She's going to know her daddy was a brilliant man," Chandra said, a smile evident in her tone. "A brilliant man," she repeated, and Sandy knew she needed another moment.

"Almost finished here," Sandy said. "How're you holding up?"

"Fine. I'm actually feeling better. Talking about it kind of lightens the load. Like sharing a burden. It—" Her voice fell away from the receiver, as if she'd turned her head.

"Ms. Tupelo?"

"It's nothing," she said, coming back on the line. "Thought I heard something. Now, where— What was your name again?"

"Detective Cameron."

"No, your real name."

"Sandy."

"Sandy. You sound like a Sandy. You sure don't sound like any cop I ever talked to before."

"I'll take that as a compliment."

"It is, honey. Believe me, I've known some cops. You call me Chandra."

"All right, Chandra." Sandy started a new page. "Do you know a Charlie Doogan?"

Chandra laughed. "Everybody knows Charlie. "Charlie's been in animation since Methuselah got acne."

Sandy laughed. Charlie Doogan certainly was a crusty old bird. "How would you describe him?"

"Angry at the world. You know what I mean?"

Sandy knew exactly what she meant.

"Besides that, he's a drunk," Chandra added. "Not a good drunk, either. A mean drunk. You know the kind—storm in a bottle."

"You don't think much of him."

"I have nothing against him. It's just difficult being around angry people. Shoot, Charlie's been angry ever since I met him."

"When was that?"

"Back in November. It was right after the funeral. That's right," she recalled. "First week in November. He came to ACN to pitch a show."

"November, you say?"

"Yes. Awful. Whatever else Charlie may've had going for him, he wasn't an 'idea man.' I felt sorry for him, considering what he was going through. I wanted real hard to like it but I had to pass." She let out a sigh. "What could I do, though? It was really a bad idea."

"Was his pitch on the same day as Parker's?"

"Might've been. Who can remember? We were taking a lot of pitches that week, many of them back-to-back."

Sandy thought about it a moment. "You mentioned a funeral."

"Yes. Actually, it was a double funeral. His wife and daughter."

"Dear God."

"That's right. He lost both of them in one day. One in the morning, one in the afternoon." She sipped her drink. "I suppose I'd be angry, too. Can you imagine?"

Sandy couldn't. "How did they die?"

"The daughter went off a cliff in a car," Chandra explained. "Mulholland, I think. She and two other kids, hopped-up on dope. It was too much for the wife, I guess. She took her life, at least that's how the papers reported it."

"I read about it," Sandy said, remembering the article. A grainy picture of wreckage at the bottom of the ravine came to mind. Beneath it were photos of the occupants, high-school pictures of two boys and one girl, each wearing the immortal smile of youth. Then she remembered the photograph of the girl at Doogan's place. No wonder the man was angry.

"Strange, isn't it?" Chandra said. "People killing themselves."

"Yes," Sandy said, not certain how to respond, or if she should.

"What in the world—" Chandra's voice again fell away from the receiver.

Sandy perked. "Is something wrong?"

Chandra came back on the line. "Jumpin' at shadows." She chuckled. "You ever think you see something out one side of your eye? Then you look and nothin's there. My momma always said it was the devil watching you."

Sandy felt a chill down her spine as a thought occurred to her. "Are your doors locked, Chandra?"

"*Doors* locked?" She laughed. "This is Valencia."

"Still—"

"There. . . . It's nothing. Just the neighbor's dog barking. Probably a coyote sneakin' around. We get plenty of them out here."

Sandy stared uneasily at her countertop, fear spidering over her scalp. "You're sure you're okay?"

"I guess I'm more tired than I thought. Maybe we should wrap this up, Sandy."

"All right, Chandra, just one more question. Do you know Annabelle Lynch?"

"Talk about a devil," Chandra said, her tone suddenly sharp and vitriolic.

"How do you mean?"

"She's evil, that woman is. Don't turn your back on her. For the life of me I don't know what he ever saw in her."

Through the receiver Sandy could hear the sound of a doorbell. Chandra's voice fell away. "Now, who in the world would be coming by at this hour?"

"What *who* saw in her?" Sandy asked.

"Just a minute, Sandy. Probably my neighbor with the mail."

Sandy heard Chandra's footsteps over what sounded like a wooden floor—*slap, slap, slap* . . .

Suddenly the hairs stood up on the back of Sandy's neck. Inexplicably—call it intuition, premonition, a synapse of terror— she yelled into the receiver, "Chandra, *wait!*"

But Chandra was already opening the door. "Why . . . Why, it's *you!*" Sandy heard her say to her visitor. "What—? *No!*"

Sandy reeled as she heard a scream, the scream masking a thump. The thump sounded like someone hitting a flour sack—a blow to someone's chest, she imagined. She heard a sharp cough, an expulsion of wind, followed by another thump, a crash, someone apparently falling back against a wall or table. Something made of glass shattered, a lamp perhaps, then a welter of crashes and guttural cries that described a brawl.

"Dear God!" Sandy dug in her purse, found her cell phone, dialed the sheriff's station and waited, a phone pressed against each ear. Dispatch picked up, Sandy reported a possible homicide in progress, and gave Chandra's address. "Hurry!"

She disconnected the cell phone, pressed her ear to the other receiver. "Chandra! Are you all right? Chandra!"

"Help!" she heard her gasp. "Somebody . . . Somebody help me!"

Sandy listened in horror to what was obviously a violent assault—the scuffle of feet and bodies. All the while the sickening *thump . . . thump . . . thump* of blows, and Chandra's weakening cries for help. Then, nothing.

A moan. What sounded like a body slumping to the floor. It was quiet for a few moments. Then Sandy heard someone moving around in the house, the indistinct movement of feet.

Silence.

A low gurgling noise broke the silence, a pathetic plea that was little more than a hoarse gasping for air. Straining to hear, Sandy could just make out Chandra's voice. ". . . Please . . . Jesus . . ."

Suddenly there was a rapid succession of thumps, the sounds slightly altered now, as if someone were punching a bag of wet plaster. Then silence.

Sandy felt sick to her stomach. "Chandra!" she called into the phone, knowing full well something dreadful had happened to her. "Are you all right?" Once again she heard someone moving, a soft shuffling of feet over the wooden floor, the wood creaking.

"Chandra, is that you?"

The shuffling halted abruptly. Sandy listened intently as footsteps approached the phone—not Chandra's footsteps, she knew by the sound of the footfalls, but the assailant's. Soft-soled shoes: running shoes, perhaps; topsiders maybe. She heard breathing.

"Chandra?"

No response, save the odd rush of wind over the mouthpiece.

"Who is this?" Sandy demanded. "This is Sergeant Cameron of the Sheriff's Department! What've you done to Chandra?"

The phone clicked . . . went dead.

Sandy reeled as if she'd been slapped in the face. She stood, staring down at the countertop as her imagination detailed different scenarios of what may have just happened. All horrible.

"God have mercy." She hung up the phone, grabbed her car keys, and raced to the door.

Chapter Eleven

By the time Sandy arrived at Chandra's house, three black-and-white units from LASO were already angled against the curb, lights flashing, radios squawking. Tim Sturdevant was questioning a small group of neighbors on the sidewalk, their faces wide with concern and curiosity.

Sandy felt cold dread in her chest as she switched off the ignition. She stared up at the house for several moments, her hands locked on the steering wheel, breathing slowly to calm herself. A part of her wanted to just drive away, ride Buster Brown into the hills and sit and stare at the moon. She took a deep, cleansing gulp of air then slid out of her car.

The night air was cool and scented with peach blossoms as she hurried up the walk toward the house, the air cool enough to bring a wave of goose pimples over her arms. She shrugged on her jacket. An officer, securing a cordon across the front of the house, turned, recognized her with a nod.

"What've we got?" she asked, fearing the answer.

"A one–eighty-seven," he said. *Murder.*

A dog barked from a nearby yard. Sandy glanced in the general direction as she continued up the walk. Probably the same dog Chandra had heard. The sound of wind chimes drew her gaze to the house, the chimes dull, sounding as if they were made of pewter. They made Sandy think of cowbells.

Frank Dutton stood on the front porch with a clipboard, his expression grave. "Hey, Sandy."

She nodded grimly. "Frank." She stopped ouside the doorway, looked in the house, and stared.

"Tim and I got here first," Frank said. "We went through the place. No one's been in since."

Sandy did not trust herself to speak.

"We didn't go near the body. Didn't want to contaminate anything."

Sandy nodded vaguely. The wind chimes tolled dully in the light breeze, almost mournfully.

Chandra Tupelo lay on her back across the foyer, her feet pointing west toward the entry wall—straight out like an open pair of scissors—her head facing east toward an open living area, with the back of her head toward the front door. From where Sandy stood she couldn't see Chandra's face, only a portion of her left cheekbone. She was wearing a black-and-navy batik shirt, head wrap, and blue jeans—a blend of African traditional and modern American. Chandra's right arm extended over her head, as if reaching for something across the floor. Her left arm lay flattened against her side, the hand clenched in a bloody fist. There seemed an inordinate amount of blood.

"You called it in?" Frank asked.

Sandy nodded. "I was talking to her on the phone when it happened," she said, hearing in her voice an airy shudder.

Frank shook his head.

She'd been at several murder scenes during her five years as a homicide detective. Most of the cases she'd worked on were either suicides, or domestic squabbles gone bad, where guns tended to be the weapons of choice. Relatively clean, considering. Knives were another matter. She'd seen a few stabbings out in Lancaster during her early years on the force, but they were usually gang-related, drug squabbles—quick, silent, untraceable. Nothing as bad as this one, though. Someone very sick had done this, someone evil. A monster. "Let's get the teams here," she said.

Frank nodded. "Okay," he said, and called it in.

"What was your TA after you got the call, Frank?" Sandy asked.

"Four minutes. We were at Jamba Juice."

Sandy knew the place, a few blocks away. Four lousy minutes. "Didn't see anyone leave?"

Frank shook his head.

"Any of the neighbors see anything?"

"Tim's with them. I don't think so."

"You check the cars up and down the street?"

Frank nodded. "Drove round the block, too. Didn't see anything."

Sandy looked down at the sidewalk. The small group of neighbors had grown into a crowd of rubberneckers. Tim and three other officers were busy taking statements. The neighborhood dog continued barking.

Sandy looked up and down the street. The streetlights cast a yellow, unearthly glow over the street and sidewalks and lighted the *Better Homes and Gardens* landscaping fronting each home. Slumpstone walls neatly separated the houses. Typical for Valencia. No way to sneak in through the backyard without climbing walls. That meant the killer probably came in from the front, as natural as can be. No one noticed but the dog. The killer was probably walking up the street when Frank and Tim pulled up in their black-and-white. "You didn't see anybody on the sidewalk?"

Frank shook his head. "Shoot, the killer could've heard us coming a mile away. We were rolling Code Three."

Sandy considered that, looked at the doorbell. "Either of you ring the doorbell, Frank?"

"No. We looked through the windows, then went straight in."

There were vertical windows on either side of the door, sheer curtains covering them. Sandy looked through the window on the right. "Door was unlocked?"

Frank nodded.

"Don't let anyone touch the doorbell," she said. "The killer rang the doorbell."

"Okay."

Sandy looked over at the front window on her right, at the shrubbery on either side of it, then stepped into the foyer, mindful of the shards of glass and blood spatters. The foyer was about fifteen by twenty. A ceramic lamp lay on its side at the base of an entry table on the left. Thick, jagged shards scattered over the floor. A vertical smear of blood on the wall, beside the table. Bloody handprints tracked out from the base of the wall, beneath the smear, and disappeared under the body, about ten feet away. Directly ahead, a wide hallway led toward rooms at the rear of the house. There were paintings on the hallway walls, undisturbed. Living room to her right. No sign of violence in there.

"The lights were on, Sandy," Frank said. "We didn't touch anything."

Sandy nodded. She looked for the phone, a point of reference from which she had talked with Chandra, then overheard her murder. Didn't see one. Then she saw the jack and cable lying on the floor at the foot of a rectangular table, about four feet long, in the living room. The table backed a sofa facing away from the foyer, about twenty feet from the front door. There was a thin film of dust on its surface. The phone was gone. Sandy could see a faint outline where it had been. "You didn't move the phone, Frank?"

"No. Why?"

"Just asking." It was a dumb question, but she had to ask it. The killer had obviously taken the phone, for reasons known only to the killer. Had to be something incriminating on the message machine. Something that warranted murder. She wrote a note to subpoena Chandra's phone records.

A faint musky scent fingered through the death smells. "Do you smell cologne or anything?" she asked. "Perfume, maybe?"

Frank leaned in through the doorway and sniffed. "I don't know. I'm not much in the olfactory department."

Sandy looked at him. "Olfactory, huh?"

Frank shrugged.

Sandy stepped carefully along the inside front wall to avoid tracking over any evidence. She stopped by the rectangular table where a half-filled glass of white wine stood on the corner. Sandy guessed it was where Chandra had set her glass down to answer the door.

She had a good view of the main living area. The layout was pretty much as she'd envisioned it. Open floor plan. Hardwood floor covered with colorfully patterned throw rugs. Cathedral ceilings. Living and dining rooms combined, stone fireplace in the east wall connecting them, bookshelves on either side of the fireplace. The kitchen opened to Sandy's right, a black stone counter separating the two living areas, probably granite. A bottle of white wine stood on the counter.

The furnishings were mostly handmade African root tables, chairs, and sofas. Sandy had taken an interior design class at Cal Arts, and found African decor wonderfully creative. Colorful *kitenge* prints covered the cushions and windows. Woven rugs covered the hardwood floor. Recessed lighting shone on wooden busts, carved animals—hippos, elephants, antelopes—probably made of African rosewood, teak, or olive. Masai masks, spears, shields, and artifacts bracketed large colorful paintings—some primitive, some impressionistic. The room suggested someone proud of their heritage, yet at ease in the modern world. It fit Sandy's image of Chandra Tupelo.

Sandy looked back into the foyer, saw the body from this angle, and felt a shudder of revulsion. Chandra's eyes, locked in death, were staring at her—wide open—her mouth a hideous yawn. Chandra's right hand extended toward her, as if reaching for the phone—for a voice on the line, for a police detective. Reaching for Sandy.

"Oh God. Why?" Sandy's right hand rose and she clasped her face, shook her head sadly. When she opened her eyes, Frank and Tim were staring at her from the porch.

"You okay, Sandy?" Frank asked.

"I'm fine," she fibbed. "Just a little tired. What've you got, Tim?"

"Neighbors didn't see anything," Tim said. "Someone heard a dog barking. Nothing out of the ordinary."

"Coyote sneaking around."

Frank and Tim looked at her quizzically.

"Just thinking out loud," she said. "Everybody know each other out there?"

Tim nodded. "Seems like. No killers lurking around, if that's what you mean."

"That's what I mean. Why don't you guys check around the house for footprints in the beds. The front window, especially. The victim heard something outside."

"Sure." Tim left.

"No sign of Nick yet?" Sandy asked Frank.

He looked down toward the street and shook his head. "Nope."

"Okay." Sandy wished he'd hurry up and get there. She turned around, wiped her palms on her jacket sleeves. *Can't fall to pieces.*

Got to keep focused. She was a cop; cops don't have the luxury of human emotions while on duty. Steeling herself, she took a deep breath. First order of business: Question the witness. *She* was the witness—a blind witness, but still a witness. Best do it as close to the event as possible, while the details were still fresh in her mind.

She walked away from the view of the foyer, away from distraction, sat down on a sofa, and opened her notebook. She needed to play it back, listen carefully to Chandra's voice as she opened the door. *"Why . . . why, it's you!"* she had said. *You!*

That was a start. Chandra had recognized the killer. A co-worker, a friend, a family member. A lover maybe. Parker Stewart was dead, but perhaps she had had others. There were many possibilities. The double *"Why"* in Chandra's greeting suggested surprise, someone she knew but didn't expect to see at her door. That could be anybody. Perhaps it was someone they'd just been talking about.

Sandy wrote down several categories; wrote names in each of the categories; wrote down bits of information she'd gleaned from her conversation with Chandra beside each name. Writing helped her to focus, to move from the emotional to the mental, something she very much needed to do. She was still a little shaky.

Sandy took another deep breath, and forced herself once again to visualize what she'd heard through the receiver. Go through it step by step.

It didn't come step by step. The scene buzzed through her mind like a whirling dervish—the rush of murder, a violent shock wave piercing quiet suburbia—furniture crashing, glass shattering, grunts, coughs, limbs flailing. A welter of confusion, the death brawl so horrible.

Sandy wrote furiously, fear gripping her as she remembered calling into the receiver. *"Chandra! . . . Are you all right?"*

She recorded from memory Chandra's pathetic cries, like those of disembodied souls, rising through the bedlam— *"Help! Somebody help me!"*—rising through the thumping cadence of the blade. She knew it was a blade now.

At that point Sandy had phoned the station, listening to the dispatcher in one ear, Chandra's cries in the other. She was in the room with her, but unable to help. Out of reach. Again she felt the rage of helplessness, panic clutching her throat.

Silence.

A gurgling noise. *". . . Please . . . Jesus . . ."*

Sandy imagined Chandra clawing for the phone, gasping for breath, then collapsing, rolling over onto her back in surrender as the killer, in a final burst of fury, stabbed the life from her body. A crimson flash . . . flash . . . flash . . .

Sandy winced, felt the blows pounding in her head, as if someone were pounding wet plaster. Once again, silence.

Chandra dead.

Sandy remembered the creak of the wooden floor. Someone moving. She imagined the killer—an amorphous collage of faces, shapes, and sex—awash in blood. An evil thing brooding over its kill. The floor creaked again, the killer looking for something. The phone. Sandy knew that now. She listened to the approach of the killer's soft-soled shoes, heard the breath of air over the mouthpiece—the killer listening to her outrage. *"This is Sergeant Cameron of the Sheriff's Department! What've you done to Chandra?"*

The line disconnecting.

Dead.

Sandy felt a jolt through her body, felt her pulse throbbing in her chest and temples. She felt light-headed, then realized she was breathing rapidly, hyperventilating. "Take it easy," she said. Then she slowed her breathing, forced herself to relax.

A cold bead of sweat trickled down her right flank. She started to wipe it, then saw that the fingers of her left hand were dug into her thigh, the knuckles white, as if she were clutching a phantom receiver.

She loosened her grip, took several more cleansing breaths, and stared down at her notes. Ten pages. Her handwriting was sharp, slanted, resembling a seismograph. Seven-point-two on the Richter scale. Somewhere in these pages lurked a brutal killer, someone who had killed at least once, possibly three times. A monster.

Sitting there, Sandy felt a mixture of shock and fear, and she felt something else, too—something indefinable. Guilt, probably. All of it churning in her stomach. The mantel clock chimed the quarter-hour.

She looked up at the sound of Nick's voice. *Nick.* He was talking with Frank on the porch. A cooling relief spread over her. She needed his strength, his big Russian shoulders to lean on. This was a bad one—bad on many levels.

Closing her notebook, she stood; her legs felt a bit rubbery as she walked into the foyer. Nick and Lieutenant Ubersahl were signing in with Frank. Nick stepped into the house first. She noticed his shirt collar sticking out of his coat, as if he'd dressed in a hurry. She smiled vaguely. Nick never could dress himself. He was looking down at the body, then he looked at Sandy and nodded grimly. It was a mess.

● ●   ● ●

Criminalists were in every room of the house, bagging and dusting and taking photographs of the crime scene that was now less than forty minutes old. People calling from room to room. Police radios squawking. High energy. Lots of noise. White index cards were marked and pinned to the wall beside each of the blood splatters, or folded in half like little pup tents and set up next to the spatters on the floor, indicating where samples had been taken for typing and DNA testing.

Jorge Ortega, the coroner's deputy, was kneeling beside the body making a careful examination. Sandy was crouched across the body from Ortega, her back to the front door. She felt—if not better—certainly more in control, now that the rhythm of the crime scene was in full swing.

From the index cards marking the blood trail she saw how the attack had gone from the doorway back into the foyer, where Chandra probably had fallen back against the table and lamp, then stood with her back against the wall before collapsing to the ground. Sandy pictured Chandra crawling on her hands and knees, then collapsing where she lay.

Sandy glanced at Chandra's feet, and noticed for the first time that one of her sandals was missing. It was lying on its side over beneath the entry table. Sandy shook her head, her mouth a grim line. She had moved from the shock-and-guilt phase to the anger phase, which helped her to focus.

Ortega must have felt the intensity of her gaze, and looked up at her. His big, watery black eyes twinkled with knowledge and sorrow.

"How're we doing, Jorge?" she asked.

"Almost finished."

Sandy noticed that the body had taken on a waxy pallor and seemed unreal. Her gaze moved to the extended right hand, the fingers curled, clawlike. "What do you think of the blood under her nails?"

"We won't know until later, of course."

Sandy knew that. Her fingers drummed anxiously against her thighs. "You'll look for tissue samples, of course."

Ortega smiled patiently.

"I'm sorry, Jorge. Tell me to shut up."

Nick stepped back into the foyer. He'd been outside talking to Lieutenant Ubersahl and Frank. His shirt collar was still sticking out of his coat.

"Anything on Weber?" Sandy asked.

"He's not at home."

"Not at home, huh?"

Nick shook his head. "We'll find the little weasel."

Sandy grunted. She'd give a week's pay to know where Weber was right now. Where he had been about forty-five minutes ago. She knew the patrol deputies would find him, and when they did, she'd be the first to jump on his chest, heels-first. She had definitely moved into the anger phase.

Jorge Ortega shook his head sadly. He was finished with his preliminary examination. "Vicious," he said softly. He lifted the blouse delicately to expose the wounds. Chandra's bra was a dark, sticky scab. "Here. . . . These are the initial attack wounds. Note the angle of penetration."

Sandy angled her head to look, forcing herself not to feel anything.

Ortega continued: "This one was probably the first wound. From the looks of it, it penetrated the right lung near the heart." He made a deliberate downward movement with his left hand to demonstrate how the wound was probably made.

"Southpaw," Nick observed.

"Perhaps. It was a clean, solid wound . . . no deflection. The victim was surprised." The little man smiled humorlessly. "This is speculation, of course."

"It was someone she knew," Nick said, glancing at Sandy for verification.

She nodded.

"It usually is," Ortega said. "These others were deflected by the victim." He indicated the wounds. "See, how she had brought her hand up to shield herself?"

Sandy observed the slashes on Chandra's right palm and forearm, a puncture wound in her left wrist.

"I would say that the murderer was probably a short person," Ortega said.

"How do you know that?" Nick asked.

"The victim is a fairly tall woman. Most of the wounds fall in a range consistent with a shorter person's reach. Again, this is speculation."

Sandy asked, "How short?"

Ortega shrugged. "Perhaps my height . . . maybe a little taller. I am five foot three." He smiled self-deprecatingly. He lifted Chandra's left shoulder, and indicated a series of slashing wounds across her side and back. "These wounds, as you can see, were made as the victim turned to flee. They were needless wounds, as the initial wound was most likely fatal." He lowered the body gently.

"What about these?" Nick indicated several stab wounds grouped high in the chest. "They're higher than the others."

Ortega sat back on his heels, pinched his lower lip with his index finger and thumb, as if studying a mathematical problem on a blackboard. "They are very interesting. They tell me much about the killer."

Sandy looked at him.

"The victim is down, you understand. She is immobile . . . dying. They were made here, as the victim lay on her back. She is no longer able to defend herself. She is no longer a threat to her assailant."

"And—?"

Ortega stood, stepped gingerly around the body. "The murderer stepped around the dying woman, as I have done." He looked at Sandy. "You mentioned that there were several moments of silence. You heard the victim begging for mercy?"

Sandy nodded.

"But the killer has no mercy. Quickly, the killer stabs the victim several times." Ortega stooped, again lifted the blouse away from the chest area, where the blood had not fused the material to the skin. He indicated the puncture wounds above the left breast. "Do you notice the angle of penetration? The punctures are horizontal to the body. That is, the flat of the blade is perpendicular to the stem of the body," he clarified. "Also, there is no slant to the blade. . . . The blade comes straight down. Like this—" He demonstrated a series of short chopping motions.

Nick nodded, scratched the side of his head.

Ortega continued: "Notice the pattern of the wounds . . . the grouping. They are grouped very close together. As I have said, there was no movement on the part of the victim. Also, the pattern coincides with the floor."

"The floor?"

"The nicks in the floor. They are the wounds of a deep anger. They were very fierce. Vicious."

"How do you know?" Nick asked.

Again Ortega smiled patiently. "As I have said, they were not necessary. They were made as the victim lay dying."

"That squares with your account, Sandy." Nick looked over at her. "Sandy?"

She remembered the sound of Chandra slumping to the ground, the pause as the killer stood over her, admiring his work. Then the final series of rapid blows. "Yes," she said, hearing the count in her head. Then silence. "There were nine blows."

"That is correct," Ortega verified.

Nick looked at Sandy, then back at the corner's deputy. "What can you tell us about the murder weapon?"

Ortega shook his head. "Very little at this point. It was a long blade, of course. Probably a common, everyday kitchen utensil. Butcher knife."

Nick glanced in the direction of the unseen kitchen.

No doubt reading his mind, Ortega said, "The killer would have brought his own weapon, of course. It was an act of premeditation."

"Sure. Can you tell us any more about the killer? If it was a man or a woman, for instance?"

"This I do not know." Ortega smiled. "It is your job, I think."

Sandy stood. "Thanks, Jorge," she said. She'd learned all she could from the body, for now—the time of death, the manner of death, the cause of death. The motive for death lay elsewhere. The message machine most likely held the answer, but it was gone.

Frank Dutton leaned into the foyer and said, "There must be a dozen reporters out here, Sandy. How soon can you give them a statement?"

She looked out the front door at the street and frowned. Media blitzkrieg. There must have been five news vans and a dozen reporters waiting for a statement. Murder was big news in Valencia. "I don't know, Frank. I'll get to them in time for the eleven o'clock news."

"Okay, Sandy." Frank left.

Sandy watched him briefly, the feeling of helplessness creeping back into her chest. The wind chimes tolled dully. She turned and stepped into the living room.

Nick followed her. "You okay, kid?"

"I'm fine." She stopped in the middle of the room, massaged the bridge of her nose. "It was like I was in the room with her, Nick. I couldn't help her."

"You did what you could."

"All I could do was listen to her cries for help." She shook her head. "It was like being in a nightmare where something's chasing you and your feet turn to lead."

Nick turned her around and held her shoulders with his big hands. "It's not your fault, kid," he said. "Get that through your head."

"Maybe if I hadn't been talking to her on the phone—distracting her . . ."

"The killer still would have rung the doorbell. The victim would've opened the door. She'd be lying in the same place she is now."

Sandy thought about it, looked at Nick. "Fix your collar."

"What?"

"Your collar. It's sticking out in back." She reached over and tucked it down into his coat. "I have a partner who can't dress himself."

He shrugged. "I got the call. I came. Who looks in the mirror?"

"She was pregnant, Nick."

"She told you that?"

She nodded. "It was Parker Stewart's baby."

"Stewart, huh? Well, I guess that ties it together. Looks like your hot flash was on the money."

Sandy did not respond.

Nick shrugged, looked back at the foyer. "I guess I'll check out the neighbor with the mail. You okay in here?"

"Nick?"

He turned and looked back at her. "Yeah?"

"I want this guy. I want him bad."

"We'll get him."

Chapter Twelve

Sandy found Chandra's purse, a synthetic leopard-skin shoulder bag, sitting on a large tribal drum beside the sofa on which Sandy had been sitting. She put on a pair of latex gloves she'd snagged from one of the criminalists. As she started to sit back down on the sofa, an object in the far right corner of the room caught her attention, an object she had not noticed before. Curious, Sandy crossed the room for a closer look.

Standing on the floor next to the bookshelves, partially hidden by a large potted palm, was a life-size wood carving of an African *Madonna and Child*. It was a magnificent piece of art. Sandy guessed the statue was carved from teak—smooth, dark, shining dully in a single beam of recessed light. It made her think of Chandra. *Beautiful.*

Then her gaze fell on a wooden object set on a pedestal next to it that gave her a bit of a start. It was a carving of a female nude, about two feet high from its base, its gleaming, reddish torso and limbs contorted into impossible positions. Its face was twisted in a mocking grimace, glaring at Sandy with crossed eyes. She stared at the thing for several long moments.

"It's a *shetani,*" a woman's voice said.

Startled, Sandy reeled and saw that Saleen Noreau, the criminalist working latent fingerprints, was standing next to her. Sandy had not heard her approach. "Don't sneak up on me like that, Saleen!" she said, catching her breath. "You about scared the life outta me!"

Saleen was a thin black woman with long, cocoa-colored hair, braided and pulled back, falling in long, beaded cords to the middle of her back, and revealing a high, sloping forehead. An exotic beauty. "I did not sneak up on you," she said, with a Jamaican accent as smooth as honey butter. "The *shetani* has captured your thoughts. It has that effect on people."

" '*Shetani*'?"

Saleen indicated the grotesque nude. "It is Swahili for 'little devil.' "

They both looked at the piece. "Mahogany?" Sandy asked.

"Yes. It was probably carved by someone from the Makonde tribe."

Sandy looked at her thoughtfully, then back at the nude. "Swahili for 'little devil,' huh?"

"You can feel the evil in it?"

"Not in that thing; it's a piece of wood. In the room . . . yes."

"Yes." Saleen glanced around the room. "There has been much evil in this house tonight. *Much* evil. I think that *shetani* has been very busy."

Sandy looked at her.

Saleen said, "I see incredulity in your eyes. You do not believe in the devil?"

"Oh yes. I wrestle with him every day." Changing subjects, Sandy asked, "How're you doing with the sampling?"

"So far, we've got two or three sets of prints. The dead woman's and a couple unidentifieds."

"One of them probably belongs to a man named Parker Stewart," Sandy said. Then she clarified: "They were lovers. Burbank PD will have his prints on file. Okay to set up shop on the coffee table?"

"Yes. It's clean."

"Good. Did you come across any financial stuff while you were dusting the kitchen—checkbooks, financial records?"

Saleen shook her head, the beads in her long corded hair clicking softly. "There's an office down the hallway, though. I'll look around."

"That would be helpful, thanks."

Saleen smiled curiously at the nude. "You think that such things are for the ignorant . . . for the superstitious, perhaps?"

Sandy shrugged her eyebrows.

"Do not disregard the cunning and power of *shetani*," Saleen said; crossed herself, then glided silently away through the kitchen toward the back of the house.

Sandy looked at the nude again, at the grotesque contortions of the body and limbs, the hideous features, and felt a chill. She rubbed her arms, frowning at the thing. Whoever carved it, hated women.

Sandy walked back to the sofa, sat down, and spread out a paper towel over the glass-topped coffee table. She was tempted to remove her latex gloves, and smooth her palms over the handwoven texture of the *kitenge* covering. Earthy textures, to ground her. Instead she emptied the contents of Chandra's purse onto the paper towel—small makeup bag, small vial of perfume, an assortment of ballpoint pens, breath mints, receipts for purchases, a wooden rosary, other odds and ends, synthetic leopard-skin wallet that matched the purse, paycheck stub, checkbook, and address book.

She picked up the vial of perfume—Obsession—removed the cap, and sniffed. Musky. She glanced into the foyer. It wasn't the same as the trace scent she'd smelled earlier. That fragrance was more like a man's cologne, but it was difficult to tell, with the other conflicting odors.

She set down the vial on the coffee table, opened Chandra's address book, and thumbed to *W*. She wanted to see if Steven Weber's name and address were recorded. A Jim Walker topped the list. L.A. address. Then Celinda Woods, likewise, and some others. No Weber.

Sandy frowned. The book was old, the edges worn. It was older than a year, by the looks of it, certainly predating Chandra's short-lived romance with Weber, eight months ago. Why wouldn't his name be listed? Perhaps she'd memorized his number, and didn't need to write it down. *Okay.*

She flipped back to *S* to see if Parker Stewart's name was listed. No Stewart. Instead she found the name *Steven* written in black ink at the top of the page, the name crossed out with three bold red ink strokes. She dialed the number on her cell phone, waited two rings. A machine picked up. "It's me, babe! You know what to do." *Beep.* It was definitely Weber's voice. Cocky. Repulsive. Not at home.

Sandy disconnected the line. Interesting. She guessed that

Chandra recorded people's names as she thought of them. *"Sandy. You sound like a Sandy."* Friends were thought of in terms of their first names, and recorded as such—even friends who later turned out to be skunks.

She turned back a few pages, to *P,* to see if Parker Stewart's name was listed as a single first name. It was. No red strokes going through it. Parker's name and address were listed beneath Bill Pender's. That made sense, since Chandra had met Pender first. Bill Pender was a two-namer. A business associate. On a whim Sandy dialed Pender's number and, four rings later, got his machine. She frowned. No one home tonight. She didn't leave a message.

She looked under *T,* for Tupelo. No entry. Sandy thought it odd that there was no listing for Chandra's parents, unless, of course, they were deceased. No siblings, either. Might have a sister under a different last name, if she was married, but if Sandy's theory held water, she'd probably be listed as a single first name. She looked under *M* for "Mom," then *D* for "Dad." Nothing.

There were other names written in the address book: most with New York addresses, several with single-name entries— Amanda, Yolanda, Carver, Sly. Chandra had had many friends, apparently. Sandy kicked herself for not asking Chandra more about her personal life. Then again, she had been investigating the death of Wendy Burgess at the time, not Chandra's.

She thumbed over to *L* to see if there was an entry for Annabelle Lynch. There wasn't. The only names on the page were Skip Louellen, Lothell, and Lucille Lemmons. She thumbed back to *A.* No Annabelle. Annabelle Lynch was neither friend nor business associate. Was she a foe? She was the last person Chandra had talked about— *"Now there's a devil for you"*—but was she the last person Chandra had seen alive?

Sandy and Nick's meeting with Lynch earlier in the day had been brief. With artists blowing in and out of her office before the upcoming MIP convention, Lynch was clearly distracted. The only information Sandy had gotten from her, concerned her relationship with Wendy Burgess—someone Lynch referred to as "a senseless little girl" (corroborating Chandra's description of Wendy as "naive"). Sandy's impression of Lynch was that of a tough professional woman: someone who, despite the chaos surrounding her, was very much in control. Whether or not she was "evil" (as Chandra had described her), remained to be seen.

Sandy finished going through the address book—more than a dozen first-namers. Weber and Stewart were the only ones from Los Angeles. The rest were from New York, any one of whom could be a brother or sister or friend. Or murderer.

She set the address book down on the coffee table, picked up Chandra's paycheck stub. According to the stub, she worked at a place called CyberLight Systems 21, in Hollywood, grossed $3,000 a week, brought home $1,750. Uncle Sam took the rest. Nice uncle. The company's address and phone number were printed on the upper left corner of the stub.

Sandy picked up Chandra's checkbook and thumbed through the carbon stubs, starting from the back of the book, to see how Chandra had spent her money over the past month. Her mortgage was $1,850; Lexus, $475; utilities, credit card, groceries, miscellaneous . . . A book from Barnes and Noble, bought two weeks ago: *The First Nine Months of Life*. Baby book. She sighed. Couldn't think about that now.

Chandra's other purchases included items from Pier One, Nordstrom's, Vons, and Trader Joe's. Nothing unusual. When she got to the front of the checkbook, Sandy saw that the first check had been written to someone named Lothell Taylor. Check number 5630—five hundred bucks.

A red flag went up. She picked up the address book and flipped to *T*. No one named Taylor. Then she remembered seeing a Lothell in the L section. She flipped back and found it. Lothell was a single-namer with a New York phone number. No address. The phone number, like Steven Weber's, was crossed out with three red pen strokes. She looked across the room at a Masai mask. "Lothell," single-namer from New York with a scratched-out phone number, had received a check for five hundred bucks. *Why?* Nothing written on the check's memo.

Sandy stood, walked down the hallway toward the back of the house, and turned into the first room on the left. Saleen was sitting at a computer desk in the far right corner, in an office with textured wallpaper and bamboo curtains that echoed the home's African motif. She was dusting the keyboard, looked up when

Sandy entered, and indicated a shoebox on the corner of the desk. "I found that for you," she said. "Looks like what you need."

There were several checkbooks and financial printouts inside the shoebox. "Thanks, Saleen. I'm taking this into the other room."

Saleen nodded.

Sandy walked back into the living room, sat down on the sofa, and found the checkbook that immediately preceded the one in Chandra's purse. Starting from the back of the book, she flipped forward, and found that Chandra had paid another five hundred to Lothell Taylor, three weeks before check number 5630. Sandy frowned. Chandra was unmarried, so it couldn't be alimony. What, then?

There were three other checkbooks in the shoebox, each one showing that Chandra had written checks to Taylor for different amounts, at irregular intervals: one for $600, six weeks ago; one for $750, three months ago; two for $400, four months back, a week apart. No earlier checks. Chandra had paid Taylor three grand over a four-month period. Why?

Sandy considered other possibilities: Payment for artwork? sculptures? Some of the pieces in the house were expensive. Perhaps Lothell Taylor was an artist, or a broker. If so, there'd be receipts. There weren't any in the purse, and there was none in the shoebox. She'd hunt for the receipts later.

There were other possibilities, of course. Blackmail? Not likely. A blackmailer wouldn't be listed on a first-name basis, unless it was under *L* for "Louse." Drug dealer? A drug dealer would handle his business on a cash-and-carry basis, no checks. Besides, it didn't square with what Sandy knew of Chandra. Concerned for the health of her unborn baby, she had been mindful of her wine intake. That didn't square with Sandy's experiences with drug users. Drug users tended to be just that—users. Self-centered. Why, then, the checks to Lothell Taylor?

Sandy dialed Taylor's scratched-out number. It was one o'clock in the morning in New York, but she wanted some answers. After one ring a phone-company computer recording stated that the number had been disconnected. No forwarding number.

Dead end. Not a dead end—wrong turn. She dialed the sheriff's station. Judy Nesbitt was on duty and picked up. Sandy told her to do a background search on Lothell Taylor, and gave his last known phone number. Judy said she'd get right on it. Sandy gave Judy her pager number, and told her to call the minute she heard anything. Didn't matter what time. Sandy disconnected the line, glanced around the house.

Behind her, Ortega, still with the body, seemed fascinated that rigor mortis was showing up on schedule. To her left, a criminalist was going through the cabinets in the kitchen. She heard voices in the back of the house, calling from room to room. Strangely, Sandy felt invigorated. Horrible as it was, this was a murder investigation, no doubt about it. All she needed to do was to hunt down clues, put the pieces together, and, hopefully, a picture of what happened— who, and why—would slowly emerge.

She looked over her shoulder as Nick walked into the room holding a small bundle of mail he'd gotten from the next-door neighbor. He walked around the sofa and stood looking down at the items on the coffee table. "Got the case solved?" he asked.

"Ten minutes ago. I'm writing my memoirs now."

"Who done it?"

"Professor Plum, in the attic, with the trained chimpanzee."

"Not the chimp again?"

She smiled at Nick for several long moments. Her friend. Partner.

He shrugged his shoulders. "What? I got something in my nose?"

"Nothing." She took the bundle of mail from him and set it on the far corner of the coffee table. "I take it the neighbor didn't hear or see anything."

Nick shook his head. "Both of them were watching television. An old movie."

"How well did they know the victim?"

"Not very." Nick opened his notebook. "They spoke when they saw each other . . . neighbor stuff. The victim was a private person. Never entertained. A white guy visited frequently. Some-times left in the morning."

"Parker Stewart?"

"Sounds like it from the description—six feet tall, reddish hair pulled back in a ponytail, paunchy. A black guy came by every so often, too."

Sandy looked at him.

Nick read her look, apparently. "Little dude," he said. "Skinny. Maybe mid-twenties, give or take. The neighbor couldn't tell. A couple of times he came over with Stewart—assuming Stewart's the white guy."

"No idea who the black man is?"

"The neighbor had no idea. Didn't want to pry."

"Sure." No one would admit to being a nosy neighbor, of course, despite the fact that not much could fly under the social radar in most American neighborhoods. Except killers, maybe; terrorists maybe. "No one resembling Steven Weber?"

Nick shook his head. "I asked her. No one fitting his description." He sat down on the sofa next to Sandy. "Why the interest in the black dude?"

She told Nick about the checks written to Lothell Taylor, his crossed-out New York phone number.

"Dope peddler."

"You think? I'd considered that, too. But I don't know—"

"Sure. Maybe the victim's from New York, like you say. She moves to L.A. but keeps her source. Why change? FedEx your fix."

"Oh, sure."

"Probably has a Website, too." She ignored him. Nick asked, "How do you know Taylor's a black dude?"

"I don't. But how many white guys do you know named Lothell?"

Nick shrugged. "I don't know *anybody* named Lothell."

Sandy looked at the check stub written out to Lothell Taylor. "Not that I'm buying the drug angle, but if it's true, how does it figure in with Wendy Burgess? Or Parker Stewart?"

"Maybe Stewart became her new source. Didn't they find cocaine in his house?"

Sandy considered it. "Yeah." Also, Charlie Doogan had informed her that Stewart threw wild doper parties. Plenty of drugs on hand. If Chandra was a user with a New York source, there would have been no need for him any longer. Three red strokes of her pen, and he's history. It was possible.

"Old source gets ticked and offs both of them. It fits."

"And Wendy?"

Nick rubbed his face. "I didn't say it fit perfectly."

Sandy frowned at the items on the coffee table—pieces in a puzzle. Maybe. "Or there's no connection at all. Taylor is from New York. Who's going to fly three thousand miles to kill someone who brought in a few hundred a month?"

"Who says he flew? L.A. is full of ex–New Yorkers." He grinned.

She thought about it. "Try this: Taylor is an ex-lover. Chandra is his meal ticket, pays him a few hundred a month. When he finds out she's having an affair with Stewart, he kills Stewart. Makes it look like a suicide. Then, in a jealous rage, he kills Chandra."

Nick shrugged. "And Wendy?"

Sandy wrinkled her forehead. "I didn't say it fit perfectly," she said, mimicking Nick. She stared down at her notes. "The MOs aren't consistent, Nick. Stewart is killed with a twenty-five auto. Suicide. Burgess drowns in her tub. Accident. And now this. How does it tie together?"

"Maybe it don't. Maybe they're three unrelated incidents."

"Maybe." Lots of *maybe*s. Sandy gazed across the room at the *shetani*. From this angle the carving appeared to be looking directly at her, laughing. It was an evil thing after all, she decided. A host for something evil, at any rate. She could almost feel evil reaching across the room toward her. She felt strangely vulnerable.

Nick put his hands on his knees to stand up.

"Nick?"

He looked at her. "Okay, what's bugging you?"

"The killer knows who I am," she said quietly. "I identified myself." She looked at him. "That was stupid, wasn't it?"

"Stupid? I don't know." Nick smiled, showed his bad dental work. "A Bible-thumper like you? It should put the fear of God into them, don't you think?"

She smiled, removed her latex gloves, placed them into the side pocket of her jacket, and stood. She followed Nick into the foyer.

Ortega and a criminalist were placing Chandra's body into a plastic body bag, Ortega gently folding her arms over her stomach.

Sandy watched them close up the bag. Suicide. Accidental drowning. Murder. What would be the motive, the connection between the three deaths? Drugs? The only known drug user was Parker Stewart. Sex? Maybe. Chandra and Stewart had been lovers— but where did Wendy Burgess fit in? Power? Sandy couldn't figure out a power angle. What else connected them? They'd all been at ACN six months ago. Then a single word came to mind.

Cartoons.

Chapter Thirteen

It was after one o'clock in the morning when Sandy entered the kitchen of her Sand Canyon home. The house was quiet. She could almost feel the weight of silence after the busy chaos at the crime scene. It felt good. The welcoming tick of the grandfather clock against the wall brought a smile to her lips.

Home. A refuge inviolate.

No more reporters shoving microphones into her face with stupid questions. No more watch commanders demanding solutions to the crime, no more stacks of paperwork.

For now.

She turned on the sconce lights, adjusted the dimmer to soften the brightness, then kicked off her shoes and walked into the kitchen, feeling the solid warmth of the hardwood floor beneath her tired feet. The red light was blinking on her message machine. The outside world wanting back in. She ignored it.

Removing her jacket, she hung it over the back of a counter stool then poured a half-glass of white zinfandel. She walked into the living room, plopped down in her favorite armchair, and leaned her head back onto the deep cushion. She smoothed her hand over the comforting texture of the fabric. No latex gloves. Yes, it felt good to be home.

A few moments later Rhubarb appeared at her feet and jumped onto her lap. Sandy scratched the kitty's neck, her thoughts drifting back over the day's events—her mind abuzz with details of the case. She needed to talk to someone, get it off her chest. Gazing up into the shadowy recesses of the ceiling, she prayed for a little while. God was a good listener. Then she set her glass down on the side table and reached for her journal. The journal fell open to the place marked by her fountain pen, and she wrote in the upper left corner of the page:

April 4. Thursday. 1:05 A.M.
Dear Paul,
A very difficult day. This morning I attended the autopsy of the young woman I told you about, and tonight I witnessed the murder of another woman over the phone. Horrible. Her name was Chandra. I liked her. Given the chance, I think we might have been friends.

I am either tracking a killer who is very clever, or these are unre-lated incidents. I marvel at the wickedness of man. You can't help but lose a little of yourself when something like this touches you. "No man is an island," as the poet said. Sometimes I feel like throwing a saddle on Buster Brown and escaping into the hills. Let the devil have it all.

Sandy paused, lay the end of the pen against her lips as she gazed across the room at the Terpning print. She wrote:

But then I think of you, Paul. Nothing lately on your case. The leads are a bit cold, as you can imagine. I'll never stop trying, though. Oh, the visions you must see. 'Bye for now.

Sandy closed the journal, closed her eyes, and for the next several moments sat in quiet reflection. She opened her eyes. She couldn't relax, couldn't let it go; the crime scene kept pushing in. Chandra's face. She glanced over at the blinking light in the kitchen. Mom or Marvin. Might help to distract her.

She set Rhubarb on the floor, stood, and walked over to the counter and pushed PLAYBACK. A computer voice, sounding nothing like "Hal" of *2001: A Space Odyssey* fame, told Sandy she had one message, gave the time of the call—11:17 P.M. Then, "Hello, this is Detective Tom Rigby. I saw you on the eleven o'clock news. I'd like to talk with you as soon as possible." He left several numbers. *Click.*

Sandy stared at the message machine. A simple thing, really.

Name, message, time of the call. Someone had called Chandra and left an incriminating message. Why else take the machine? Why else kill for it?

She played back Rigby's message and wrote down the numbers: office (she already had his home number), boat, and cell phone. She wondered how crime fighters back in the twentieth century had managed to solve crimes without cell phones. Then again, Dick Tracy had his two-way wrist radio, didn't he? Roy Rogers had Trigger. They'd managed.

She looked at her watch—1:12 A.M.—debated whether or not to call Detective Rigby, tapped her pen on the notebook. He had said as soon as possible, hadn't he?

She tried Rigby's home number. A groggy male voice answered on the fourth ring. "Hello?"

She recognized his voice. "This is Detective Cameron from LASO."

"Who?"

"Detective Sandy Cameron. You left a message on my machine. Did I wake you?"

"Wake me?" There was a pause. "No, I was just reading the back of my eyelids."

Sandy bit her lower lip. "I woke you. I'm sorry."

"That's okay. . . . Glad you called." Sandy heard what sounded like material rustling. Bedcovers, she guessed. Then he said, "Busy day, huh?"

"You heard."

"It's all over the news. Sounds bad."

"It was." Sandy heard something crash through the receiver. "What was that?" No response. She listened to objects clanking against hard surfaces, heard Rigby cuss. "Detective Rigby? Are you all right?"

"There," Rigby said, coming back on the line. "Pulled my stupid phone off the nightstand."

Sandy raised her eyebrows. "Listen, I can call you back first thing in the morning."

"No, really. I'm glad you called. What's up?"

" 'What's up?' You called me."

"Right. I watched you on the news."

"You already said that." Sandy waited a moment for Rigby's head to clear, thinking it had been a bad idea to call him. "You think there's a connection between our cases?"

"Possibly. The victim—what was her name?"

"Chandra Tupelo."

"That's it. She worked at ACN, right?"

"Yes. So did Wendy Burgess."

"Well, there, you've got it."

Sandy beat him to it. "Each of the victims—if Burgess and Stewart were victims—either worked at, or visited, ACN during the first week of November."

"Seems pretty coincidental, don't you think?"

"I told you, I don't believe in coincidences."

"I remember."

Sandy looked down at the phone. So far, she wasn't getting anywhere with Mr. Sleepyhead. "What did you want to talk about, Detective?" She dug her notebook out of her purse, opened it to a clean page. "Do you have any theories?"

"Theories? None that hold water. But I'd like to get together and go over the cases with you."

Sandy closed her notebook. "All right. How about first thing in the morning?"

"How about now?"

Sandy's head bobbled. "Now?"

"This *is* the first thing in the morning, isn't it?" Rigby's voice was suddenly alert, even perky. It annoyed her. "I'm up, you're up," he said. "I can be there in twenty-five minutes."

"Where, *here*? To my house?"

"No, we can meet at a bar or something. There should still be a couple of them open."

Sandy frowned. "I don't do bars."

"Restaurant, then."

"It's after one." Sandy hadn't even considered meeting with Tom Rigby at this hour. A quick phone call, yes, followed by a hot bath and then bed. She was tired, whipped both emotionally and physically. She didn't want to meet with anyone, not now.

"What about it?" Rigby asked. "We could meet at the Tupelo crime scene. I'd like to check it out."

Sandy had no intention of checking out the crime scene again; she'd had enough of the place. She tapped her pen, looked at her watch—1:20 A.M. *No rest for the wicked.* None for the righteous, either, if she was going to catch them. "There's a Coco's, off Highway Fourteen. Sand Canyon exit."

"I know it. My stepdad used to take me shooting out that way when I was a kid. It was Denny's on the way out, Coco's on the way back."

Sandy couldn't've cared less. "Twenty-five minutes, you say?"

"Twenty, if I 'Code Three' it."

"I'll see you in twenty." She hung up the phone and stared across the once-quiet serenity of her home, shattered now. She looked down at the clothes she'd been wearing for eighteen hours straight, then glanced down the hall where her bathtub and master bedroom were, and shook her head. "This is nuts."

Rhubarb rubbed against her legs and mewed plaintively.

"Gotta go, sweetie." Sandy shrugged on her rose-colored jacket, stepped back into her crosstrainers, still warm, grabbed her purse, and was at it again.

● ●   ● ●

Nursing a cup of coffee in a corner booth, Sandy had a view of the restaurant parking lot and waiting room. No one was waiting, except her. There were a few night owls perched in various nooks—a couple of truckers hunched over the counter. An old couple chatted quietly across the aisle. Toward the rear of the restaurant, a man wearing a rumpled business suit stared down into his coffee cup. Sandy drummed her fingers on the table, thinking of her warm bed, a million miles away.

A pair of headlights swung into the parking lot, flashed through the restaurant, swung away, and, through the blinds, Sandy saw Rigby's Bronco pull into the space next to her Roadster. Rigby got out of his vehicle, closed his door, and looked over at her car. He made his way around the corner of the building toward the entrance of the restaurant, looking in through the blinds. He didn't see her.

Entering the restaurant, Rigby waved off the waitress as he glanced over the patrons. Sandy waved. He nodded when their eyes met, and walked toward her, his gait confident. He was wearing a pair of blue jeans, Docksiders, no socks, and a beat-up aviator's jacket over a white T-shirt. His hair was a mess. He was holding a manila envelope and a spiral-topped notebook in his left hand. "Sorry I'm late," he apologized. "Forgot I had to throw on some clothes."

"No problem," Sandy said, looking at her watch. He'd made it in twenty-two minutes. "You must've flown."

"I stepped on it a little. Thanks for meeting with me, Detective Cameron."

"Likewise." She shook his hand. Warm.

Rigby slid into the booth opposite her, set the envelope and notebook down on the table, smiled, then he looked out through the blinds at her Roadster again. "Nice ride."

Sandy smiled. She wasn't in the mood for small talk.

"Stick, huh?"

"Five-speed," she said; then: "Lieutenant Ubersahl wanted me to contact your department . . . see if we couldn't work together on this. Consider yourself contacted."

Rigby seemed about to say something when the waitress, a heavyset woman with short, curly blonde hair and dark circles under her eyes, appeared at their booth and handed him a menu. She looked at Rigby. "May I get you anything?"

"I don't know." Rigby looked at Sandy. "What're you having?"

"Coffee."

"I gotta have something to eat." He glanced quickly over the menu. "Let's see. . . . I'll have the chicken-fried steak, mashed potatoes and gravy. Do biscuits come with it?" He looked closer at the menu. "Yeah, there it is. Biscuits. Blue cheese on the salad."

Sandy's mouth watered. She realized she hadn't had a bite to eat since she had been waiting for Rigby at the marina so much earlier that day, and suddenly she was famished. "Make that for two."

The waitress wrote it down. "Two chicken-frieds. Anything to drink, Sugar?"

Rigby shrugged. "Just water."

The waitress smiled, turned to leave, and behind Rigby's back gave Sandy the thumbs-up. Sandy looked at Rigby. Brown hair that looked as if he'd combed it with a lawnmower. Pillow creases on his right cheek. He needed a shave—unless the stubble was intentional, that is. *Oh yeah, a living doll.* "So, Detective Rigby—"

"Tom."

Sandy nodded. "Okay. Tom." She opened her purse and removed her notebook. "Let's get down to cases."

"Sure." The waitress brought the salads. Tom sprinkled salt and pepper over his, then started into it. He opened his notebook. "Where would you like to begin?"

"Tell me about Parker Stewart."

Tom slid the manila envelope across the table. "You look at these while I eat."

Okay, Spunky. Sandy withdrew an inch-thick stack of color, eight-by-ten photos from the envelope: the Stewart crime scene— different angles of the death room, desks, position of the body, photos showing the powder burns on the left hand, the scorched temple. She looked at each photo carefully. "Not much blood," she said.

Tom shook his head, took a sip of water. "Small caliber, no exit wound."

"What caliber?"

"Twenty-five auto. Beretta Minx."

Sandy found the photo of the gun. Twenty-five automatic— stainless-steel barrel and action, black plastic grips. Two words dropped into her mind: *woman,* and *gangbanger.* She knew that women favored the weapon because of its low recoil and compact size—it could be easily concealed in a purse or bra. Gangbangers also favored its compact size, as well as its low cost: the Beretta was around two hundred dollars; knockoffs could be had for under a hundred. Plus, it was relatively noiseless. The dead man chewing carpet was evidence enough of its effectiveness. "Is the gun Stewart's?"

"No way to know. It's a Pre-'68."

"Ah." Sandy frowned. She knew that Stewart may have purchased the gun new in the early 1960s, or that he may have bought it secondhand at a gun show or from a private party. Loose records, or no records. Whichever, there would likely be no way to match the serial numbers on the gun to his, or anyone else's, name. "The ME ruled it a suicide, huh?"

Tom nodded, chewing.

"But you think otherwise."

"I'm leaning that way." He told her about the suicide note on the computer, the odd placement of Stewart's fingerprints on the keyboard, and the granules of sand found in the carpet.

"Sand?"

Tom indicated the photos with a sharp nod. "It's in there."

Sandy found a close-up shot of the carpet, the base of a swivel chair showing in the photo to give it scale and spatial relationship. An index card with writing on it leaned against the chair leg— placed there, she guessed, by one of the detectives or forensics people. "This it?"

Tom looked at the photo, nodded. "Couldn't find sand anywhere else in the house. Nowhere outside the house, either. Toenail scrapings don't match."

Sandy looked down at her salad. *How lovely.* She pushed the plate away and studied the photo.

"That's beach sand, by the way," Tom said. "Same kind you might find out in Malibu, for example."

Sandy looked at him. His eyes were a color of blue that seemed to change its hue with his moods. That afternoon at the marina they had been a gray-blue, flat, distant, edged with pain. Right now they were dark, searching, intense. Detective's eyes. Whatever pain she had seen in them earlier, was gone or well concealed. "Interesting," she said.

"We thought so. The sample I took from Doogan's place matches."

Sandy considered the implication. She knew from her interview with Doogan that there was no love lost between the two animation directors. She also knew that there was about five hundred miles of California coastline covered with lots of pretty sand. She regarded the photo. "Do you think the killer tracked it in?"

"I don't know." Tom shrugged. "It was just in the one area by the desk. Curious."

Sandy agreed. If someone had tracked in the sand, there would be a sand trail leading from outside the house. Curious indeed. "That sand could've been there for some time."

"We thought of that, too. Stewart had a cleaning lady that came in once a week: Maria Gonzales. If she vacuumed the carpet regularly, then the sand was a new addition to the carpet. It could mean something."

"Like what?"

Tom shrugged. "We're just trying to connect the dots." He finished his salad, pushed the plate to one side. He folded his hands on the table and looked at Sandy with a searching gaze. He seemed to be studying her.

Sandy bristled. She guessed he was gauging her competence level. After all, female detectives with looks couldn't possibly have brains, too.

"What's interesting to me is the ACN connection," Tom continued. "At the marina you said that Parker Stewart and Wendy Burgess met at a pitch."

Sandy set the photo on top of the others. "I didn't say Burgess was *at* the pitch. I said she probably met Stewart the day of the pitch. *Big* difference. Chandra Tupelo confirmed that with me on the phone. Wendy was in Business Affairs at the time, and may have come in contact with Stewart in her office."

"Was Tupelo at the pitch?"

Sandy nodded. "She and Bill Pender."

Tom's eyes were dark and penetrating. "Three people in the same building on the day of Stewart's pitch turn up dead six months later." He opened his hands, massaged the meat of his right palm with his left thumb. They were expressive hands, moving continually as he talked. "Must've been *some* pitch," he said. "The pitch from hell."

"Could be."

Tom reached into his notebook, withdrew a piece of paper, and slid it across the table. In doing so, his fingers brushed against hers. Sandy thought nothing of it. Two cops going over their cases in a restaurant. "Take a look at this."

"What is it?"

"It's a copy of something we found in Stewart's scanner."

Sandy looked at it. A drawing. "A rabbit in a space suit?"

"That thing's been bugging me since I laid eyes on it. Driving home this afternoon, I got to thinking about Stewart and Burgess meeting at ACN. When I saw you on the eleven o'clock news, first thing I thought about was the drawing."

"You think it has something to do with Stewart's pitch?"

"Who knows? There were other drawings in his house—bears, mice, girls. Some funny stuff. Any one of them could have been his pitch." Tom gestured to the drawing. "I just know that people I show that drawing to, get a case of clampjaw."

"Who'd you show it to?"

"So far, Charlie Doogan and Annabelle Lynch, the president of Empire Films. You should've seen her face when I showed it to her—looked like she'd seen a ghost."

"Maybe she did." Sandy wrote it down in her notebook. "Pender passed on Stewart's pitch, by the way. According to Chandra, it was too soft."

Tom frowned. "Did she tell you what it was about?"

"No." Sandy regretted that she hadn't pushed Chandra about it earlier; now she may never know. She looked at the drawing, saw something in the lower left corner. "What's this number five here?"

Tom gave her the nickel tour on animation, explained how the animator drew the initial extremes of a cartoon character, then made the little chart for the breakdown artist and in-betweener to follow. "Fascinating stuff," he said.

Sandy watched him as he talked. He seemed an intelligent man, serious about his work, a bit intense, perhaps, but she sensed it was a cover. Men were good at covering their vulnerable parts. They'd probably gotten it from Adam, back in the Garden; he was the original coverer-upper.

"There are twenty-four frames of thirty-five–millimeter film per second," Tom said. "Figure it out: You might have twenty-plus drawings every second. Multiply that by sixty for every minute of film. A half-hour cartoon show could have well over thirty thousand drawings. Very labor-intensive."

Sandy shook her head. It was mind-boggling. "One man couldn't do it by himself."

"No way. Not unless he had all the time in the world." Tom leaned back in his seat. "I'd sure like to know the whereabouts of drawings one to four. Or six to who-knows-what-number, for that matter."

Sandy thought about the drawing. "It might have been in the scanner for some time."

"Sure. We thought of that."

Sandy indicated the drawing. "May I keep this?"

"That's why I brought it."

"Thanks." Sandy set the drawing down as the waitress brought over their meals. The waitress cleared away the salad plates and left. Sandy leaned over her plate and breathed in the warm vapors. "Smells delicious."

It was. They ate in silence for several minutes. Sandy's mind was working; she guessed Tom's was, too, between heaping forkfuls of chicken-fried steak and mashed potatoes. She liked to watch a man eat. Tom must have felt her gaze on him, for suddenly he looked up from his meal. "What? You got something?"

Sandy felt her cheeks flush. She quickly dipped her biscuit in the gravy, and took a bite to cover her embarrassment. "I don't know, Tom," she said, glancing at the drawing. "The pitch may not have anything to do with their deaths."

"True. You got any theories?"

"Steven Weber." She took a sip of coffee. "He, Wendy Burgess, and Bill Pender had a love triangle going . . . blamed Chandra for breaking them up."

"How, 'blamed'?"

"He knocked her around for it. Got a four-one-five call from the neighbors."

Tom raised his eyebrows.

Sandy nodded. "That's what I'm saying. The pitch may be incidental." She told Tom about Weber's assault on Wendy Burgess a week ago, and his loathing for Bill Pender. "He doesn't like being crossed."

"You think Weber's our boy?"

"I don't know. Both women are dead now."

"Hmm." Tom cut a wedge of chicken-fried steak with his knife and ate it. "Do you have anyone watching him? Pender, I mean. He might be in some danger."

It was a possibility, of course. If Weber was the killer, killing Pender would bookend the set. Sandy picked at her food. She'd ask Lieutenant Ubersahl about it in the morning. Maybe he'd cut loose a surveillance car to watch Pender.

When she looked across the table at Tom, he was staring at her this time. A glimmer of light played over his eyes, the intense blue softening for a flicker of time. She caught a glimpse of something she'd seen earlier, at the marina, the ghost of something hiding in the corners. "What are you thinking?" she asked.

The color in Tom's eyes changed, once again darkening in hue. "I'd like to know who else knew about the pitch."

Sandy regarded him a moment. *All right, Mr. Elusive.* "Charlie Doogan did, remember? He was the one who told me about Burgess possibly meeting Stewart."

"Right. Anyone else?"

Sandy shrugged. "Any number of people, I suppose. Chandra said they were taking back-to-back pitches that whole week. ACN should have a record of it."

Tom looked out the window.

Sandy picked up the photo of Stewart's coffee table, looked closely at the single-bladed razor and baggie of white powder that were set on top of a square-shaped mirror. "How much cocaine was found in Stewart's house?"

"Why?"

"I'll tell you if you tell me."

Tom looked at her. "Just the dime bag. He blew a nickel's worth up his nose. Some marijuana butts were found in the bedroom. Your turn."

"That's it, huh?"

"Your turn," Tom repeated.

"Were Stewart's prints on the razor?"

Tom nodded. "Left hand."

"No one else's?"

"Nope."

"No signs of anyone else in the room?"

"We got some shoe imprints, but the carpet is so old and threadbare it's hard to make anything of them. Could be Stewart's. Could be the live-in's. Could be anyone's. Your turn."

Sandy frowned. "What live-in?"

The waitress appeared with a coffeepot. Sandy held her hand over her cup without looking at her. "What live-in?" she repeated.

"We're working on it. Hasn't been seen for a couple of weeks or so."

Sandy was incredulous. "Any descriptions?"

Tom grunted. "Too many." He rattled off the several conflicting descriptions from earnest eyewitnesses—brunette, redhead, blonde, between five-four and five-eleven. "About all we know for certain is that it's a white woman, between twenty and forty-five."

Sandy knew that eyewitnesses weren't always what they were cracked up to be. Ask four people to describe a peacock, and you'd get something that would drive the Audubon Society batty. "What about the cleaning lady . . . Maria Gonzales? She'd have seen her."

"She's dropped off the radar. We're pretty certain she's the one who made the nine-one-one call. From a phone booth," Tom added, apparently reading her look. "We're combing the barrios for her."

"A live-in, huh?" Sandy leaned back in the seat, looked across the aisle as the old couple got up to leave. The old man helped the woman with her coat. Sandy watched them leave. A different generation—courteous, good morals, low divorce rate, been through most of the horrors of the past century, some new horrors in this one. She considered Stewart. "Maybe the neighbors are describing more than one woman," she said.

Tom looked up from his mashed potatoes, his brows pinched. He set his fork down, and wrote something in his notebook.

"Any of your witnesses mention a black woman?" Sandy asked.

"No. Why?" He looked at her. "Chandra Tupelo?"

Sandy nodded. "She and Stewart were lovers."

"You're serious."

"She was carrying his baby."

Sandy could almost see the wheels turning in Tom's mind. "The live-in finds out about them," he said. "Clears out of Stewart's house, comes back later and kills him. Makes it look like a suicide. A few days later, she kills Tupelo . . . changes the MO to make it look like a burglary gone bad. Anything missing from her house?"

"The phone machine."

"The phone machine?"

Sandy shook her head.

Tom doodled in his notebook. His expression changed. "It still works. The live-in phoned Tupelo after she discovered the affair, maybe left a threatening message."

Sandy considered it. "I don't know, Tom. That takes care of Chandra and Stewart, but why kill Wendy Burgess?"

Tom said nothing. He rubbed his face, and Sandy heard the stubble of his beard beneath his fingers.

"Every time I get two angles of the triangle working, the third one comes up square," she said. "The only scenario that works for me so far is Weber."

"Weber, huh?"

She shrugged. They each backed into their separate corners. Tom drew more doodles. Sandy glanced down the aisle at the man in the rumpled suit. He was still staring into his cup, his eyes lost, and she wondered what he saw there.

Tom broke the silence. "Why'd you ask about the drugs?"

"It's just an idea. It may be nothing." Sandy told Tom about the checks paid to Lothell Taylor, his crossed-out New York phone number. Her partner Nick's theory that Taylor may have been a possible source for Chandra, one that she left out to dry once she connected with Stewart.

"What's Taylor got to do with Burgess?"

"I don't have the vaguest idea." Once again, Wendy Burgess was the odd angle out. Sandy looked into her coffee cup. "Maybe she slipped and cracked her head on the tap, just like the ME said."

Tom wasn't buying it.

"I'm just trying to connect the dots, as you say," Sandy said. "The rabbit drawing bugs you, Chandra's checks to Taylor bug me. Toss in an unknown live-in, and we've got a real puzzler."

Tom consulted his notes. "The checks go back four months, you say?"

She nodded.

"Nothing before that?"

"No."

"Maybe he's a relative—got laid off and needed some help?"

" 'Taylor' doesn't exactly rhyme with 'Tupelo.' "

Tom shrugged. "Same mom, different dad. Maybe he's a step-brother, or a cousin or something."

Sandy had to admit it was a possibility. "Okay," she said, and wrote it down in her notebook. "Taylor's a loser on the family dole."

"Was the Burgess girl a user?"

She shook her head. "Not that we know of."

Tom's eyes narrowed. "I don't know. The drug angle's a bit of a stretch. The ménage à trois is interesting, but leaves the Burgess girl out."

"Unless the live-in, or -ins, factor in somehow," Sandy added. "For all we know, Wendy Burgess may have had a thing going with Stewart on the side that Chandra Tupelo knew nothing about."

"Certainly fits his MO."

She looked at Tom and sighed. "So what've we got?"

"We've still got three people who met at ACN. Six months later, one drowns accidentally, one supposedly shoots himself, one is stabbed to death. Three MOs. One pitch." Tom fiddled with his fork. "I think it has something to do with the pitch."

Sandy felt it was connected on a sexual level. But how? She had no idea. Jorge Ortega had described Chandra's killer as "vicious." Sandy found the photo of Parker Stewart and gazed at it. Relatively clean. She thought back to the body of Wendy Burgess, submerged in a tubful of water. Clean.

Sandy placed the stack of photos into the envelope, handed it to Tom. "It's late, Tom. I'm bushed."

"Okay." He smiled at her.

Sandy smiled at him. An awkward moment passed between them—a boy-girl thing. His eyes, a brilliant cobalt blue, seemed to be boring into her. She felt strangely disquieted inside. Somehow vulnerable. She could not hold his gaze, and looked away, picked up the drawing of the space rabbit, and said, idly, "Funny drawing."

"Funny," he agreed. "Maybe we can connect again tomorrow."

"You mean later today?"

"Right."

Sandy placed the space-rabbit drawing into her notebook, put the notebook into her purse. "Right now all I can think of is a soft pillow."

End of meeting.

Sandy was about to signal the waitress for the check, when she felt her pager vibrating on her hip. She recognized the number. "Just a sec."

She dug out her cell phone and dialed the number. Nick

Ivankovich picked up. "What're you doing at the office, Nick? You should be home in bed." She listened. "I'm at Coco's. Working on the case," she added. She listened. "Detective Tom Rigby." Listened. "No kidding? I'll be right down." Listened, frowned. "Tom Rigby. He's a detective with Burbank PD. Check it out."

She disconnected the line, folded her cell phone back into her purse. She was suddenly wide-awake. She took a last sip of coffee, glancing at Tom over the rim of her cup. His eyes were two blue question marks. "Weber," she said. "We've got him in a cage down at the station. DUI. He's been in a fight—seems he's bloodied up pretty good. I'm heading to the station."

Tom signaled the waitress for the check. "Mind if I tag along?"

Sandy slid out of the booth. "We're after the same killer, aren't we?"

Chapter Fourteen

Tom held the door open for Sandy as she stepped into the booking room of the Santa Clarita Sheriff's Station. She nodded a thank-you then squinted in the glaring brightness. The room was a clutter of file cabinets and desks. Dominating the center was the jailer's desk, a large L-shaped command center cluttered with papers, police manuals, in/out boxes, and a computer. The strong smell of coffee permeated the room.

Nick was standing beside the jailer's desk, talking to Senior Deputy Ken Abrams, who had the duty. Mark Kelso and Mark Weinman, otherwise known as the "Mark Twains," were the arresting deputies and stood to Nick's right. Sandy returned their smiles, then looked at Nick.

Nick was wearing a navy windbreaker over gray sweatpants, his shirttail showing below the jacket. He was not wearing socks. His hair stood up in dark wiry tufts. "Look what the cat dragged in," Sandy grinned.

Nick frowned. The harsh overhead lights glared off his face and washed out his dark skin tones. His eyes were puffy and red-rimmed. Nick looked awful when he was wakened from his sleep. His temper would likely follow suit. He mumbled something under his breath then noticed Tom. "Who's he?"

"Detective Rigby," Sandy said. "The one I told you about. We've been comparing cases."

Nick stared at her deadpan, checked the time on his wristwatch.

Sandy put her hands on her hips. "That's *cases,* Nick, not *etchings.*"

Tom stepped forward and touched Sandy on her arm. "Actually, Sandy, we *were* looking at etchings."

She looked at him.

Tom was smiling. "Technically, a drawing is an etching."

She rolled her eyes, walked over to the desk, handed her purse to Abrams, and signed in. "Got to lose your weapon if you want to go in the cell, Tom."

"Sure." Tom reached behind his jacket and unclipped an automatic from his waist. He handed it to Abrams.

Abrams, a beefy man with short-cropped strawberry-blond hair, and a Howdy Doody face that was difficult to take seriously, looked it over. "A Sig, huh?" he said, with a voice affected to sound deeper. "Nine-millimeter? Not enough stopping power. I carried one for a while until I switched to my Glock forty-five. Can't beat it."

Tom nodded politely.

Sandy noticed the men eyeballing Tom as he signed the log— Nick, in particular. "Burbank PD, huh?"

Tom grinned. "That's right. Got a badge and everything." Tom handed the log back to Abrams. "You can ask Sandy about the etching. It's quite good."

Nick grunted, shoved his hands in his windbreaker pockets.

Sandy looked at the Mark Twains. The men were in uniform— beige short-sleeved shirts, olive green trousers—both bald on top, buzzed around the ears, with serious blue eyes, and, by the look of their arms, lifted truckloads of weights. Both men had asked her out in the past, but she had declined on the grounds that she wanted to keep her working environment free of emotional snags. "Pulled him over on a deuce, huh?" she asked.

Kelso, the taller of the two Marks, nodded. "He was weaving a rug down Soledad."

"Flunked the FST," Mark Weinman added.

Sandy knew that most drunks would submit to the Field Sobriety Test, thinking they could beat it. Most didn't. "Did he submit to a Breathalyzer or a urine test?"

"Breathalyzer," Weinman said. "Flunked it, too. Point–one-two."

Blitzed. "What time'd you pick him up?"

"About one-fifteen."

"How'd he act?"

The Mark Twains looked at each other. Kelso said, "Defensive at first, wouldn't you say, Mark?"

Weinman nodded. "Then surly."

"How surly?" Sandy asked.

"He wouldn't get into the cruiser." Kelso grinned. "We got him in."

Sandy was certain they had fun doing it, too. "You ask him what he was doing out at that time?"

Kelso nodded. "Says he was at a bar. We asked him which bar, and he said he'd made the rounds and didn't remember. After that he put on the lip clamps. Demanded to see his lawyer."

"That's our boy." Sandy held back a surge of anger. "Lawyer on the way?"

Weinman shook his head. "Couldn't reach him."

Good. "You didn't mention the murdered woman, did you?"

"No. That's your angle."

Yes, it was. Sandy wanted to see Weber's face when she told him. She went to the Mr. Coffee machine on the table against the back wall, and poured a cup. She held the pot up to Nick and Tom, and they both shook their heads. Sandy set the pot down, took a sip, and winced. She looked at Abrams.

He shrugged. "I like it strong."

"Tastes like train oil." Sandy looked at the two deputies. "You didn't notice a telephone in his vehicle, did you? By that, I mean a loose phone that he might've taken from a house?"

The Marks looked at each other. "No. Didn't see a phone."

"You look around the trunk?"

Kelso nodded. "Didn't see a phone. Just a gym bag."

Nick rubbed his eyes wearily. "It isn't likely he'd carry the phone around with him, kid."

Sandy realized that but had to ask it anyway. "What was in the gym bag?"

"Just some sweats and sneakers," Kelso said. "I rummaged around but didn't see anything suspicious."

Nick dragged a thick hand across the back of his neck. "Okay, let's get this over with." He looked beat.

Sandy took another sip of coffee, shuddered, then walked over and set the cup on Abrams's desk. "Next time add some meat-tenderizer."

Abrams led the three detectives into a hallway that opened off the east wall of the booking room. Sandy walked ahead of Nick and Tom, kept close to Abrams's right elbow. She was looking down at the floor, her eyes glaring at phantom images of Chandra Tupelo. She couldn't help it. Their footsteps echoed as they made their way through a maze of cement hallways. With each footfall she felt tension mounting in her chest, anger rising through it and pricking against her diaphragm. She knew she could not allow her emotions to get ahead of her, and took several cleansing breaths. She had to keep cool. *Keep cool.*

There were two detention cells ahead on the right. The first cell was empty, the door left open, a strong antiseptic odor drifting out into the hallway. Abrams unlocked the second cell, went into the cell and looked around, then came back out and said it was all right to enter. Sandy went in first, and straight off was smacked in the face by the sour stench of alcohol, dirty clothes, and bodily fluids.

The cell was about twenty by twenty. The walls were made of cinderblock, and painted a drab white—the color of nothing, like the zeros that frequented the place. The floor was made of concrete, and likewise painted. A concrete bench went around three walls. The cell door shut behind them with a heavy clank of metal on metal that Sandy felt through her body.

A Latino boy, maybe eighteen or nineteen, squatted in the far right corner, and stared across the room from two dark holes beneath a rake of greasy black hair—dark, feral eyes that seemed to be fixed on a point in another universe. His head rocked back and forth to music no one else heard; his back thumped against the wall.

The sound of someone retching pulled Sandy's gaze to her immediate left. There she saw a middle-aged white man, wearing a suit coat and trousers, crouched over the toilet in the corner. The man was shoeless. The seat of his trousers was soaked through—probably urine, by the smell. Then Sandy smelled a scent, fingering through the stench, that reminded her of the foyer in Chandra Tupelo's house. She looked toward the far left corner. Weber.

Abrams gestured with his thumb. "We can move him to the first cell if you want."

Sandy shook her head, her eyes fixed on Weber. "No, that's okay."

Weber was slumped on the cement bench, his elbows planted

on his knees, his head bowed between his shoulders, supported by his hands. He was wearing black trousers, a pale blue shirt, black leather jacket, his hair a riot of spikes. No sunglasses. Sandy glanced at his feet. Black leather shoes, crepe soles. A small pool of viscous fluid between his feet.

Sandy felt a cold worm of revulsion crawling up her throat as she walked across the cell and stood in front of him. "You been out celebrating, Mr. Weber?" she said, forcing herself to sound friendly.

Weber looked up at her—his eyes glassy, dark, ranging. He didn't seem to recognize her. His left eye was bruised and swollen.

"How'd you get that mess under your eye, Mr. Weber?" Sandy asked.

He squinted at her. A glint of light rose from somewhere deep in his watery eyes, played dully over the surface, then flashed. He chuckled, his head wobbled, swung away from her with the over-compensating movement of a drunk, then settled heavily in the cradle of his hands. "Don' haffta talk t'you."

Sandy noticed that the knuckles on both hands were bruised and bloodied. There were blood spatters down his shirt. Anger pushed through her revulsion. "What happened to your hands, Weber? Beating up on women again?"

No response.

"Mr. Weber?"

Weber chuckled, extended the middle finger of his right hand and held it alongside his nose.

Sandy felt a prickling of rage. "That's very interesting—is that your hat size? Where you were at around nine-forty, this past evening?"

Weber chuckled, tapped the finger against his nose. He was a real funny boy.

Sandy smiled facetiously. "I'll break it if you don't put it away."

Nick stepped forward, opened his hands, palms out, to Weber. "She means it, sonny-boy." With an added shrug of his big shoulders, he said, "My partner would like a little respect, Mr. Weber. We hope you will cooperate."

Weber grunted. The finger retracted slowly. He made a hissing sound through his teeth, yanked his head toward the wall, and wrapped his arms around himself in a ball of childish petulance.

Sandy wanted to hit him. "I take it you don't know where you were at around nine-forty," she said. "I find that interesting."

Weber continued making a hissing sound, his shoulders bouncing.

Sandy squatted in front of him, glared into his bloodshot eyes. His breath reeked of alcohol, and vomit. The heavy cologne he was wearing wrapped it up in a disgusting stench of filth. "Maybe you didn't hear me?"

"Back off," he growled, swung his head away.

Sandy mirrored him. "No, Mr. Weber, I'm not going to back off. Not until you answer my question."

He narrowed his eyes. "I said, back off."

Sandy got within a foot of his nose. "Are you getting tough with me?"

Weber averted his eyes to Nick. "You get her off me, or I swear—"

"You swear *what?* You swear you're going to take a poke at me?" Sandy laughed. "Go ahead. I don't think you're *man* enough."

Weber stood slowly, wavering, to his feet, his fists clenched.

Sandy stood with him, still in his face, still grinning at him. She was several inches taller, and stepped forward to emphasize it. "You're nothing but a little man with a big ego."

Weber made a movement with his hands. Sandy straight-armed him back against the wall, so that the room echoed his impact. Regaining his balance, Weber lunged at Sandy but she caught him in the solar plexus with a well-aimed right. Weber doubled over, held his stomach in pain. He puked.

"Wonderful," Nick said with a deadpanned expression.

"You want to try it again?" Sandy growled, her fists cocked.

Weber glared at her, groaned. He dragged a sleeve over his mouth. "You think you're pretty tough . . . with your buddies in here."

"They won't interfere, will you, boys?"

Nick and Tom shook their heads.

"It's just you and me, little man," Sandy said. She wanted him to take a swing at her. She'd talk to God about it later, but right now she wanted a pound of flesh. "You like to beat on women, don't you? Well, come on, then."

"Sure." Weber stood straight, his fists opening and closing slowly.

Sandy could almost see the thought processes at work behind his hateful eyes. "Go ahead, creep, give it your best shot."

Weber's gaze slanted toward Nick. "You better tell her to back off."

"*You* tell her." Nick turned around. "I don't mess with her."

"Where were you at nine-forty, Weber?" Sandy demanded. "You told the deputies you were at a bar. What bar?"

"None of your business."

"Oh, but it *is* my business. I don't think you were at a bar at all. I think you went over to Chandra Tupelo's house and killed her."

Weber stiffened, his face drained of color—same color as the drab white walls. The color of nothing.

Sandy thought he might puke again. "That's right," she said. "She was murdered. But you knew that, didn't you? Where were you at nine-forty?"

"No." Weber blinked at her, his face pale. "I didn't—"

"Of course you didn't. How'd you bust up your hands, Weber?"

He looked at them, fear pushing through the alcohol. "I—"

"Did Chandra give you that bruise under your eye?"

"That's not what happened."

"No? What happened, then, Weber?" Sandy jabbed a finger in his chest. "I think you killed her. You didn't like her telling Wendy what a creep you were, so you killed them both."

Weber backed away, was stopped by the cement bench. "*Both?* No!"

"Where were you at nine-forty?" Nick asked.

Weber swung his head at Nick. "I . . . I was at a bar."

"What bar?" Sandy demanded.

"A bar."

"Somebody would've seen you. What bar?"

Weber's eyes darted around the cell. "Wait a minute! It's, uh . . . It's . . ." He scratched his head, looked at Tom, Nick. "Wait, it was . . . It was . . ."

Sandy pressed, "What bar, Weber?"

"I can't think of the name."

"Because you weren't at a bar, were you? You were at Chandra Tupelo's house." Sandy jabbed at him. "You killed her, didn't you?"

He glared at her, swallowed hard.

Sandy jabbed at him again. "Didn't you?"

"You got it all wrong."

Jab. "Didn't you?"

"I wasn't there!" Weber's voice crashed against the cement walls, then thinned away to the *thump, thump, thump* of the Latino boy marking time against the wall behind her. The man with his head in the toilet moaned.

"It'll go better for you if you spill it," Sandy said.

A shade crossed Weber's face, color returning. His eyes narrowed coldly. "You're trying to get me to say something." He started to sit, misjudged the last six inches of air space, and sat down with a jolt. He blinked at Sandy then a sneer curled along his lip. "I'm not saying another word. Not another word until my lawyer gets here."

Sandy stood glaring at him for several long moments, every nerve in her body tingling hot. Weber swung his face to the wall. The toilet flushed. Interrogation over.

"Let's go," Nick said.

Abrams opened the cell door, and the detectives shuffled silently back to the admitting room. Sandy's mind was still in the cell with Weber, the cold hiss of his breath whistling in her ear, the stench of his cologne clogging her nostrils. She felt nauseous.

"Isn't he a dirty word," Abrams said, as he walked around the desk. He opened the drawer and handed back their guns.

Tom clipped the Sig to his waist, covered it with his aviator's jacket. "What do you think?"

Sandy shook her head. She didn't know what to think. "Nick?"

Nick picked up his service revolver off the desk, and shoved it into his windbreaker pocket. "You got to put him in her house."

Sandy knew that, of course. So far, her case against Weber was circumstantial. She needed a smoking gun. "What about his cologne? Same stuff I smelled at the crime scene."

Nick shook his head heavily, started toward the door. "You're grasping at straws, kid."

Sandy stood in the middle of the room. She felt helpless, tired.

Numb. Angry. She looked at Tom. His look said it all: They had nothing on Weber, nothing concrete.

The telephone rang and Abrams picked up. "Abrams," he said, his voice dropping a manly octave. He listened. "Yeah, she's here." He handed Sandy the phone. "Judy Nesbitt. Says she has something for you."

Sandy pressed the phone to her ear. "What's up, Judy?" She listened. "*Really?* Any idea when he took off?" She listened. "You're serious. Four months ago, huh? No, this has been helpful. Okay, thanks, Judy. You win the gold star for the day." She handed the phone back to Abrams.

Tom and Nick were looking at her.

"Lothell Taylor," she said. "He's wanted by the NYPD."

"Why?" Tom asked.

"He jumped bail four months ago." Sandy slipped the strap of her purse over her right shoulder. "It appears he sold a dime bag of coke to a narc. When the narc badged him, Taylor pulled a knife." She waited for their minds to register the implication, then added, "A big one."

Nick grunted. "Whaddaya know."

Tom looked at Sandy, his eyes that intense shade of blue she'd seen in the restaurant. "Four months ago, huh? That'd be about the same time the checks started, wouldn't it?"

"Yes, it would."

Chapter Fifteen

Tom sat in the expansive lobby on the penthouse floor in an ergonomically designed, low-slung, cushy leather chair that held his rear end about three inches off the deck. He felt the chair was designed to make visitors sitting in the waiting room feel like lesser mortals. People buzzing through the lobby seemed to tower over him in a forced perspective: he looking up at them; they looking down at him. He didn't like the feeling. He got the idea he wasn't meant to.

The walls in the lobby were twenty-five feet high—proud gray walls with burgundy veins fingering through them, nine-inch molding running along the base and crown. Quite a contrast to Empire Film's outdated primary colors. Dominating the wall in the elevator bay was a magnificent bronze sculpture of the Panda logo. Suspended four feet off the floor, the logo was twelve feet in height, twenty feet in width, and projected out a foot from the wall on hidden steel rods, so that it appeared to be levitating. The delicate lace of ornamental cane and Japanese maple accenting the lobby niches, softened its bold, masculine lines. Light from bronze shell sconces shone on its polished surfaces and radiated a burnished glory: a graven image to be worshiped as people stepped off the elevators.

Tom was not in a worshipful mood. He tossed a copy of *Newsweek* onto the coffee table, his eyes immediately hunting for another distraction. He'd already thumbed through the usual waiting-room offerings—*Time, People, National Geographic*. A splash of color caught his eye.

Angled on the corner of the glass coffee table, shin height, was a copy of the *Hollywood Reporter*. The issue was devoted solely to the animation industry, and to the upcoming MIP-TV convention in Cannes. It was dated last Friday. On the cover was a full-bleed color photo of a man sitting at his desk with an orbit of cartoon characters whirling around him, and wearing a grin that paled that of the Cheshire Cat. The man was Bill Pender, CEO of Panda Productions—the animation industry's "Man on the Move."

Tom flipped open the magazine and found the feature spread on Panda's two dozen offerings for the upcoming MIP-TV fun fest. Ranging from a preschool digital cutie named *Scootapie,* to a Saturday–morning lineup—crammed with 2-D and 3-D monsters, witches, space aliens, and a pair of techno/turbo superheroes called *Nutz and Boltz*—Panda appeared to have all its kidvid bets covered. Topping its stack of chips was a prime-time *Simpsons*-buster called *Rocket Rodents*—a family of goofball rodents battling a spaceship full of scantily clad, half-girl, half-fox aliens, bent on conquering the world. Tom grunted. They were more likely to ignite the libidos of adolescent boys.

According to the write-up, Panda's skein of characters was mostly drawn in a spiky, Anime approach—a style derived from Japanese cartoons. The word "edgy" was used more than once, as were the phrases "pushing the envelope" and "cutting-edge technology." With the multibillion-dollar merger pending between Panda Japan, Quality Toys, and ACN Children's Network, Panda Entertainment was hoping to upend Disney and Nickelodeon. It was a high-stakes game, and Bill Pender, the creative dynamo driving the machine, had all the chips on black. The man on the cover appeared confident in his game.

Tom looked at his watch. He glanced to his left at the guard, sitting at the power desk by the lobby entrance, a balding bug of an old coot in a dark blue uniform and white shirt, too big around the collar for his scrawny neck. "Would you mind ringing Mr. Pender again, please?"

The guard nodded, picked up the phone and pushed four buttons: *bee-bee-baa-bo.*

The guard spoke to someone. Ten minutes later Tom, more than a little annoyed, was about to stand up and arrest everyone on the floor, when an attractive redhead appeared at the guard's desk. She looked down her pointed nose at Tom, and said, "Mr. Pender does not wish to see anyone at the moment. Sorry." She started away.

"Excuse me, Miss ————?"

The redhead whirled. "*Ms.* Ms. O'Neill."

"All right, *Ms.* Ms. O'Neill—" Tom, with a grand total of two fitful hours of sleep under his belt, worked his way out of the tail-dragger, and said, "I take it you're on some inside track around here?"

"Excuse me?"

"You heard me."

O'Neill's eyes flashed. "I'm Mr. Pender's assistant. Don't you need a search warrant or something?" She spoke with a lilt that might be appealing, were it not edged with an air of superiority. "You can't just come in here and see people."

Tom smiled facetiously. "You tell Mr. Pender that we can either meet in his office now, or in mine. I'm just down the street. Great view of the freeway, if you don't mind hiking up to the roof."

O'Neill regarded Tom icily, her hip cocked as she clicked her fingernails on the guard's desk. Her hair was short and spiky, her mouth a full red poutiness, her eyes a startling shade of green. She was wearing a burgundy knit minidress that looked as if it had been knitted over her body. Nice figure—compact, curvy, no wasted space, all the way down to her glossy red toenails. Tom guessed her to be in her mid- to late twenties. "Very well, then," she said. "I'll see if he can spare a few minutes. Wait here."

"I think I'll come with you." Tom tossed the *Hollywood Reporter* onto the coffee table. "I've learned more than I ever cared to know about *Beavis and Butt-head.*"

O'Neill bristled, swung around, and jiggled down the wide hall. Tom followed at a respectful distance, negotiating the heavy, two-way traffic of worker bees over the plush gray carpet. The 405 had nothing on this place.

"What is this regarding?" O'Neill demanded, jerking her head back just enough to reveal the point of her nose.

"That information is on a need-to-know basis."

O'Neill shook her head with a grunt, quickened her pace.

Tom followed her into an open office at the end of the hall, where a spectrum of pretty girls—one of each color—were ticking away busily at computers. The room smelled like the perfume counter at Robinsons-May. The girls looked up from their keyboards in unison and stared at Tom. Tom nodded politely.

O'Neill wheeled abruptly, and with a sharp nod of her head indicated the sofa against the wall. Tom looked at it—a knockoff of the one in the lobby—and assumed she meant for him to have a seat. He declined.

She jerked away and Tom followed her through huge double oak doors into a large office. Sitting behind a chrome-and-glass desk in the center of the office, was a handsome black-haired man—the man on the *Reporter* cover. Bill Pender. He was simultaneously talking to someone on the telephone while watching what appeared to be a newscast on one of several wall monitors adjacent to his desk. The strong profile of his brow and jaw were angled in sharp relief against the shuttered wall of glass behind him.

O'Neill stopped in front of the desk and flicked her nails. Her buttocks flinched spasmodically. Tom could almost feel bolts of electricity shooting out from her fingertips as he crept up behind her. He looked at the monitor and saw the ACN news interview with Sandy Cameron outside the home of Chandra Tupelo. It was the same coverage he'd seen last night on the eleven o'clock news. Nothing new, except that now he found himself watching Sandy Cameron with more than professional interest. She was truly a beautiful woman. Tough cop, too.

Tom glanced out the shuttered glass wall, at the foothills bathed with golden morning light. Best time of the day to see Burbank. Then his gaze swept the opulent appointments in the office: black leather chairs and sofas, miles of plush gray carpeting, accented with tiny diamonds of burgundy, wainscoting ascending two-thirds the height of the walls—the walls covered with photographs of celebrities, both entertainment and political. There were no cartoons, no action figures lining the shelves, nothing to betray (and *betray* seemed the proper word) that Bill Pender—"Man on the Move"—was the CEO of a major cartoon studio. Instead, the office evoked an image of corporate élan, technological savvy, and success. Then a single word came to mind. *Power.*

The man behind the glass-and-chrome desk glanced quickly at O'Neill, then back at the newscast. "I'll get back to you later, Hiroko," he said into the receiver. "It seems I have company. Yes, what a tragedy. Later." He hung up the phone.

Pender watched the news a few moments longer, before clicking off the set with a remote. "I can't believe it," he said, staring blankly at the monitor. "Chandra Tupelo—dead."

O'Neill's fingernails clicked to a halt. "Chandra?"

"Yes. She was murdered."

"Murdered? You're kidding!"

"She just got back from a vacation and someone killed her."

O'Neill stared at the blank monitor where the news coverage had been showing. "Wow, Chandra Tupelo. I used to see her at ACN. She was nice."

Pender looked at her, started to say something, when he noticed Tom off her starboard beam.

O'Neill, snapping out of her reverie, said, "I'm sorry, Bill, but there's a detective outside who insists on speaking with you. I tried to get rid of him, but he's very rude."

Tom stepped forward and whispered in her ear, "I also pee in the shower."

O'Neill whirled. *"You—!"*

"Me." Tom grinned. "I've considered joining an encounter group for rude people. Know of any good ones?"

Her eyes flashed angrily then froze—two slits of emerald ice. She swung away. "Bill!"

"Sharon, baby, it's all right. I've got a few minutes."

O'Neill gave Tom a look that could strip paint.

Pender stood, walked around the desk, and held her. "There, there," he said, his voice a comforting baritone. "Be a dear and see that the caterers have the proper directions to my house tonight. I don't want any foul-ups."

Her body seemed to go lax in his arms. "Whatever you say, Bill." Then, shooting Tom a sneer, she stalked across the room, every inch of her body vibrating.

"Don't mind Sharon," Pender said, as she closed the door. "She's a good soldier. She's been doing two jobs since my assistant passed away this week."

"Wendy Burgess."

"That's right," Pender said, smiled graciously, and extended his hand. "Bill Pender."

Tom guessed his height at well over six feet. He was wearing a short-sleeved black polo shirt over sea-foam–green slacks, and Italian loafers. He looked to be in his mid-forties, was trim, tanned, and looked as if he could handle himself. Ladies' man; man's man. Certainly a man who got what he wanted. Tom shook his hand. "Detective Rigby. Burbank PD."

"Ah, one of our neighbors. What can I do for you, Detective? Is this about Chandra Tupelo?"

"Actually, I'm here to talk about Parker Stewart. But since you brought it up . . ."

"Parker, huh? There's a tragedy." Pender gestured to a leather chair in front of his desk.

"No thanks," Tom said. "I've done enough sitting for one day."

"Would you care for something to drink? Coffee? Juice? I have a wonderful juice bar."

Tom was certain he did. He probably had a hot tub that opened in the floor, and a California King bed that twirled out of the ceiling. "I'm fine, thanks." Tom declined. "How well did you know the Tupelo woman?"

"Chandra? Not well." Pender leaned back against the desk and crossed his legs. "We worked together at ACN, of course. She was a wonderful lady. Very bright . . . caring." He glanced over at the blank wall monitors. "I can't believe it. How strange."

"How do you mean?"

Pender looked at him, his eyes serious. "First Parker takes his life, then Wendy dies accidentally, and now Chandra— What? *Murdered?* All in one week."

"It *is* strange," Tom agreed. He opened his notebook. "You wouldn't mind telling me where you were last night around nine-forty?"

Pender's thick black eyebrows rose. "Why? Am I a suspect?"

"Routine. Last night?"

"Nine-forty? That's easy. I was at a meeting with a representative from Quality Toys."

"Quality Toys? The toy company Panda is merging with?"

"That's right. They're a Japanese entity with an office in Santa Monica. Global penetration of the market. We've been strategizing over a few ideas we're taking to Cannes next week."

"Nutz and Boltz?"

"I see you've been reading the *Reporter.*" Pender smiled. "Do you watch cartoons, Detective?"

"Sure. For my intellectual stimulation. How late did your meeting go?"

"Late. Well after midnight. It's been quite hectic, as you can imagine." Pender frowned. "I'm really sorry to hear about Chandra," he said, shaking his head. "She was a decent person . . . *really* decent. Too decent for this cutthroat business. Was it a robbery or something?"

"What makes you think it was a robbery?"

"Oh, I don't know." Pender shrugged. "First thing that popped into my head. What else could it be? Chandra didn't have an enemy in the world. She had quite a collection of African art, though. Some of the pieces were quite valuable."

"You didn't know her well, yet you knew about her collection?"

"Just about everyone knew about it—at least the people at ACN knew about it."

"Why is that?"

"Because every Thanksgiving the network would put on an art exhibit. Wine-and-cheese kind of thing. String quartet. Employees could bring whatever they wanted—paintings, drawings, sculptures. Chandra would always bring in several pieces from her collection. They would always get the most attention. She was quite proud."

Tom wrote it down in his notebook. "Every Thanksgiving, you say?"

"A week or two before, usually. During pitches."

Tom looked at him.

"It was always a busy time," Pender said, apparently reading

Tom's look. "The exhibit helped everyone to relax . . . socialize. Enjoy the finer things in life. You know"—he twirled his hand in the air—*"joie de vivre!"*

"Right. Did Chandra exhibit her art pieces last November?"

"Of course. Do you think that was it, then? A robbery?"

"The case is being handled by LASO."

"You mean Detective Cameron?" Pender flashed a set of perfect teeth—the Cheshire Cat grin. "Isn't she a goddess?"

Tom nodded politely, felt something stir in his chest. Anger, maybe. "Could I have the number for Quality Toys?"

"Certainly."

Tom watched Pender scribble the number and address on the back of a business card. Right-handed.

Pender handed the card to Tom. "Is that all you wanted to ask me, Detective? You mentioned Parker Stewart."

"That's right." Tom removed the space-rabbit drawing from the manila folder, handed it to Pender, and watched for a reaction. There wasn't one.

Pender shrugged. "Is this supposed to mean something to me?"

"That's one of Parker Stewart's drawings. I was wondering if you could tell me anything about it."

Pender looked at the drawing again, shook his head. "Sorry. It certainly looks like Parker's work." He handed the drawing back to Tom. "It's a rabbit in a space suit. What else can I tell you?"

Tom placed the drawing in the folder, mindful of Pender's newly acquired prints on the edges of the plastic covering. "Six months ago Stewart pitched an idea to you while you were still at ACN. Do you remember?"

"How did you know that?"

Tom said nothing; the question remained.

Pender smiled. "And you'd like to know if that drawing had anything to do with the pitch?"

Tom nodded. "Something like that."

"Why?"

"Three people are dead who were there that day—Parker Stewart, Wendy Burgess, and now Chandra Tupelo."

"You think there may be a connection?"

"Who else was at the pitch?" Tom asked.

A glimmer of light flickered in Pender's deep-set blue eyes, then darkened. "I see what you mean," he said, considering the implication. "No. No, there was no one else at the pitch. Just Chandra and myself."

"Steven Weber wasn't there?"

Pender gazed across the room, lost in thought, apparently, and didn't respond.

Tom cleared his throat. "Was Steven Weber at the pitch?" he repeated.

Pender looked at him, a dark scowl creasing his brow. "No. Weber was strictly lower-level. He handled the follow-up."

"Follow-up?"

"Right. If we green-lighted an idea, we'd kick it down to a lower-level executive to handle all the face-to-face work. Track the production with the show runner."

"Show runner?"

"Point man . . . creator of the show, usually."

Tom wrote it down in his notebook. "Since you passed on Stewart's idea, would Weber have come in contact with it afterward?"

"No. Chandra and I handled everything on the spot with Stewart."

"Why'd you pass on his idea?"

Pender shrugged his shoulders. "Too soft. Didn't have enough *edge* to it. Stewart wouldn't consider modifications, either. He was an *artiste,* you see. No one modifies the work of an *artiste.*" He grunted. "He was a man who'd clearly outlived his time."

Tom looked at him. "That's one way of putting it."

"You know what I mean. You either bend with it, or you take it down the road."

"What was his idea?"

Pender pinched his lip and frowned. "Some nonsense with dragons. Dragons didn't make the cut this year. Who knows about next year? Probably have dragons coming out the wazoo."

Tom wrote the word *dragon* in his notebook. "Do you have a copy of the pitch?"

"No. Stewart took it with him. He gathered up his drawings, uttered a few niceties, and left. He took it on down the road.

What a shame. Maybe if I'd bought it . . ." He left the thought hanging.

"When was the last time you saw him?"

Pender thought about it for a moment. "I guess it was at the pitch. Yes, that was it."

"So, no one else at the network would've come in contact at all with Stewart's pitch? Just you and Chandra Tupelo?"

"I didn't say that. Our people in Business Affairs would've seen it. They'd have to."

"Why is that?"

"The network required artists or studios to sign a submission agreement before looking at anything. We live in a litigious age, Detective—got to cover yourself."

"Who in Business Affairs would've handled it?"

"Wendy Burgess." Pender again stared across the room. "She was there that day, too. Three people dead." He looked at Tom. "Do you think the pitch had something to do with their deaths?"

Tom saw something in his eyes—fear maybe. "Why?"

"Oh, I don't know. It just seems odd, don't you think? Three people dead. I mean, I was there, too."

"Do you think you're in some kind of danger?"

Pender shrugged his eyebrows. "I guess I never thought about it before. You don't think about people wanting to kill you."

"The world is an evil place, Mr. Pender." Tom folded his notebook, started to leave, then stopped. "By the way, where were you the night before last, around six-thirty?"

"Tuesday?" Pender looked at the floor. "The past two nights I've been in meetings with Quality Toys. Why?"

"How about Sunday afternoon around five o'clock?"

Pender shook his head. "I don't have a clue. With all the meetings I've been having lately, I don't know if I'm coming or going." He turned around and picked up a day planner off his desk, flipped back several pages. "Oh, that's right. I was in a videoconference with Quality Toys, Panda Japan, and ACN. The merger. Went most of the afternoon and well into the evening, as I recall. I know it was dark when I left. Why do you ask?"

"Where was the conference?"

"Here." Pender gestured to the adjoining room. "I have a video setup, so I don't have to fight the freeways."

From where Tom stood, the room appeared to be a duplicate of the main office—foxhunts on the walls, a jungle of potted plants, and a television monitor facing a conference table. A video-conferencing device atop the monitor was connected to a tabletop unit by a black cable. "Anyone else with you in the room?"

Pender flashed his teeth—again the Cheshire Cat grin. "Not unless you count the board of directors in Tokyo, the people at QT, and the president of ACN."

The intercom on Pender's desk buzzed. "Excuse me one moment," he said, reached across the desk, and pushed a button. "What is it, babe?"

"It's Cannes," O'Neill said, her voice edged with panic. "They need to talk to you immediately."

"Tell them to hold, I'll just be a moment."

"It's quite urgent."

"Thank you, babe. Everything's going to be all right." Pender disconnected the line. "Don't mind Sharon, detective, she's busy keeping twenty plates spinning."

"Uh-huh." Tom turned to leave. "I think that should just about do it, Mr. Pender."

Pender extended his hand. "Bill. My friends call me Bill. Can you see yourself out? I need to take this call."

"Sure." Tom crossed the room, opened the door, and looked back into the office. Pender was already leaning back in his chair, his jaw thrust proudly at the ceiling, grinning at someone on the phone. Tom imagined an orbit of cartoon characters whirling around him, shook his head, and closed the door.

Sharon O'Neill was sitting in Wendy Burgess's cubicle, talking on the phone. She was checking with the caterer for a party that afternoon. Three people in the industry are dead: Throw a party. Yipee skipee! She hung up the phone, but before Tom could speak she pushed a speed-dial button, clicked her nails impatiently, then once again hung up the phone with a frown. When she saw Tom, her eyes narrowed into two green slits. "We are quite busy, as you can see."

Tom stepped over to the cubicle opening. "Just one question."

O'Neill's mouth became a small rose of truculent flesh—an inflamed hemorrhoid came to mind. "Could you please tell me where Mr. Pender was around five o'clock, this past Sunday afternoon?" Tom asked.

"How should I know?"

Tom looked at the horizontal plaque on the cubicle wall. "The sign here says that you are an executive assistant. Don't executive assistants keep records of their bosses' meetings?"

"I wasn't his assistant then. Wendy was."

Tom stood staring at her, his eyebrows arched slightly. He wasn't going anywhere.

O'Neill rolled her eyes, slapped opened a day planner on her desk, and clawed back several pages. She slapped her palm down on the book, found the entry. "Sunday afternoon. Mr. Pender was in a conference with Tokyo, Santa Monica, and ACN." She glared at Tom. "Happy?"

Tom grinned. "Must've been a big room." The humor escaped her, of course. Ms. O'Neill did not strike Tom as one who frequented karaoke bars or comedy clubs. "How long did the conference last?"

"Quite late. They usually do."

"Were you here?"

"No."

"Was Wendy?"

"How the hell should I know?" O'Neill clapped the day planner shut, shoved it to one side of her desk. "Now, is there anything else, Detective, or Sergeant, or whatever you are?" She leaned her head on one side and gave Tom a smile that said, *Drop dead*.

"You've been quite helpful," Tom said. "Toodles." He smiled at the spectrum of beauties that were staring at him from their computers, then left.

Tom exited the building, took the buildingwide flight of granite steps down, two at a time, and walked briskly across the broad terrace, streetscaped with ornamental pears, Chinese pistache, and a maze of lush planters. Reaching his Bronco, parked in the yellow zone in front, he opened the driver's-side door and slid into the seat. He was about to turn on the ignition when his pager vibrated on his hip. He looked down at the number, grabbed his cell phone, and dialed. Dan Bolt picked up. "We've got the cleaning lady, Tommy. She's sitting across the table from me."

"Maria Gonzales?"

"The same."

Chapter Sixteen

"I am afraid."

"Why are you afraid?"

"I see him lie there," she said. "I think he is sleeping, you know? Mr. Stewart sometime sleeps on the ground. It is not so strange. Then I see his face. I see the blood here." She pointed at her left temple. "I know he is dead. I see things like it on TV, and I know he is dead. His eyes are open."

"You are afraid because he is dead, or is there another reason?"

Maria Gonzales did not answer. Her eyes were black—all pupils—and they moved with the wariness of a cornered animal. They were strained and red-rimmed, as if she had not gotten a lot of sleep lately. That made two of them.

"Miss Gonzales?"

"I am afraid."

"I know." Tom guessed her to be in her mid-thirties, although he had a difficult time guessing the ages of Hispanics. She was short and thin, with long black hair pulled back off a round forehead into a ponytail. Flat nose. Grim mouth. Brown, leathery skin, as if she spent her time out in the sun when she wasn't cleaning house. "You didn't call the police," Tom said.

Her gaze jerked sharply to the tape recorder in the middle of the table, then down at her brown, callused fingers that tapped a nervous choreography on the edge of the table. "No," she said. "When I see that he is dead, I am afraid and run. I drive away. Pretty soon I feel bad inside, so I call." English was not her first language, but she spoke it well enough. Better than Tom, or anyone else in the room, spoke Spanish. She would not look at either Dan or Lieutenant Stenton.

"What made you feel bad?" Tom asked.

Gonzales glanced at him quickly, shook her head. "I do not know."

She knew. The four of them were sitting at a rectangular table in the windowless briefing room on the first floor of the Burbank police station. Everything new. The tabletop still shiny, like something out of *"Better Cops and Squad Rooms."* No cigarette burns. No chewing gum underneath. Very un-coplike. Tom sat across the table from Gonzales so he could see her face. Dan, wearing his usual ill-fitting brown-on-browns, was sitting to her left, eating a Snickers bar. Dan said, "You called from a booth at Western and San Fernando?"

"Sí." She did not look at him.

Lieutenant Stenton was sitting at the far end, holding his head up with the palm of his left hand. He looked lousy. He'd been out with the stomach flu the past couple of days, but had come in to hear Gonzales's testimony. He should've stayed home in bed. "Why didn't you leave a name?" he asked.

Gonzales continued looking at Tom. Tom was safe. "I was afraid."

"You said that," Stenton said. "Why?"

She looked at the tape recorder with nervous black eyes, then back at Tom.

Tom nodded at her to continue, added a quick smile to put her at ease. Something had put the fear of God into her, and it wasn't the corpse of Parker Stewart. "Tell us why you were afraid, Miss Gonzales."

Her fingers were trembling. She lowered her hands below the table, out of sight. "Because . . ." she said tentatively. "I did not want him to know that I see him."

"'Him'?" Tom's eyes narrowed with interest. "There was someone else in the house?"

She looked at him, jerked a fast look at Dan and Lieutenant Stenton.

"There was someone in the house that frightened you?" Tom pressed her. "Was it a man?"

Gonzales answered with a sharp nod.

"What's his name?"

"No," she said, shaking her head. "I am afraid."

"There's no reason to be afraid, Miss Gonzales. No one is going to hurt you. What is the man's name?"

Her eyes were intense, frightened, searching Tom's face. She leaned forward slightly. "Rudy," she said, just above a whisper.

"Rudy?"

She nodded.

"That wasn't so hard, now, was it? Rudy *what?*"

She shrugged.

Tom wrote it down. "Tell us about Rudy."

She regarded Tom a moment. Her hands fluttered to the table, patted the surface as if to test its solidity, then retreated to her lap. She began twisting her fingers. "He . . . He killed Mr. Stewart."

Tom stared across the table at her. Dan took a bite of the Snickers bar and chewed slowly, looked across the table at Tom and made a face—a face that Tom understood clearly. *We've just cracked the case. Let's head home and crack open a couple brewskis.* Tom said, "This Rudy . . . Why do you think he killed Mr. Stewart?"

Gonzales twisted her fingers into white knots. "As I am coming to the house, I see him leave."

"You saw him leave the house?"

"*Sí.*"

"Did you see Rudy kill Mr. Stewart?"

"I see him leave," she repeated, more forthrightly. "He kill Mr. Stewart."

"Okay. This was Monday morning, right?"

"*Sí.* Monday. I come to clean Mr. Stewart's house every Monday."

"Not Sunday afternoon?"

Gonzales waved her hand. "No, Monday. I do not work Sunday."

Tom doodled in his notebook—circles, curves. Stewart was killed Sunday afternoon around five. If Rudy was the killer, then he had come back for something Monday morning, the proverbial returning to the scene of the crime. Pretty gutsy. "Okay. You saw Rudy leave Mr. Stewart's house. Did he see you?"

"No. I am in my car. I am reaching for my purse as Rudy is

getting in his car. I am down low." Gonzales demonstrated how reaching for her purse put her head just above eye level to the dashboard, the tabletop being the dashboard. "He look at my car, but did not see me, I think."

Tom smiled. "Then there's no reason to be frightened, is there?"

She looked at him, again searching his eyes. She shook her head, and the fear and tension seemed to drain from her limbs and shoulders. "No."

"You were parked behind Rudy's car?"

"*Sí*."

Tom made a quick sketch of Stewart's house in relation to the street, drew an arrow to indicate north. The street in front of Stewart's house ran east and west. "What time did you arrive at Mr. Stewart's house?"

"At nine o'clock. Every Monday at nine o'clock. I am always on time."

Tom believed her; Gonzales seemed a credible witness. Scared but credible. He tapped his pen on the table. At nine o'clock the sun would've been in her face. If Rudy was the killer, he very easily could have seen her. "Okay. So you go into the house and see Mr. Stewart dead on the floor. Did you touch anything?"

She seemed puzzled.

"Did you touch anything in the room where Mr. Stewart draws?" Tom clarified. "Move anything on his desk, for instance?"

She shook her head. "I do not touch anything."

"You come in every Monday?"

"*Sí*. Every Monday."

"To clean the whole house?"

"*Sí*."

"Dusting, washing clothes, vacuuming? Things like that?"

She nodded.

"Do you vacuum the carpets every week?"

"Oh, *sí* . . . every week," she said, her voice infused with obvious pride. "I am a good housecleaner. No dust. No dirt. Mr. Stewart likes his house clean."

"Even his drawing room?"

"*Sí*. Every room. Vacuum and dust. I clean very good."

Tom was certain that she did. He looked at Dan. "Did you print her yet?"

Dan crumpled up the Snickers wrapper and tossed it into a trash receptacle in the far corner by the blackboard. Two points. He shook his head, still chewing. "We'll print her afterward."

Gonzales swung her head at Dan, her eyes wide. "I am arrested?"

"No, ma'am," Dan said. "We need a set of your prints for elimination purposes."

Gonzales blinked at him. "You do not arrest me, but you take my fingerprints?"

"That's right," Tom said. "We fingerprint everyone who goes in the house. Lieutenant Stenton, Detective Bolt, and I have already been printed."

Gonzales nodded warily at Tom, her dark eyes once again resembling those of a rodent testing a possible trap. "I am not arrested?"

"No." Tom smiled. "We only arrest bad people. You're not a bad person, are you?"

Gonzales shook her head vigorously. "No." She glanced quickly at Lieutenant Stenton and Dan, then back at Tom. Her hands settled quietly in her lap. "I feel bad so I make the call. I come here to tell."

"You did right," Tom said. He looked at Dan. Dan had no questions at this point. "All right, then, let's see what we have," Tom continued. "You walked into the house, saw your boss lying dead on the floor, then you left. Right?"

"*Sí*."

"And I take it you've seen Rudy in the house before?"

"*Sí*. Many times. Rudy and Mr. Stewart work together on the drawings."

Tom looked up from his notes. "Rudy and Mr. Stewart were working together?"

"*Sí*. They work many weeks. Rudy brings drawings for Mr. Stewart to check, but always they fight. Terrible fights."

Tom looked at Dan. "You find any checks in Stewart's checkbook written to a 'Rudy'?"

Dan shook his head. "He might've paid him under the table with cash, though. We're assuming that Stewart paid Rudy."

"Sure." Tom considered that. He considered also that their working relationship might not have been based on monetary exchange. A *joie d'art*, as Bill Pender might say. "Miss Gonzales, do you know what these fights between Rudy and Mr. Parker were about?"

"*Sí*. Mr. Stewart says his drawings are no good." Gonzales shrugged. "Always they fight about the drawings. Mr. Stewart was very—how you say?—*artístico*."

Tom connected the squiggles of his doodle with a couple of curved lines, added details here and there. "You said Rudy brings drawings for Mr. Stewart to look at. Did Rudy ever take drawings with him when he left the house?"

"He always carry a big case. A black one . . . you know?" She drew a large rectangle in the air with her index fingers.

"A portfolio?"

"*Sí*, portfolio. Maybe he take drawings with him, I don't know."

"When you saw him leaving the house on Monday, was he carrying the portfolio?"

"*Sí*."

"What's the big deal with the portfolio, Tom?" Lieutenant Stenton asked. He appeared to be fading.

"Drawing number five."

Stenton nodded. "Oh."

Tom could see that it meant nothing to him. "Rudy may know what happened to drawings one to four," he clarified.

"Right."

Tom turned to Gonzales. "Miss Gonzales, did you ever happen to see what Mr. Stewart and Rudy were working on? The drawings, I mean."

She shrugged. "They are drawings. Cartoons."

"What kind of cartoons? Were they people cartoons, or animal cartoons?"

"Animal and people cartoons." She nodded. "You know, like Bugs Bunny."

Tom pulled the space-rabbit drawing from his manila envelope and slid it across the table. "Did the cartoons look like this one?"

Gonzales bent over and looked at the drawing. "Maybe so. I never look too close. Mr. Parker does not like me in the room when he is looking at Rudy's drawing."

Dan peeled a banana and cleared his throat. "These fights—they had them often?"

"*Sí*. Big fights. Then they smoke marijuana and are quiet."

"That would do it." Dan took a bite of the banana. "Was there—" He swallowed, cleared his throat. "Was there ever any hitting?"

"I do not see hitting. I hide in other part of the house and wait till they are quiet. Then I smell the marijuana and I know everything is okay." She looked at Tom seriously. "I think they like to fight, so they can smoke the marijuana."

Tom smiled. "You think Rudy killed Mr. Stewart because of the drawings?"

She shrugged. "Rudy gets very angry when Mr. Stewart says bad things about his drawings."

"Did you ever hear Rudy threaten Mr. Stewart?"

She shook her head.

"Okay." Tom tapped his notes with the end of his pen, worked his doodle some more. "Miss Gonzales, do you know what cocaine looks like?"

She pointed to her nose and sniffed.

"That's right. Have you ever seen Rudy and Mr. Stewart doing this with cocaine?"

She made a shrug with her mouth. "No see. But I see the white powder later. It is cocaine, I think."

The detectives thought about that for a moment.

"What's this Rudy character look like?" Dan asked. "How tall is he, for instance? What color hair? What race is he?"

Gonzales looked down the table at Lieutenant Stenton, who appeared to be going down for the third time. "He is like that man."

Stenton's eyes jerked open. "What man? Me?"

"*Sí*. He is a black man like him. Only, Rudy is not so big."

Tom said, "I'll have Fitz work up a computer sketch with her, Joe. We'll get her to look at some mug shots. Who knows?"

Stenton nodded, laid his head back on his hand.

Dan's mouth turned up wryly at one corner. "Say, you really don't look so good, Joe." He picked up the banana. "You want any of this before I toss it?"

Stenton did not open his eyes. "Shut up, Bolt."

Tom gazed intently at Gonzales. "So, Rudy is a black man, and he's not as big as the lieutenant?"

"Not so big. Rudy is very small." She put her hand out to her side to suggest his height. He couldn't have been much taller than a dwarf, if her scale was correct. "I am afraid of him, though."

"Because of the fights?"

"*Sí*. I no like Rudy. He has the evil eye, you know—?" She touched the side of her head. *"Loco en la cabeza."* She looked at Tom earnestly. *"Diablo.* I am afraid he will come after me with his knife."

All three men looked at her. "Knife?"

"Rudy's knife." Gonzales was aware she'd just said something important. She nodded. "He carries it in the portfolio. One time after Rudy leaves, I see it on the table when I clean. He uses it for the cocaine, I think."

"Is it a pocketknife?" Tom asked. "You know—the kind that folds in half and you can put in your pocket?"

Gonzales shook her head. "No. . . . Is no pocketknife. Is big knife." She extended both of her index fingers in front of her. The space between them was about fifteen inches. Big knife.

Tom tore a blank page from his notebook and slid it and a pen across the table to her. "Do you think you could draw a picture of the knife?"

Gonzales shrugged. "Maybe so."

While Gonzales drew, Tom flipped back through his notes, found the place where he and Sandy had been discussing Lothell Taylor. He drummed his fingers on the table.

"What's up, Tom?" Dan asked.

Tom frowned at his notes. "We need to run those John Doe latents against a Lothell Taylor."

"Who's he?"

"New York jumper on a cocaine bust. Knew Chandra Tupelo. Carries a knife."

Gonzales nodded vigorously. "*Sí,* a big knife." She slid the page back to Tom, pleased with her handiwork.

It was a crude drawing, but it had the look of a bowie knife—long blade, single cutting edge, a concave cutaway at the tip, characteristic of its namesake. Tom held it up to Dan and Lieutenant Stenton. "I'll fax a copy of this to the ME, and see if it could be the same type used on Tupelo."

Stenton nodded. "Good idea, Tom. Do you think Rudy and Lothell Taylor could be the same man?"

Tom shrugged. "There are some similarities. Both men are black. Both are cocaine users. Both carry a knife."

"You've just described half of South Central," Dan said.

"That were on a first-name basis with Chandra Tupelo?"

"Lothell Taylor was on a first name basis," Dan corrected. "We don't know if she knew Rudy."

"She knew Stewart, Stewart knew Rudy. It's not that much of a reach that she knew Rudy, too."

Dan thought about that. "Okay," Dan conceded. "Still, it could be two men, Tom."

"Only one way to find out. I'll call New York and have them fax us a photo of Taylor. We'll compare it to Miss Gonzales's description. If they match, we may have a break in this thing."

Tom looked at Maria Gonzales. "You're doing great." She smiled meekly. Tom opened his briefcase and pulled out the Stewart crime-scene photos. He found the one of the Beretta and slid it across the table to Gonzales. "Have you ever seen a gun in Mr. Stewart's house that looks like this?"

She looked at the photo. "It looks like the gun on the floor beside Mr. Stewart."

"That's right. Have you ever seen it around the house before?"

"No."

"Did Mr. Stewart own any guns that you know of?"

"I never see guns."

"How about Rudy?"

She shook her head. "Knife."

Tom added a couple of lines to his doodle, then realized he'd drawn a picture of a woman, no one in particular. He scribbled over it. "Okay, Miss Gonzales," he said. "There's just one more matter we'd like to discuss with you. We understand that there was a woman who lived with Mr. Stewart. A white woman, maybe forty years old. Do you know anything about her?"

She nodded. "Oh, *sí*. Miss Annabelle."

"Miss Annabelle?" Tom had not expected that answer. "Annabelle Lynch?"

"*Sí*. Miss Annabelle. She lives with Mr. Stewart."

Tom sat back in his chair and stared at Gonzales. He and Dan exchanged looks.

Lieutenant Stenton perked up. "Annabelle Lynch? She's the production head at that studio, right?"

"Empire Films," Tom said, not taking his eyes off Maria Gonzales. "Think, now. Does Miss Annabelle actually *live* with Mr. Stewart, or does she just come over for visits?"

Gonzales raised her eyebrows. "I am only there on Mondays. When I clean, I think maybe she is there all the time."

"Why do you think that?"

"For many years there are only Mr. Stewart's clothes in his closet." She shrugged. "Then one day I am cleaning and I see there are woman's clothes, too. Miss Annabelle's clothes. Also, I find two toothbrushes in the bathroom. There are other things, too. Woman's things . . . you know? For the monthlies."

Tom wrote the name *Annabelle Lynch* across the top of the page then underlined it. "How long ago did Miss Annabelle's clothes appear in Mr. Stewart's closet?"

"I don't know. . . . Many months ago, I think."

"This is very important, Miss Gonzales. I want you to think hard. How many months? Try to be specific."

Gonzales blinked at Tom several times, then stared down at the table. "I don't know. It is before Christmas. I think." She brightened. "*Sí*, it is before Christmas. I go away to visit my family in Mexico. Miss Annabelle is living there many weeks."

Dan took a bite of banana. "Whaddaya know?"

Tom wrote it down in his notebook. "When you came back from Mexico, was Miss Annabelle still living with Mr. Stewart?"

"*Sí*. I think maybe she and Mr. Stewart get married soon. But then I see Mr. Stewart with the black woman and I do not think they will get married now."

"Black woman?"

"*Sí*. She comes when Miss Annabelle is not there."

Tom and Dan exchanged looks.

"Do you know this black woman's name?" Tom asked.

Gonzales shook her head. "No."

"You have never heard Mr. Stewart call her Chandra?"

"No."

"You're sure?"

"*Sí*, I am sure."

"Can you describe her then?"

"*Sí*. She is tall. *Muy bonita* . . . very beautiful," Gonzales clarified. "She wears very pretty clothes . . . African clothes, I think."

Gonzales had just described Chandra Tupelo. "Did you ever see Rudy and this black woman together?" Tom asked.

"No, I don't think so."

"Are you sure? Think back."

Gonzales frowned. "No, I do not see them together. I see her with Mr. Stewart." She shook her head reproachfully. "Is no good what he is doing, but I don't say anything to her."

"Say anything to whom?"

"Miss Annabelle. I think Mr. Stewart and this black woman are . . . you know?"

"Having an affair?"

"*Sí*. Is no good."

"Do you think Annabelle knew about it?"

Gonzales nodded seriously. "One day she catches the black woman with Mr. Stewart. They are in the bedroom . . . you know? I am in the kitchen cleaning. There will be much trouble, I think." She shook her head at the thought of it. "Much trouble."

"What happened?"

"I try not to listen but I cannot help it. I hear Miss Annabelle say something, then she comes into the kitchen and gets whiskey. She takes very long drink. Then the black woman comes in. She is leaving. I am sure Miss Annabelle is going to hit her, but she just looks at her. Is a bad look. The evil eye. The black woman leaves house and Miss Annabelle goes back into the bedroom. I hear much fighting."

"Was there any hitting?"

"I don't know. I think so. I hear a slap. Miss Annabelle comes back in with suitcase and Mr. Stewart follows her. I see a red mark on his face." She pointed to her right cheek. "I leave the kitchen very fast, but I can hear them. He is very angry with her."

"Because of the black woman?"

She shrugged. "I don't think so. He say some things I don't understand. . . . Something that makes Miss Annabelle very scared."

"Scared?"

"*Sí*. Mr. Stewart says he maybe call the police. Is something very bad, I think. She said, 'Prove it.' I remember those words. . . . Then Miss Annabelle leaves." Gonzales shook her head solemnly. "Very bad."

"How long ago did this happen?"

She frowned at the table. "I don't know. . . . Maybe three weeks. Maybe longer."

"Have you seen Miss Annabelle since then?"

She shook her head. "No."

Dan took a bite of the banana and tossed what was left of it onto the table. "Whaddaya know."

Chapter Seventeen

Tom drummed the top of the steering wheel as he waited for the car ahead of him to move. Traffic was heavy. Always was in the Valley, no matter what time of the day. There were twelve cars ahead of him. Tom calculated three changes of the light. Twelve minutes.

He opened his briefcase, took out the NYPD photo of Lothell Taylor and once again compared it with the computer sketch of Rudy. "Rudy" was a black man who appeared to be in his late twenties. His head was shaved and he had the thin, sunken face of a doper that narrowed to a pointed goatee. Small nose. Small ears. Thick eyebrows. Something crazy in the eyes. No wonder Maria Gonzales was afraid of him. He was certainly scary-looking. He was also a dead ringer for Lothell Taylor. The NYPD had faxed Taylor's photo and fingerprints, the latter matching several John Doe latents in Stewart's house. Lothell Taylor was their man. Tom had had his photo circulated among the Burbank black-and-whites, LASO sheriff's deputies, and CHPs. Maybe somebody would get lucky and spot him.

Lynch's house was single-story, ranch-style with a weathered wood-shake roof covered with pine needles and eucalyptus leaves. Tom climbed a short, steep flight of cracked cement stairs, bracketed by a low-trimmed hedge of Japanese boxwood, then took the front walk in about six steps, and stepped up onto the porch. He rang the doorbell and waited, glanced at the shrubs—junipers, mostly. He rang the bell a second time and waited. He could hear music playing in the house—a mambo of some kind.

Annabelle Lynch appeared at the door in a white bathing suit, tying a colorful cotton wrap around her waist. She was wearing sunglasses over her eyes. Her hair was wet and combed back, as if she had just taken a swim. "Hello, Detective," she smiled, recognizing Tom. "Are you here socially, or is this business?"

"Business."

"Pity." She pushed her sunglasses on top of her head, glanced around Tom. "Where's the sack of potatoes you brought with you last time?"

"Dan? Collecting for the policemen's ball."

She smiled. "How lovely. Shall we go inside?"

Lynch's house was an eclectic blend of traditional and modern furniture. Burgundy-colored chenille sofa and chairs. Knickknacks and doodads lined the shelves and tables. Wall-to-wall white Berber carpet. Colorful, abstract wall hangings. A framed Tommy Tortoise cel hung over the white painted brick fireplace; three Emmys stood on the mantel. The place reeked of stale cigarettes and booze.

Lynch glided rhythmically across the room to the driving beat of a Gloria Estefan mambo. Tom remembered her as being an angular woman, but in her bathing suit he saw she had her share of curves. She had some moves, too. Tom followed her out through a sliding glass door onto a sun-drenched brick patio.

A tiny bean-shaped pool took up most of the deck space, behind which the hill, lush with vegetation and pines, rose steeply from a brick-and-cinderblock retaining wall. Cushioned wrought-iron chaise lounges and deck chairs faced the pool, magazines piled beneath one of the lounges. Cape honeysuckle formed an impenetrable barrier on the eastern boundary of the property; towering eucalyptus screened the west and scattered leaves over the patio and pool. An automatic pool sweep was shimmying along the edge of the water, sucking up leaves and bugs. The smell of chlorine permeated the close air.

Lynch paused by the tiled bar and with tongs put ice into a glass tumbler, rocking her hips to the steel drums knocking through the outside speakers. The backs of her legs, glistening with suntan oil, were tinged with red, as were her back and shoulders. Tom guessed she was trying to build a base tan before heading to Cannes. The ice crackled as she poured Jack Daniel's into the tumbler. "May I get you anything?" she asked. "Bourbon? Gin? I have beer, if you'd like."

"No thanks."

She danced around the bar, reached under the counter to what had to be an outside stereo unit, and turned down the volume. She indicated a deck chair. "Won't you have a seat?" she asked, then lowered herself into a chaise next to it. She parted her wrap, exposing her long, muscular legs to the sun, and to Tom's eyes. She wiggled her toes.

Tom sat in the chair and gazed steadily at Lynch. The sun was in her face and softened the angular planes, highlighted the silver in her short, mousy-blonde hair. Her blue eyes, once cold and hard-edged in her studio office, seemed to sparkle with mischief. She reminded him of Lauren Bacall—a dangerous beauty. The bathing suit probably had something to do with it. The Jack Daniel's helped a little, too, no doubt.

"Detective Rigby, wasn't it?"

"That's right," Tom said, adjusting his seat. A gurgling sound drew his attention toward the pool, where the sweep breached the water surface.

"What can I do for you?"

"I have a few follow-up questions."

She set her drink down on the side table beside her lounge, reached for a cigarette, and lit it. She blew a cloud of smoke over their heads. "I hope I'm not in some kind of trouble."

"Why would you think that?"

She picked up her drink and smiled playfully.

Tom was a bit confused. Lynch was a different woman now than the one he'd met at Empire Films. That woman was all business—a tough, no-nonsense boss lady. The jury was still out on this one. She was a little drunk, Tom guessed, as he opened his notebook. "Why didn't you tell me you'd lived with Parker Stewart?"

She gazed at him levelly, the mischief in her eyes cooling briefly, then leaned her head back onto the flowered lounge cushion. She closed her eyes and angled her face to the sun. "You didn't ask me."

"I'm asking you now."

"I didn't see it as any of your business. Is that a no-no?"

"A man is dead, Miss Lynch—a man you were living with. We suspect it wasn't by his own hand."

She rolled her head lazily toward him and squinted, gently

twirling the glass tumbler between her thumb and middle finger. "But I thought—" She took a sip of her drink. "You're saying Parker was a victim of foul play?"

"It's very possible. Where were you last Sunday afternoon around five o'clock?"

"You think I killed him?"

Tom let the question stand.

She groaned playfully. "And here I thought this was going to be fun. Am I going to need my lawyer?"

"You have that right."

She looked at him over the rim of her glass. "I don't think that will be necessary. I was at the beach with Eric—you remember my assistant Eric?"

Tom did. The Jack La Lanne poster boy. "He'll verify it, I'm sure."

She smiled. "Why wouldn't he? Zuma," she added, watching Tom write it down. "We were there all afternoon."

"Zuma Beach?"

"That's right. You know—*Beach Blanket Bingo*. Annette Funicello, Frankie Avalon. Lousy surf." Lynch crossed her legs at the ankles and bounced her right foot, a thong sandal dangling from her toes, mischief back in her eyes.

"How long ago did you move in with Stewart?"

"A couple months. Why?"

Tom regarded her for a moment. Cool cookie. She hadn't blinked, hadn't averted her eyes. Either she was lying, or Maria Gonzales was lying. "A couple of months ago, huh?"

She shrugged. "That's right."

"Try again, Miss Lynch."

"I beg your pardon?" She squinted at him, then chuckled throatily. "Uh-oh, something tells me I've made a boo-boo."

"Answer the question, please."

"I will if you tell me why."

"That's not how it works."

"You're not being very neighborly, Detective. I invited you in, remember? I didn't have to."

"That's right. We can do this poolside, or we can take a trip downtown. Your choice." Tom was getting a little tired of her routine.

"You can't do that."

"Try me."

She studied his face, smiled humorlessly, and took a drag of her cigarette. With her right arm she reached blindly for the ashtray sitting on the side table, and set it on her stomach. "I liked you the other day," she said coolly. "I don't think I like you anymore."

"It breaks my heart."

"I can see that." She tapped her cigarette against the ashtray. "All right, Detective, I moved in with Parker back in December."

"Don't you mean November?"

She shrugged. "It may've been November—who knows? It was late last year. What's this all about?"

"I understand that you and Stewart had words a few weeks back."

She shrugged, blew out another cloud of smoke.

Tom knew she wasn't going to answer. "Miss Lynch, I know that you and Parker had a blowout the day you left his house. I'd really like to know what it was about."

A bee, attracted to the colors in her wrap, landed on her thigh, and she waved it off. "It was about the usual relationship blues— too much this, not enough that. I didn't kill Parker. I may've wanted to on occasion, but I didn't kill him."

"No one is accusing you."

She lowered her sunglasses over her eyes. "Like hell you aren't." She bounced her foot, the sandal slapping against her heel. "I told you once before that Parker was mercurial. We fought often. So do lots of people. That doesn't mean they kill each other."

"Did your fight have anything to do with the drawing I showed you?"

"What drawing?"

"The one of the rabbit in a space suit."

"Oh, that." She rattled the ice in her glass. "Why would I fight with him about that?"

"You tell me."

"There's nothing to tell." She removed her sunglasses, kicked off her sandals, and stood. Walking to the edge of the pool she untied her wrap, let it fall, and dove into the water. She surfaced halfway across the pool, swam the breaststroke to the opposite end.

She was a good swimmer. She pushed off backward, back-paddled to the middle of the deep end, and treaded water. "The water's lovely, Detective," she said, smoothing her arms over the surface. "Why don't you come in?"

"I didn't come here to swim."

"No, you came here to fish." She laughed, went under feet-first, came up out of the water with her head back, to set her hair, then swam to the ladder.

Tom watched her climb out of the pool. He got the feeling she was stalling, regrouping, working through a strategy.

She glanced sideways at him, gave him the Lauren Bacall smile, then walked over and grabbed a towel off one of the deck chairs and began toweling herself dry.

Tom removed the computer sketch of Rudy from its folder and showed it to her. "What can you tell me about this man?"

She toweled the water from her ears and grunted. "Isn't he a car wreck?"

"Do you know his name?"

"Rudy. Julian Rudolph—Rudolph as in the Red-nosed Reindeer." She laughed. "He had a red nose, all right."

"From coke?"

"Certainly not from the cold."

Tom wrote the name *Julian Rudolph* in his notebook. "His real name is Lothell Taylor."

She picked up her drink from the side table and took a long swallow. "Doesn't surprise me. What is he, some kind of underworld character or something?" She angled her face to the sun as she ran a comb through her hair.

Tom put the printout back in the folder. "Do you know where he lives?"

"Don't have a clue. Don't want a clue."

"He and Stewart were working on something together?"

She lit a cigarette. "A Webisode."

"For the Internet, right?"

"That's right." She stood looking at him, smoking her cigarette. "Don't ask me what it was about. Parker never told me, and frankly, I was too busy getting ready for MIP to care."

Tom didn't believe her. People don't live with each other and not have a clue what the other is doing, who their friends are, what makes them tick . . . their likes, dislikes. Then he looked down at his feet and made a correction. He'd lived the past five years with a stranger, hadn't he? *Go figure that, Tommy.*

"Something troubling you, Detective?" Lynch was staring at him over the rim of her glass. "I hope it wasn't something I said."

Tom looked up, grunted. He was thinking of Sandy Cameron. He didn't have a clue why. "Do you think this Webisode had something to do with Stewart's pitch at ACN?"

She picked up her glass, rattled the ice as she walked over to the bar to freshen her drink. "I have no idea. But then, I've already told you that, haven't I? Will this inquisition go on much longer?"

"Did Stewart hire Rudy?"

"Yes. Don't ask me what the arrangements were, Parker kept his finances to himself. Sure I can't get you something to drink?"

"No thanks." Tom flipped the page in his notebook. "Your fight with Stewart wasn't about Chandra Tupelo?"

She looked back at him sharply, her eyes narrowed. "That witch?"

"The witch is dead, Miss Lynch. Did you kill her?"

"Good heavens, no. Why would I?"

"She was sleeping with your roommate."

"Which one?" She laughed as she filled her glass with bourbon. "If I killed every girl he slept with, half the women under twenty-five in this town would be compost by now." She turned around and leaned back against the bar, her elbows resting on the counter. She gave Tom a sly look. "You'll have to do better than that, Detective."

"Okay. Where were you last night, around nine-forty?"

"Do I have to answer that?"

"No, you don't. 'You have the right to remain silent. Anything you say may be used against you in a court of law.'"

Her eyes widened in mock surprise. "Are you arresting me, Detective?"

"If you don't cooperate, I may have to. This isn't a cartoon studio, Miss Lynch. Three people are dead. They won't jump up in the next scene and make you laugh. I'd like to know where you were last night."

She pushed away from the bar. "I can't tell you."

"All right, then." Tom stood, pulled out his cell phone and pushed a series of buttons.

"It's not that I don't want to cooperate," Lynch said. "I can't. If it gets out, it could ruin the deal."

Tom put the phone to his ear.

"It concerns a toy company," she said. "That's all I can tell you."

"Hey, Dan," Tom said into the receiver. "Yeah, I'm at her house now. Don't know yet. Might need a cruiser out here."

"Mr. Park."

"Hold on a sec, Dan." Tom looked at Lynch. "What was that?"

She folded her arms across her chest, glass in one hand, her other hand holding the cigarette away from her face. "I was with Mr. Park," she said, flicking the filter with her nail. "I took him out to dinner. Satisfied?"

Tom spoke into his phone. "Hold off on the cruiser, Dan. You get anything from the probate lawyer?" He listened. "A million bucks, huh? Yes, that ups the ante a bit, doesn't it? All right. I'll get back to you if I need you." Tom folded the cell phone back into his coat pocket.

Lynch's blue steelies slanted at him through a filter of smoke. She was the boss woman back in her office now. All angles. Not so drunk, after all.

"So you were meeting with Mr. Park," Tom said. "He that Korean fellow at your office the other day?"

"Yes." She padded over and sat down on the edge of the chaise lounge. "You can verify that I was with him, but you can't go public with it. Not until after MIP."

Tom remained standing. "If it's material to the case I can't make any promises. If not, I don't see any reason why we can't keep it quiet. Where'd you take Park to dinner?"

"Going to verify my alibi?"

He smiled.

"Le Chêne's."

"You mean the little French restaurant out in Agua Dulce?"

She nodded. "Mr. Park wanted to see Vasquez Rocks. He's an amateur geologist. I figure, 'What the hell. He wants to climb rocks, we'll climb rocks.' Besides, I didn't want to chance anyone seeing us in the Valley." She picked up a folder and leafed through it. "I must ask you to leave now, Detective. I have oodles of work to do before the weekend."

"Okay." Tom gazed down at her. The jury was *in* on Annabelle Lynch: There was only the one woman, the woman he'd met at Empire. Tough broad. Corporate man-eater. She was only wearing a different power suit. "Did Stewart threaten to blow your deal with Park?"

She looked over the top of the folder at him.

"Is that why you fired him?" he asked. "Stewart got something on you and threatened you with it. You said once that you didn't like airing your dirty laundry. Maybe he found a pile somewhere?"

She stubbed out her cigarette in the ashtray, picked up a bottle of suntan lotion. "You're fishing again."

"Just connecting dots, Miss Lynch."

The corners of Lynch's mouth jerked upward in a humorless smile. "Please connect them elsewhere. I'm busy." She lay back in the lounge, covered her eyes with her sunglasses, and smoothed lotion over her arms.

Tom left without comment, feeling a sudden disgust for the human race. He slid into the front seat of his Bronco and headed back to Burbank, his mind troubled; not because of Lynch—he'd already dismissed thoughts of her the moment he'd stepped foot off her porch. His mind was troubled because of Sandy Cameron. He couldn't stop thinking about her.

Chapter Eighteen

Tom pulled into the basement parking lot of the Burbank station, parked, and took the back stairs two at a time. The smell of beer nuts smacked him in the face as he walked into his office. Tom really hated the smell of beer nuts. Corn chips, another of Dan's snacktime favorites, were a close second. Dan was on the phone, his "searchlight" showing as he scribbled in his notebook. He looked up at Tom, pointed at the phone, and gave him the thumbs-up. Breaking news.

Tom hung his coat on the back of his chair, sat down at his desk, and leaned back. He massaged the bridge of his nose with his thumb and index finger. With only two hours' sleep the previous night, the weight of the day was finally taking its toll. He was beat.

Dan had left a yellow Post-it on his desk. Sandy Cameron had called at eleven forty-five, asking if Tom wanted to go to Bill Pender's party with her, around four o'clock. Dan had drawn a string of *x*'s and *o*'s after the message. Tom set the note down on the desk, and gazed up at the Stewart crime-scene photos tacked onto the bulletin board. Over the past few days he had committed the details of each one to memory. He had assembled the pieces into various scenarios, none of which completed the puzzle. There was always a piece or two missing.

He closed his eyes and allowed a thought to drift into his mind. He wasn't thinking about the crime scene, though. He was thinking about Sandy Cameron.

Again.

Dan hung up the phone and said, "Hey, Tom. You get that note from that blonde detective?"

Tom opened his eyes. "What's that? Yeah, I got it. Herb give us any word yet on Bill Pender's prints?"

"You mean, did Herb find any matches to the latents in Stewart's house?"

"That's what I mean."

"Not a one. You gonna call her?"

Tom looked across the desks at Dan. Dan had a look on his face—an ironic smugness—that he had perfected over the years, specifically to annoy Tom. Tom ignored it. "So, Stewart's mother stands to inherit a million bucks, huh?"

Dan popped a handful of beer nuts into his mouth and waved him off. "Chump change. You're not going to call her?"

"Who was that on the phone?" Tom smelled a fresh wave of beer nuts and narrowed his eyes.

Dan offered Tom the bag. "Want some? No?" Dan grazed and crunched as he talked. "That was a guy named Rosenfeld. Stewart's entertainment attorney."

"What've you got?"

"The guy stood to make a truckload of dough on one of his cartoon series."

"What guy?"

"Stewart. Apparently there's a revival of his *Punching Judy* cartoons in Europe." Dan glanced at his notes, munching. "A syndication/toy deal is pending at that MIP-TV thing in Cannes."

"For *Punching Judy?*"

"That's right. Some company called Bruemann Entertainment is leading the charge. German conglomerate with holdings all over Europe and the Pacific Rim—Tokyo, Seoul, Manila, Taipei."

Tom was confused. "*Punching Judy* is—what?—twenty-plus years old."

Dan shrugged, fished the corners of the bag for strays. "There is a feature in the works, apparently. It's a complete package."

Tom thought about it a moment. "Empire Films doesn't own the rights?"

"Not anymore. The rights reverted back to Stewart last December, after Empire failed to renew its option. The deal was hush-hush until Stewart secured the rights. In light of what's potentially at stake, it seems like a bit of an oversight, if you ask me. Empire was caught napping."

Tom nodded his head thoughtfully. "You mean Annabelle Lynch was caught napping."

"Or so it appears."

"The deal still goes through, even with Stewart dead?"

"According to Rosenfeld, it will." Dan emptied the bag of beer nuts into his mouth, crumpled the bag, and tossed it into the trash receptacle beside his desk. "He wasn't too broken up about it, either. He's in for fifteen percent."

Tom looked at him.

Dan shook his head with a wave of his hand. "I know what you're thinking, Tommy. Rosenfeld was in France meeting with the Bruemann people at the time of Stewart's death. I checked. He just got in yesterday."

"Who collects the eighty-five percent?"

"His mother."

"The mother with Alzheimer's."

Dan nodded.

Tom thought about it. Mother offs son for his dough then forgets why she killed him. Maybe it wasn't supposed to make any sense. "A bundle, huh?"

"Millions and millions," Dan said with a voice imitating Carl Sagan. "An artist has to die in order to make money, I guess. Nothing new." Dan put his feet up on his desk and folded his hands behind his head. He was clearly pleased with himself, and deservedly so. It was good police work.

Tom knit his eyebrows together. It put a different slant of light on the Stewart death, which, he allowed, may have had nothing to do with the ACN pitch after all. If Stewart was sitting on a deal that was potentially worth millions, then it opened up the stage for a different cast of suspects. Another thought occurred to him, one that concerned Annabelle Lynch and her rock-climbing Korean buddy, Mr. Park. "You say this Bruemann outfit has offices in Seoul?"

"That's right. Up and down the Pacific Rim, it looks like."

"Need to find out who the big kahuna is in Seoul."

"That shouldn't be too hard. Why?"

"Don't know yet. It may be nothing." Tom crumpled Sandy's

note and threw it in the trash. "Good work, Dan. I'm thoroughly confused."

"What else is new? You gonna call her now?"

"Who?"

Dan grinned. "You know who."

Tom looked away. "Later."

"Suit yourself. Her name ring a bell to you?"

"Whose?"

"Sandy Cameron. Something about the name rings a bell. Something in the news a while back."

Tom looked at him.

"Cameron," Dan repeated. "No? Okay, what'd you get from Lynch?"

For the next fifteen minutes Tom briefed Dan on the Lynch interview. Dan swung his feet off the desk and sat forward, his gaze serious. "You think Lynch was lying?"

"Lying?" Tom thought back over the interview, Lynch's cagey responses to his questions. "Let's just say she was a little fuzzy around the truth. I got the feeling she was hiding something . . . especially when I asked her why she'd moved in with Stewart right after the ACN pitch."

"It may have nothing to do with the pitch," Dan suggested. "Empire blew the copyright renewal. That's got me thinking. Lynch dropped the ball, big-time."

Tom frowned. It didn't figure. He couldn't imagine Lynch dropping *any* ball, not in a man's game. Correction: *If* it was a man's game. "Did Fitz drag any more off Stewart's hard drive?"

"Nothing yet."

A silence fell over them, each man looking at different corners of the room. "You're thinking Lynch may've popped Stewart?" Dan asked.

Tom shrugged, glanced over at the photo of the Beretta that had killed Stewart. "She had the opportunity, and maybe the motive. A double motive, maybe."

"The Tupelo woman?"

"Right," Tom said thoughtfully. "She catches Stewart playing footsie with her. She could've taken them both out."

"A woman scorned."

Tom leaned forward and doodled on a piece of notepaper. "Still leaves Wendy Burgess out of the loop. She doesn't fit any of the angles."

Dan shrugged, spread his hands wide. "Maybe she don't fit, Tommy. Maybe she just slipped, like the ME said. You gotta figure that."

"Sure. And Stewart popped himself, too, right?"

"Can't rule out that possibility, either."

"With a multimillion-dollar deal brewing." Tom didn't believe it, not a bit of it. They were connected somehow; he felt it in his gut. There was an unconnected dot just beneath the radar—maybe a couple of dots. Best thing to do was to get out on his boat, step back from the trees, maybe gain some perspective on the forest. He resolved to do just that.

"What're you thinking, Tommy?"

Tom tossed his pen on the desk. "Not a thing, Danny-boy. Not a thing." He was about to go for a cup of coffee when his phone rang. Tom picked up the receiver, frowned at his desktop. It was Sandy Cameron.

"Did you get my message?" she asked.

"I was just going to call you," Tom lied. He looked across the desks at Dan. Dan was leaning on his elbows, wearing his idiot grin. Tom covered the mouthpiece with his hand. "You got gas or something?"

Dan chuckled.

Tom spoke into the receiver. "What's up, Sandy?"

"How would you like to go to a party?"

"A party?"

"Bill Pender is throwing a little soirée this afternoon for a short list of his friends. I've got a few questions for him."

"Concerning the Tupelo murder?"

"That's right. I can't shake the fact that two people who worked with him are dead. Two women."

Tom heard something in her voice. "Stewart didn't work with him," he said. "How do you figure that angle?"

"I don't. Not yet."

Tom thought about it for a moment. "A short list, huh?" He grinned. "I guess I didn't make the cut."

Sandy laughed, her voice an airy fluttering, almost a release. "Neither did I. I'm crushed. I thought maybe we'd crash it and see what we could stir up—see who's on the A-list. What do you say?"

"What time are you headed over there?"

"Around three-thirty. You game?"

Tom glanced at the clock on his desk—two thirty-five. Not a chance. Allowing for travel time during the peak of rush hour, he couldn't see finishing up at Quality Toys until well after four. "I'm on my way to Santa Monica," he said. "I don't think I'd get back in time."

"What's in Santa Monica?"

"Bill Pender's alibi."

"Oh?"

Tom told her about Pender's meetings with Quality Toys over the past two nights, his videoconference last Sunday. Tom wanted to verify his story. Something about the guy was a little too clean, too pat. Sandy agreed. "I'll let you know if everything checks out," Tom said.

"Thanks, Tom. Call me as soon as you hear, okay?"

Tom heard it again in her voice. "Are you all right, Sandy?"

"All right? Sure. Why do you ask?"

"You sound a little jumpy."

Sandy was quiet for a few moments. "Maybe I am," she admitted. "I just came from the Tupelo autopsy. I always get a little nervy—this one, especially. Thank you for asking."

"Sure." Tom didn't know where to take it from there. "By the way," he said, changing tacks, "I've got a line on your bail-jumper."

"Lothell Taylor?"

"He's living out here now under the name of Julian Rudolph. Goes by 'Rudy.'"

"How do you know that?"

"I got a positive ID on the guy." Tom briefed her on his meetings with Maria Gonzales and Annabelle Lynch: that Rudy/Lothell had been working with Stewart on some kind of animation project—a Webisode, according to Lynch—that he was a cocaine user, and that he was seen coming out of Stewart's house Monday morning, carrying a portfolio. "Did the ME give you a picture on the murder weapon?" he asked.

"As much as he could. It was a large, single-edged blade, apparently, about twelve inches long, and two inches wide at the haft. Butcher knife, most likely. One in every kitchen. Why?"

"How about a bowie knife?"

"*Bowie* knife? Sure, Tom. A bowie knife would be consistent with the kind of wounds made. Why?"

"According to Maria Gonzales, Rudy carries a large bowie knife."

"Hmm."

"That's right." Tom told her that Annabelle Lynch had been Stewart's live-in, and that according to Maria Gonzales, she'd caught him in bed with Chandra Tupelo. Then he gave Sandy a brief rundown on the interview at Lynch's house, how he had probably caught Lynch in a lie. "She didn't want me to know the date she'd moved in with Stewart."

"Interesting."

"I think so. Lynch connects Stewart and Tupelo." Tom drew a triangle next to the scribbled-out doodle, then wrote the names *Stewart* and *Tupelo* beside two of the corners. "It still leaves Wendy Burgess out of the loop, though."

"No it doesn't, Tom. Wendy and Lynch knew each other."

"How do you know that?"

"I got it from Steven Weber. Wendy was in awe of her, apparently. She used to hang around Lynch when she would come to the network and pitch shows."

"No kidding?" Tom wrote the name *Lynch* in the middle of the triangle, then added Burgess's name in the third corner. " 'In awe,' huh?"

"Maybe after I nose around Pender's a bit, we can get together," Sandy said. "Grab a bite to eat or something. We need to go over this."

Something stirred in Tom's chest—a breath of wind over a becalmed sea. "Sounds like a plan."

"Where would you like to meet?" she asked.

"How about at the marina? I was planning on heading down to the boat later. There's a restaurant next to my dock."

"That would be fine."

"I hope you like seafood," Tom said, hearing something in his own voice now.

"I love seafood."

"Good. Give me a ring when you wrap it up at the shindig."

"You got it. Tom—?"

"Yeah?"

She didn't answer.

"What's wrong, Sandy?"

"The killer stabbed her *twenty-seven* times," she said. "We're after a monster."

Tom nodded grimly. As far as he was concerned, all killers were monsters. "I'll see you later," he said, then disconnected the line. For several moments he stared down at the phone.

Dan cleared his throat.

Tom looked across the desks at him; he had forgotten Dan was still in the room.

"Well?" Dan asked.

" 'Well' *what?*"

"What did *Sandy* say?—if you don't mind me asking."

"Why should I mind? She told me that Lynch knew the Burgess girl. What's with you?"

"Oh, nothing," Dan said, the corners of his mouth impishly turning up into the look that so annoyed Tom. "It sounded kind of chummy there toward the end. Like you were planning a date or something."

Torn shook his head. "You're an idiot."

"Chopped and channeled." Dan chuckled, opened the top drawer of his desk and found his car keys. He stopped in the doorway on his way out of the office. "All kidding aside, Tommy, that detective from LASO is the real thing. I can tell. A classy lady. Not to mention drop-dead gorgeous."

Tom didn't say a word.

"Did you hear me, Tommy?"

Tom looked at him, started to say something, stopped; then: "Good work on the Bruemann angle. Might mean something."

"Sure. You never know." Dan patted the doorjamb then walked away.

Tom stared at the bulletin board, but his mind was on a tiny dockside restaurant in Marina del Rey, Sandy sitting across from him, candlelight reflecting in her beautiful hazel eyes, as the two of them talked cases. The image made him feel strangely disquieted, his emotions in conflict, churning, as though caught between tides—part of him looking forward to the evening with Sandy, another part of him wanting to avoid it at all cost.

The bulletin board came into focus. The Beretta. Stewart's contorted face staring at him. The suicide note: THAT'S ALL, FOLKS! Tom took a deep, cleansing breath. "Let it ride, Tommy. Not on the rebound."

Tom removed Bill Pender's business card from his wallet, found the number for Quality Toys written on the back, and dialed it. A woman with a heavy Japanese accent picked up. Tom identified himself, asked to speak with someone who had been in the video-conference last Sunday with Bill Pender.

"You need talk with Hiroko."

"Hiroko?" Tom remembered that Bill Pender was talking to someone named Hiroko when he'd busted in on him that morning. "Who is Hiroko?"

"Hiroko Fujiyama. She not here now."

"How do you spell that?" Tom asked, writing slowly as the Japanese woman struggled with the American alphabet. "Where is Hiroko now?"

"She went to party—Bill Pender house."

Tom disconnected the line and stared at his hand still holding the phone. Cameron. Sandy Cameron. The name did have a familiar ring to it. There had been something in the news, now that he thought about it. Years ago. A shooting. Once again he felt the pull of forces inside him, and none of that mattered anymore. "Nuts," he said, picked up the receiver, and dialed Sandy's cell phone. She picked up after the first ring. "Want to go to a party?" Tom asked.

"Is that you, Tom?"

"It's me."

"What happened to Santa Monica?"

"Santa Monica must be on Pender's short list."

Sandy laughed. "Super. I'll pick you up, around quarter to four. Are you at the station?"

"Do you mind if we meet at the marina? It'll save us having to drive back and forth across the Valley later."

"Okay. Same place as before?"

"Sure."

"See you in about an hour, Tom."

Tom hung up the phone, Sandy's voice still gliding through his mind like a dance. He leaned back in his chair, folded his hands behind his head and stared up at the ceiling, the day's work drawing a curtain of exhaustion over him. He was beat. For several minutes he tried thinking of nothing. Hard to do. The day kept pushing in—his interviews with Bill Pender, Maria Gonzales, Annabelle Lynch—encroaching from every side. He built a mental dam against them. Then, at some point, he allowed a thought to slip through, a breach, felt the sudden movement of tide, and steeled himself against it. Too late.

"Nuts."

Chapter Nineteen

Tom drove into the parking lot at the marina and saw the little blue Roadster parked against the curb. Sandy stood on the cement walk that went along the docks. She was looking out at the boats, leaning forward slightly into the offshore wind, one hand holding her shoulder bag behind her back, the other shielding the breeze from her face. Tom parked next to her car, got out, and stood there watching her.

Sandy turned and, seeing that it was Tom, smiled and waved, abandoning her hair to the wind as she walked toward him. She was wearing a pair of pink pedal pushers that showed off her legs, a sleeveless pink-and-white polka-dot blouse, and a pair of cloth espadrilles, the sun showing the glowing freshness of her face and her hair wildly insouciant. Tom started to say something.

"You look nice," Sandy said, stealing his thunder. "Those colors go well with you."

Tom automatically looked down at his clothes. Navy-blue sports coat, khaki trousers. Docksiders. He shrugged and, looking up, made a quick sweep over Sandy's figure, starting from her pretty feet, then over a choreography of curves that brought a rush of emotion to his throat. "You too," he said.

"Thank you." She tossed her head back, closed her eyes, and breathed deeply. "Don't you just love the salt air? It's so clean." She stood, face upturned to the sky, offering the clean line of her throat—the sun firing a million shades of yellow through her hair.

"Yes," he said, and quickly looked down at his boat bobbing in its slip, pulling against its moorings. He felt a similar pull of the current in himself, his feelings held by an uncertain mooring.

"It makes you feel alive, doesn't it?"

They looked at each other several moments, her hazel eyes bright as she seemed to study his face.

"We'd best go," he said.

She broke from his gaze as a seagull swooped low, screeching. "Yes—if we must," she said playfully. "Don't want to be *too* fashionably late, do we?"

Tom felt something give way inside him. "It would be a scandal."

She laughed, tossed her keys to him, and said, "take my car?"

"Fine by me," Tom said. And it was.

● ●   ● ●

Bill Pender lived in a multilevel cliffside dweller off Mulholland, situated on a rise of mounded hilltop. There were large, seven-figure–dollar homes to the east of Pender's house: some cantilevering out from the hillside; others carved into the side of the mountain—occupied by industry executives, celebrities, investment bankers, and dot-com wizards.

Tom pulled the Roadster into the wide circular drive, parked next to the granite fountain, and, seeing one of three red-jacketed valets stepping out from a booth, left the motor running and got out. The valet slipped a ticket beneath the windshield wiper, handed Tom the stub as he slipped into the driver's seat, and wheeled around the drive.

Tom met Sandy at the base of the stairs. He gazed up at the house—a glass-and-stucco monster that he guessed was at least ten thousand square feet—and whistled.

Sandy smiled. "Shall we? Mustn't keep Bill waiting."

"No, we mustn't."

They climbed a series of slate terraces that cut through the middle of an expansive cross-cut lawn, the grounds meticulously groomed and landscaped with stands of conifers, white birch, liquid ambar, and flowering fruit trees. Tom heard music playing inside the house as they approached the double front doors that were twelve feet high, carved oak. "I believe Bill has started without us."

"Impossible!" Sandy arched an imperious brow. "See if *I* come to one of his parties again." She rang the doorbell.

A girl with short, flaming-red hair, wearing a black French maid's outfit with white lace trim, greeted them. Her face was small and pointed, her eyes large and liquid brown, her thin lips a cherry-red gloss. Her nametag read: FIFI. *"Bonjour."* She smiled demurely. *"Comment appelez-vous?"* She spoke French in a dialect that probably traced its origins to Van Nuys. She was no Fifi.

Sandy stepped forward. "Detective Sandy Cameron."

Fifi the hostess ran her finger down a guest list of well over two hundred names. "Let's see. . . . Cameron. Cameron."

Tom leaned toward Sandy and whispered, "Short list, huh?"

She dropped a hand playfully at him as if to say, "really, darling," picking up the game they had begun at the marina. "You know how it is when you're on a budget."

Fifi looked at Sandy, her smile fallen a bit. "Uh . . . I don't see your name on the list." Definitely Van Nuys. She looked at Tom.

Tom fanned a thumb at Sandy. "I'm with her."

"Did Bill invite you?"

Sandy flashed her badge.

Fifi's eyes widened. *"Police?* It's too early for a complaint." She glanced past them, as though trying to locate a scowling plaintiff on the front lawn.

Tom smiled. "Could you tell Mr. Pender we're here, please?"

Fifi blinked at him then looked over her shoulder as a second girl, wearing an identical maid's costume, approached. "Oh, good, Chelsea will take you down," Fifi said, relief breaking through her heavy makeup. "Chelsea, these people are the police."

Chelsea, a slim girl with a cadaver-like complexion—dark lipstick, dark nails, and blue hair—looked at Tom and Sandy with open boredom. "Oh?" Her nametag read, YVETTE.

"They're here to see Bill," Fifi said.

"Bill's down by the pool," Chelsea/Yvette said, wheeling perfunctorily. *"Entrez, s'il vous plaît!"* Yvette sounded as though she hailed from the Bronx.

"We're supposed to follow her," Sandy whispered.

"Gotcha."

Yvette took them through a series of large rooms, each with a panoramic view of the Santa Monica Mountains and the San Fernando Valley. Tom's gaze swept over polished granite floors with enormous squares of wine-colored carpet.

Waiters wearing blue-and-white–striped Riviera shirts, white trousers, and black berets, carried trays of drinks back and forth into adjoining rooms, where clutches of people—standing, or sitting in sofa groups—talked loudly, to be heard over the violin and accordion music blaring from hidden speakers. It seemed there was a Riviera theme to the party. Tom and Sandy followed "Yvette" down a wide flight of stairs, passed a darkened room on the left, which appeared to be a small theater. A cartoon was showing that Tom didn't recognize. No one was watching it. "What's playing?" Tom asked.

Yvette shook her blue head. "Don't ask me. I'm in live-action." Definitely the Bronx.

A spacious game room opened at the base of the stairs. The room was smoky, and filled with noise that came from a television over the bar against the left wall. Men and women sat hunched over the counter, drinking and smoking as they cheered a soccer match. Two men in shorts and sports shirts, smoking big cigars, were playing pool. A current of blue smoke eddied through the shuttered light streaming in through the wall of glass doors. Video games and pinball machines lined the east wall. No one was playing them.

Finally the game room opened onto a spacious patio terrace, made of flagstone and gray slate. As they stepped out onto it, Tom heard the Riviera music again, the music having been momentarily upstaged by the din in the game room. The air was suddenly clean to breathe.

An Olympic-sized swimming pool, irregularly shaped, with rock bridges and steps, dominated the expansive backyard. Men and women lay sunning in a double row of chaise lounges around its slate edge. Some were swimming laps or clinging to the pool's edge, talking, while others floated in aimless, glistening circles on air mattresses.

At the far end of the patio—a football field's length away, it seemed—a waterfall, spilling from a small mountain of rock built into the hillside, cascaded down into several smaller pools, before finally spilling a continuous pane of water into the deep end. Three diving boards jutted from rock platforms at the one-, two-, and three-meter marks. Stands of palm trees, stilting over sandy grottoes of lush vegetation around the patio, gave the pool grounds the appearance of a tropical island. Sandy clucked her tongue. "I say, we *are* slumming it today."

Fifty yards beyond the pool, the crosscut lawn fell off abruptly into a canyon. It seemed as though Pender's property line ran along the edge of the world, beyond which lay a killer view of the San Fernando Valley.

"There's Bill, over there," Yvette said, pointing a black-nailed finger in a vague direction across the pool.

A crowd stood on the patio beneath three large green-and-white–striped Cinzano umbrellas, to the left of a glass-and-stucco pool house. Bill Pender was in the middle of the crowd, head and shoulders above everyone else. "I see him," Tom said. *"Merci,"* he added with a grin. "I learned that from a Peter Sellers movie."

The girl made a face. Clearly she'd never heard of Peter Sellers. She flounced away.

"She's in *live-action,*" Sandy said, raising her nose a little, in affected boredom.

"Riffraff," Tom said. "I see you didn't invite the Hendersons."

"We had to draw the line somewhere, didn't we?" Sandy raised an eyebrow. "The Hendersons, yet."

As they made their way toward the umbrellas, waitresses in French-cut bathing suits carried trays of drinks to and from the pool-house bar. A large U-shaped barbecue stood in front of the pool house. Caterers basted tri-tips, halibut steaks, chicken, and carved meat, and had set out plates on the counter for a line of people. Tom and Sandy stood on the edge of the group, watching Pender. "Give him a minute, then put the cuffs on him," Tom said.

"I was going to shoot first."

"Fine with me."

Pender, wearing a short-sleeved white Mediterranean shirt over mauve-colored slacks and leather sandals, appeared to have stepped out of a Euro-magazine spread, his teeth flashing as he discussed the upcoming trip to Cannes.

Tom looked across the pool as a diver sprang off the three-meter board with a clatter and executed a flawless triple-gainer before knifing into the water. Applause awaited him as he broke the surface.

"That is André Mollier," Bill Pender said, walking over to Tom. "He was on the French Olympic diving team."

Tom looked over as Mollier climbed up the chrome ladder, the diver's hair sleeked back like an otter's, water shedding off his body as a second wave of applause warmed him onto the patio. "Kind of puts the finishing touch on things around here."

Pender smiled. "You noticed our Riviera theme. Yes, it gets us in the mood for Cannes." He looked at Sandy, his electric-blue eyes charged with interest. He looked her over; a flash of teeth. "You get lovelier each time I see you."

Tom felt something jump in his chest. Definitely anger.

"Would you care for something to drink?" Pender asked Sandy.

"Perrier with a twist of lime, if you have it."

Pender nodded at a waitress.

Tom started to order, but his request was cut off as Sharon O'Neill appeared out of the crowd.

"There you are," she said, jiggling up to Pender with a camera. "Smile." She took his picture. She was wearing white shorts, a red-and-white–striped T-shirt with quarter-sleeves, and high-heeled block sandals. A black beret tilted rakishly over her left eye. "I think Cannes will be wonderful, Bill," she said, then followed his gaze to Sandy. Her eyes narrowed coldly. "What are you doing here?" she demanded. "This is a private party."

"And we're public servants, Ms. O'Neill," Sandy replied politely. "We're investigating a murder."

Tom grinned. "We really are."

O'Neill glared at him. "They shouldn't be here."

Pender put his arm around O'Neill and patted her shoulder. "Now, babe, they're just doing their jobs." He smiled at Sandy. "What can I do for you?"

"Mr. Pender—"

"Cease." He put up his hand. "This is my house. This is my party. What must I do for you to call me Bill?"

"Answer some questions regarding your relationship with Chandra Tupelo."

The waitress appeared with the Perrier. "There you are, my dear," Pender said, handing Sandy the drink, then clasping her hands. "Chandra? What a horrible thing."

"Yes," Sandy said. "I've just a few questions."

Pender released her hands with a soft pat. Barracuda grin. "Of course."

Tom felt a sudden, visceral dislike for the man. He glanced over the crowd, spotted a group of Asians across the pool. "I understand that Hiroko Fujiyama is here today?"

Pender continued looking at Sandy. "Yes. She's here some-where," he said. "Sharon, could you see to our guests, please? I won't be a minute." He guided Sandy toward the opposite end of the pool.

O'Neill watched them walking away, her hand on her hip, holding the camera; then, turning to face Tom, she thrust a finger at him and snapped, "I trust your presence here will not be dis-ruptive."

"Oh, you can count on me," Tom said, crossing his heart three or four times. "Scout's honor." He swung his head toward the food table and rubbed his stomach. "Say—you got any beanie-weenies?"

O'Neill turned with a snort of contempt, her hind parts quiv-ering like mounds of Jell-O as she headed toward the house.

Tom glanced once more at Sandy and Pender, and shook his head. He definitely did not like the man.

The pool house was noisy inside—people coming and going, laughing, talking loudly, calling out their drink orders to the bar-tenders. Tom squeezed between two men and put his hands on the bar. "I'll take a Heineken, if you got it."

Dumb question. As Tom stepped away from the bar, sipping his beer, he felt a tap on his shoulder.

"Excuse me?" a woman's voice said.

Tom turned and standing behind him was an attractive Asian woman. "Detective Rigby?"

"That's right."

"My office informed me that a Detective Tom Rigby had called and wished to speak to me."

"If you could spare a couple minutes," he said, looking her over.

She had dark, almond-shaped eyes, exotic cheekbones wrapped with smooth, honey-colored skin, and her thick black hair fell in a single length below her tiny waist. Very curvy, her figure accented by a floral wrap and matching bikini top; and she spoke better English than Tom did.

"You are Hiroko Fujiyama, I presume?"

"I am not David Livingstone." She smiled, delicate curls rising at the corners of her small, pouty lips. She extended her hand and he shook it. Long, cool, femininely tapered fingers. "Please call me Hiroko," she said, and he felt the tips of her fingers slide from his grasp like a sable brush. "What may I do for you?"

Tom stepped aside to allow three men and a woman, all in bathing suits, the woman laughing hysterically, to squeeze past him into the already-crowded pool house. "Get me out of here, for one thing," he smiled.

"Follow me."

Tom followed Hiroko onto the patio. She led him toward a table set back in a quiet, palm-shaded retreat, her black-felt thongs flapping softly against her heels as she glided over the flagstone. Tom set his drink on the table and sat facing the pool. Hiroko took the chair next to him, so that their chairs were spaced about two feet apart. Very cozy.

Tom heard the music shift to a New Age jazz instrumental, looked at Hiroko. He guessed she was in her mid- to late twenties, and she seemed very sure of herself. Her shapely legs, crossed at the ankles, extended toward the pool. "Thank you for taking time to meet with me," he said.

She smiled, spread her toes. She seemed to be studying him. "You don't look like a policeman."

Tom guessed it was a mild come-on. "Really," she said, sipping her drink. She sat back in her chair, leaning sideways on her right elbow; her left hooked back over the chair back, holding her drink between her thumb and middle fingers, rattling the ice. "I expected a fat, bald dude, chewing a cigar."

Tom smiled. "I like a good cigar, now and then."

"I do, too." She raised a finger at a waitress with a wedge of gold hair and ordered a rum and Coke. The waitress asked if Tom would like another Heineken.

"No thanks," Tom said, raising his bottle. "Still working on it." He sipped his beer, looked across the pool where Sandy and Pender stood talking by the waterfall. Pender was leaning slightly forward, hawklike.

"She is very beautiful," Hiroko said. "I think Bill is taken with her."

Tom looked at Hiroko, set his bottle down, and opened his

notebook. He could care less what Bill Pender thought of Sandy. . . . But, that wasn't true. He wrote *Hiroko Fujiyama* across the top of a clean page. "What is it that you do for Quality Toys, Ms. Fujiyama?"

"Call me Hiroko." She was smiling at him with her eyes.

"All right, Hiroko. What do you do for Quality Toys?"

"This is exciting. I've never been interrogated by a detective before. Will you give me the third degree?"

"If you don't answer the question, I might."

"Oh, good. I am the Director of Product Development," she said, clearly enjoying herself. "I locate film and book properties that can be optioned, and maybe, turned into toy lines. I guess you could say I am a troubleshooter."

"Sounds fun."

"It is. I am also the liaison for the parent company in Tokyo— a bridge, as it were, between QT and Panda. Other companies, too, of course."

Tom wrote it down in his notebook. The waitress brought Hiroko a rum and Coke, smiled at Tom as she left. "I understand your company and Mr. Pender have been spending quite a lot of time together lately," Tom said.

Hiroko tested her drink. "Oh, yes."

"You had a meeting last night?"

"Yes." She removed the little umbrella from her drink and set it on the table. "We met with the board from about seven P.M. until ten."

"The board?"

"The QT creative board. We met in Bill's office. There were six of us."

"And your meeting went until ten o'clock, you say?"

"Yes. Afterward, Bill and I went out for a late dinner, then continued the meeting here."

"Here?"

She smiled at him over the rim of her glass.

He turned the page in his notebook. "Where did you eat dinner?"

"At the Elephant Bar in Burbank. We go there for drinks."

Tom had eaten at the restaurant many times; it was just down the street from the station. He knew the manager and a couple of the waiters. "Is there someone who can verify this?"

"Our alibis, you mean?" Hiroko set her glass down and leaned forward conspiratorially, resting her chin on the back of her folded hand. She was definitely having a good time. "Are Bill and I in some kind of trouble?"

"We've asked these questions to everyone who knew any of the deceased."

"The deceased. . . . Yes." A shiver of excitement seemed to pass over her. "Shall I write you a list?"

"I would appreciate it."

She extended her hand. "I'll need a sheet of your notepaper."

Tom tore out a sheet of paper and gave her his pen. She angled her head to write, left-handed, her long straight hair sliding back off her shoulders then falling in a mass to hang down one side like a sheet of black satin.

She giggled. "I've never had to write out my alibi before."

Tom glanced at the waterfall, but Sandy and Bill Pender were no longer there. He found them sitting at a table across the pool. Pender was leaning across the table, his hand poised on the back of her chair. Too cozy. Tom felt another surge of anger. The guy was getting on his nerves. Tom took a quick sip of his beer, set the bottle down, and removed a second pen from his coat pocket. "What time did you leave the restaurant?"

"What time?" Hiroko continued writing. "Let's see. . . . We left the restaurant around eleven-thirty . . . arrived here around midnight or so. I left this morning at eight-thirty."

"This morning?"

She smiled up at him, a scolding slant in her eyes. "We're consenting adults. Would you like Bill's and my itinerary for the night Wendy Burgess died? It will save you having to ask me about it."

"That would be fine." Tom sipped his beer.

"Every night this past week, Bill and I have been in meetings with the board, in Bill's office," she said. "The meetings have usually ended around ten or so. After the meetings, Bill and I went out to dinner. Here you go." Hiroko handed Tom the list with a flourish. "Our alibis! Everyone who saw us on each one of the nights."

"Thank you." Tom read through it quickly. The first four

names were those of Japanese men, with a phone number written beside each name. "These are their work extensions?"

"Yes. I don't know the numbers for the restaurants."

Below the names were two restaurants—the Elephant Bar, and BJ's. There were three names listed beneath each of the restaurants. Tom would call each of them to verify her story. "Thank you," he said, folding the page into his notebook.

When he looked at Hiroko, she was circling the rim of her glass with her middle finger. "This is fun." She leaned forward, onto her hand. "Is that bulge in your coat your gun, or handcuffs?"

"Could I have my pen back?"

"Of course."

Tom placed the pen in his coat pocket, holding it by its push-button end. He would have her prints taken and checked against the John Doe latents found in each of the three dead persons' houses. "Let's talk about last Sunday."

She brightened. "All right. Last Sunday."

"Ms. O'Neill informed me that Bill Pender was in a videoconference with Quality Toys and Panda Japan. Is that correct?"

"That's right." She sipped her drink. "It seems like ages ago, doesn't it? Wendy had set it up. Poor thing."

"How many people were in the meeting?"

Hiroko tapped the corner of her mouth. "Let's see. There were about four of us at QT. A roomful of people in Tokyo . . . perhaps a dozen. And Bill."

"No one in the room with Pender?"

"Just Bill . . . larger than life. Oh"—Hiroko smiled, reached across the table, and touched his hand with her fingertips—"and, of course, Mickey Mouse," she said, giggled, and withdrew her hand. "Ask me another question."

Tom smiled politely. Three people were dead, probably murdered, and to her it was nothing more than a party game. "Do you remember when the meeting started?"

"Oh, yes. Five o'clock P.M. sharp."

"You seem pretty sure of the time."

"I am. You can verify it with any of the board members. All our meetings start precisely at five."

"Why is that?"

"To allow for the time difference in Japan. Five o'clock P.M. here, is nine in the morning in Tokyo."

Tom nodded. "How long did the meeting last?"

"Several hours, as I recall." She shrugged. "I believe it went until nine P.M. or so."

"You're certain about that?"

"Quite certain."

"Did you and Bill get together afterward?"

She brushed her left index finger over her right one. "You're a naughty boy," she said, frowning playfully at him. "That wouldn't have been kosher, would it? With Wendy still alive."

Tom looked at her. "What exactly do you mean by that, Hiroko?"

She shrugged. "I mean that Bill and Wendy were a couple. Believe it or not, Bill is a one-girl-at-a-time kind of guy."

"Are you his girl now?"

"I'm my own girl," she said, twirling the little drink umbrella between her fingers. "I like to keep my options open."

"Fair enough." Tom glanced across the pool and saw Pender talking on the phone. Sharon O'Neill had joined them and was standing next to Pender. It appeared as though Sandy was asking her own questions.

● ●   ● ●

"I got out of my routine, with Wendy gone," O'Neill answered, defensively. "Normally I go to the gym after work. Last night I went out to dinner." She glanced down at Pender, who had turned around in his chair for privacy while he talked on the phone. The call was from Cannes.

"What restaurant did you go to?" Sandy asked.

O'Neill looked at her, her face flushed with anger. "Why? You think *I* killed Chandra Tupelo? She looked around quickly, realizing that she had said it too loud. She looked back at Sandy and leaned forward, confidentially. Why would *I* kill her?"

"These are routine questions, Ms. O'Neill. We have to ask them."

"Well, you don't have to ask them here. Can't you see Bill is busy? There are a lot of very important people here. Clients!"

Sandy saw the veins along Sharon's neck and thought she might blow a gasket. "So, you went out to dinner last night?"

O'Neill folded her arms across her chest.

Sandy placed her hands on the edge of the table. Two could play at that game. "Ms. O'Neill? If you want me to go away, then please answer the question."

Their eyes were locked. Then O'Neill broke away with a grunt of contempt. "I ate at the Macaroni Grill. I sat in the bar. If you don't believe me, check it out."

Sandy had every intention of doing just that. "The one out in Valencia?"

O'Neill nodded sharply. "Plenty of people saw me."

"Did you eat by yourself?"

"There's no crime in that, is there?"

"If there is, then *I* ought to be arrested." Sandy smiled. Sharon O'Neill apparently didn't get the joke. "What time did you leave the restaurant?" Sandy asked.

"I didn't look at the clock."

"All right. Then what did you do after your dinner?"

O'Neill looked over at Pender. Pender was turned away from the table with his finger in his ear. "I went to the gym," O'Neill said.

"Right after dinner?"

"Not right after—that'd be stupid. I went home first and watched TV."

"Anything good on?"

"No. Just some stupid Hitchcock flick. It was so boring I went to the gym. I've been under a lot of stress lately. I needed to burn it off."

Sandy frowned. "Don't we all?" Clearly, the woman's exercise therapy wasn't working. Sandy looked at her notes. "You live off Soledad?"

O'Neill frowned. "How'd you know that?"

It's called a "preliminary background check," sweetie, Sandy did not say. *I also know your age, height, weight, Social Security number, and that you probably aren't going to win any Miss Congeniality awards in the near future.* "What time did you get to the gym?"

"I didn't look at the clock."

"Can you give me an approximate time?"

"I don't know—nine-thirty . . . quarter to ten or so. How many more questions are you going to ask me? I have guests to entertain."

A waitress with flaming red hair stopped and asked if anyone would like a drink. Sandy shook her head. O'Neill flicked a hand at her, as though shooing a fly.

"Did people see you at the gym?" Sandy asked.

O'Neill waited until the waitress was out of earshot then threw her hands onto her hips. "I don't believe this," she said, anger pinched in her voice. "You really think I killed her, don't you? Why would I kill her?"

"I don't know why. You tell me."

O'Neill's face contorted slightly. "I hardly knew her. She was Wendy's friend, not mine!"

"Did anyone see you at the gym?" Sandy repeated, very politely.

"I didn't sign autographs or anything."

"So, no one saw you?"

"A bunch of people saw me," O'Neill said, her voice quavering. She seemed on the verge of tears. "I said hi to the manager. Ask, if you don't believe me."

Sandy intended to. "Which club?"

"Twenty-four-hour Fitness."

"The one next to Costco?"

O'Neill answered with a sharp nod of her head. "Please"—her expression changed abruptly, and Sandy knew she was going to lose it—"this has been a terrible week," O'Neill said, bringing her hands up to her face. "I'm trying to do my job as well as Wendy did. It's not easy." She looked at Sandy, her eyes wet with tears.

Sandy handed her a tissue from her purse.

"Thank you," O'Neill said, dabbing her eyes and composing herself. She blew her nose. "Are you almost done? Really, Bill has important guests. He can't be sitting here talking to you all day."

"I won't keep him. I'm finished with you, though."

Pender disconnected the line he was on, turned around in his chair to face Sandy. "Sorry to keep you waiting."

Sharon O'Neill stepped forward. "I told her you had guests, Bill. She needs to wrap this up."

Pender put his hand on Sandy's arm. "We're about finished, aren't we?"

"Just about," Sandy replied, recoiling from his touch.

"That's what she said earlier, Bill." O'Neill once again seemed on the verge of tears. "She's ruining the party."

"Now, now, babe," Pender said, patting her rump. "You attend to the guests while I finish up here with the lovely detective. All right?"

O'Neill stood, glaring at Sandy, shook her head, and left.

"Now, where were we?" Pender said, flashing his perfect smile. "Wait a sec. Would you like a drink?" Without waiting for Sandy's reply, he hailed a waitress.

While Pender ordered, Sandy looked over at Tom. He was looking at her. So was the Asian girl he was sitting with. Hiroko Fujiyama, she presumed. Sandy waved her fingers at him.

● ●   ● ●

"Is she your girl?"

Tom looked at Hiroko.

"The beautiful blonde," Hiroko clarified. "The way you've been looking at her every two minutes." She smiled. "The way she looks at you, too."

Tom turned the page in his notebook. "You said earlier that your company did business with other companies. What other companies?"

Another enigmatic smile curved along her small, sensuous mouth. "That is a trade secret."

"This is a murder investigation," Tom said. "I would appreciate it if you would answer the question."

Hiroko set the little umbrella down and picked up her drink. "Do you have a court order?"

"Do I need one?"

She continued smiling at him, rattled the ice in her glass. She wasn't going to say a thing.

"Okay," Tom said. "What do you know of a German company named Bruemann Entertainment?"

Hiroko blinked. Her eyes had the sudden dark cunning of a panther, a vague shadow passing over them. Tom wasn't sure if it was the overhead palms, or something else. One thing he *was* sure of: the game had changed. She leaned back in her chair. "Do not do business with them," she said coolly.

"Why not?"

"They are our competition." The corners of Hiroko's mouth twitched up a little. It might have been an attempt at a smile. Then again, it might've been a frown. She sipped her drink, shadows playing over her face.

"Can you tell me anything about them?"

She shrugged noncommittally. "What's to tell? Bruemann acquires shows that are already produced, and repackages them." She took a long pull of her drink. "Mostly Anime crap."

"Anime is Japanese-style animation?" Tom asked.

"Yes. Bruemann buys up a bunch of shows at a time, throws them against the wall, and sees which ones stick. QT is only interested in first-run shows. Hard to package a toy deal with hand-me-downs."

"*Punching Judy* is not a Japanese-style show."

The glass froze in Hiroko's hand. Her eyes went flat, without depth, a dull sheen glazing over them that reminded Tom of a one-way mirror. She could see out, but no one could see in.

"Hiroko, *Punching Judy* is not a Japanese-style show," Tom repeated.

She continued staring at him. He got the feeling she had left him sitting there for a few moments, talking to her body, while she had gone off somewhere. "What's your point?" she asked, an edge to her tone.

Tom shrugged. "No point. Do you know a woman named Annabelle Lynch?"

She held her glass out to the side, again rattled the ice. "No. . . . Sorry. Should I?"

"She's the president of Empire Films. Big animation studio in town. I would've thought in your toymaker troubleshooting, you would've come across her."

"You asked me if I knew her, and I don't. Not personally." She averted her gaze, brushed a piece of something off her wrap. "She's the one who is running Empire Films into the ground."

Tom looked at her. "How do you mean?"

"She hasn't had a hit series in quite some time, has she? The word I hear is that the company's on shaky ground. So is Lynch."

"How so?"

"She's incompetent. She couldn't pick a winner if it sat down in her lap." She covered her mouth playfully. "Did *I* say that?"

"Yes, you did. What do you mean by it?"

She leaned back in her chair, took a sip of her drink. "This is a party," she said, her smiling fading. "I don't mean anything by it."

"Really?" Tom didn't believe her. "It sounds to me like you've had dealings with her."

"You think so?" Hiroko finished her drink, gently set the glass down on the table. "If I had dealings with her, then I would know her personally, wouldn't I?"

Tom conceded the point. "All right, then. Do you know a Parker Stewart?"

"Who's Parker Stewart?" she asked with a straight face. She waved a hand at him. "Oh, that's right. He's the dude that killed himself the other day, isn't he? I read something about it in the trades."

"We think he was murdered."

"Murdered?" She clucked her tongue. "Such a world."

"You haven't answered my question, Hiroko."

"No, I don't know him. Personally or otherwise. Are you about finished, Detective? I would like to go swimming now." Without waiting for a reply, she stood, untied her wrap, and folded it across the back of her chair as delicately as if it were made of orchids. She stood looking down at Tom. "Well?"

Tom didn't know if she was asking to be excused, or if he should comment on her spiffy bathing suit. "I've got what I need for now. Thank you."

She stepped out of her thongs and walked away from him on the balls of her feet, and, as she stepped down into the shallow end of the pool, her hair became a spill of black ink over the surface.

Tom folded his notebook, drank off the last of his beer, and sat staring at Hiroko's folded wrap. He suspected that she knew Lynch. She knew about the *Punching Judy* deal, too. Something screwy was up. *What?* He glanced over at the opposite side of the pool and caught Hiroko staring at him. Her back was against the pool wall, her elbows hooked over the edge, her outstretched legs scissoring slowly in the water. The corners of her mouth were upturned slightly, but her eyes held that same flatness, behind which she might be calculating some mystery deal, some wickedness—or she might not be there at all. She might have left the scene. Then, as if reading his thoughts, Hiroko waved her fingers at him, giggled, and, pushing away from the side, brought her hands together and submerged.

Tom shook his head. It was all a game.

The clatter of the springboard drew his gaze to the deep end of the pool, in time to see André Mollier knife cleanly into the water, then climb, shedding water, up the ladder to rigorous applause. Sandy and Pender were not at the table. He looked around the pool, stood, then looked toward the house. She was nowhere in sight. Neither was Pender. Then he saw her threading through the crowd under the Cinzano umbrellas to his right, men and women turning to stare at the long-legged beauty as she walked along the edge of the pool. Alone. When their eyes met, Tom was not prepared for his reaction.

He felt a thrill.

Chapter Twenty

Dear Paul,
It seems so silly. I can't stop thinking of him. Even now, as I write,
I'm thinking of him. I feel like a schoolgirl. I haven't told you about
him yet, but his name is Thomas Rigby. Tom. He's a bit gruff on the
outside, but that's all fake. I can see it's all fake; he's actually sensitive.
He can be funny, too, if I coax him into it. Did I mention that he's
quite good-looking? (I feel stupid writing this.) I think you'd like him,
Paul. Not because of his looks, but because he's genuine.

Sandy reread what she'd just written, tore out the page, and
crumpled it. "This is silly," she said aloud. The house was quiet,
except for the ticking of the grandfather clock, and hearing her
own voice when she was alone was a little startling. She actually
glanced up to see if anyone had heard. Even sillier.

She drew her legs up into her chair and chewed on the end of
her pen. Through the French doors, she could see the sun nestling
behind the saddleback; her gaze went far beyond the mountains,
though. She was seeing the light come alive in his eyes across the
table from her as they sat in a quiet booth of the restaurant, the two
of them talking through the case, then no longer talking about it.
Laughing. The talk was different than it had been yesterday at
Coco's. She redated the entry.

Dear Paul,
I went out to dinner tonight with an interesting man. He's a Burbank
detective. We ate dinner at this nice little place on the dock at the
marina. I had Alaskan king crab. I thought of you, Paul, unsuccessfully
working the crab tools that weekend we went up to Morro Bay together.

*Do you remember? You got so frustrated you started cracking the legs
with your teeth, and tearing out the meat like a caveman. I thought we
were going to be asked to leave.*

Sandy laughed, leaned her head back into the chair, looking out
and seeing the sun lower now. Paul always made her laugh, sometimes so hard she'd dribble a little in her pants. She shook her head,
the laugh trailing, then she felt a tear trickling down her cheek.

Paul . . .

The kettle whistled. Sandy set her journal aside, got up, and
went into the kitchen. She turned off the gas, took the kettle off
the range and poured herself a cup of herbal tea. Herbal tea would
help her settle into the evening.

Spooning in a little honey, she looked out the window over the
sink, facing the road. A black Corvette was parked across from her
house. Nice car. Someone visiting a neighbor. A face appeared in
the car window briefly, then disappeared. She didn't see who it
was. She glanced at the grandfather clock. Late. Probably someone
lost, looking at a map or directions.

Sandy lived on a secluded street; the homes—custom ranches,
Mediterraneans, contemporaries, French provincials built on two-
to five-acre lots—were far apart. There were no street lamps, or
addresses marked on the curb. People often drove up her street,
having made the wrong turn off Sand Canyon—pizza deliveries,
mostly—cruised along the street, reading mailboxes, then, realizing
their error, drove back down the hill.

Sandy sipped her tea. No delivery boy she'd ever seen drove a
new 'Vette like that one, though. She smiled down at Rhubarb.
"It's too nice outside to be cooped up in here, Rhub. What do you
say we go out and see Buster Brown?"

The kitty mewed.

"That's the stuff." Sandy glanced once more at the Corvette
then stopped out the back door of her house onto the patio. She
smiled inwardly at a thought.

● ●   ● ●

When Tom got back to the boat there was still plenty of light left
in the day, and he made the calls to the restaurant. Hiroko's story

checked out. The managers and waiters remembered seeing Pender and her there each night. They were good tippers. Also, they could not help but notice Hiroko. The two of them left each night around eleven, eleven-thirty, or so. Tom then put in a call to Panda Japan, and through an interpreter learned that the videoconference on Sunday checked out as well. It had begun precisely at nine o'clock in the morning, Tokyo time, and had concluded approximately four hours later. Pender had been in the meeting the entire time; so had Hiroko. So far, their alibis checked out. He would call each of the Quality Toys board members in the morning.

Tom changed into a pair of jeans and a sweatshirt. He took the pen from his coat pocket and carefully placed it into an evidence bag. He'd have the lab boys lift Hiroko's prints, compare them with the John Doe's still unaccounted-for in Stewart's place. He got the feeling Hiroko was hiding something. It was only a hunch, but his hunches were fairly reliable.

Tom grabbed a St. Pauli Girl from the refrigerator, went back to the stern, and lay back against the seat cushions. The air was cool. It felt good to be on the boat, feeling the teak deck beneath him, the rolling surges, the smell of the sea, and all of the harbor sounds that went with it. He would sleep on the boat tonight. On the boat he could think, and he very much needed to think. His feelings toward Sandy troubled him. What was his hunch about her?

He sipped the beer and looked out beyond the breakwater as a skein of widgeons, beating a northerly course, showed black against the setting sun. Lying there he heard, then saw, a large Chris-Craft motoring up the channel. A minute later he felt the swell, then tug of the lines, then cushion of the bumpers as the boat nudged against the dock.

Feeling the old ache in his chest, he leaned his head back against the cushion, watching the sun touch the horizon, watched the shimmering boil of red-and-yellow light as it sank into the sea. He took a sip of beer, rested the bottle on his stomach, and felt the cool air sweep over the world that seemed to bear a great sadness. He decided it would probably be a pretty good idea to see Sandy as little as possible.

● ●   ● ●

Sandy felt the solid pack of Buster's muscles as she patted his neck. "Hey, boy," she said. "Maybe we'll go for a ride tomorrow. Would you like that?"

Buster nibbled at her sleeve with thick, prehensile lips.

"None of that," she scolded.

Rhubarb was busy with a rat in the bales. She smiled, found a rake and began mucking out the corral, Buster watching curiously as she shoveled the manure through the pipe rails into a wheelbarrow. She enjoyed the work. It was therapy. It freed her mind to think—to think about Tom Rigby. She found herself drawn to the man, felt emotions moving in her heart she had thought long dead, emotions that both excited and frightened her.

She placed the rake on top of the manure pile in the wheelbarrow, felt the forward heft of weight as she guided the wheelbarrow along the sloping gravel path that went along the northern edge of her property, and down toward the Dumpster near the street. Wheeling around the corner of the house, she saw the Corvette still parked across the street. She was level with the car and, approaching from the rear, the driver was hidden by its high back and roof. She saw a movement through the rear window, so she knew the driver was still sitting there. Something about the setup was strange.

If someone was lost, they would have gotten their bearings by now, or they would've gone up to a door and asked for help. Then she saw a reflection of the driver's face suddenly profiled in the side mirror. It was Steven Weber. He was looking up at her house. Weber wasn't lost, and he was certainly no delivery boy. He was stalking her. She knew she'd gotten to him at the jail last night. She'd cornered his masculinity—a dangerous thing to do, considering his track record.

Her scalp prickling, Sandy set the wheelbarrow down easily on its rear supports, reached instinctively for her pistol before remembering that she'd left it on the kitchen counter. Chiding herself, she glanced up at her house and thought about retrieving it, then walking down to the street to confront Weber. Maybe provoke him to do something. An image of her pistol-whipping him came to mind. She frowned when she saw Weber's reflection slide back off the mirror. He might be leaving, no time for the pistol.

She looked down at the manure rake and shrugged. Somehow it seemed fitting.

Gripping the rake like a rifle at port arms, Sandy approached the Corvette from the rear, keeping in Weber's blind spot. But when she got to within twenty feet Weber's face reappeared in the mirror. He was looking straight at her, his eyes wide.

Sandy quickened her pace, heard the engine turning over, roaring to life, and the Corvette peeled away with a squeal of tires. Sandy ran after him, brandishing the rake. "You creep!"

She stopped amid a cloud of exhaust and burning rubber, stood glaring at the Corvette until it disappeared behind the oaks along the bend of the road. She could hear it going down the road to the corner, heard its progress up Sand Canyon, the roaring climb of the engine, rubber in each of the gears, then the sound of the engine fading. Then it was quiet.

The neighborhood was peaceful in the twilight, Venus brightening on the horizon. Sandy could almost hear her heart pounding in her chest. She could certainly feel it. She looked down at the rake in her hands, her knuckles white, then realized she was standing in the middle of the road. She felt silly and started toward her house. But as she reached the front door, a thought occurred to her that sent a chill over her arms. She turned and looked down the street, waves of chills now racing up and down her spine.

Weber knew where she lived.

Chapter Twenty-One

The next morning Tom drove into the office and made the calls to Quality Toys. Hiroko's story checked out. She and Pender had been in meetings both nights, the meetings beginning at seven and ending around ten like she had said. Tom gave the pen with Hiroko's fingerprints on it to Herb Walters, the latent-fingerprint technician. Walters, a thin, nervous man with short wiry red hair and colorless eyes, said he would get to it as soon as he could. He told Tom that the prints on the beer bottle he'd taken from Charlie Doogan's house matched a partial they'd gotten from the corner of Stewart's computer desk.

"It's just a partial, Tom," he said. "But it belongs to Doogan. He was in Stewart's house. Don't know when, but he was in there."

Tom stared at the carpet. Doogan had told him he'd never been in Stewart's house, so he had lied. Why?

Walters shrugged. "Hope that helps."

"It may. Thanks, Herb." Tom stopped by his office, grabbed his coffee cup and walked down the hall to the break room. Dan and a couple of detectives were watching a high-speed chase on the television mounted on the wall. Dan's feet were up on the table, crossed at the ankles. He was eating a bag of Frito's. "Look at this, Tommy," he said. "Those are our boys!"

Tom glanced at the television. A helicopter-mounted camera traced a small red import that was weaving recklessly in and out of traffic along Glenoaks. Several Burbank units were in pursuit, their lights flashing.

"The guy's nuts," Dan said. "He's already hit three vehicles."

Tom looked at his watch.

"Oh, don't worry about what time it is, Tommy," Dan said,

watching the television. "I'm done for the day." He slid a file across the Formica-topped table. "I've been doing all the crime-fighting around here."

"I can see." Tom picked up the file. It was fairly thick. "What's this?"

Dan grinned. "I get the prize today. Take a look."

Tom did. There were police photographs of a wrecked car, a newspaper clipping of the same photo with three photos of high-school kids. There were other photos, autopsy reports.

Dan popped a handful of corn chips into his mouth. "You're so lucky to have me as a partner, Tommy."

Tom allowed a smile.

"Look at that!" one of the other detectives howled.

Dan swung around. "What? Oh, *man!*"

The fleeing vehicle had just sideswiped a truck, and was hopping the median into opposing traffic. It caromed off the front left fender of an oncoming semi, spun a brody across the road, and shuddered along a cement curb, where it came to a stop, steam pouring from the hood. The semi jackknifed and two vehicles rear-ended its trailer. Other cars skidded to avoid collision. The driver of the red import, apparently unhurt, jumped out of his car and raced into the Bob's Big Boy across the street. Several black-and-whites pulled into the scene. The helicopter camera widened to show uniformed officers dashing from their units into the restaurant.

"Hey! I just ate breakfast there this morning," one of the detectives said.

"They're going in there for takeout," Dan said.

"What? They open a new run-thru counter or something?"

"No, there's a run on doughnuts."

The detectives laughed.

The Bob's Big Boy was only a few blocks from the station.

Tom went back to his office and read through the file. Inside was a stack of eight-by-ten color photos taken at the scene of the crash. The driver, an eighteen-year-old boy, had been crushed against the wheel. There were two kids in the backseat, obviously dead. One of the victims was a seventeen-year-old girl named Brittany Doogan. There was a fourth person involved, a high-school senior named Ronnie Trueblood, who had been thrown clear of the vehicle as it tumbled down the ravine. Miraculously, she had suffered only a few cuts and bruises.

The ME's report indicated that each of the victims had had significant levels of cocaine in their systems. In her statement to the police, Trueblood had confessed that they had just left a party where they'd gotten the drugs. The party was at the home of Parker Stewart, a cartoon director. Charges were filed against Stewart by Charles Doogan, but were dropped because of a lack of incriminating evidence. Distraught over the loss of their daughter, Doogan's wife Cynthia had hanged herself in her bathroom later that day, a photo of her daughter pinned to her chest.

Tom looked at the eight-by-ten of Brittany Doogan, a duplicate of the one he'd seen on the side table in Doogan's Malibu home—a pretty girl smiling at the world. Wasted. He closed the folder. Dan got the prize.

Tom picked up the phone and dialed Doogan's house. The machine picked up. Tom did not leave a message. He dialed Empire Films, got the receptionist with the face metal, and asked the receptionist if Doogan had come in. She said no. Tom gave her his pager number, told her to call him if Doogan came in. She said she would be happy to. He disconnected the line and looked down at Doogan's file. Then he looked over at the photographs on the bulletin board, paid particular attention to the one of the carpet with the granules of sand. Sand consistent with the sample he'd taken from Doogan's front stoop.

Tom heard a rush of footsteps in the hall. Moments later, Dan stuck his head in the door, all excited. "Tommy, it's our guy!"

"What guy?"

"The crazy on the TV. It's Lothell Taylor—Rudy, or whatever his name is. One of our boys IDed him from the NYPD photo. They've got him holed up at the Holiday Inn!"

Tom was already in motion.

● ●   ● ●

Black-and-white units surrounded the Holiday Inn on Third and Angelo, in downtown Burbank, their lights flashing. Uniformed officers secured the exits, guns drawn; others kept a gathering crowd of onlookers at bay and directed traffic. Three news vans screeched to the corner, doors sliding open, their crews hitting the ground running with Betacams aimed. News helicopters hovered overhead, like vultures circling carrion, more approaching in the distance.

Breaking news!

Tom and Dan badged their way into the hotel lobby, headed to the elevator bay, where uniformed officers kept a clutch of puzzled guests from entering. "What floor?" Tom asked the nearest uniform.

"Sixth. He's got a hostage. A cleaning lady."

"Thanks."

Tom and Dan took the elevator to the sixth floor, made their way down a hall crowded with policemen and inquiring guests. It was a zoo. Too many policemen with nothing to do but wanting to be close to the action. Any action. Tom understood: It was why they were cops, but right now they were between him and where he needed to be.

"Back up, fellahs. Back up," Dan said, pushing through the crowd ahead of him. Just like in the old days on the varsity squad.

Tom and Dan stepped around a fallen cleaning cart outside the room where the action was apparently taking place. Sergeant Dickerson, the watch sergeant on duty, was at the door, looking into the room, talking to someone on his radio. The watch lieutenant, Tom guessed. "What've we got, Sam?"

Sergeant Dickerson, a thirty-year man with curly gray hair and a paunch, said, "He's got a woman hostage in there, Tom. Got a knife to her throat."

"Making any demands?"

Dickerson shook his head. "Not yet. He's scared to death."

Tom glanced into the room, saw the backs of two uniformed officers. He recognized them, Rob Feld and Kyle Platchett. Both officers were crouched with their guns drawn and pointed. Tom couldn't see their target, Lothell Taylor, aka Julian "Rudy" Rudolph. Bail jumper from New York, handy with a knife.

"He's around the corner there, Tom," Dickerson whispered.

"Okay." The room was typical of many moderately priced hotels. A bathroom on the right cut into the living space, giving the entryway and bedroom areas an upside-down L shape, with the leg of the L opening to the right. A queen bed was pushed against the right wall, all but the foot hidden by the bathroom wall corner. The bed was stripped of linen, which lay in a bundle at the foot. There was a mirrored bureau against the left wall, opposite the bed, a TV on the far side of the mirror. Tom saw Taylor's reflection in the mirror, an unmistakable match with the NYPD mug shot. The black man was backed into the far right corner behind a heavyset Mexican cleaning woman, holding what appeared to be a large bowie knife to her throat. "I'll cut her!" he said—almost a screech. The woman was crying. It looked bad.

"He grabbed her and ran into the room before we could nab him," Dickerson said. "That the guy you been looking for?"

"That's him."

"How do you want to handle this, Tommy?" Dan asked.

"I don't know yet." Tom did not want to upset the delicate balance of power between the two officers and the man holding the knife, but they had to do something. Taylor was a known doper, he sounded desperate—scared to death, as Dickerson had put it. Maybe hopped-up. With a knife pressed against the woman's throat it was a dangerous combination. A delay might exacerbate an already-volatile situation; push Taylor to do something stupid. Then again, giving it some time might help diffuse it. Hard to tell. Tom frowned. It looked bad all around.

"What do you think?" Dickerson said. "You want my men to back out? You and Dan take over?" Tom could hear the tension in Dickerson's voice.

"Yeah, that's probably best," he said, hearing it in his own voice, too. "When we move in."

"Okay." Dickerson looked into the room. "Feld . . . Platchett?"

The officer on the right, Platchett, angled his head slightly without taking his eyes off Taylor.

"Get ready," Dickerson said in a stage whisper.

Platchett nodded, understood.

Dickerson's radio squawked. He listened. "Ten-four. Chopper's on its way, Tom," he said quietly. "ETA, two minutes."

"Okay." There was a large window in the wall directly ahead, with a view of the Golden State Freeway. Tom could see the rubbernecking traffic already bunching up. "The drapes are open, that's good." The rifleman on board the chopper would have an unobstructed view of his target. "You ready?" Tom asked Dan.

Dan unholstered his Beretta .40, his expression tense. "Walk in the park."

"Walk in the park." Tom drew his Sig auto, kept it pointed at the ceiling as he entered the room, stepping cautiously toward the officers, his gaze fixed on Taylor's reflection in the mirror. He felt a surge of adrenaline, his senses heightened as if he were going into combat. He was. He felt Dan behind him, a little to his left. "Okay, fellahs," Tom said to Feld and Platchett. "Back out nice and easy. We'll take over here."

The officers, their weapons trained on Taylor, allowed Tom and Dan to pass by them, Tom on the right, Dan on the left, elevating their pistols once they stepped in front. Tom and Dan leveled theirs as they rounded the corner.

Tom was maybe fifteen feet away from Taylor and his hostage, who were backed into the far right corner by a small round table, the bed separating them. Taylor was a small black man, five foot six (according to the NYPD jacket), and skinny—no doubt the result of drug use. He was wearing black pants and short-sleeved black T-shirt that revealed tattoos on sinewy arms. Black biker boots. Weedy goatee. Something crazy in the eyes. He held the woman in front of him like a shield. The bowie knife pressed against her throat looked like a small machete. Tom did not have a clean shot.

"Hey, what's goin' on?" Taylor shrieked, observing Tom's and Dan's approach. "Who are you?"

"Detective Rigby." Tom held up his left hand. "I just wanna talk. Nobody's going to get hurt here."

Taylor's eyes were nervous, druggy. Definitely hopped-up. He made a threatening gesture with the knife at the woman's throat. "Don't come any closer, man! I'll cut her! So help me, I'll cut her!"

The woman shrieked, babbled something in Spanish. She stared wide-eyed at Tom. Her savior.

Taylor's left arm was diagonally across the woman's hefty bosom, his hand clenching her right shoulder, holding her back against him, a little off-balance. His right hand held the big knife to her throat, the flat of the blade pressed into the flesh, so that with a little jerk it would puncture the skin. She was shorter than Taylor, but outweighed him by fifty pounds or more. "I'll cut her!" he repeated, his eyes glaring at Tom.

Tom could smell fear in the room, like an animal can smell fear. He could see it in the glaring eyes of the black man holding the knife, in the wide-eyed terror of the woman, who looked as if she expected to die at any second. "Take it easy, Lothell," Tom said calmly, sighting over his automatic at the top of Taylor's head. No, he did not have a clear shot. Dan would have a shot if he could get around more to Tom's left, which he was doing, sidestepping slowly.

"Don't you come any closer!" Taylor growled. "I'll kill her! I swear it, man, I'll kill her!"

Tom believed him. Both detectives stopped. "There's no need for this," Tom said. "Let her go."

"No way, man." Taylor pressed the flat of the blade deep into fleshy throat tissue. The woman jumped, choked on an intake of air, jerked her eyes downward to see the blade, which she could not see. Taylor hefted her back against him, clearly struggling, like he was wrestling a greased hog. He certainly had his hands full.

Tom's gaze went from Taylor's eyes, to the knife, back to Taylor's eyes. Crazy eyes. Occasionally he would dart a look at the Mexican woman, but mostly he watched Taylor, trying to read his intent. "Let her go, Lothell," he said calmly. "You're in enough trouble without adding to it. Put the knife down."

"I didn't kill him!" Taylor snapped, his voice tight with rage. "Man, I don't believe this is happening. He was already dead. I *swear!*"

"No one said you killed him. We'd like to talk to you about it."

"I didn't kill him! Stewart was dead when I got there, man!"

"I'd like to believe you, Lothell. But it doesn't look good with you threatening this woman's life with a knife. Chandra Tupelo was murdered with a knife. A knife like you're holding."

Taylor's face contorted. "Chandra was my sister, man!" He began to cry. "Oh, man!"

Tom frowned. "She was your sister?"

"My half-sister, man, you dig? Why would I kill my sister?" Taylor shook his head in anguish. "Man, you need talk to that *Lynch* broad. You need to talk to *her* about this!"

"What about Lynch?"

Taylor's eyes filled with hostility. "You just talk to her, man! She's the one had reason to kill them! *Both* of them!"

"Why is that?"

"She caught them in bed, I don't know! She's a crazy woman!"

"I'd like to believe you," Tom said. "Let the woman go so we can talk about it."

Taylor shook his head. "Man, I don't believe this is happening."

Tom thought he was going to lose it. "Take it easy, Lothell. I want to hear your side of the story. Why were you at Stewart's? Were you doing some work together?"

"That's right, man. I was gonna show him some drawings."

"I believe you, Lothell. His cleaning lady told us."

"Yeah? Did she tell you how Stewart cut Lynch out of the deal? Man that was stupid."

Tom could see Dan sidestepping out of the corner of his left eye, a few inches at a time, his gun pointing at Taylor. "What deal?" Tom asked.

"You don't mess with a witch like that." Taylor noticed Dan, jerked the knife at the woman's throat. "You stay where you are, man!"

Dan froze. "All right. Take it easy. No one's going to hurt you."

Taylor's eyes bulged with rage. "So help me, I'll cut her throat!"

The woman shrieked, straining again to see the knife at her throat.

"Take it easy," Dan said, patting the air with his left palm.

"What deal?" Tom repeated, wanting to get Taylor's mind off of Dan.

Taylor jerked his eyes to Tom, jerked back to Dan, whom he clearly did not trust. "Lynch had a deal with Stewart. She let him buy back the rights to his show, on condition that she could be a silent partner."

"Punching Judy?"

"That's right. Some German company was behind it, but didn't want to deal with Empire."

"Bruemann Entertainment?"

"That's it."

Tom wanted to keep him talking. Maybe talking would use it all up; maybe he'd put down the knife. Tom wasn't banking on it, though. "I didn't know that. Interesting."

Taylor nodded vigorously. "Damn straight, man. Lynch knew Empire was going down and she wanted a place to land. Stewart was her pad."

"Why would Lynch want to kill him?"

"Stewart showed her the gate, that's why."

"He double-crossed her?"

"I guess you could say that." Taylor hefted the woman to better secure his grip on her bulk. "He was fed up with her. She wanted to control everything. Stewart wouldn't go for it."

"Is that why Lynch fired him?"

Taylor barked a laugh. "Did *she* tell you that? She's a liar! Stewart *quit,* man! He wanted nothing more to do with her, you dig?" Taylor clenched his teeth, and Tom saw the change in his eyes. Bad. "Oh, man, Chandra—I can't believe she's dead."

Tom inched along the bed.

"It's all bad," Taylor moaned. He jerked the knife against the woman's throat. She whimpered, her eyes wide open.

"Lothell!" Tom watched Taylor's eyes . . . the knife . . . his eyes. Dan was a little to the left of Tom now. "Take it easy, pal," Tom said, again calmly. "Why don't you let the woman go?"

"No way, man. I ain't lettin' you take me. No way I'm going to jail."

"You hurt the woman, you're going down for the count."

"Who cares, man! . . . It's all bad!" Taylor's voice changed; became less pinched, calmer. "Ain't nothin' I've ever done turned out good."

Tom knew Taylor was resigned to a decision. "What would Chandra say about this?" he asked. "Is this what she'd want you to do?"

Tears streamed down Taylor's cheeks.

"Don't do it, Lothell," Tom said.

Taylor said nothing.

Tom sighted over his gun. Taylor's eyes . . . knife . . . back to the eyes. "Put the knife down and no one gets hurt."

"Taylor shook his head, his eyes fixed. "It's all bad."

The room filled with shadow as the sudden dark bulk of a police helicopter lowered into view, the deafening thunder of its rotors vibrating the window and floor. Taylor jerked his head toward the window, looked back at Tom. "What's that?" he yelled over the noise of the helicopter.

"It's just a newscopter," Tom said. He could see the rifleman in the bay scoping for Taylor.

"Tell it to go away!" Taylor shouted.

"Let the woman go, Lothell!"

"Tell it to go away!" Taylor pressed the knife against the woman's throat, drew blood. "I'll kill her!"

The woman sobbed.

Tom crouched. Eyes . . . knife . . . eyes. Taylor was going to kill her.

Dan crouched.

Tom yelled, "Look out, Lothell!"

Taylor jerked his head toward the window. The Mexican woman screamed, swung away from him, and cleared a sight picture for the detectives. Tom saw Dan's pistol buck in his peripheral vision, felt the concussion as the room shuddered with the report. Taylor's body was lifted back against the wall, twirled and crashed into the corner table, his knife clattering to the floor. The woman stopped and looked down at him, stunned, terrified, then bounded over the bed, jumped down and ran screaming out of the room.

Tom stepped around the bed, his gun trained on Taylor's chest, and kicked the knife away with his foot. The room behind him filled with uniformed officers. The situation was contained. Dan stepped over to the window and signaled the helicopter to abort. The chopper pulled away, the noise level dropping immediately.

Tom felt himself breathing.

Taylor was slumped against the wall, blood oozing from a hole in his right shoulder where Dan's bullet had struck him. His legs kicked at the floor, as though he was trying to retreat into a hole in the wall. He wasn't going anywhere.

Tom knelt beside him and patted for weapons. He was clean. Tom holstered his gun and stood. "Way to go, Danny-boy."

Dan holstered his piece. He said nothing.

Kyle Platchett, a medium-built man in his early thirties with short black hair, and a thin Clark Gable moustache, walked up beside Tom and Dan and indicated Taylor. "This the dude you guys've been looking for?"

"That's him," Tom said.

"We pulled him over for an out-of-date registration, then recognized him from the photo you guys circulated. Had a feeling he was going to rabbit. Sure enough. . . ."

"You done good." Tom felt his pager vibrate on his hip, looked down and read the number in the little window. It was the receptionist at Empire Films.

Chapter Twenty-Two

Tom and Dan drove to the Empire Films building in Toluca Lake, and parked along the curb in front. There were no artists lounging on the front strip of grass, or in the lobby, as they went inside the building. Tom walked over to the receptionist with the face metal; Dan headed for the security door. The girl wearing a purple tank top looked up from her film magazine. "Hello!" she said, brightening when she saw that it was Tom.

"You said Charlie Doogan came in?"

"Yes. He hasn't gone out yet." She reached for the phone. "I'll ring him for you."

Tom put his hand on top of hers. "No phone. We'll just see ourselves in."

Her face changed. "But you can't just go in. Not unescorted."

"We'll escort ourselves." Tom smiled. "We're the police. What room?"

"Room?" She looked down at a company phone list automatically, her face a blank of perplexity as she drew her finger down the list, found the number, and told him. "Second floor. But—"

"Thank you." Tom walked over to the security door where Dan stood waiting. "Could you buzz us through, please?"

Dan opened the door as the buzzer sounded. Tom followed him up the dingy stairwell to the second floor. He could hear the sound of ruffling papers as they neared Doogan's office. The room was small and crowded with bookshelves and file cabinets. Late-morning light streamed in through a single window in the back wall, played over a clutter of papers and folders on a table-and-desk setup beneath the window, then up onto the adjacent wall covered with animation drawings and painted backgrounds.

Doogan was bent over an animation desk that faced the wall to the right of the door, his big arms draped on the inclined drawing surface of the desk. He was animating a scene, his unshaven face cast in strange shadow and light as he gazed down at the drawings over the lighted window of the animation disk. Wearing a buttoned short-sleeved Hawaiian shirt over a pair of faded blue jeans, he was sitting on a padded metal chair, the green vinyl cushion flattened beneath his heavy bulk. The room reeked of cigarettes and booze. No sea air to cut it.

"Good morning, Mr. Doogan," Tom said. He and Dan stood inside the door, waiting to be acknowledged. "We'd like to ask you a few questions."

Doogan continued drawing as if he was alone in the room.

"Mr. Doogan—?"

"Wait a minute!" he growled.

Tom felt a prickling of anger over his scalp. He had prepared himself mentally for this interrogation, had warned Dan about the man's belligerence, but still he felt his chest constrict with cold hostility. He and Dan exchanged looks.

Doogan chuckled. Tom was not certain if he was laughing at his drawing, or because he was ignoring them. The light through the animation glass cast Doogan's eyes in shadow, hollowing out the sockets like a skull. "What can I do for you characters?" he said with open contempt.

"You were in Stewart's house," Tom said.

"Oh?" Doogan did not look at him. He rotated the animation disk a quarter-turn counterclockwise and continued drawing, rolling a small sheaf of drawings held between the thick fingers of his left hand, while studying the flow of action of the under-drawings. He added details to the top drawing with his right hand. Tom had seen Parker Stewart using the same drawing technique in the video he had watched at the station. Doogan leaned back slightly, angling his head at the top drawing, then rotated the disk back a quarter-turn. "You have proof, I suppose?"

"That's right," Dan said.

Doogan looked over the top of his half-glasses at Dan, as though seeing him for the first time. "Who's the sidekick? Barney Rubble?"

"No, I'm Deputy Dawg."

Doogan chuckled. He put his pencil into an automatic sharpener sitting on the flat surface of the desk to the right of his slanted drawing board, held it in there for a couple of seconds. The pencil seemed ridiculously tiny in his meaty hand. He looked at the point, blew on it, then continued drawing. "You're in my light."

Dan did not move. He was clearly ticked-off about the "Barney Rubble" crack.

"We found one of your thumbprints on Stewart's desk," Tom said. "Got the match off the bottle you handed me the other day."

"Oooh, a *thumb* print." The chair creaked as Doogan adjusted his seating position.

"Puts you at the scene."

Doogan shrugged his eyebrows and continued flipping his drawings, his enormous belly showing through the gaps between the buttons of his shirt.

"You have anything to say, Doogan?" Tom was growing tired of the routine.

Doogan chuckled, continued drawing.

Tom noticed that Doogan had removed the bandage from his right hand, saw the scabbed cut across the knuckles. "You told me you'd never been in his house."

"I must've made a mistake. You're still in my light, Barney."

Dan did not move. "I'm about ready to get in your face."

Doogan once again lowered his head and looked over his glasses at him with pale blue, unblinking eyes.

Dan squared himself. "You got something to say?"

A sudden cold hostility filled the room.

Doogan set his pencil down in the gutter that went along the base of his drawing surface, then took off his glasses.

"Any time you want to jump, froggy," Dan said. He was ready for a fight.

"All right," Tom intervened, waving Dan to back off. "It's in your best interest to cooperate, Doogan. We can do it here, or in Burbank."

Doogan continued looking coldly at Dan. "Why don't you stick it where the sun don't shine, sonny?"

"Okay, if that's how you want to play it." Tom was finished with the routine. "Read him his rights, Dan."

"You bet." Dan pulled out a small card from his coat pocket and began reading: " 'You have the right to remain silent. Anything you say can and may be used against you in a court of law.' "

Doogan looked at Tom, shook his head. "So you're arresting me."

Dan continued reading. " 'You have the right to speak to an attorney, and to have an attorney present during any questioning.' "

"Fine." Doogan pushed back from his desk, put his hands on his knees. The wheels on the chair squeaked plaintively over the linoleum floor. "What's the charge?"

" 'If you cannot afford a lawyer, one will be provided for you at government expense.' " Dan put the card back in his pocket.

"I got a right to know what the charge is."

"Let's start with the murder of Parker Stewart," Tom said.

"I didn't kill him."

"You threatened him publicly a couple of days before his death. You lied about being in his house. And you had a motive. We know about your daughter."

Doogan's face burned red with anger. His thick brow flattened over his eyes as he stood up deliberately. He seemed somehow bigger to Tom in the small confines of the office. His arms were all forearm, thick and powerfully built, and ended in two club fists the size of grapefruits. He looked as though he knew how to use them. "You keep my daughter out of this."

Dan stepped behind Doogan and set himself.

Tom, hoping it would not come to blows, removed his handcuffs from the back of his belt. "You got a beef with the world, Doogan, that's your problem. Go pound sand. Are you going to come peaceably, or do I have to use these?" Tom held up the cuffs.

Doogan's lower eyelids sagged away from bloodshot corneas, showing little hammocks of red skin in which two menacing bull-eyes stared dully at Tom. "I didn't kill him."

"No? How'd you get those cuts on your right hand?"

Doogan looked quickly at his hand, brought it up slowly, and rubbed it.

Tom said, "I'll lay you ten-to-one odds they match Stewart's teeth."

"I didn't kill him."

"Tell it to a jury. Let's go."

"Wait a minute!" Doogan continued rubbing his knuckles. "All right, I was there. But I didn't kill him."

"No? You lied to me once. Why should I believe you now?"

"I don't care if you believe me or not. I went over there to get a scene—*this* scene," Doogan said, indicating the stack of drawings secured by the metal pegs at the base of the animation disk.

"When?" Dan asked.

"Last Saturday. I'd taken over the show from him and I needed the layouts for the main title sequence."

Tom looked at the drawings. The top drawing showed a girl in a space suit with a tiny body and a disproportionately large head and big, cutesy-girl eyes, firing a ray-gun at a mechanical plant monster. He found it hard to believe that a misanthrope like Doogan could draw something so well.

"When I got to Stewart's house he was higher than a kite," Doogan said gruffly. "I told him I needed the scene. He laughed—told me to go to hell. Can you beat that?" Doogan grunted. "Standing there looking at him, all I could think of was my little girl. My little girl in his house." His eyes watered. He looked down at the ground quickly, brought his hand up and massaged his eyes.

Tom glanced over at Dan.

Doogan squeezed the water from his eyes with his thumb and forefinger. "You cops," he said, his voice thick with emotion. "Never around when you're needed. I got no use for you."

His eyes lowered to a framed photograph sitting beside the pencil sharpener, the anger gone from his face. There was only pain now. The photo showed Doogan with his arms around his smiling wife and daughter, bedecked in snow attire, standing in front of a ski lodge. "Stewart killed her, as sure as if he drove her off the cliff himself."

Tom watched his eyes. "Did you kill him?"

"I wanted to kill him," Doogan said evenly. "I lay awake at nights dreaming how I would have done it. All I could see was my little girl at the bottom of the ravine and my wife hanging in the bathroom. If I had a gun I would've blown that smirk off his face."

"What did you do?"

"I hit him. I swear, I just hit him. He went down and I stood over him. He was pathetic. Looking at him I thought how easy it would be to kill him. Do *something* to him . . . get *something* back. Do the world a favor. But I didn't. I went into his studio and found the scene on his desk. He was still alive when I left the house."

"Were there any other drawings on his desk?"

Doogan looked at Tom.

"Like the one I showed you of the rabbit in a space suit," Tom clarified.

"There might've been. But I was only looking for this scene."

"All right. Where were you Sunday afternoon between four and five?"

Doogan put his big hands on the seatback of his chair, gazed down at the vinyl seat.

"Where were you, Doogan?" Tom pressed.

"I was at the cemetery."

"Which one?"

"Forest Lawn. Hollywood Hills. I go there every Sunday afternoon. The broad in the flower shop can vouch for me."

"What's her name?"

Doogan told him. He looked at Dan, then back at Tom, his expression changing. "I hear they're planting him this afternoon."

"That's right," Tom said. "Are you planning to attend?"

"I'll pay him a visit on Sunday." Doogan chuckled, the hostility surfacing in his face. "I thought I might water some lilies." He pulled the chair behind him and sat down heavily, the shock of his weight vibrating through the floor. "Are you cops going to arrest me? If not, get out of here."

Tom returned the handcuffs to their pouch.

"Check it out," Doogan said. Sitting on the chair, his legs walked him forward to the desk, the wheels protesting over the floor. "You don't believe me, ask the flower-shop broad."

"We will."

As Tom and Dan left the office, Tom heard Doogan blow his nose. Then he heard the muffled riffling of papers, the only sound in the hall; a sad, lonely sound. He imagined Doogan hunched forward on the desk, his big right hand smothering the pencil, his face eerily lit, eyes hollow, peering at the drawings as he flipped them back and forth with his left: Animator in his habitat.

It wasn't funny.

Tom and Dan walked up two more flights of stairs, then down the wide hall to Annabelle Lynch's office, passing cubicles of artists drawing silently at their desks. A heavyset girl with curly black hair, neatly dressed in a navy-blue pantsuit, was sitting at Eric Getz's desk. She had the look of a temp. She looked up from her keyboard, smiled perkily. "May I help you?"

"We're looking for Annabelle Lynch," Tom said.

"She won't be in this afternoon. Did you have an appointment?"

Tom produced his badge. "Where is she?"

The girl, clearly out of her element, blinked at them. "A . . . A funeral," she stuttered. "She went to a funeral."

● ●   ● ●

Forest Lawn was nestled in a verdant escarpment of the Hollywood Hills, along a fairly easy stretch of the Ventura Freeway. Pulling up to the cemetery entrance, Tom asked the guard where the Stewart service was being held. The guard was a lanky black man in a black suit with an old weathered face and deep wrinkles radiating out from kind gray eyes. "At the Old North Church, sir," he said with a warm, Southern-accented voice. He smiled like he meant it, showing his white teeth as he stepped off the curb and pointed. "You just follow the signs, sir. Take you right to it."

"Got it. Where's the flower shop?"

The guard indicated a building to the left of the gate. "Right over there, sir . . . next to the mortuary there."

"Thank you." Tom drove over and parked in front of the flower shop.

He and Dan went inside, talked to the kind-faced woman at the counter, and minutes later they came outside. "Doogan could've bought the flowers, then gone over to Stewart's house, Tommy," Dan said. "Nobody's logging in times in there."

"I know." Tom slid into the front seat of the sedan, started the engine, and calculated the time it would have taken to travel from the flower shop to Stewart's house on a Sunday afternoon.

Half-hour, tops. Well within the margin of the coroner's time of death. Doogan had motive and opportunity. Strangely, Tom empathized with the man.

He drove into the cemetery, past the magnificent fountain on the right, the road winding up through rows of neat, ground-level headstones, mature trees shading the slopes on either side of the road. There were clutches of people standing looking down at headstones; others alone, placing flowers. Many of the graves were still decorated from Easter.

Tom didn't like cemeteries for obvious reasons—they made him think of death. The rows upon rows of headstones made him feel as though he was getting away with something, that he was somehow tricking death. He almost felt the need to apologize to someone—to the dead, maybe. Maybe that's why people put flowers and trinkets on graves; maybe they were guilt offerings, little apologies.

"My grandparents are here," Dan said, looking out his window. "I don't remember what section, though. I guess I'll be here one day."

Tom looked over at him.

"You ever think about dying, Tommy?" Dan asked, still looking out his window. "I do. I think about it all the time. Dumb, huh? I guess you think about it when you get older."

Tom grinned. "Older, huh? You still get acne."

"That's right," Dan agreed. "But it's *older* acne. My zits have been around the block."

Tom shook his head. The Old North Church was directly ahead, a redbrick edifice set against the lush green of the hills, its white-painted wooden steeple penetrating the bright blue expanse of sky. Pretty. Tom saw a steel-blue BMW Roadster parked along the curb below the church and pulled in behind it. Sandy and Nick were standing in the shade of the church.

"Looky there, Tommy. Who's the gorilla with her?"

"Nick Ivankovich. Her partner."

"Looks like he could crush walnuts between his knuckles. Look at the size of that brute."

As they walked up the wide steps to the church, Sandy stepped away from the shade into the sun. She was wearing a teal-green jacket over faded blue jeans, and as the sun struck her hair, Tom could see the corona of light encircling her head, and the million colors of her hair. Seeing her, Tom felt both a thrill and a pang of remorse.

They all shook hands.

"I saw you on the morning news," Sandy said to Tom. "You're getting famous."

Tom couldn't hold her gaze, looked away at the double doors of the church. "I would've called you but things developed pretty quickly."

"It's not your job to call me."

Tom looked at her. He wasn't sure of her tone.

"You've got Taylor in custody?" she asked.

Tom nodded. "Down at St. Joe's. Thanks to Dan here."

Everyone looked at Dan. Dan smiled, shrugged. "I guess you were right about Chandra being his half-sister," Sandy said to Tom. "Any word on the checks?" There was a definite change in her tone.

"She was supporting him. He had an apartment in Sylmar."

"What do you make of it?"

"I don't think he killed her," Tom said, his gaze moving over her features, touching her eyes, then averting. "He's certainly capable of violence, but I think he acts out of fear . . . or when he is cornered. He was cornered this morning." Tom got the feeling they were talking to each other across an alley. "No, I don't think he killed her."

"What about Stewart?"

Tom shook his head, smoothed his toe over a crack in the cement. "It doesn't make sense. Stewart was his meal ticket. Besides, there's no connection to the Burgess girl. None that we know of."

Their eyes met and locked. "I should've called you," Tom said.

"Yes, you should've, Tom."

A silence fell between them.

Dan cleared his throat. "I'll just see what's shaking inside," he said, and left.

Nick walked to the edge of the smooth brick patio, his big hands folded behind his back.

Sandy was looking over the grounds of the cemetery. A man on a tractor was mowing a slope, the sound of the tractor motor muted by the distance, the smell of cut grass breezing back on the cool spring air.

"How'd you know we'd be here?" Tom asked.

"I called your watch lieutenant," Sandy replied, her tone still vague and distant. "What'd you get from Taylor?"

Tom told her about Stewart's deal with Bruemann, his side deal with Lynch, and how he had double-crossed her. "That sheds a bit of a light on it, doesn't it?" Sandy said, writing the details in her notebook.

"I'd say so."

"She's here, I take it?"

Tom nodded. "According to her secretary."

She looked at him. "My, you *have* been busy. I've had my hair done and filed my nails."

Tom met her gaze. What he saw in her eyes was not anger or disgust, but disappointment. Yes, he should have called; Taylor's statement had a direct bearing on her case. He'd had plenty of time and opportunity to call, but he had let it slide. He knew why, too. Last night, after walking along the docks with her, feeling the first glimmer of hope mounting the dead coals in his heart like a single tongue of fire, he had gone back to his boat and tried to extinguish that hope. He had tried to convince himself that she was an emotional rebound. But seeing her now, seeing the disappointment in her eyes, and how it made him feel toward her, he knew it was a lie.

"I thought we had an agreement," Sandy said.

Tom was about to say something, when Dan walked over to them. "Here we go," he said.

A solemn, wintry-haired man in a black suit and with a face long enough to hit his knees, opened the arched door with perfunctory gravity. Taking his post at the church's entrance, holding his long hands, one draped over the other, he smiled benignly at a vague point on the ground. First to exit the church was a middle-aged, stocky, Nordic-featured woman wearing a white nurse's uniform, slowly wheeling Stewart's mother in a chair. The old woman sat slumped, staring down at her hands folded in her lap, the palms up, fingers upturned like dead spiders, her mouth agape, a dollop of spittle swinging off her chin. She seemed clueless as to what was happening.

A handful of people followed them at a respectful distance, and stood in somber little groups on the wide brick patio. A couple of people lit cigarettes and stood blowing smoke over their shoulders. It seemed a sorry showing for a creative genius. No one else came out of the church and Tom thought it might be a bust. Then another group of people exited, then a few more stragglers, and, finally, Annabelle Lynch, dressed handsomely in a black dress suit and dove-gray blouse, walked out of the church on the arm of Eric Getz. Stepping to one side of the doors, she reached into her purse for a cigarette and Getz lit it.

Getz, wearing black shirt and trousers, noticed Tom and gestured to Lynch.

"We'll need to break this up a little," Tom said to the detectives. "Dan, Nick, why don't you question Mr. GQ there. I'd like to know where he was the last few nights. Sandy and I will handle Lynch."

Dan and Nick nodded.

The four detectives walked over to Lynch. "May we have a word with you?" Tom asked.

Lynch blew a cloud of smoke at them. "You couldn't wait until he was in the ground?"

Tom shoved his hands in his pockets. "We can wait, if you'd like."

Lynch arched her brow at the other detectives. "I see you've got the Mod Squad with you."

Tom ignored the remark. "We'd like to discuss a little matter of a deal between you and Stewart."

Lynch slanted her eyes. "And what deal would that be?"

"*Punching Judy.*" Tom caught a flicker in her eyes. This time there was no pool to jump into.

Lynch took a drag from her cigarette, tapped the ash. "*Punching Judy,*" she said, her voice flat.

"That's right." Tom saw there were people staring at them. "Could we step over here, where we will have a little more privacy?" Tom pointed at Getz. "Not you, Sparky. These detectives have a few questions for you."

Getz looked at Lynch, who nodded her approval.

Tom, Sandy, and Lynch walked over to the edge of the patio, away from the others. Lynch stood eyeing Tom skeptically. "All right. What's this all about? I thought we'd covered everything in our last inquisition. Do I need my lawyer?"

"You have that right."

Lynch smiled at Tom through a twist of smoke. "Let me see the trailer first, then I'll decide."

Tom opened his notebook. "I understand you sold Empire's rights back to Stewart."

Lynch grunted. "You just cut to the chase, don't you?"

Tom made no reply.

"It was in all the trades," Lynch said. "What business is it of yours?"

"We think it might be relevant to Stewart's death," Sandy said.

"Oh?" Lynch continued looking at Tom. "How so?"

Gauging it by her reaction to Sandy, Tom got the feeling Lynch did not like women—especially other women in authority. "Did Empire know about Stewart's deal with Bruemann Entertainment at the time you sold him back the rights?"

Lynch stared at him levelly, flicking the end of her cigarette. Lothell Taylor's information must've been right on the money: Lynch looked as if she'd gotten caught cheating on an exam.

"I take it they didn't," Tom said. "Did they know about your side deal with Stewart?"

Lynch laughed, shaking her head. "I don't know what you're talking about."

"I think you do."

Lynch took a final drag of her cigarette, dropped the butt to the pavement, and crushed it with her toe. "The trailer was bor-ing," she said; then dismissed Tom with a stick-it-in-your-ear smile, and started to leave. "You got any more questions, talk to my lawyer."

"I'll talk to your superiors at Empire first."

Lynch whirled. "Listen, pal! You go mouthing off about this, I'll slap a libel suit on you so fast it'll set your hair on fire!"

"That go for me, too?" Sandy asked.

Lynch ignored her.

"You needed a fallback position," Tom said. "You knew Empire's financial situation was on shaky ground. You needed a soft landing in case the studio went belly-up, so you sold Stewart back the rights to his series with the proviso that you become partners."

Lynch stared at him a few moments then drifted back toward them, her curiosity piqued. She put her hands on her hips and smiled. "Very amusing."

"You're the only one amused," Sandy said.

Lynch shot her a dirty look. "I'm talking to *him*, sister, not you, so butt out!"

Sandy's face flushed with anger, her hands closed into fists. Tom waved her to back off. "I can't imagine Empire allowing its top executives to moonlight," he said. "Especially if there were conflicts of interests. And there *was* a conflict of interest, wasn't there?"

Lynch lit another cigarette.

"You probably had a handshake deal with Stewart," Tom said. "You knew that sooner or later Empire would get wise to what you had done, but they'd have nothing that would stand up in court. Pretty smart on your part. Only one problem, though. Stewart. You didn't trust him. People who are devious tend to think everyone else is devious, too, so you moved in with him to protect your interests. Sound about right, Miss Lynch?"

Lynch grunted. "You're fishing again."

"You think so?"

"This is really very amusing." Lynch laughed. "Still, I fail to see a connection between any of this nonsense and Parker's death."

"Chandra Tupelo is the connection," Sandy said. "You found Stewart playing footsie with her one fine afternoon, and you realized that he'd been playing you for a fool."

Lynch's expression changed.

"Is that why you fired him?" Tom asked. "You *did* fire him, didn't you? You showed me the very spot in your office where you did it—don't you remember?"

Lynch looked away, flicking her cigarette.

"You lied," Tom said. "Stewart quit, and he took all the marbles with him. Nothing you could do about it, either."

Lynch narrowed her eyes. "Are you finished?"

Tom held up his hands and wiggled his fingers. "You told me that people kept touching the magic dust on his wings until he couldn't fly any longer. I think *you* were the one touching his wings. I think he had just enough dust left on his wings to fly away. You couldn't have that happening, so you killed him."

"You're insane." Lynch looked over at Getz. "Eric?"

Sandy stepped in her path. "Something wrong, Miss Lynch? You don't like it when someone takes away your toys?"

Lynch stabbed her finger in Sandy's chest. "Get out of my way, sister, or—!"

Sandy grabbed the finger and bent it back, causing Lynch to grimace in pain. "Or *what*, 'sister'?" Sandy said, then released her grip.

Lynch rubbed her finger. "I'll see you in court for that."

"You assaulted a police officer, Miss Lynch."

Lynch glared at Sandy for a few moments, threw her cigarette down at her feet with a grunt. "You either arrest me for something, or get the hell out of my way!"

Tom shook his head at Sandy. Sandy stepped aside.

Lynch waved at Getz. "Eric, we're leaving!" She strode down the walk toward a silver Mercedes convertible. Getz ran after her, opened the driver's-side door, and Lynch dropped into the seat. Getz closed the door, ran around to the other side and jumped in. The Mercedes coughed to life, then sped away with a squeal of tires that could wake the dead.

"I don't like that woman," Sandy said.

"I don't think she likes you, either," Tom said. "Definitely not the kind of person you want to double-cross."

"I should say not. What do you think?"

Tom frowned. "She's certainly got motive."

Dan and Nick walked over to them. "What'd you get?" Tom asked.

"Says he was at the beach last Sunday," Dan replied. "His alibis for Tuesday and Wednesday nights are a little sketchy. Claims he was at the gym both nights. Gave us some names to prove it."

Tom put away his notebook, his mind elsewhere.

"What do you think, Tommy?"

"I think he's a good little soldier," Tom said. He looked at Dan. "Could you give us a minute, please?"

Dan looked at Sandy, then back at Tom. "Sure, Tommy. Why don't I just wait for you in the car?"

"Good idea."

Nick picked up on the hint, and Tom watched the two men walk away toward their vehicles. A gorilla and a pile of stones. He glanced over the patio. People were gradually dispersing. A few headed across the road to where the internment service would be held. Others drifted toward vehicles parked along the curb.

Tom looked up at the sky—bright blue and cloudless. A gentle warming breeze was blowing from the coast.

Sandy put her hands on her hips. "You look like a thought searching for a word."

Tom looked at her. "I should've called you."

"We've already covered this ground."

"I was wrong."

Sandy angled her head inquiringly. "That sounds vaguely like an apology."

"It is." Tom knew now that the rebound business was a lie. He just felt a little clumsy with the truth, with his emotions. He knew he cared for this woman. She was decent, friendly—"the real thing," as Dan put it. Not to mention drop-dead gorgeous. "I thought, maybe, you'd like to have dinner with me on the boat tonight."

Sandy raised her eyebrows.

"We could do a little sailing afterward," Tom said. "That is, if the weather holds out."

" 'If the weather holds out.' " She'd said it with a straight face. "Are you asking me out on a date?"

Tom looked at her. "A *date*?"

"You know—boy meets girl. Boy's not quite sure if he likes girl, so he asks her out to dinner or a movie. Girl thinks he's kind of handsome—in spite of his past transgressions—thinks he might be fun, and agrees. A date. It's an American original."

Tom smiled. "I'm a little out of practice."

"No excuse. What time?"

"I don't know. How about around six?"

"Six it is." Sandy got out her notebook. "Let me give you

directions. If we're going out on a date, you're going to pick me up at my house. No meeting at the marina. Here." She tore off the page and gave it to him. "Why is your partner staring at us?"

Tom looked down at their vehicles. "Same reason yours is."

Chapter Twenty-Three

A smile tugged at the corners of Sandy's mouth. She was looking forward to the evening, actually felt a thrill as she opened her back door. First time she felt like that in a long while. But as she stepped inside the mud room, closing the door behind her, she inexplicably felt the hairs on the back of her neck stand up, a sensation not related to the evening's promise. It was as though someone had crept up from behind and breathed hot breath behind her ear.

Her gaze went from a basketful of laundry, piled next to the washing machine, to the garage door through which she had just entered. There was nothing. She walked into the adjoining kitchen, set her purse and keys down on the granite counter, and glanced down the hall to the bedrooms, glanced across the living room. Nothing. The house was quiet, save for the quiet ticking of the grandfather clock. Afternoon sun shone in through the French doors in the far wall. From where she stood, she could see the pool, sparkling in the afternoon light, the barn beyond it surrounded by stands of cottonwoods and oaks, the San Gabriels in the distance with the sun well above them.

There was no sign of foul play; still she felt a strange tingling over her scalp, as though hidden eyes were watching her. She glanced out the kitchen window at the street. No cars parked in front of her house. She walked back into the mud room and dead-bolted the garage door, then went through the house, bolting out-side doors, opening hall closets, and checking behind doors. She felt foolish but that didn't stop her. It was a compulsion that, once it got ahold of her, she could not shake until she ran it into the ground.

When she was a little girl she'd wake up from a bad dream and couldn't go back to sleep until her father had made a visual inspection of the entire house, little Sandy following close behind with her own flashlight. Her childhood fears had been irrational, perhaps, but real. Her older brother Paul, then an avid reader of Marvel Comics, used to tell her it was her "spider senses" tingling—a heightened sensory perception of danger. Never once, though, did her dad discover a bogeyman or monster lurking in the shadows.

So far, Sandy's inspection of the house had likewise failed to turn up anything with claws or fangs. She tiptoed down the hallway, looked in each of the spare bedrooms, then continued on down into the master at the end of the hall.

She glanced over the spacious room. Her queen bed was against the wall to her left, bracketed by distressed-wood nightstands, and a large wood chest at the foot, in which she kept spare blankets. Sunlight streamed in through double French doors on her right, which opened, as did the living room, onto the patio. The sun lay over the carpet and the chest, making a rosy glow over the carpet and the distressed-wood texture of the chest. Then she felt a breeze, looked quickly across the room to the raised sitting room. She saw that the window between the stuffed reading chairs was cracked open, and once again her skin crawled—her spider senses tingling like crazy. It was the same feeling she'd had when talking to Chandra Tupelo on the phone.

She opened her purse, removed her Colt and crept over to the window, her gaze roving over the room, under the bed, back down the hall, seeing a portion of the living room and front door at the far end. No bogeys. Then she remembered she had opened the window. Last night had been unusually warm, so she'd cracked the window to let in some cool air. She had forgotten to shut it this morning before leaving for work. Her sigh of relief was aborted as something hairy brushed against the back of her leg. She swung around, her pistol pointing at—

"Meow!" The kitty completed a tight figure eight at her feet. "Rhubarb! You almost scared me to death! I could've shot you!"

Rhubarb hissed then stalked away, head slung low, shoulders hunched, with the hair on her back standing up in a roach. She leaped onto the chest and lay in the sun with her paws over the edge, flicking her tail, a low growl rattling in her throat, as though a Doberman pinscher was in the next room.

"What is it, Rhub?" Sandy closed the window, stepped down warily into the bedroom and passed by the chest. "Do you sense something, too?"

The kitty followed Sandy with her green-eyed gaze, eyes blinking slowly as she whipped her tail against the top of the chest.

Sandy rounded the corner of the bed. There was only one room she hadn't checked.

The master bath was straight ahead, through an arched opening, in which a vanity stood against the left wall of an alcove passageway. A walk-in closet opened opposite the vanity. Sandy opened the mirrored slider cautiously, her scalp still tingling, turned on the light, and poked her head inside. The closet was a ten-by-twelve cedar-paneled room, lined with dresses, blouses, and work suits. A shelf for hats and winter clothes went around the top. A shoe rack went around the base. She saw nothing out of the ordinary.

Sandy came back into the bedroom, holstered her pistol, and set it on the nightstand. "I go crazy once a month, Rhub. What's *your* excuse?"

The kitty continued flicking its tail against the chest.

Sandy undressed, hung up her clothes in the closet, and dropped her undies in the hamper, already stuffed. She frowned, remembered the pile of laundry in the mud room. *Mañana.* Stepping into the bathroom, feeling the cool terra-cotta tiles under her feet, she turned on the brass taps, then poured fragrant bath oils into the tub, swirling the water with her hand. The floor creaked behind her. Sandy whirled, half expected to see some fiend in a hockey mask, holding a chainsaw. There was no one.

She turned off the taps and listened. She could only hear the swirling movement of the water in the tub. She crept back into her bedroom, glanced around the room, lifted her head when she smelled a trace odor of perfume in the air. Was it musk? She sniffed the bottle of bath oils she was holding. Maybe. Then she looked down at herself and realized she was standing in the altogether. If there were an intruder, what did she plan to do? Massage him to death? "This is ridiculous," she scolded herself. However, on her way back into the bathroom, she was mindful to take her Colt with her.

She folded her bath towel into a pillow and laid it along the back edge of the tub, turned off the taps, then slipped into the hot water. She lay her head back against the towel and closed her eyes, feeling the soothing, atomatic heat enveloping her, the day's tensions easing from her body.

Once again her thoughts forwarded to the evening ahead, the corners of her mouth curling upward into a smile. Dinner on a boat, followed by a moonlit cruise up the coast sounded deliciously romantic. Had to be better than attending a lecture on old-world primates with Marvin. Of course, an ingrown toenail would be less painful than that.

A part of her hoped something meaningful might develop with Tom. Another part didn't know what to think about the guy. Tom could be friendly and charming one minute—a very likeable person. The next minute he could be a real boob. It was clear he was battling demons. Did she want to risk becoming collateral damage? What did her spider senses tell her about him? *It's just a date, silly.*

The floor creaked in the other room. Jerking open her eyes, she swung her head toward the bedroom and listened intently. Another creak. Reaching for her pistol, she aimed into the bedroom. "Who's there?" Dumb question.

No response.

Then she felt it. She saw the surface of the water shimmering along the edge of the tub, ringing out from the middle. The walls began shuddering. The medicine cabinet popped open; a bottle of Advil fell onto the sink counter.

One of her pet phobias was taking a bath during an earthquake. Think what the neighbors would say if she went running outside with nothing on but a towel. Scandalous! Normally she would feel the initial jolt of primal terror common to all animals, then ride out the steady, climaxing build of the tremor wave, waiting anxiously to see if it was going to be small, or a big one like in '94. That one had felt and sounded like a freight train rolling through her bedroom. Quite a wakeup call.

The tremors subsided quickly—no freight train this time. It had been a relatively small one—a trolley car—maybe 3.8 on the Richter scale. Strangely, knowing it was an earthquake, and not something with two legs and a machete, she was relieved.

Rhubarb leaped onto the edge of the tub, her fur standing up all over her body.

"It's okay, baby," Sandy smiled, setting her pistol down. "It's over."

Peace descended upon her domicile.

Finishing her bath, Sandy wrapped herself in a towel, sat down at the vanity and turned on the lighted mirror. After she had put on her makeup, she stepped into the closet and turned on the light. Dinner on a boat. What to wear? She did not want to dress too formally; neither did she want to underdress. She should have asked Tom what he was going to wear. She selected a colorful print dress and laid it across the bed.

The doorbell rang. Sandy looked at her watch—five-forty. Tom was early. She put on a bathrobe and padded down the hall, a little annoyed. She peeked through the eyehole in the door but didn't see anyone. She cracked open the door and peered outside. No one was on the porch. That's odd. "Tom?" She opened the door a tad more and called, "Is that you, Tom?"

No Tom.

She was about to close the door when Tom appeared from around the side yard.

"Sorry!" he said, waving. "I didn't see your car in the driveway, so I checked the garage. Hope I'm not too early." He stepped up on to the porch. "I never know how to judge the traffic, so I'm either real early or real late."

"You're real early."

Tom grinned apologetically. He was wearing a pair of faded blue jeans, a black polo shirt, and Docksiders. Casual. "I'm not presentable," she said. "Give me thirty seconds, then come on in."

Tom looked at his watch. "Ten-four."

Sandy hurried back to her bedroom, closed her door, and moments later heard the front door shut. "Did you feel the earthquake?" she called out.

Tom did not answer.

Sandy hung up her dress and got out a clean pair of jeans and a peach-colored cotton blouse. "Tom?"

"Earthquake? We had an earthquake?"

"About fifteen minutes ago."

"I was in the car. Didn't feel a thing."

Sandy dressed quickly. "Make yourself at home. I've got some mineral water in the refrigerator. No beer, sorry."

"That's okay," he said. "Nice house. You live here by yourself?"

"All by my lonesome. My dad built it for me."

"Nice dad."

"He's a contractor. Builds commercial, usually."

Tom was quiet for a moment. "Any relation to Cameron Construction?"

Sandy buttoned up her blouse. "That's my dad. I guess you've seen his trucks around town."

"Who hasn't? He's built half of Southern California."

"Not quite." Sandy touched Shalimar behind her ears, on her breastbone, on the insides of her wrists, rubbed them together. Selecting a pair of white crosstrainers, she came out into the bedroom and sat on the wood chest, slipped her feet into the shoes and tied them. She felt as if she were dressed for a ball game. She brushed her hair in the dresser mirror, retrieved her Colt and put it in her purse. You never know who you might need to shoot at a ball game.

As she came into the living room, Tom's back was to her. He was straightening a photograph on the wall that the earthquake had apparently jostled. "That's my family," she said, walking up beside him.

"I can see the resemblance. You have your dad's eyes." Tom pointed. "Who's that?"

"That's Paul. My older brother."

"Oh yeah? I'd like to meet him." Tom chuckled. "Your dad build him a house, too?"

"No. Paul was killed ten years ago."

Tom's expression fell. He looked at her, looked back at the photo. "Oh . . . I'm sorry."

She could see he meant it. "It's all right; you didn't know."

"Still, it was a jerk thing to say.

Sandy smiled, pointed. "Look—that's Buster Brown. Isn't he beautiful?"

They both looked at the photograph. Sandy was seated on a

sorrel gelding, a flower lei wrapped around the horse's neck, and a blue ribbon dangling from his silver headstall. "He sure is," Tom said, his voice still contrite.

Sandy's father, mother, and brother were lined up smiling at the camera; Paul, brown-haired and blue-eyed like his mother, half a head taller than his father, was standing next to Sandy holding a large silver cup. Tom glanced over at the cup sitting on the fireplace mantel. "That the cup?"

"That's the cup. Shall we go?"

"Sure, if you're ready." Tom looked at her, did a mild double take. "You look nice," he said, his voice normal again.

Ball game or not, she liked the way he looked at her. "You look nice, too," she reciprocated, and meant it. She had not seen him before without a jacket. He had a good build—broad shoulders, narrow waist, muscular arms. Not too beefy. "Will I need a windbreaker or something?"

"It might get a little cool. Whoa!" Tom jumped, looking down at his feet. "What's that?"

Sandy laughed. "That's Rhubarb." The kitty brushed against Tom's legs. "She likes you."

Tom squatted, nuzzled the kitty's fur. "Hey, Rhubarb. Hey, kitty-kitty."

"You've done it now," Sandy said, walking over to the foyer closet. "She'll be your Velcro buddy for life." As she removed a light-blue windbreaker from inside the closet, she felt an aftershock. The crystal chandelier over the dining-room table tinkled. "There's another one!"

Rhubarb bolted down the hall, looking like a porcupine with its quills on fire.

"Felt the earth move that time," Tom said, smiling at Sandy with a look that suggested a double meaning to his words. "What would you say . . . about a three-point-niner?"

"No way. Three-four, tops." Sandy punched in the code to arm the security system—something she rarely did, living in her quiet, ruralesque neighborhood. Looking back into the house, she closed the door behind them and locked it.

● ●　　　　　● ●

Sandy sat on a cushioned canvas seat in the stern of Tom's 42-foot sailboat. She glanced over at the other boats bobbing in their slips, their masts reminding her of huge metronomes. "Paul had just been elected to the city council," she said. "We were all so proud of him. He was going to make his mark in the world." She smiled wistfully. "Local politics, then state . . . then, who knows? He was very civic-minded. He cared about people."

"So does his sister," Tom said.

Sandy looked at him. *Way to go, fellah.* She liked to hear things like that.

Tom had set up the hibachi and a portable table in the middle of the deck, and was barbecuing a meal of shish kebabs and jumbo shrimp. He looked up from what he was doing. "You said he was killed?"

"He was murdered."

Tom frowned, compressed his lips together in thought. "I remember something about it in the news." He laid out the shrimp on the grill. "A robbery, was it?"

"That's what they said."

"What happened? Do you mind talking about it?"

"Not at all." On the contrary. It was a pleasure talking with someone who seemed genuinely interested in the case for a change. Even Nick, after years of her pulling his ears, had grown weary of it. "Paul left home to take care of some business at city hall. Somebody was lying in ambush, apparently. Paul was the mark. The killer took his wallet and his Rolex. They found his wallet in a Dumpster, half a block away. No prints."

"I take it they never found the killer."

Sandy shook her head. "Some local thugs were brought in and questioned, but no one was indicted. We were told it would be next to impossible to find a killer without a motive."

"Robbery is a motive."

"Yes, but without hard evidence to connect the killer with Paul, there was little to go on. Nothing, really. In time the trail went cold, and that was the end of it. Unofficially, of course. Officially, the case is still open." Sandy took a sip of wine. "But you and I know that police files are full of unsolved murders."

Tom raised his eyebrows. "Too many."

Sandy watched Tom turn the shish kebabs with a pair of tongs, then brush some kind of buttery garlic sauce over them, the smoke rising off the grill then slanting in the breeze and dissipating. "Chances of ever finding Paul's killer after these many years are pretty slim, I suppose," she said. "Nick tells me I'm tilting at windmills."

"How was he killed?"

"One shot, close range. Nine-millimeter." She did not mention that it had been a head shot. That part was still too difficult to talk about. "No casings were found," she continued. "So, either the killer used a revolver . . . or if he used an auto, he picked up the casing."

"No slug matches with other crimes?"

"No. Ballistics never turned up a thing."

"Anyone hear the shot?"

Sandy shook her head. "That's the weird part. Here it is, not even five in the afternoon . . . people still coming and going, and no one hears a thing. Not so much as a car backfiring."

"Silencer?"

"How many parking-lot robbers do you know that use silencers?" Sandy let the point sink in.

Tom glanced at her—point taken—took a sip of Heineken. "I take it you're not buying the random robbery."

"Honestly? No."

"Who had the case?"

"Lieutenant Ubersahl," Sandy answered, a note of regret in her voice.

"Ubersahl, huh? Your lieutenant?"

"He was a sergeant then. I suppose he did everything he could," she said, unconvincingly.

Tom set his beer down with a grunt, turned the shrimps over on the hibachi. "Do you think Ubersahl bought the 'random robbery' theory?"

"Who knows what he bought? I just didn't like how quickly the case was shelved."

Tom picked up the basting dish and delicately brushed each of the plump shrimp. "Is that why the daughter of a wealthy contractor becomes a cop?"

"Something like that." Sandy smiled humorlessly. "It's been years now, and nothing's turned up. I guess Nick was right—I've been tilting at windmills." She watched carefully for Tom's reaction.

There wasn't one.

"Do you think I'm crazy?"

Tom looked at her and grinned. "Crazy? I don't know you well enough yet. Give me a couple more minutes. But for now, I think the world could stand a few more windmill-tilters." He made a goofy face, pointed the tongs into the air, and yelled, *"Charge!"*

Sandy laughed. It felt good to laugh. Really good. She leaned forward and sniffed the air. "That smells delicious, by the way," she said, changing the topic.

The shrimp were now a pinkish brown, slightly burnt around the edges and where the grill had made stripes, the meat white in the middle. The kebabs, marinated in teriyaki sauce, were just about ready. Tom indicated her glass. "You doing okay there?"

"I'm fine," she said, the barbecued shrimp and kebab smells mixing with the sea air. "This is lovely." She leaned back into the cushion and took a sip of wine. There were a few clouds to the west, just enough to provide a backdrop for a colorful sunset. Boat riggings rapped quietly against tilting masts in the soft, cooling breeze; the muted cries of seagulls, swooping and dipping to some ancient song. Yes, it was lovely.

"I come out here as much as I can," Tom said. "The world is a million miles away."

"Yes." Sandy enjoyed watching him cook. His hands were constantly in motion, picking up utensils, slicing and dicing vegetables, lemon wedges, wiping his fingers on the towel he kept on the seat next to him. They were strong, masculine hands, but, observing how delicately he handled the food, capable of much tenderness.

Their eyes met, held for a moment. She looked away, following the glide and swoop of a pelican landing awkwardly on a piling next to Tom's boat. She chuckled. It seemed to her that God had made pelicans as an afterthought, and had used spare parts. Nothing quite fit. The bird began sawing away under its wing with its too-long bill.

"That's Henry," Tom said. "I think he likes you. He's making himself presentable."

"Hello, Henry."

"Actually, he's hoping you'll give him a shrimp."

She frowned. "Get your own shrimp, Henry."

Tom tossed the salad in a large wooden bowl, pouring in Caesar dressing, then tossing it until everything was mixed together. He dropped a handful of croutons on top then disappeared below deck to check on the rice pilaf.

"Can't I do anything?" Sandy called down to him. "I feel so helpless."

"Good." Tom came back up with the pan of rice pilaf, brought the bowls of salad over to Sandy, then, arranging lemon wedges and garnish on the edge of the plate, brought over a steaming plate of kebabs and shrimps and rice pilaf.

Sandy closed her eyes and sniffed. "Oh, this is delicious."

"You haven't tasted it yet."

"I can smell, can't I?" Sandy blessed her meal. Then she picked up a shrimp by the tail and bit into it, the meat firm on the outside, tasting of garlic butter and herbs, then tasting the sweet, firmly tender meat in the middle.

Tom watched her, his eyes anticipating a response.

"Oh, this is too good!" she said. "Oh—" She fanned the heat out of her mouth, took a quick sip of iced chardonnay.

Tom smiled, pleased. "They're hot."

"Hot, yes. Oh, they're delicious!" She took another bite.

Tom squeezed a lemon wedge over his shrimp and rice pilaf. "Try the lemon."

Sandy did. The lemon cut through the garlic, butter, and herb tastes, teasing her taste buds with a delectable mix of flavors. She drank the last of her wine, the cool fruitiness of the wine cleansing her palate. "Where'd you learn to cook like this?"

Tom filled her glass. "I'll make somebody a good wife someday, huh?"

"I'll say." Sandy cleaned her plate. "I think you've missed your calling. You should've been a chef."

"There's plenty more kebabs and shrimp," Tom said, beaming.

Sandy shook her head. "Oh, no. I'm stuffed." She looked over at the piling. "Where's Henry?"

"He shoved off about fifteen minutes ago. I don't think you scored any points with him."

Sandy made a sad face. "I'm sorry, Henry." She giggled, then sat looking out over the harbor, sipping her wine, feeling wonderfully sated. "This was a terrific idea, Tom. Really."

Their eyes met. "Then I'm forgiven?"

"For what?"

"For not calling you earlier."

"This is now," she said, adding more meaning to the words than she had intended.

Tom smiled at her appraisingly. "Yes it is."

Sandy felt her cheeks flush. She didn't know if it was from the wine, or because of the way Tom was looking at her. "Here, let me take your dish," he said.

Sandy started to get up. "Let me give you a hand."

Tom waved her down. "Sit. You're my guest. I want you to enjoy the view." He took the trays of dishes down into the cabin.

Sandy lounged in the stern of the boat, her legs stretched out and crossed on the cushioned seat, listening to the water lapping at the pilings as the boat bobbed rhythmically on the gentle swells. Strangely, hearing the muted clinking of plates below, she felt lonely for Tom to return. She wasn't quite sure what to make of that. "Sure you don't want any help, Tom?"

No response.

The sun was behind the clouds now, shooting radiant shafts of golden light into the water. Two fishing boats motored down the channel from the breakwater. Behind them came a troop of seagulls, dipping and floating in looping arcs; their strident cries piercing the evening quiet.

A chill went over Sandy's arms. Rubbing them, she called down into the cabin, "Tom?"

"Here I come."

When Tom appeared at the top of the stairs, their eyes met and locked. Something unspoken passed between them. Sandy wasn't quite sure what it was, but she felt her heart suddenly beating. It felt good. The evening showed promise.

"Would you like to do a little sailing?" Tom asked, stepping out onto the deck. He suddenly looked as awkward as Henry the pelican, a smile groping his face for a place to settle. "We've still got some daylight."

"You're the skipper."

Tom stepped over to the pilot's console, pushed a button to start the blower, then turned on the motor.

Just then Sandy's cell phone rang. She glared at her purse. *Let it ring.* "What can I do?" she asked. "I'm not much of a sailor. You have to teach me."

Tom shook his head. "Not much you can do until we get out of the harbor. Isn't that your phone ringing?"

Sandy narrowed her eyes. "Yes."

"Aren't you going to answer it?"

"No." The phone stopped ringing. "There. . . . See? It's gone." Ten seconds later, the phone started ringing. Sandy frowned. "Just a second."

She dug the phone out of her purse and flipped it open. This had better be good. "Hello? Frank?" Sandy felt the blood drain from her head. She swung her feet off the seat and planted them on the deck. "You're *serious.* When? I'm on my way." She glanced at her watch. "I'll be there in about forty-five minutes. Call Nick."

She disconnected the line and stood. "I'm sorry, Tom," she said, reaching for her purse. "I'm going to have to take a rain check on the sailing."

Tom turned off the motor, his concern obvious. "What's wrong, Sandy? You look as though you've seen a ghost."

"Someone's broken into my house."

Chapter Twenty-Four

Sandy jumped out of the Bronco before it came to a complete stop, felt her legs moving, her heart pounding, felt the earth pounding up through the soles of her feet into her jaw, as she ran toward her house. In the blurred sweep of her peripheral vision were two black-and-white cruisers parked in her driveway, the forensics wagon up the street, Nick's car behind it. Deputy Frank Dutton stood on the front porch next to a security guard from her home protection agency. "What've we got, Frank?"

Frank's expression was solemn. "I'm real sorry, Sandy."

She stepped past the men into her house, stopped in the foyer, and glanced quickly over the living room and kitchen. It took a moment for her to collect her bearings. Everything was changed.

There were broken dishes scattered over the kitchen floor, cupboard doors left open, boxes of cereal dumped over the counters and floor. Pictures were off the wall and lay haphazardly about the living room. The glass case where she kept her silver buckles was smashed, the trophies on her fireplace mantel knocked to the floor. Her initial impression was that there had been another aftershock. A big one.

Then she saw the throw pillows, slashed open, the stuffing torn out and strewn about the room, as if by some childish caprice. No earthquake did *that* to pillows. She smelled the same musky scent she'd smelled in Chandra Tupelo's home, felt a thousand tiny spiders crawling over her scalp.

Sandy stepped forward and felt something break beneath her feet. She looked down at the floor. Shards of glass everywhere. The photograph of her family standing beside Buster Brown was smashed over the tiles. Someone had slashed her face.

Sandy looked at Frank. "Can you believe this?" she asked, her voice an airy flutter of disbelief.

Frank lowered his head, dragged a hand over his pockmarked face. There was something in his eyes that disturbed her. "What, Frank? What is it?"

He gestured down the hall.

Sandy stepped over the broken glass, mindful of her feet, and walked quickly down the hall toward her bedroom. The first bedroom was empty. Saleen Noreau was in the second room, dusting for fingerprints. The Jamaican woman stopped what she was doing, and gazed at Sandy for several moments. The look in her eyes conjured in Sandy's mind the image of a female nude woodcarving, its torso and limbs contorted with grotesque proportions.

Shetani.

Swahili for "devil."

Sandy felt its evil presence touching her, felt a sudden panic clutching her throat, a shudder of terror. Quickly she ran into the master bedroom, looked toward the bathroom and saw Nick coming toward her, his expression grim. "Nick?"

Nick held out his hands. "Best not go in there, Sandy."

She frowned, hurried past Nick into the bathroom. Immediately her gaze went to a small pool of blood on the tiles. She looked up and saw some scraggly thing hanging by a cord from the overhead light. At first, she could not make sense of it—a dark, shiny mat of hair. Wrong color. Her mind was a riot of thoughts. Then she saw it, saw that the cord was tied around the tail, the head pointing down with a wicked slash across her kitty's throat. "Oh God, no."

Sandy felt the blood drain from her head.

Nick put his hands on her arms. "Come on, kid," he said, easing her back. "Let's go in the other room." His voice sounded strangely distorted, slightly ephemeral, as though it was being played back at a slow speed.

Sandy, glaring at Rhubarb, saw spots pinging before her eyes, a high-pitched whine stretching taut through her head, the pitch rising. Nick's voice called down to her, as though from the edge of a deep, deep well. . . .

"Sandy? Hey, Kid . . . Are . . . you . . . all . . . right?"

The light dimmed as two shapeless hands closed over her face. She felt herself falling, falling into a bottomless shaft of inky blackness.

● ●   ● ●

The world was a gray spot in the center of a black pool—a single pinpoint of light oscillating in a vast universe of nothingness. The gray spot grew larger, spread outward from its epicenter, rising upward at the speed of light, as though from infinity. The spot became a gray haze, smeary-edged with black. Inchoate shapes moved in the haze, head shapes gathering light, color, pushing the darkness to the edges. Garbled noises wavered through the haze like strange, watery creatures. *"Here she comes,"* a voice spoke, as if from a great distance.

"Sandy? Are you all right?"

"N—Nick?"

"Right here, kid."

Nick's big Russian face hovered vaguely over her. Sandy rolled her head slowly from one side to the other, as if it held a great weight, images clearing, coming into focus. She was lying on her back. Her feet elevated on a pillow. There were people in the room—her bedroom, she saw now. Tom was stooped beside her; he was patting her hand, his expression grave. "What happened?" she asked, blinking up at him.

"You fainted," Nick said.

She rolled her head toward Nick, confused. "Fainted?" Then she remembered. Closing her eyes, she groaned, "Rhubarb. Oh, Rhub." She saw everything in her mind. "Who did it?"

"We're working on it."

Sandy opened her eyes with a start, struggled to sit up. "Buster!"

Nick pushed her gently back down. "He's fine, kid. Take it easy."

"Thank God." She lay there thinking, then once again tried to sit up. "I'm okay now. Let me up!"

"Rest a minute," Nick said.

"I'm all right, Nick. Let me up!"

Tom and Nick helped her to her feet. She felt woozy and leaned against Nick. "I'm okay. Just give me a sec."

Minutes later Sandy was sitting in the stuffed chair in her living room. Frank Dutton and Tim Sturdevant, first to arrive on the scene, stood to her right. Nick and Tom were on her left. "Your neighbors didn't see anything, Sandy," Tim said.

"No black Corvette?"

Tim shook his head.

"What black Corvette?" Nick asked, his thick bony brow pinched over his eyes.

Sandy took a sip of water. "Tell me what happened, Frank."

"We got a call from your home security company," Frank said. "Tim and I took a look around and found your door open."

Sandy looked across the living room.

"That one," Frank said, pointing to the French doors opening onto the patio. "The security panel showed the perp came through there."

"What's this about a black Corvette?" Nick asked.

Sandy stared across the room at the doors. "Was the lock forced?"

Frank shook his head. "Not a scratch."

Sandy looked at him. "But I locked it. I made sure. . . . I even dead-bolted it." A thought wormed into her mind.

"What is it, Sandy?" Tom asked.

Sandy rubbed a chill off her arms with a nervous laugh. "My 'spider senses' tingling," she said quietly. She stared down the hall toward her bedroom. "He didn't break in."

"What do you mean, 'He didn't break in'?"

Sandy saw herself standing in the middle of the room, naked, holding a bottle of bath oils in her hand. She imagined a pair of hidden eyes watching her every move, leering at her. She could still smell his cologne. Feeling a shudder of revulsion, she drew her arms over her chest and bent forward.

Tom stooped beside her chair, patted her arm. "Sandy, what do you mean?"

"What's going on?" Nick asked.

Sandy continued staring down the hall at the wooden chest at the foot of her bed, the one place she had not inspected earlier for bogeymen. "He didn't break in," she repeated. "He broke out. He was in the house the whole time I was getting ready."

"Who was?" Nick asked, frustrated. "And what about this 'black Corvette'?"

Sandy lowered her head, covered her face with her left hand, feeling a sense of shame and anger and helplessness. She had been violated. Emotionally raped.

The *shetani* had done its work.

● ●   ● ●

Two hours later the criminalists were finally leaving. Jorge Ortega had left earlier with Rhubarb's body. Tom thought it would be helpful to compare the knife wounds with those inflicted on Chandra Tupelo. Ortega agreed. The kitty may have scratched her assailant with her claws. It was certainly worth a look.

Standing at the front door, Sandy handed Saleen a list of people who had been in her house over the past month, for the purpose of eliminating prints. Saleen told her that from what they could determine, the intruder had worn gloves. The list would be helpful, though. As Sandy said goodbye, their eyes met briefly, and she knew what Saleen was thinking: *There has been much evil in this house.*

There was no doubt about that.

Sandy closed the door, feeling a sense of relief. At least that part of the investigation was over. Tom and Nick were the only people left in the house. "You sure I can't make you guys some coffee?" She smiled wanly. "At least they didn't break the coffee machine."

Nick shook his head. "So, Weber was here last night?"

She nodded. "Parked in front of the house. I chased him off with a rake." She chuckled humorlessly. "No word from Frank and Tim yet?"

"Not yet. Don't worry, we'll find him. This time we'll keep him in the cage for a while." Nick studied Sandy.

"Don't give me that look, Nick," she said. "I'm fine. Whoever did this isn't coming back tonight."

"I'm staying here with you."

"No you're not. You're leaving." Sandy pushed him toward the door. "I already have a mother, thank you."

Nick leveled a dark look at Tom. "What about *him?*"

Tom smiled lamely. "We're on a date."

"Date, huh?" Nick grunted, looked back at Sandy. "You call me if you need me."

"I will. Get going."

Nick shrugged resignedly. "I'm real sorry about Rhubarb. She was a nice kitty."

"Thank you, Nick."

"You call me."

"I will. I promise."

Sandy watched Nick shuffle heavily down the front walk to his car, his head lowered. It was dark and quiet outside. Peaceful. Still, he'd worry about her all night, she knew. Poor Nick. He climbed into his car, started the engine, cast a helpless look at her as he drove slowly away. Sandy waved then closed the door.

Tom and Sandy were alone. "Why didn't you tell me about Weber?" he asked.

A twinkle of humor came to life in Sandy's tired eyes. "Same reason you didn't call me about Lothell Taylor."

Tom grunted.

Sandy glanced over her house, put her hands on her hips. "Look at this mess." The latent-print technicians had left a fine, talcumlike powder covering lamps, tables, counters, picture frames. The house would take hours to clean.

"Are you going to call your parents?"

"Tomorrow." Feeling numb and emotionally exhausted, Sandy stooped, picked up a broken plate, and gently placed smaller shards of plate and glass onto it. She stood and set the plate on the counter. She picked up several more broken pieces and likewise set them on the counter. "I need a box," she said, dazedly.

Tom stood watching her. "That can wait until tomorrow, Sandy."

Sandy continued picking up broken pieces of glass. "I can't go to bed with the house like this."

"You're staying at my place tonight."

Sandy shook her head.

"I'm serious," Tom insisted. "You can't stay here. You're staying at my place, and that's final."

She looked up at him. He was frowning, but she could see the tender concern in his eyes. He reminded her of her father. She stood, felt something give way inside her chest. A release.

"I've got an extra bedroom," Tom said. "I'll fix you some hot apple cider." He smiled. "You think my shrimp were good, wait'll you taste my cider. It'll knock you out."

Sandy felt her legs moving toward him, felt his arms wrap around her, pulling her close to him where her cheek pressed against the warmth of his chest. She felt small in his arms, like a little girl wrapped in a world of strength and safety. His heart beat strong and steady.

"Let it go," Tom said, patting her back.

"I can't."

"Yes you can."

"No." Then she was crying. "What kind of person would do this, Tom?"

He pulled her close and let her cry.

Chapter Twenty-Five

Saturday morning, 8:14 A.M.

Tom stood over the stove in his kitchen cooking breakfast—sausage and eggs, country potatoes, pancakes. Coffee. Saturday-morning breakfast was his favorite meal of the week.

Tom lived in a modest two-bedroom apartment, off Glenoaks Boulevard, in Burbank, the bedrooms small but adequate. The kitchen and living room were essentially one room with a Corian-topped counter separating the two living areas. A large couch and reading chair faced the television and stereo against the far wall in the living room, so that Tom, standing behind the counter, could watch television while cooking or washing dishes. Sunlight slanted through a single large window in the south wall, splashed over the rope-colored, wall-to-wall Berber. Though a far cry from the three-bedroom Tudor he'd shared with Carolyn, his apartment was at least comfortable and quiet.

Seeing that a new episode of *Pinky and the Brain* was starting after the commercial break, Tom hit the MUTE button on his remote. *Pinky and the Brain* was his favorite, that and the old *Bugs Bunny* and *Yosemite Sam* cartoons. Carolyn disliked cartoons; hated them in fact. She thought they were dumb. Her word. It was the cause of their first real fight. They had been married less than a month and only had one television set. Tom was watching a *Road Runner* cartoon and she had wanted to watch something on the Lifetime Channel. It was a power struggle that ended with a day of silence, a night of making up, and a second television set—a 35-inch Mitsubishi that Tom had managed to keep in the divorce settlement.

Tom poured six buttermilk-batter coins onto the skillet, felt a tingle of excitement when the door to his bedroom opened. Sandy padded barefooted into the kitchen wearing a pink bathrobe and a sleepy smile. Her hair was tousled and she had that early-morning look that women hate but men find sexy. "Good morning," Tom said. "You look nice."

She shot him a look of incredulity, combed her hair with her fingers. "You must be joking."

"I never joke on Saturday mornings. How'd you sleep?"

"Like a log." Sandy grabbed two fistfuls of air and yawned. "What'd you spike that cider with, anyway?"

Tom smiled. "Just a little rum."

"A little rum, huh? I don't remember hitting the pillow." Sandy folded her arms across her chest and stood looking at Tom. She was not fully awake yet. "Look at you—you're all dressed."

Tom was wearing charcoal-colored Dockers, a short-sleeved blue-and-white–striped oxford shirt, and Bass Weejuns. "I hope I didn't wake you with my shower."

"You didn't." She looked at what he was doing. "That smells delicious."

"Want some coffee?"

"*Would* I? I'm dead until I have my first cup."

Tom poured a cup and set it before her. "How do you take it?"

"Black and hot." Sandy picked up the cup and sipped. "Mmm . . . good," she said, then looked over at the couch where Tom had folded the extra blankets and pillow. "You didn't sleep in the second bedroom?"

Tom shook his head. "All my junk's crammed in there from the divorce. Ever try to fit ten pounds of garbage in a five-pound bucket?"

Sandy frowned. "Why didn't you tell me? I could've slept on the couch."

"That wouldn't have been very chivalrous, would it?"

"You don't need to be chivalrous."

Tom flipped the pancakes. "I wasn't all that chivalrous. . . . I've logged many hours on that couch. Why don't you have a seat?"

Sandy sat down at the counter, looked over her shoulder at the television. "What are you watching?"

"Pinky and the Brain." Tom picked up the remote. "I'll turn it off."

"You don't have to do that. I love *Pinky and the Brain.*"

"You too?"

"Sylvester and Tweety are my favorites, though." She smiled.

Tom noticed her eyes clouding momentarily. Pain. "Are you okay?"

Sandy brightened. "I'm fine." She took a sip of coffee and looked back at the television. "What's that in the corner?"

"The news," Tom said. "That's my PIP feature."

"PIP?"

" 'Picture in picture.' "

"So you can watch two shows at the same time, huh?"

"Actually, six." Tom pushed the PIP button and another picture-in-picture rectangle popped onto the screen. Then another.

Sandy shook her head. "I don't know how guys do it."

"We're from Mars, remember? Martians have zero attention spans." Tom placed the sausage and eggs on her plate beside the potatoes, added a sprig of parsley. "Here you go." He slid a short stack of buttermilk pancakes onto a side dish. "Would you like some O.J.?"

"Please." Sandy sniffed her meal. "I can see I'm going to get fat around you, Tom."

Tom smiled at her from the refrigerator. He liked the way she'd said that. He poured two glasses of orange juice, then watched admiringly as Sandy lifted each of her pancakes, slabbed butter over them, then poured syrup over the top. "Where'd you learn to cook?" she asked, cutting a pancake wedge. "You didn't answer me last night."

Tom shrugged. "When I was a kid, if I didn't cook, I didn't eat."

Sandy looked at him.

Tom drank his juice, held up his hand. "You don't want to hear about it."

"Yes I do."

"Later."

"All right, later. But I'm going to hold you to it." As Sandy bit into the eggs, her eyes widened. "What did you do to these eggs? Why don't my eggs taste like this? You can't eat like this every day."

Tom smiled inwardly as he fixed a plate for himself then stood behind the counter, eating. "Normally, I just have a bowl of All-Bran or something." He grinned. "Nature's broom, you know? But Saturday mornings are special, so I splurge."

" 'Nature's broom,' huh? What a lovely thought."

They ate in silence for a few minutes, both of them watching the cartoon. They laughed at the same places. "Why don't you sit on the couch?" Tom asked. "You'll get a crick in your neck."

"I'm okay."

From where Tom stood, he was able to watch the cartoon and at the same time cast furtive glances at Sandy's profile. Every so often he'd see her eyes lower, her smile drop, and he knew she was thinking about her kitty. She was clearly hurting and doing her best to cover it. Tom wished he could hold her until all of the pain was gone. He watched the cartoon. "Pretty funny, huh?"

"What's that? Oh, yes."

Something on the screen caught Tom's eye. "Wait a second." He picked up the remote and pushed the PIP button. *Pinky and the Brain* shrank to a small rectangle in the upper left corner, at the same instant a news program enlarged to fill the screen. The news anchor was reporting a fire in South Central L.A. Over his left shoulder was a graphic of a building on fire. Tom stared a moment at the graphic, a thought surfacing through a haze.

"What is it?" Sandy asked. "A fire somewhere?"

Tom frowned. "Maybe a dot coming up on the radar."

"A what?"

"There, it's gone." The cartoon was over. Brain's Napoleonic megalomania once again had been thwarted by Pinky's stupidity, and the world was spared. Tom hit the MUTE button. "By the way, your partner called."

Sandy looked at him. "Nick? I didn't hear my cell phone ring. I must've really been out."

"He called on my phone. Three times. Twice last night after you went to bed, and once this morning. He'll make someone a fine mother-in-law."

Sandy smiled. "What'd he say? Any word yet on Weber?"

"Nope. He's disappeared again."

Sandy shook her head. "I don't believe it."

"We'll get him."

"You think he's our guy?"

"I don't know. I still can't get Annabelle Lynch out of my head. You didn't score any Brownie points with her yesterday."

"That's an understatement."

Tom grabbed his jacket off the back of the counter stool, looked at Sandy. The sun coming in through the living room window shone in her hair, highlighted the tousled strands that strangely moved him. She looked vulnerable. Beautiful. "You sure you're okay?"

"Where are you going?"

"I gotta go down to the office for a bit. Dan and I are meeting with Stewart's lawyer to go over the Bruemann deal. Shouldn't take too long." Tom shrugged on his jacket. "I'll be back in about an hour to give you a lift home. I figured you'd like to have the place to yourself to get ready. There's clean towels in the bathroom. New bar of soap. It ain't the Ritz, but, hey—"

She smiled.

Tom opened the front door. "I'm a phone call away if you need anything."

"I'll be fine, Tom. Really. . . . Tom?"

He looked back at her. "Yeah?"

"Thank you. For everything."

Tom wasn't sure how to button the conversation, without sounding either mushy or glib. "Later," he said with a warm smile, then left.

● ●   ● ●

Sandy sat for a moment looking at the closed door, quiet enveloping her thoughts. Thoughts of Tom. He was a good man—caring and sensitive and, she suspected, loyal. A part of her was growing fond of him; another part was still unsure. After all, they were still relative strangers. She knew nothing about his religion, or politics, his family, or his dreams. Then she chuckled. She knew he liked *Pinky and the Brain,* so he couldn't be all bad. She glanced around the small apartment, the whole place no larger than her garage. No, it wasn't the Ritz, but right now the Ritz couldn't compare.

She padded around the counter into the kitchen and started to pour another cup of coffee. She set the pot down and gazed across the room, as an image of Rhubarb batting a paper wad across the floor crossed her mind. Tears leaked down her cheeks. "Not now," she told herself, wiping her eyes. There would be time for grieving later. Right now she needed to stay focused.

She called Nick's cell phone but it was out of service; must be roving. Then she called the station to see if there was any further word on Steven Weber. Sergeant Jim McNaulty was the watch commander on duty. "Nothing yet," he said. Weber hadn't shown up at his house last night, or in the morning. Wasn't at work, either. Nick had deputies scouring the highways and byways. They'd find him. Black Corvettes are not easy to hide.

Sandy frowned. "Okay," she said, told McNaulty to call her on her cell phone the minute they had anything. "Oh . . . and if you hear from Nick, have him give me a call."

"You got it. How're you doing, Sandy?"

"I'm fine."

"You sure?"

"I'm sure."

"Sorry about your kitty."

"Thanks, Jim." She hung up the phone, shook off a shudder of revulsion as a gruesome image of Rhubarb hanging in her bathroom flashed in her mind—couldn't give in to that now—and began rinsing and stacking dishes in the dishwasher.

As she headed toward the bathroom she noticed two photographs mounted in the hallway. The one on the left showed a middle-aged policeman with his arm around a boy of about nine or ten. The boy was holding a football, his gaze fierce. Young Tom. Sandy had no idea who the policeman was. Tom's dad, maybe. Tom kept his past close to the vest, so Sandy could only guess.

The photo beside it was one of an older Tom and a woman— his ex-wife, she presumed. They were standing on the dock in front of Tom's boat, both of them grinning, cigars in their mouths. Sandy guessed they must have just purchased the boat. Tom looked as though he was standing on top of the world. Sandy studied the wife. The wife looked . . . well, she looked—pretty.

Sandy grunted. She walked into the bathroom, showered, then

put on a pair of faded blue jeans and a rust-colored cotton blouse. After she had cleaned up the bathroom, made the bed, and packed up her things in her overnight bag, she walked out into the living room, sat down on the couch, and began channel-surfing. She stopped when she saw the spinning ACN logo. A Panda cartoon. Curious, Sandy decided to give it a minute or two.

The main title music pulsed with a driving erotic beat, evoking a mental image of she-devils in heat. Within the first thirty seconds of the cartoon, a scantily clad prepubescent girl had kicked a bad guy in the groin, kicked the teeth out of another one, blasted a squad of zombies to smithereens with an automatic, then morphed into a nine-foot-tall Amazon babe, wearing leather tights and a chrome brassiere, and kicked tail on a horde of robomonsters. Body parts flying everywhere. *Isn't this fun, kids? Stay tuned!*

Commercial break. Selling sugar.

Sandy shook her head. And people wonder why children brought weapons to school. She switched the channel to an oldies cable station. *Casablanca* was playing. The morning showed promise. She got up and poured another cup of coffee, then came back, drew her legs up onto the couch, and settled in to enjoy the movie. Not much to do until Tom got back.

Casablanca was one of Sandy's favorite movies. She enjoyed the political intrigue and suspense, the great character acting, and, of course, the sexual tension between Bogie and Bergman. The filmmakers in those days knew how to evoke passion without showing writhing body parts. Take that scene from *It's a Wonderful Life,* where Jimmy Stewart and Donna Reed are talking on the phone, their faces inches apart—not touching, yet touching—the scene heating up like a blowtorch. No graphic sex, yet it was one of the most erotic scenes in all of film history. Or those fireworks between Cary Grant and Grace Kelly in *To Catch a Thief?*

Suddenly the world passed by in black-and-white, sounds falling away to a distant murmur. Sandy felt that the murders were connected on a sexual level; money had had nothing to do with it. The pitch may have had something to do with it, but the killer was more likely motivated sexually. Norman Bates came to mind, from *Psycho*—someone profoundly disturbed. Someone evil.

Sandy did not know at what point the shift in her thinking took place, but she was no longer watching *Casablanca*. She was gazing out the window, her thoughts miles away. It was as though a series of mental tumblers were falling into place, one after the other, until a door eased open in her mind. She frowned. Wait a minute. . . . How could—?

She leaned over, hit the MUTE button on the remote, and picked up the *TV Guide* off the coffee table. It was the past week's issue, the same one she presently had in her house. She thumbed through the guide and found what she was looking for. Wednesday. Nine P.M. *To Catch a Thief*. Cary Grant and Grace Kelly.

She stared at the entry for several moments, feeling a prickling over her scalp as she reconstructed a conversation she'd had only yesterday. Turning each word over in her mind, as carefully as she might hold a piece of bone china in her hands, she looked at the implications from every angle. Then she saw it—part of it, at least—a revelation that caused her to gasp. She looked at the television set, Sam the piano player playing their song, Sandy's spider senses tingling as she reached for the phone.

● ●   ● ●

Sitting in the briefing room, Tom hit the REWIND button and viewed the Parker Stewart tape for the umpteenth time. Young Stewart was sitting in his studio, answering a raft of questions from an unseen interviewer as he animated a scene. When asked about the in-between drawings, Stewart's response was axiomatic: *"The eye is very forgiving. It sees what isn't there, fills in the flow of action to give an illusion of motion."* Clearly bored with the interview, Stewart declined comment on his concept, grinning arrogantly at the camera. *"It's all about ideas, isn't it?"*

Tom turned off the machine. So, tell me something I don't know. He popped out the tape and went back to his office, thoroughly flummoxed. The message light on his phone was blinking. He ignored it. Something was worming through his subconscious, a dot struggling to surface into his radar. But it was elusive. Each time he thought he'd caught sight of it, it would lower out of screen like a child playing peekaboo. Annoying.

Tom sat at his desk and stared up at the Stewart crime photos until they became a blur. He rubbed his eyes. *"The eye is very forgiving."* Terrific. His eyes could see nothing to forgive.

He thought through various scenarios, drawing triangles in his notebook, adding names and motives, then crossing out names and adding new ones. Finally he tore out the page and threw it into the trash. Nothing fit. He was looking at it too hard. *"It sees what isn't there."*

He thought about Sandy sitting at his kitchen counter in her bathrobe, her hair tousled and sexy, the look on her face when he was getting ready to leave. He felt their relationship—if it could be called a relationship—was definitely moving in a personal direction. She was a beautiful woman, inside and out. He missed her. Strange. He didn't think it would be possible to care for anyone after Carolyn. But he did. It was both exciting and scary.

". . . to give an illusion of motion."

Tom looked at his watch. Dan was late. He glanced at the message light, started to reach for the phone, but looked back at the crime photos instead. Something was there, staring at him, taunting him. He sensed he had all the puzzle pieces on the table, he just needed a corner piece to get it started. *Get the corner in place, and the rest of it will begin to take shape.* So the theory goes.

An illusion of motion.

Just then Dan walked into the office, looking as if someone had just swiped the last cookie from the jar. He was eating a banana.

"What's with you?" Tom asked.

"Stewart's lawyer blew us off. If we want to meet him, we have to head over to LAX. He's catching an early flight to Cannes."

Tom was staring at the crime photos. *An illusion . . .*

"Did you hear me, Tommy?"

Tom stood with a grunt. "I gotta pee."

He stared at the white tiles about two feet from his nose. The boat would be good for her. He'd drive her home and help clean up the place, then they'd head over to the boat. How long could the cleanup take? With both of them working at it, a couple hours maybe. Sailing would help clear it out. Some of it, at least.

He finished his business, walked over to the sink, and lathered his hands. He checked his image in the mirror, looked down at his hands as he rinsed them.

An illusion . . .

Blip.

A dot came up onto his radar screen. Solid. Tom raised his head slowly and looked back at his image. A mirror is an illusion. A deceptive image; two places at the same time—one real, one illusory. *"The eye sees what isn't there."* Tom stood staring at his image, his mind miles away at a poolside interview as he reconstructed their conversation. "What did she say?"

Tom wiped his hands, playing the interview back in his mind. He went over it carefully, mindful not to leave out any details. "Sure. . . . If you just had one of those devices." He thought through a possible scenario, added names to an imaginary triangle. "Sure. Why not?"

Dan was just hanging up the phone as Tom hurried into the office. "That was Sandy Cameron, Tommy."

"Wait a second, Dan." Tom did not want his train of thought derailed. He stood studying the crime photos, thinking through the scenario he had begun in the bathroom. The dots were connecting. Not all of them just yet, but enough of them to get a corner started. "There we go."

Dan walked over to him. "She thinks she knows who the killer is."

Tom tapped his finger on a photo. "Right there. Two places at once." A picture in a picture—PIP. "It's been staring at us all along."

Dan glanced at the photos, shrugged. "Did I tell you Sandy thinks she knows who the killer is?"

Tom shook his head at the photos. He was fairly certain how the murder was committed—the broad strokes, at least. It was certainly no suicide. "Talk about your cold-blooded killers," he mused. The motive fits, too. *"It's all about ideas, isn't it?"* An idea potentially worth millions.

"Did you hear me, Tommy?"

Tom grinned. "I was right, Dan. It had to do with the pitch."

"Sandy has a pretty good idea who the killer is."

Tom grabbed his coat and started for the door. "So do I, Danny-boy. So do I."

"Sharon O'Neill, right?"

Tom looked back at him. "Sharon O'Neill? No."

Dan shrugged. "Well, that's who she's gone off to arrest." He followed Tom down the hall. "If O'Neill isn't the killer, then who is?"

"Mickey Mouse."

Chapter Twenty-Six

The taxi pulled over to the curb in front of Sharon O'Neill's condo on Soledad. Sandy paid the driver and stepped out onto the sidewalk. Nick was walking over to her from his vehicle parked in the visitor's spot. He was wearing a navy-blue windbreaker over blue jeans and a gray Eddie Bauer sweatshirt. "You get the warrant, Nick?"

Nick tapped his breast pocket. They walked toward the security gate.

"You just get here?" she asked.

"Two minutes ago." Nick looked at her. "*To Catch a Thief*, huh?"

"O'Neill told me she watched a Hitchcock film Wednesday night. *To Catch a Thief* was the only Hitchcock film slated." Sandy's gaze was intent on the wrought-iron gates of the condominium complex. "She said it was boring."

"And . . . ?"

"It had been preempted, Nick. I'd like to know why she lied. The judge give you any static?"

"Nope. I think she likes me."

"You think all the girls like you."

Nick shrugged his big shoulders. "'Where there's smoke, there's fire.'" He pushed the buzzer on the gate. "It's my Brooklyn charm." He pushed the buzzer a second time. A woman's voice came through the speaker.

Sandy identified herself, told the woman to let them in.

"Police?"

"That's right."

"Has there been a complaint?"

"Let us in *now.*"

The gate buzzer sounded, Sandy and Nick pushed through the gate and headed on up the walk. A short, middle-aged woman with a wedge of frizzy salt-and-pepper hair met them at the office door. She eyed Sandy's badge nervously. "I hope it's not those musicians in thirteen-C again."

"Could you show us the way to Sharon O'Neill's apartment?"

"Sharon O'Neill?" The woman walked behind a desk and referenced a tenant list. Sandy and Nick stepped into the office. "I think I know her," the woman said. "She's a redhead, right?"

Sandy nodded. "What number?"

"Here we are. . . . Fourteen-B. That's on the second level." The woman pointed out the window. "You can use those stairs over there, if you'd like."

Sandy saw the stairs across the courtyard. "Do you have a master key?"

The woman looked at her.

Nick grinned. "We don't want to have to break down the door, if we don't have to."

"We have a warrant," Sandy said.

"Yes, of course," the woman said nervously. She opened a drawer behind the desk and handed Sandy a key. "What's she done?"

Sandy turned away without comment. Feeling her adrenaline pumping, she led the way with a quick stride into the warming coolness of the cement courtyard. She felt certain O'Neill was the killer. Sandy had no concrete proof as yet, other than the lie about her whereabouts on the night Chandra was murdered. That was pretty good, though, for starters—that, and the fact that after a couple of quick calls her alibis seemed to be coming apart at the seams. It wasn't much, but it was enough to convince Judge Eikleberry of probable cause, and to issue a search warrant. Maybe Nick's Brooklyn charm had done the job, after all.

Nick caught up to her. "You okay, kid?"

"I'm fine, why?"

"Just asking."

It was a fairly new condominium complex, with dormers and gray masonite siding and white trim that gave the place a Cape Cod look. Stands of white birch and flowering plum softened the angular lines of the building. A beefy pool man cleaning the small rectangular pool looked over as Sandy and Nick made their way along the courtyard.

Sandy and Nick climbed up the stairwell to the second level, saw how the numbers went along the balcony, and stopped at 14-B. Nick rang the doorbell. "How do you want to play this?"

Sandy stood glaring at the door. "How about you hold her while I beat a confession out of her."

"The soft approach. Okay." Nick rang the doorbell a second time. "I don't think she's home."

Sandy couldn't see anything through the lace curtains. "Let's give it a look-see." She tried the door. Locked.

She unlocked the door with the master key, and put her head inside. "Ms. O'Neill?" No response. She went inside, immediately smelled the heavy scent of musk, and felt her skin crawl. "Come on, Nick."

The layout was fairly typical of many midrange condos. Fair-sized living room. High ceilings with track lighting. Gas fireplace against the right wall. Dining area straight ahead, off the living room. An L-shaped tile counter separated the living room from the kitchen and dinette. Light filtered into the living room through the lace curtains fronting the courtyard. There were a couple of large prints on the wall—one showed a rainbow line of ballerina feet; the other one was James Dean.

Sandy stepped cautiously through the room. "Ms. O'Neill?" No response. There were two rooms on the left—bedrooms, she guessed. A guest bathroom opened at the end of a short hall past the kitchen. "I'll take the first room."

"Okay." Nick took the second bedroom.

Sandy stepped into the first room and stopped abruptly. It was the master, apparently, judging by the queen-sized bed taking up most of the floor space. The walls were covered with photographs of Bill Pender: some framed, some mounted on stiff cardboard backing. There were framed photos of Pender on the dresser, a "Man on the Move" blowup of him from the cover of the *Hollywood Reporter* on the right wall. Sandy felt she had walked into a shrine. Creepy.

She continued into the room and looked closely at the pictures. There were black-and-white and color photos—eight-by-tens and larger. A couple of them showed Pender, alone, grinning charmingly at the camera; in others he was posing with O'Neill at parties, or at the studio. The rest were candid shots of the man—on his boat, by his swimming pool, on the beach, on the town—the field images compressed and slightly grainy, as if taken with a telephoto lens. An image of a stalker came to Sandy's mind, a paparazzo with a single celebrity mission.

There was something odd about several of this latter group of photos. Their compositions were wrong. Instead of Pender being centered in the composition, there were large areas of negative space to the left or right of him. Sandy guessed it was because there was some other person with Pender, and when O'Neill took the photo (if she was the photographer) she did not wish to include them. Clearly O'Neill was obsessed with her boss, and didn't want to share him.

A framed eight-by-ten glossy of Pender kissing O'Neill on the cheek at a party stood on the nightstand beside the telephone. Sandy looked closely at the picture. Wendy Burgess, Annabelle Lynch, and Chandra Tupelo were in the background, talking. Interesting.

She made a cursory inspection of the dresser drawers but found nothing incriminating. The closet yielded only O'Neill's taste in clothes and footwear—L.A. chic on a budget.

The musk scent was particularly strong in the adjoining bathroom as Sandy entered. Same scent she had smelled in Chandra Tupelo's house; same scent she'd smelled in her own house yesterday; same scent she'd smelled on Steven Weber. A bottle of Calvin Klein CK-1 stood on the tile counter, a unisex brand for both men and women. Sandy picked it up and smelled it. The thought of O'Neill in her house yesterday (if it had been O'Neill), hiding in the wooden chest while Sandy was getting dressed, sent a chill through her. Then she felt a surge of anger.

"Get a load of this, Sandy," Nick called from the other bedroom.

"Be right there." Sandy set the perfume bottle down, checked the contents inside the medicine cabinet, then left.

The second bedroom was set up as an office. A computer desk and return stood against the back wall. A reading chair and lamp stood next to a bookshelf that O'Neill probably had purchased at Ikea. A print of Marilyn Monroe trying to hold down her dress blowing up over the subway grille was the only wall hanging. Nick was standing by the computer. "What've you got, Nick?"

"Take a look."

On the monitor was an image of O'Neill in a bikini, her arms wrapped around Bill Pender—the latter standing behind the large chrome wheel of a sailing yacht. There was something wrong about the picture.

"Check this out," Nick said. A scanner, similar to the one Sandy'd seen in the Stewart crime photos, was set up next to the computer. With a handkerchief Nick raised the lid. Facedown on the glass surface was what looked like an eight-by-ten photograph. Looking at it from the back, Sandy saw that a small oval, about an inch and a half long, had been cut out, and another oval added and taped to it.

Picking the photo up by the corner, Sandy saw that it was the same photo showing on the screen. She also recognized it as the same photo she'd seen in the silver frame on Wendy Burgess's office desk. Wendy's head had been cut out. Inserted in its place was O'Neill's head. O'Neill apparently had stolen the photo, cut out Wendy's head, and replaced it with her own.

Sandy looked at Nick and read his mind. Nick hummed the *Twilight Zone* theme: *"Doo-dee-doo-doo . . . doo-dee-doo-doo."*

Sandy looked at the computer screen.

"She used Photoshop," Nick said. Sandy saw that the image on the screen was an airbrush-rendered version of the two photos, at first glance an almost seamless marriage. "Pretty snazzy, huh?"

"Pretty sick, you mean." Sandy was looking at the face of O'Neill; now that she really studied it, she saw that the light was all wrong, and the angles off.

Nick grunted. "You think she killed the Burgess girl, too?"

Sandy shook her head thoughtfully at the screen, O'Neill smiling happily at the camera. "Wendy was certainly in her way, wasn't she?"

"How does it jibe with Chandra Tupelo?"

"I don't know yet. First things first." She glanced around the office. There were some boxes in the closet. "We'll need to get a team over here."

"I'll call it in." Nick snapped open his cell phone and pushed a series of buttons.

Sandy opened the file drawer in the return and found the camera—a Nikon N50. A 135-millimeter telephoto lens was attached to it. There were other lenses and camera stuff in the drawer. She closed the drawer, opened the one above it, and stared briefly at a stack of photographs. Removing a handkerchief from her purse, she began looking through the photos. They were pictures of Wendy Burgess. *Bingo.* "Take a look at this, Nick."

Nick, still talking on the phone, glanced at them and raised his thick eyebrows.

They were mostly candid shots taken with a telephoto lens— Wendy shopping at the mall, at the gym, at lunch with co-workers. A few nightlife shots with Bill Pender. There were several photos of Wendy with Pender in town; a couple showing them in compromising situations, poolside. They appeared to be taken at dusk, from a perch somewhere on the shoulder of the hill overlooking Pender's house and backyard. Sandy imagined O'Neill creeping through the yucca and sage until she found a vantage point from which to shoot, undetected. She was clearly a stalker. A predator. Proof that she killed Wendy Burgess? No—but it definitely tilted the scales in her direction.

Sandy set the photos on the desktop, then noticed a One-Hour Photo envelope in the back of the drawer. She opened the envelope, half expecting to find photos of Chandra Tupelo inside. But as she worked through the pictures, she felt a finger of cold fear working over her scalp. "Nick."

Nick folded his cell phone into his jacket. "What've you got, kid?"

The first photo was a picture of Sandy at the marina, looking out over the harbor. From the outfit she was wearing, Sandy knew it had been taken Wednesday afternoon, the day she first went to the marina to meet Tom.

"That's you," Nick said.

"Take a look at these." The next couple of photos showed

Tom tying off his boat, then carrying a cooler up to his Bronco, then the two of them talking—arguing, actually. Each of the shots favored Sandy; Sandy was the target, not Tom. There were shots of Sandy driving her car, entering the station; one of her sitting poolside with Bill Pender, one with Nick at Parker Stewart's funeral.

Nick grunted. "She got my bad side."

"Very funny." Sandy stared at the next photo with mounting revulsion and rage. "I can see I'm going to have to start closing my drapes."

Nick held out his hand. "What is it?"

Sandy slid the photo into her purse. "For my eyes only."

"That's 'withholding evidence,' kid."

"Tough darts." The last photo caused Sandy to frown.

"For your eyes only?"

Sandy handed Nick the photo. "Take a look."

Nick studied the photo, the creases between his eyebrows deepening into a dark scowl. "How in the world . . . ?"

"From the bushes on the slope behind my house. Look at it closely."

Nick angled the photo toward the light. The photo showed Sandy mucking out her corral, Buster Brown leaning over the rails watching her. Her house was in the background, the street just visible in front. Partially hidden by the front left corner of the house was a black Corvette. Nick looked at Sandy.

"What do you make of it?" she asked.

Nick shrugged. "You think they're in it together?"

Sandy didn't answer. She took back the photo and studied it. It would certainly connect a few dots, as Tom would say. "The team on its way?"

"Should be here in about five minutes."

"Good." Sandy walked out of the room, seething. She envisioned herself slamming O'Neill over the hood of her car and cuffing her, maybe bouncing her head a couple of times for fun. Walking into the kitchen, she spotted O'Neill's telephone on the counter, the light blinking on the answering machine. With the tip of her pen, she hit the MESSAGES button.

Computer voice: *"You have one message. Ten-fourteen A.M."* Beep.

"Hey, babe. Sorry I missed you." It was Bill Pender's voice. "Just wanted to let you know I'm leaving for Cannes today instead of Monday. Don't worry, I already took care of the arrangements. Need you to—"

Someone picking up the receiver interrupted the message: "Bill? It's me." O'Neill's voice, slightly out of breath. "I was in the other room."

"Did you hear what I said?"

"You're leaving for Cannes *today?*" Airy giggle.

"That's right, babe. Thought I'd take an early flight. Catch a little nightlife before the slugfest, you know." Shallow laugh.

There was a pause.

"Bill, I thought *I* was going with you to Cannes." O'Neill's voice sounded strained, a giggle fluttering around the edges.

"I never said that, babe."

"Yes, but I thought I was going. I just figured—"

"I never said it. Sorry you got your signals crossed. I'm taking Hiroko. Business, you know. Be a good trouper and look after things while I'm gone, won't you? Any problems, you can reach me at the hotel."

"Bill . . . are you at home?"

"Yes, I'm packing."

Breathing sounds.

"Sharon? Are you there?"

"You *owe* me, Bill," O'Neill said. There was a definite change in her voice—a low, flattening edge of something very sinister, as though a different person had got on the line.

" 'Owe' you?" Pender laughed. "I give you a paycheck every week, babe. What more do you want?"

More breathing sounds.

"Sharon—?"

Click.

Sandy stared down at the phone, feeling a sense of déjà vu. It was as though a scene was being played out before her eyes in slow motion. She could see O'Neill standing over Chandra's body, a bloody knife in her hand, then walking over to the phone and breathing into the phone receiver. She felt another wave of chills.

" 'Booga-booga,' " Nick said.

Sandy rubbed her arms, looked into the office. "There's no phone in there?"

Nick shook his head. "Didn't see one."

Sandy reconstructed the scene. O'Neill, attaching her own head to Wendy's body on the computer, hears the phone ring, ignores it until she hears Pender's voice. She runs out of the office and picks up the receiver, gets an emotional jolt from Pender, morphs into "Ms. Hyde," hangs up the phone, and leaves. Sandy looked at her watch—10:35. The call had come in at 10:14. "We just missed her."

"Think she's headed over to Pender's?"

"What do you think?"

Sandy opened her notebook, found Pender's number, and dialed it on her cell phone. Busy signal. She disconnected the line and stared at O'Neill's bedroom shrine. Sandy could not shake the feeling that she was in the middle of a slow-moving dream, where something dreadful was about to happen and she was powerless to stop it. She started for the door.

"We'd best get over there."

Chapter Twenty-Seven

Tom and Dan were stuck in bumper-to-bumper traffic on the westbound 134, in their unmarked sedan. The 101 connector was directly ahead, where the road narrowed and generally caused a slowing in traffic. The traffic they were caught in, however, was more than just a narrowing of lanes. "So, you think that's how it went down?" Dan asked.

"Pretty sure of it." Tom looked to see around the car in front of him. "This is Saturday—what gives? Can you see anything ahead?"

"Not a thing." The car in front of them showed its taillights. "Best hit the lights, Tommy. We ain't ever gonna get there."

Tom felt a wind was at his back driving him forward—into what, he could only guess. "Do it."

Dan turned on the police lights, causing them to flash, then put a call in to Dispatch, gave their location, and asked why there was a traffic jam on Saturday morning. A minute later the radio squawked. "David one-sixteen . . . David one-sixteen. You've got a sig-alert at Laurel Canyon. The left two lanes are blocked."

Tom banged the wheel. "Terrific."

"Thank you, Doris," Dan said to the dispatcher. "David one-sixteen, out." He switched off the radio. "About a half-mile ahead, Tommy. Should clear up after that."

"Okay." Tom edged right into the next lane. What was it that had tipped Sandy toward Sharon O'Neill? A part of him had doubts, now that the three murders were connected—two separate murders and an accidental drowning. Another part of him felt certain they did connect. But how? How did Parker Stewart's killer figure in with O'Neill? Were they in it together? Maybe. It would certainly fill in some blanks.

Tom frowned at the wall of red taillights; the vehicles ahead of them doing their best to get out of their way, but unable to move because of the jam. Suddenly he felt an inexplicable premonition of danger. "Try Sandy again."

Dan dialed Sandy's number on his cell phone. "It's ringing." He gave Tom the thumbs-up. "Sandy? Dan Bolt. Dan Bolt," he repeated. "I can hardly hear you."

Tom looked at him. "Ask her why she thinks O'Neill is the killer."

"Tom wants to know why you think O'Neill is the killer." Dan spoke into the receiver. He listened. "No kidding. Seriously?"

"What?" Tom wanted to know.

"On the *computer?*" Dan listened. "Spooky."

Tom looked at him. "What's spooky? Where is she now?"

"Tom wants to know where you are right now." Dan put his index finger in his ear. "Where? Can't hear you—breaking up. 'Victory,' you say?"

Tom reached for the phone. "Here, gimme that."

Dan bent away from Tom. "Where, Sandy?"

Tom grabbed his arm. "Gimme the phone, Dan."

Dan handed the phone over. "Oh, sure, Tommy. Would you like to use the phone?"

Tom put the phone to his ear. "Sandy? What's this about Sharon O'Neill? . . . What? I can't hear you, Sandy, the connection's breaking up. I'm losing you." Static. "Terrific." Tom slammed the phone down on the seat. "These stupid things are useless. What'd she say to you?"

Dan was looking out the window, turned to him with an innocent look. "Oh . . . Were you talking to me?"

"Knock it off."

"She's on the southbound four-oh-five at Victory."

"Victory? Where's she headed? Get her on the radio."

Dan looked at him with a sarcastic expression. "Why don't I just get her on the radio?"

"Please." Tom made his way across three lanes of traffic and finally got onto the far right shoulder. He sped up past several cars on his left, then came to an abrupt halt. A stalled vehicle was block-ing the shoulder ahead. Tom slammed his fist on the steering wheel. "What *is* this?"

Dan was talking to the Burbank PD dispatcher. "That's right, Doris, see if you can't patch us through to their vehicle."

Tom worked his way around the stalled vehicle, got back onto the shoulder and punched it.

The radio squawked. "David one-sixteen . . . David one-sixteen. I've got the watch commander from LASO on the line. Go ahead."

"Sergeant McNaulty here."

Tom glanced at the radio. "Sergeant McNaulty? Detectives Rigby and Bolt."

"Right. What can I do for you?"

"Can you patch us through to Detective Cameron?"

"Please," Dan added. Tom shot him a look.

"Sorry," McNaulty said. "She and her partner have no radio access. They're in a private vehicle. I can tell you where they're headed, though."

"We'd appreciate it."

● ●   ● ●

"Look at that," Nick said, as he drove into the circular driveway of Bill Pender's palatial estate. A red Nissan was parked carelessly in front of the entryway walk. A tire mark showed where the front right wheel had rolled up over the curb and landed in the planter of ivy. The driver's-side door was left open. Clearly the driver had been in a big hurry. "Do you know what O'Neill drives?"

"No, but I have a pretty good idea."

Nick pulled his vehicle up in front of the Nissan and parked. They got out of their vehicle and checked the Nissan for keys and registration. The keys were gone. The vehicle was registered to Sharon O'Neill. A small red purse lay on the passenger seat. "I don't like this, Nick," Sandy said. "Best call for backup."

"Good idea."

Sandy could feel her heart pounding as she and Nick made their way up the front walk.

● ●   ● ●

Rolling Code Three, Tom turned right off Coldwater Canyon and raced up Mulholland. "I got a bad feeling about this one, Dan. See if you can't scare up a couple of black-and-whites in the area."

"You got it." Dan's expression was intense as he flicked the switch on the radio. He must've felt it, too.

● ●   ● ●

The front door was ajar. A set of keys dangled from the lock. O'Neill had obviously let herself in, unannounced. Sandy, holding her Colt .38 at the ready, toed the door open and peered inside. There was no sign of Pender or O'Neill. Nick stepped past her. "Gentlemen first."

Sandy followed Nick into the foyer. Broad shafts of sunlight slashed over the floor and walls of the expansive house that seemed even larger to her than it had two days ago. "Mr. Pender?" Sandy called out.

No response.

Sandy led off, Nick a step behind on her right, her gaze sweeping the length and breadth of the upper level for signs of life. A haunting melody by Roberta Flack echoed through the halls and rooms. *"The first time . . . ever I saw your face . . ."*

The voice—sad, longing—like a lost soul drifting through a deserted mausoleum.

Sandy felt a breeze. Diaphanous sheers covering a dozen windows, two stories high, fluttered into the enormous hall like monstrous wraiths, the breeze carrying the music from a source seemingly miles away, and with it, a trace scent of musk. Sandy's "spider senses" tingled.

"Look at this place," Nick said, awed by its size. "Reminds me of an airport terminal."

"This is just the summer cottage," Sandy joked, to relieve the tension in her voice. It didn't help. She could feel it mounting in her throat as she continued forward. No one in the bar area to the left. The kitchen and family-room areas beyond the bar appeared empty, too. There might be other rooms beyond them. She paused, considering a direction. "What do you think, Nick?"

He shrugged. "The music's coming from somewhere ahead. I say we go forward."

"Okay." They followed the music. The scent of musk was stronger ahead, too—a finger of scent beckoning them like something out of a Pepe le Pew cartoon.

A weight room opened off a short hall on the right, the wall mirrors giving it a sense of infinite depth. Farther ahead was a library, the double doors opened to show stuffed black leather chairs, a chrome-and-glass desk, and floor-to-ceiling bookshelves spanning the length of the room.

She had not paid much attention to this section of the house when she and Tom had come through the other day, since "Yvette" from the Bronx had seemed on a rail to get down to the pool. Maybe that's why the place appeared larger to her now. The music seemed to be originating from a wide hallway just ahead. "This way."

When they turned down the hall, the volume of the music jumped up a couple of decibel levels.

Sandy felt her pulse quicken.

The hallway was as wide as four bowling lanes. Sunlight lanced in through skylights, two stories above the floor. There were photographs of Bill Pender with Hollywood celebrities, mounted in silver frames along the wall, Pender's teeth flashing in each one. Rooms opened on either side of the hall—bedrooms, bathrooms, a sitting room that looked out over the San Fernando Valley. A double set of doors was set into an alcove at the end of the hall. The doors were open. "Mr. Pender?" Sandy's voice sounded fluttery.

The first bedroom on the right was empty. They started toward the second bedroom on the left, shooting looks up and down the hall. "Mr. Pender?"

Sandy peered into the second bedroom, pointing her revolver. Empty.

Nick shook his head. "You could fit my whole house into one of those rooms."

Sandy could hear a flutter in Nick's voice as well. She stopped and looked down at something on the polished granite floor. She stooped over. "Nick . . ."

A drop of blood. Fresh.

"There's another one," he whispered, pointing a couple of feet up the hall.

"There's one behind us." Sandy looked toward the double

doors at the end of the hall, then back toward the main living area.

"Which way is the trail going?"

Nick looked up the hall. "Let's check out the room at the end."

They crept down the wide hall toward the double doors. Sandy paused outside the door, her pistol raised, her heart pounding faster. She looked at Nick. He nodded.

Sandy stepped into the room, sighting over her pistol as she gave the room a quick visual sweep. She looked quickly at something on the left—a body. To the right was the master bath and sitting area, a stereo tower, potted palms and ferns adding color to the white-and-gray tones of the walls and floors. A bank of floor-to-ceiling windows in the master bath allowed for panoramic views of the San Fernando Valley. No one else in the room. "Nick."

"I see her."

A woman with long black hair lay facedown on the king-sized bed against the wall, her head and left arm dangling over the side, her upper and lower back gleaming in a shaft of overhead light, naked. The rest of her body, covered by a tangle of maroon-and-gray bed linens, lay diagonally across the bed. She wasn't moving.

Nick came up on Sandy's left, stood guard while Sandy stepped quickly over to the bed. The woman's back a honey gold color where it wasn't covered with blood, the blood oozing down her left side and soaking into the bedsheets. She appeared to have been stabbed at least a dozen times—within the past few minutes, Sandy guessed.

Mindful of a small pool of blood in the carpet below the woman's bloody fingertips, Sandy pulled back the long mass of hair covering her face. It was Hiroko Fujiyama. Sandy felt for a pulse. Hiroko was quite dead.

"Sandy." Nick indicated blood spatters on the right side of the bed, on the pillow, drops of blood tracking out of the room.

Considering the evidence, Sandy speculated that O'Neill had surprised Pender and Hiroko in bed, stabbed Hiroko, and most likely had stabbed Pender as well. Pender, bleeding, had fled for his life. "A fifty-one–fifty," Nick said seriously.

Sandy nodded. "Let's find them."

Sandy and Nick hurried back down the hall, following the trail of blood, and turned right into the main hall. Sandy glanced back into the bar and kitchen areas, saw nothing, and, with her pistol at the ready, continued toward the rear of the house. "Here's another drop," she said, pointing.

"And another," Nick added.

They were headed in the right direction.

Sandy looked ahead. She was intensely aware that they were stalking a brutal killer, someone emotionally and mentally unhinged. A 5150, as Nick had said. Crazy person.

He pointed at the floor.

Sandy nodded, stepped clear of a large spatter, and moved forward, her senses sharpened by the increased flow of adrenaline. She could feel beads of sweat trickling down her sides. She looked over at Nick.

Flattened beneath thick Russian brows, his small dark eyes glistened warily, shifting from side to side. His powerful shoulders were hunched, his head thrust forward, the muscles flexing in his heavy jowls, his mouth a grim line, like a scar. Nick was clearly tense. Before joining the NYPD he had been a guard at Bellevue. He'd lasted three months—crazy people spooked him. "How do you figure crazies?" he'd once said.

Sandy narrowed her eyes. *How* do *you figure crazies?* O'Neill had had opportunity, but what was her motive? Even crazy people had reasons for doing things, didn't they? *Look at me wrong, I kill you. Take my marbles, I kill you.* In O'Neill's case, it appeared she was obsessed with Bill Pender, insanely jealous of anyone she viewed as a threat. Wendy Burgess and Hiroko had been sexual threats, so Sharon O'Neill had killed them. What about Chandra? Perhaps she had posed a different kind of threat.

And what about herself? Sandy was on O'Neill's hit list, too. Why? She didn't have an answer for that one. *How do you figure crazies?*

A strong breeze blew through the house, lifting the sheers from the windows—the wraiths protesting, warning. Somewhere in the far reaches of the house a door slammed shut. Sandy jumped, then shot a quick look at Nick.

Nick grinned. *Booga-booga.*

Sandy shook her head, took a deep breath. The blood trail led to the head of a wide flight of stairs, which Sandy knew led down into the spacious entertainment room and out onto the patio and pool. The scent of musk was stronger now.

Again Sandy felt her scalp tingling. She angled her head, listening for sounds—voices, sounds of struggle, footsteps. All she heard was the last line of the song. The music thinned to a whisper, died; then all she heard was a haunting quiet and the breeze fingering through it.

Sandy and Nick crept down the stairs to a second-level landing. The sun was on the other side of the house so it was shadowy and cool. Shivery.

Sandy peered into the dark theater on the left, reached inside the door and turned on the lights, and saw no one. She waited while Nick checked a couple of rooms off the landing to the right. Nick was a good partner. She relied on his strength, trusted his street-savvy; she couldn't think of another man she'd rather be with in a tight situation.

Nick came back shaking his head.

Sandy looked downstairs, saw the foot of the pool table. She gripped her revolver with both hands and continued cautiously down the stairs, her pulse racing. "Mr. Pender?"

Someone moaned.

Sandy froze. The moans came from somewhere around the bar that went along the left wall. Sandy stepped down into the entertainment room, Nick just behind her. The pool table dominated the center of the room—a triangle of balls racked and ready. The glass sliding door to the patio was open. Sandy glanced quickly at the video and pinball machines along the wall to the right, saw nothing. O'Neill must have heard their approach and fled out the slider.

Sandy stepped forward and saw a pair of bare feet sticking out from behind the corner of the bar. She crept past the pool table, her pistol pointing at the legs, moving up the length of the body. Bill Pender was leaning against the wall, wearing nothing but his BVDs, his left hand pressed against a bloody mass on the upper right part of his chest, blood seeping through his fingers down his side. He was grimacing in pain.

Sandy stepped toward him. "Mr. Pender?"

Pender opened his eyes, struggling to focus.

Sandy could see relief spreading over his pained face. The scent of musk was very strong. "Where is she?"

Pender shook his head slowly from side to side. His eyes widened.

Nick came up behind Sandy, a shadow thrust against the wall. "I'll check outside," he said. Then he coughed—a barking expulsion of wind.

Sandy felt the weight of Nick's body slamming against her, the jolt knocking her off-balance. She reeled, saw Nick fall to his hands and knees. "Nick? . . . What—?"

She whirled in time to see the blade. Instinctively, Sandy threw her arm up to block it, felt a sharp jolt of pain in her wrist as it connected with the wrist-bone of her assailant, the blow severe enough to knock her revolver, twirling, from her fingertips. Sandy heard it clatter over the hard granite floor.

Time slowed to a crawl.

A corridor of light connected Sandy and the diminutive form of Sharon O'Neill. The woman's face was twisted—human, but not human. Devilish.

Sandy frowned. Sharon O'Neill must have been hiding under the pool table, or behind one of the machines. Assuming that she had fled outside had been a costly mistake—that is what a sane person would have done. But Sharon O'Neill was not a sane person.

She came at Sandy with the knife, howling like a banshee, the howl disembodied and distorted in the unreal slowness of time. Details of color and sound jumped out of a slur of motion—spikes of red hair, blood-spattered T-shirt, faded blue jeans, crazy green eyes. A glint of light over a bloody blade.

Sandy set herself, drove her fist at a blur of white face, felt the jolt through her arm and up into her teeth. It was a solid hit. O'Neill fell back several feet, her nose pushed to one side of her face, obviously broken. Blood gushed down her face and into her mouth. Sandy looked around quickly for her gun, saw it on the floor about ten feet to her left, and started for it.

O'Neill rushed Sandy with a loud shriek, and hit her with the force of an NFL linebacker. Sandy flew back and struck her head hard against the leg of the pool table. A flash of light blinded her momentarily, followed by searing pain. Immediately she felt herself sinking into darkness and fought hard to maintain consciousness. To lose consciousness would be to die.

She jerked open her eyes, caught O'Neill's wrists in time to stop the downward thrust of the blade. O'Neill was on top of her, straddling her body with her legs. She held the handle of the knife with both hands, the bulk of her upper-body weight behind the knife, her legs spread out for support, pushing forward with her toes as she drove the blade downward at Sandy's chest, snarling in her face like some enraged jungle cat.

Clearly at a disadvantage, Sandy fought savagely. She bumped upward with her body, hoping to push O'Neill off-balance, but her timing was off, and O'Neill toed her leg out fast, like a wrestler, to steady her hold. *"No, no, noooo,"* she sang in a deranged voice. *"Can't let you do tha-at."*

Sandy could see the point of the knife below her chin, and knew it must be mere centimeters from her chest. She held back the knife but her strength was waning. The blow to her head had weakened her. Pain stabbed behind her eyes, she felt sick to her stomach, and feared that any moment she might black out. She swung her head to her right: "Help me, Nick!"

Nick was prostrate on the floor, coughing up blood as he groped sloppily for his gun that was lying about a foot from his fingertips. Blood flowed out from his body.

"He's dead!" O'Neill chortled. She pumped the knife at Sandy's chest, chanting, *"Dead, dead, dead . . ."*

Sandy felt a sharp stab of pain in her left shoulder as the knife-point pricked her skin. She pushed the blade free, felt a warm, wet flow from the wound trickling down into her armpit. She knew she could not hold the blade back for long. She was tiring quickly.

O'Neill seemed invigorated, possessed of superhuman strength. She pumped up and down with the knife, strange guttural sounds chuckling deep in her throat. Bloody bubbles blew out of her broken nose and washed over her teeth, a bloody slaver slinging off her chin into Sandy's face. The foul stench of her breath and perfume was nauseating.

Sandy cried out as the knife pricked her chest a second time. She felt the blade penetrate deep into her body tissue, shuddered in pain as the knifepoint probed against her rib cage. Panicked, Sandy pushed desperately against O'Neill's unyielding wrist. *Oh Jesus . . . Help me, Jesus. . . .*

The blade edged reluctantly upward.

O'Neill, growing angrier and angrier that she was not getting her way, redoubled her efforts, chanting, *"Die! Die! Die!"*

Then Sandy felt her grip sliding, and with it, her will—her fighting instinct steadily giving way to flight.

O'Neill shrieked exultantly as she pumped downward with the knife, her eyes glowing with madness. "Here we go. . . . Here we go. Just a little more."

Sandy could not hold her back. She was losing.

O'Neill pumped, chanting—almost tenderly—*"Come on. . . . Be a pal. . . . Die."*

Tears leaked from the corners of Sandy's eyes. She wanted to let go, end the struggle. It would be so easy, so quick.

"Die!"

Yes.

"Did you . . . like . . . what I did . . . to your . . . kitty?" O'Neill hissed through gritted teeth, pumping the knife. "Wasn't it . . . lovely?"

Sandy felt a surge of adrenaline. Her mind cleared, filled with anger. "No!" *It was not lovely, and you will pay for it.* She waited until O'Neill thrust downward, brought her right knee up sharply against O'Neill's backside. Great timing.

O'Neill bucked forward, off-balance, like a novice horseback rider, her face inches from Sandy's. Sandy drove her right fist up into O'Neill's face, knocking the woman tumbling over the floor. Sandy rolled over onto her elbows, looking for her revolver, but saw O'Neill already reaching for it.

Sandy jerked her head at Nick. Nick wasn't moving; his gun was out of reach. There was nothing to do but flee. Sandy leapt to her feet and, running for the slider, heard two overlapping explosions, saw the bullets smash through the glass panes on either side of her, peppering her arms with bits of glass.

Sandy ran zigzagging onto the patio and made for the pool house, which was the only available cover. It was a good 50-yard dash—the pool on her left, nowhere to go on her right—too far to outrun a bullet. She expected to feel the slam of a .38 slug in the middle of her back at any moment.

She heard the gun report, ducked instinctively as the bullet smacked the cement, yards in front of her—a splatter of lead. Suddenly her right leg buckled forward, as though a mule had kicked her from behind, and she felt herself going down. She hit the pavement hard, felt the stinging slap of cement against her palms, and rolled several feet before coming to a halt, facedown.

Sandy blinked dazedly at the pavement as a drop of blood fell from her chest and spattered there. She could hear running footsteps, closing behind her. She scrabbled backward across the patio, dragging her right leg, but it was no use. After about ten feet she stopped, sat up, and grabbed her thigh with one hand to stop the bleeding, pressed against the knife wounds in her chest with the other hand. Then she knew it didn't matter.

The fight was over.

O'Neill had slowed to a long, striding walk, bent forward, pointing the revolver at Sandy with both hands. Her eyes were wild, her face a contortion of parts twisting grotesquely around the flattened, bent-over nose. The lower part of her face dripped with blood, her mouth opening as a strange, *"huh-huh-huh"* giggling sound jerked from the back of her throat.

Sandy knew then she was going to die. For some reason, she was not afraid. Instead she felt a balm of peace spreading over her mind and body—a peace that surpasses understanding, as her Bible read. She'd had an incredibly blessed life. There were regrets, of course: She would have liked to have had a baby. But the rest of it was clean. "Don't do it," she said calmly.

O'Neill, still giggling, pulled back the hammer on the revolver with both thumbs, the muzzle wavering as she did so. "All right, smarty-pants."

"Think what you're doing. I'm a police officer."

O'Neill stepped forward, pointing the muzzle at Sandy's chest. "Uh-huh, huh-huh, yeah . . . a dead one."

Sandy closed her eyes and waited. She thought of seeing Paul. *BANG!*

Chapter Twenty-Eight

Tom and Dan heard gunshots just after entering Pender's home. Tom, drawing his Sig auto, hit the stairs leading down to the entertainment room at a run. Halfway down the long flight, he heard a third shot. It sounded different from the first two, as though it had come from outside. He took the last dozen stairs two at a time, and hit the ground in a quick stride. His gaze went to Nick Ivankovich lying in a puddle of blood behind the pool table; he didn't appear to be breathing. A bloody butcher's knife lay on the floor. Tom gestured to Dan. "Check him out!"

Tom saw Bill Pender slumped against the bar's wall in his briefs, his right flank covered with blood. His face was drawn and sallow, and he looked to be in a lot of pain. Tom ignored him, striding toward the bullet-riddled glass sliding door as a fourth shot sounded.

Tom tried to imagine a scenario that would leave two big men badly wounded—Nick maybe dead—bullet holes in the slider, and now, gunshots outside. He ran out onto the patio, expecting to see Sandy standing over the body of Sharon O'Neill. He pulled up abruptly, stunned.

Everything was upside down.

The two women were about twenty-five yards away, on the pavement next to the pool. Sandy was lying on her back, Sharon O'Neill stepping toward her with a drawn gun. O'Neill was covered with blood. She leaned warily over Sandy as though inspecting a rattlesnake she'd just shot.

Tom started to shout a warning, when O'Neill pointed the gun at Sandy's head, as though to put an end to the snake. Tom snapped into a crouch and fired, saw the bullet smack into O'Neill's right shoulder. She whirled as though she'd been struck by a sledgehammer, swung around and steadied her footing, a bewildered look on her face. Her right hand, still holding the gun, hung limp at her side, her shoulder smashed.

Sharon O'Neill looked at her shoulder, touched the blood with her fingers as though touching a new stain on her clothing, then blinked stupidly at Tom. She did not appear to be in any pain.

Tom walked steadily toward her, his sights trained on the center of her chest. "Drop the gun, O'Neill! Now!"

Tom recognized Sandy's Colt in her hand. His gaze shifted quickly to Sandy—she looked badly hurt—back to O'Neill. "I said, drop it!"

O'Neill didn't move. Her mouth fell open as though a jaw hinge had broken. Then she cocked her head a little to one side, like a bird inspecting a worm, and Tom saw all the madness surfacing in her eyes. He knew she had decided. Her face screwed up into a twisted grin, she giggled, then took the gun with her left hand and raised it at Tom.

Tom fired, saw the impact of the 9-millimeter slug hitting high in her chest.

O'Neill fell back to the pavement. Seemingly unfazed, she jumped to her feet and ran, pointing the gun at Tom, making a weird giggling noise: *"Huh-uh-huh-huh-huh—"*

Tom fired again, hit her abdomen, and O'Neill fell back, spinning, to the ground. She got up as fast as she'd gone down, running at him again, pointing her gun and giggling, louder and crazier. *"Huh-huh, uh-huh—"*

Tom fired twice more, fast; saw each of his hits in the ten ring. O'Neill bucked off the ground as though she'd been hit with a pile driver, corkscrewed into the pool with a big splash. She floated briefly on her back—her arms and legs spread-eagled, her eyes staring dully at the sky—before rolling over into a dead man's float. It had all happened in the span of a few seconds.

Tom ran over to Sandy, holstering his Sig. She was lying on her back, her arms out at her sides, palms up, fingers twitching spasmodically; her right leg, cocked over the other, was bleeding. Tom's heart sank when he saw the bullet wound in her chest. He stooped, leaned close to her. She was alive. *Thank God.* "Sandy, can you hear me?"

Sandy coughed, grimaced. She was having a difficult time breathing.

There were other wounds below her left shoulder, a bullet wound in her right thigh, but the one in her chest had Tom's full attention. The sucking sound he heard meant the bullet had penetrated a lung. "*Dan!*"

Dan appeared at the door and started toward Tom, his expression grim.

"Sandy, can you hear me? It's Tom."

Sandy's eyes opened sluggishly, took a moment to focus. She seemed disoriented. "Tom?"

"I'm right here, Sandy. Can you breathe okay?"

She winced. "It . . . It hurts."

"I know." Tom unbuttoned her blouse. "Gotta take a look," he said. Sandy watched his eyes as he examined the wound.

The bullet hole was above her right breast, a trickle of blood leaking from the hole. As she struggled to inhale, the hole was sucked inward, like a porpoise's blowhole, then blew out a pink froth of blood around the edges as she exhaled.

Dan huffed up to Tom, took one look at Sandy, and shook his head. "Oh, man, Tommy."

"What's the ETA?"

"Ten minutes."

Tom frowned at the wound. It was almost in the same place where he himself had been hit. He knew that, with a sucking chest wound, there was imminent danger that the air pressure outside her body would separate the parietal and visceral pleura lining her lungs and rib cage, and collapse her lungs. There was also the danger of internal bleeding and shock, both of which could kill her. There were probably a host of other dangers that he'd forgotten, and didn't care to remember. His main objective was to stabilize her until the cavalry arrived. Ten minutes seemed a lifetime. "I'm going to roll you over a bit, Sandy," he said. "Take a look-see, okay?"

Sandy nodded, wincing again.

"I'll be gentle, I promise." Tom carefully rolled her onto her side to see if there was an exit wound. There wasn't. Sandy probably used hollow-points in her revolver. Bad news. Hollow-points were designed for minimum penetration and maximum stopping power. The slugs, once they struck bone or tissue, became little lead mushrooms, propelled by hundreds of foot-pounds of energy that tore through the body like a meat cleaver. He gently rolled Sandy onto her back, mindful of her cervical column.

She blinked at him. "Is it bad?"

Tom forced a smile. "You're gonna be fine," he said, hoping it was true. He inspected the wounds below her left shoulder. They looked like a knife had made them, and were not bleeding terribly. They could wait. He glanced at her wounded thigh. Didn't look like an arterial bleeder, so he'd attend the chest wound first. First priority was to make an airtight bandage. He looked at Dan. "You got any of those beer nuts?"

"Beer nuts?" Dan felt in his coat pockets, a puzzled expression screwing through his face. "Sure."

"Give me the bag—quick. Open it first."

Dan opened the bag and handed it to Tom.

Tom took hold of the bottom corner and flung out the contents. He glanced around the patio, saw what he needed, twenty feet away. "Rinse it off with that hose over there! We need a hermetic seal."

Dan ran over to the garden hose by the planter, hosed off the bag, then ran it back to Tom. "Not very sanitary, Tommy."

"Tough." Tom waited until Sandy exhaled, then placed the empty cellophane bag over the wound and held it there with his hand. He could feel her lungs pulling against the wrapper, her chest rising as it filled with air. "How's that?"

Sandy coughed up a little blood, clenched her eyes shut against a painful tremor.

"Sandy?"

Her teeth chattered as she struggled to breathe, her complexion paling. Tom was worried she might go into shock. "Elevate her legs."

"Ten-four." Dan tore off his coat and carefully folded it under Sandy's legs, inspected both sides of her injured leg. "The bullet passed through, Tommy. Doesn't look like it hit an artery. I'll get the first-aid kit." He got up and started running toward the house.

"Dan—?"

"I'll get the blankets, too!"

"Right." Tom heard several sirens' wails mounting in the distance—police cruisers, by the sound of them.

Sandy's eyes fluttered open, ranged about for focus, then rolled back into their sockets. She was shivering.

"Sandy?" Tom patted her cheek. "Come on—Sandy!"

No response.

Tom patted her cheek, his eyes taut. "Sandy! Can you hear me?" *Don't die. Please don't die.* "Come on, Sandy—wake up!"

Sandy coughed up more blood. Then her eyes rolled open; it seemed she had come back from a long distance. She blinked dully at him. "Tom . . .?"

"Right here, Sandy. Hold on. Rescue ambulance will be here in a minute."

Sandy struggled for breath, winced. "Oh . . . Jesus, help me."

Tom felt the urgency of time. "Sandy, I'm going to roll you back onto your side. It'll help you to breathe a little better." Still holding the cellophane bag in place over the bullet hole, he rolled Sandy onto her wounded side. "How's that?"

Sandy nodded, her eyes and hands clenched shut, holding back the pain. Her breath came in shudders, but she was breathing.

Tom smoothed the hair back from her forehead with his free hand. He knew from personal experience that she was in excruciating pain, that she was incredibly brave. "You're going to be fine."

Sandy's eyes jerked opened. "O'Neill!"

"Don't worry." Tom had forgotten about her. Sharon O'Neill was floating facedown in the pool, drifting toward the edge, a pinkish film spreading over the water's surface. Sandy's gun was still clenched in her dead hand, pointing at the bottom of the pool. Tom shook his head in amazement. Senior Deputy Ken Abrams was right: The 9-millimeter didn't have enough stopping power. "She must've been on PCP or something," he said. "I hit her five times."

"*Shetani,*" Sandy whispered, her teeth chattering.

Tom looked at her. " 'She-what'?"

"Devil." Sandy closed her eyes, coughed, and spat up more blood.

Tom heard police sirens in front of the house. "Shouldn't be long now."

Sandy's breathing became shallow and erratic, her cheeks fluttering as she breathed through the pain. Tom laid the back of his hand against her cheek. Her skin was cool, her pulse rapid. He could see her beginning to sink. "Sandy?" He patted her cheek. "Don't go away. Come on, Sandy—don't quit!"

She came back as though from a long deep sleep, her eyes rolling open, settling, staring dully through Tom. "Nick?"

"It's Tom. Hold on, now." The high/low sirens' blare of a rescue ambulance and an engine company mounted in the distance. "Here they come," Tom said. "Thank God."

"Yes. . . . Thank God." Sandy's voice was barely a whisper. "Tom?"

"Right here, Sandy."

"But *why* . . . are you here?" Sandy clamped her jaw against intermittent stabs of pain. "Did you . . . follow me?"

Tom wiped a dribble of blood off her chin. "We'll talk about it later."

A weak smile formed at the corners of Sandy's mouth. "I like it . . . when you follow me, Tom." Sandy's lips were beginning to turn blue, her skin a ghostly pallor. She needed oxygen. Then her smile faded, her eyes released their focus, and Tom saw that she was going away.

"Sandy? Stay with me, Sandy!" He felt her carotid artery. Weak pulse. "Please stay with me." He could see her eyes rolling beneath her lids. "Come on, Sandy—fight! *Fight!*"

Chapter Twenty-Nine

Burbank. St. Joseph Medical Center.
Saturday afternoon.

Tom stared numbly at the gray-blue carpet between his feet. He was sitting in the waiting room down the hall from the OR, where the surgeons had been working on Sandy for over three hours. There had been no word on how the surgery was progressing. He felt hollow inside. He had not eaten since breakfast, but he was not hungry. The hollowness he felt came from worry and fear that ate away at his hope.

The weather had changed since the morning. Dark clouds pushed through the sky and moved over the sun like huge gray barges, drawing intermittent gloom over the room and over the square of sunlight that moved imperceptibly over the carpet. He sat there, elbows bent on knees, head low between his shoulders, holding back the dread of Sandy dying with all the force of his will.

There was a large television set in the corner of the room. The sound was turned off but he could see a news reporter in front of Bill Pender's house. Tom had already seen the report several times. There was a circus of police, paramedicals, and news media in front of the house. Inset photos of Pender, O'Neill, and Hiroko Fujiyama appeared in the upper right corner. The reporter went on talking without sound as photos of Nick and Sandy replaced the first photos. Tom had memorized the report.

The reporter gave a brief history of Nick's public service and his family; then went on to report that Sandy was in critical condition, that she was the daughter of a successful contractor, and that her brother Paul had been murdered ten years ago and the case was still open. At this point the report showed Sandy being rushed out to the rescue ambulance, with Tom extending his hand toward one of the cameras. Finally the coverage shifted to a helicopter shot of Pender's house and backyard, the body of Sharon O'Neill in a bag on the pavement by the pool, looking small, police officials from LASO and Burbank milling about. An inset photo of Tom appeared in the upper right corner, then the coverage ended with the reporter in front of the house, speculating on what had happened and why. They would likely be showing the report all day. It was big news.

Tom glanced out the window to the left of the television at the Santa Monica Mountains—the skyline of hills dulled by a fine brown haze—then once again looked down between his feet with the feeling of dread heavy upon him. He was glad that the sound on the television was turned off.

"You're Detective Rigby, aren't you?" a female voice asked.

Tom looked up and stood. "Yes."

An attractive woman, probably in her mid-sixties, smiled at him. She had been sitting across the room with her husband. Tom recognized them from the photograph in Sandy's home, but had not wanted to disturb them, as he himself had not wished to be disturbed. "I knew it was you from the news report," the woman said.

Standing behind her was a man about Tom's height. He could see Sandy's features in each of their faces. "You're Sandy's parents."

The woman nodded. "Yes. I'm Connie." She took Tom's hand and held it with both hands, looking up into his face. She was wearing blue jeans and a sweatshirt, her sandalwood blonde hair cut shoulder-length with streaks of gray, her eyes a smoky blue-gray. Tom could see where Sandy got her looks.

"I'm Tom," he said, extending his hand toward Sandy's father.

Mr. Cameron stepped forward. "Max," he said. He was a big man, maybe 220 pounds. His face was tanned and weathered from the sun; his hands were callused; and he shook hands like he meant it.

"They won't tell us anything," Connie said.

"No." Tom shook his head. "I'm really sorry about this. If only I had got there sooner."

"The officer downstairs told us you saved her life." Connie's eyes were suffused with tears. She looked away. "I said I wasn't going to do this." She shook her head. "It's just the waiting." She smiled, holding her hands. "We must have faith, mustn't we?"

Tom did not respond.

Max took his wife's arm. "Come on, honey. Tom must be exhausted." He walked her back across the room, where they sat down.

Tom felt lousy. He walked out into the hall, looked down at the double doors of the operating room. An orderly was pushing a cart of linen toward him. He walked back into the waiting room and sat down. There was a crucifix on the wall, but it meant nothing to Tom since he was not Roman Catholic. He didn't know what he was, for that matter—a spiritual mongrel, perhaps. He stared at the floor, his lips moving silently over the words: *Not for me, God, but for Sandy.*

A cloud passed outside and the room winked in the half-light, the temperature cooling, then warming as sunlight spilled back in through the window. Tom heard footsteps in the hall. Moments later, Dan walked into the waiting room holding a cardboard box with sandwiches and two cans of soda. "Any news?"

Tom shook his head.

Dan set the box down on the table next to Tom. "Brought you some lunch."

"No thanks."

"You gotta eat. Here." Dan handed Tom a sandwich.

Tom took a bite and set it back down in the box.

"She'll be okay, Tommy," Dan said, eating.

Tom touched the fingertips of one hand against the other, making an image of a spider on a mirror. "Any news on Pender?"

"They've got him in an ICU ward at Cedars-Sinai. He's not going anywhere."

"Mr. 'Man on the Move.'" Tom rubbed his hands together, looked across the room, and saw Connie's eyes closed. Max was staring at the muted television.

"Those her parents?"

"Yes."

"I figure God has to be some kind of shortstop, fielding all those prayers coming at Him, fast and furious. Some of them are bad hoppers, too, I'll bet."

Tom didn't want to talk about it. "Did you find anything in Pender's office?"

Dan was watching the television. "It was just like you said, Tommy."

Tom grunted. His mind was not on the case, but on how Sandy was doing. They were taking an awfully long time. He heard footsteps outside in the hall. A nun and a nurse walked by, going the opposite direction. Then two men walked into the room: Lieutenants Stenton and Ubersahl. Stenton was carrying a briefcase with one hand and blowing his nose with the other. He looked miserable. His face was drawn, his eyes red and watery; he was in the head-cold phase of whatever it was that was going around. He was wearing gray sweats, sneakers, and a red wind-breaker, a definite breach from his sartorial protocol.

"He looks like he's bucking for sainthood," Dan said. "Maybe he figures one of the nuns will put in a good word for him."

Stenton wiped his nose. "How're things going, Tom?"

"Okay."

"This is Lieutenant Ubersahl from LASO."

Tom nodded. "Lieutenant."

Ubersahl was standing broom-handle straight, his head shaved except for a half-inch buzz on top, his eyes a gunmetal-gray intensity that seemed to be a challenge to any other male in the room. Tom could almost feel his chest hairs bristling from the sudden influx of testosterone.

"No news on Detective Cameron?" Ubersahl asked.

"Not yet. Sorry about your man Nick."

Ubersahl nodded sharply, looked over at the Camerons, who were watching them. "He was a good man."

Stenton gestured vaguely with his hand. "The lieutenant's got something that will tie this together, Tom. Shows pretty solidly that O'Neill killed both Chandra Tupelo and Wendy Burgess."

Ubersahl handed Tom a manila folder then put his hands on

his hips, elbows cocked at crisp, 45-degree angles. "What you have there is the transcript from Chandra Tupelo's phone machine."

Tom looked at him.

"We found it in a Dumpster behind O'Neill's condo," Ubersahl said, then headed toward the coffee machine against the back right corner. "It was sitting in a box with a bag of trash over it. Can you beat that?"

Tom glanced through three pages of single-spaced typing, then forcing himself to concentrate, went back and read it carefully. Wendy Burgess had made the call to Chandra Tupelo at 3:58, Monday afternoon, from her office phone. According to the transcript, Burgess had come back to her office the previous Friday evening to finish up some work for the upcoming MIP convention, and while there, overheard a heated argument between Parker Stewart and Bill Pender in Pender's office. Stewart had read something in the trades that day, and accused Pender of stealing his rabbit pitch. He was going to expose Pender with a lawsuit, when his lawyer got back into town from a pre-MIP business junket. When Burgess had learned of Stewart's death on Monday, she'd assumed Pender had had something to do with it.

Tom remembered reading an article in the *Hollywood Reporter,* dated the Friday before Stewart was killed. Tom cocked an eyebrow. So that *was* it, after all. Pender had stolen Stewart's pitch then murdered him to seal the deal—had to act quickly before Stewart spilled the beans to his lawyer.

Dan took a bite of sandwich. "It corroborates what we found in his office, Tommy. Seals up the motive, doesn't it?"

Ubersahl came back, sipping coffee from a Styrofoam cup. "You read the last line?"

Tom was just coming to it.

BURGESS: Please give me a call as soon as you can, Chandra. I don't know what to do about this. Should I go to the police or what? After all, I love him—*Wait!* What is it, Sharon?

O'NEILL: I wanted to show you this schedule. For MIP.

BURGESS: How long have you been standing there? *(Phone disconnects. End of transcript.)*

Tom glanced back through the pages.

"O'Neill had motive and opportunity," Ubersahl said.

"What motive?"

Ubersahl removed a One-Hour Photo envelope from his coat pocket and handed it to Tom. "This is a sampling of photos we found in O'Neill's condo. Motive's pretty clear."

Dan looked on as Tom flipped through the photos. The first four showed walls of photos of Bill Pender. "Sandy was right about the shrine, Tommy," Dan said. The next photo showed a fuzzy image of Pender and O'Neill on a computer screen. "Take a look at that."

Tom grunted. The rest were mostly candid shots of Wendy Burgess: a couple of Burgess and Pender on the town, one showing the happy couple skinny-dipping in his pool. "O'Neill wanted Pender. Burgess was in her way."

"Right." Ubersahl sipped his coffee. "The transcript reveals she posed a threat to him. Take a look at the next one."

Tom found himself staring at a photo of Sandy sitting at a poolside table with Pender, the photo favoring Sandy. Sandy was the subject. It was a good picture of her, the sun on her face showing the beautiful lines of her profile. Tom held back a groan.

"That's just one of a whole roll," Ubersahl said, cocking his free hand on his hip. "Pretty clear she was stalking Sandy."

"You said she had opportunity? O'Neill told Sandy she went to the gym after work on Tuesday."

"She lied. Co-workers said she left work around six. We know from her phone records that she called Chandra Tupelo from her house at ten after seven. That's thirty minutes or so after Burgess's death. That leaves a window of an hour and ten minutes, from the time she left the office to when she made the call. Where was she? She wasn't seen at the gym—we checked. An hour and ten minutes is just enough time for her to drive to Burgess's house—allowing for traffic—shove her into the tub, then drive home and make the Tupelo call."

Tom made a mental calculation. The drive time fit. "You're not buying the Steven Weber theory?"

"Not anymore."

Dan washed down his sandwich with a swig of soda. "He must've gotten there right after O'Neill left."

Ubersahl nodded sharply. "That's the way we figure it."

Tom thought about it a moment. "Now she needs the phone machine."

"Right. She proceeded to call Tupelo's number every fifteen, twenty minutes, straight through the night, and throughout the next day. Sometimes five minutes apart. The calls stopped Wednesday night, at nine-ten. At nine forty-two, Tupelo's dead." Ubersahl paused to let Tom fill in the blanks.

Tom grunted. The evidence was circumstantial, but the pieces fit. O'Neill had heard Burgess leaving Tupelo a message—a message threatening her would-be lover, Bill Pender. Burgess knew that Chandra Tupelo was out of town (Tom remembered Pender mentioning it to her in his office); hence the phone vigil. She had to either stop Tupelo from hearing the message, or from doing anything about it if Chandra did hear it. Once O'Neill knew that Tupelo was back in her house, she had a window of about twenty minutes to drive across town and kill her.

Stenton stifled a sneeze. "Seems pretty straight-up, Tom."

Tom frowned.

Ubersahl's fingers drummed against his hip. "Something wrong with the scenario, Sergeant?"

Tom felt the lieutenant's eyes probing him. He was in no mood to play I'm Alpha Male, You're Not. He handed the photos back to him. "Why did she kill Chandra Tupelo? Why didn't she just break into her house and steal the phone machine?"

Stenton looked at Ubersahl.

Ubersahl shrugged. "We know that Pender hit on her when they were both at ACN. With Burgess out of the way, maybe O'Neill figured Pender would cook it up again. He 'missed her,' according to Detective Cameron. Who knows? The photos show that O'Neill was a stalker. She planned to eliminate anyone she thought was a threat to her relationship with Bill Pender."

Stenton sneezed.

Dan shielded himself. "Oh, man, Joe!"

Stenton blew his nose. "Sorry." He looked like death warmed over. "What do you think, Tom?"

Tom didn't want to talk about O'Neill anymore. He looked at Dan. "You said you found something in Pender's office?"

Dan thumbed at Stenton.

Stenton opened his briefcase and extracted a file. "Here you go. The first one is a copy of Stewart's pitch that we dragged off his computer. The second one is a copy of Pender's *Rocket Rodents*. Check 'em out. The two concepts are nearly identical."

Tom glanced through both pitches. It was true. The heroine was described almost verbatim. Same cast of bad guys, more or less. Same arsenal of technohardware guaranteed to sell billions of toys. The names were changed, but hey: *"A cartoon of another name would sell as many toys."*

Dan and Stenton blinked at him.

Tom raised his eyebrows. Okay, it fit: all three angles. Bill Pender had murdered Parker Stewart for his idea. Sharon O'Neill had murdered Wendy Burgess and Chandra Tupelo to protect him—a love triangle with an edge of crazy. Tom and Sandy were both correct: It worked on both the pitch and sexual levels. The rest of it—Hiroko and Pender, little Rhubarb—was the work of the devil. *Shetani.*

"You guys've been busy," Tom said, closing the file.

"The DA wants to move quickly on this," Stenton said. "It's pretty clear that Pender stole Stewart's idea then killed him for it."

Ubersahl tossed his empty coffee cup into a trash receptacle. "So, that drawing you found—drawing number five—had something to do with Stewart's pitch?"

"Looks like it." Tom handed him the file.

Ubersahl glanced through the file, shaking his head. "A lousy cartoon."

"It's all about ideas, Lieutenant—cartoons or missile systems, doesn't matter. If someone will pay money for it, someone will kill for it."

Dan grinned. "Tell him about Mickey, Tommy. Tell him how the mouse ratted on him."

Tom heard footsteps in the hall. A tall, olive-skinned man in scrubs came into the room, his mask pulled down off his face. It was Dr. Wharton, the chief surgeon. He looked whipped. "Mr. and Mrs. Cameron?"

The Camerons stood and stepped forward tentatively, Max's arm around his wife. They were both looking at the doctor. Everyone in the room was looking at the doctor. Tom searched his face for any indication of success or failure.

The man would've made a good poker player.

Chapter Thirty

Five days later

The nurse in ICU told Tom they had moved Sandy into a room on the fourth floor. A good sign. He went into the gift shop, bought the most expensive flower arrangement available, then headed to the elevators. Once upstairs, he walked down the hall, turned into the room, and saw Connie and Max Cameron sitting at the foot of the bed, next to the window. Max was reading a magazine; Connie smiled as he entered. They looked tired but happy.

Sandy was lying in bed, sleeping, her upper body slightly elevated in a square of sunlight. Her head was bandaged; her arms were at her sides over the blanket. An IV tube was attached to her right wrist; there was an oxygen tube clipped to her nose. Tom stood at the foot of the bed, watching her sleep. She opened her eyes, focused dully on Tom. "There you are," she said weakly.

Tom cleared his throat of emotion. "How're you feeling?"

"Better." There were hollows in her cheeks, the skin around her eyes was dark, her eyes glassy with medication. She looked very tired.

Tom remembered his flowers with an embarrassed shrug. "These are for you," he said.

She followed him with her eyes as he walked over and set the flowers on the table next to her bed. There were balloons and "Get Well" cards and other floral arrangements from friends and fellow officers. She was a popular lady.

"Thank you," she said, talking slowly and sounding slightly nasal from the oxygen tube. "They're very pretty."

Tom stood beside the bed, looking down at her. Her color was better, and he felt his heart move, seeing how beautiful she was in the light streaming through the window. He was very happy that she was all right.

"Have you been sailing?" she asked.

"How did you know?"

"I'm a detective, remember? You're wearing your windbreaker. And your hair is all messy."

Tom combed his hair with his fingers. "How's that?"

Sandy smiled. "You still owe me a trip, you know."

Tom looked over at the Camerons. Connie was smiling at him; Max was looking at him over his reading glasses.

"You've met my parents?"

Tom nodded. "The other day."

"Tom has been here round-the-clock," Connie said. "We sent him home last night—didn't we, Max?"

Max lowered his magazine. "Couldn't get rid of him."

Sandy looked at Tom. "Really?"

He shrugged. "You were sleeping."

Connie made to get up. "Have you come to relieve us?"

Tom shook his head. "You don't have to leave."

"Nonsense." Connie patted Sandy's feet and stood. "We're going to go and have lunch, dear. We'll be back in a little while."

Max looked at his watch. "Is it time for lunch already? Oh . . . right, lunch."

Tom watched them leave, then stood for a moment in the quiet of the room, feeling a bit awkward.

Sandy patted her hand on the blanket. Tom came around and sat down in the chair by the window. "You gave us quite a scare," he said.

She rolled her palm open toward him and he took her hand. Her hand was cool; her fingers folded inside his like a wounded bird. They were content looking at each other without speaking.

After several moments, her gaze ranged away from him, found a focus somewhere beyond the ceiling. Tears trickled down her cheeks and spilled upon the pillow. "I can still see Nick shrugging those big shoulders."

Tom patted her hand.

She blinked back the tears. "Poor Mary. Those lovely children." She swallowed then touched her throat, wincing.

Tom leaned forward. "Are you all right?"

"I'm fine. That tube they stuck down my throat—" She rolled her head toward him. "What happened, Tom?"

"We don't have to talk about it now."

"I want to know. It's all such a blur." She touched his hand. "How did you know we were going to be at Pender's?"

"I didn't."

She frowned. "I asked you this before, didn't I?"

Tom smiled. "Dan and I were on our way there to arrest Bill Pender. He killed Parker Stewart."

She blinked at him sleepily.

"He used a videoconferencing device." Tom could see she didn't understand. He grinned. "The idea came to me when I was looking at myself in the mirror."

"Aren't you clever?"

"I'm a genius." Tom smoothed his fingers over her hand, feeling the smooth texture of her skin as he briefed her on the case. He began with Stewart's pitch. "Pender must've known Stewart was going to steal it from the beginning."

"That's why he passed on it?"

"Right. Pender needed a winner to launch his production career at Panda. Stewart's idea was a winner." Tom explained the *Rocket Rodents* concept and how Stewart had learned about it in the trades. "Pender couldn't risk being exposed with a messy lawsuit, so he killed Parker Stewart."

"How did he do it?" Sandy asked. "With that video thingie?"

"That's right. He needed to act quickly, before Stewart's lawyer got back from France . . . make it look like a suicide. He also needed to establish an alibi, in case we didn't buy it, so he cooked up the videoconference idea. That way, he could be in two places at the same time—one real, one illusory."

Sandy frowned.

"The coroner estimated that Stewart was killed around five o'clock. At five o'clock Pender was in a videoconference with Japan and Hiroko Fujiyama, supposedly miles away in his office. Only, he wasn't in his office; he was in Stewart's studio."

Tom saw Sandy struggling to stay awake. "I'm listening," she said. "Two places at the same time. What gave him away?"

Tom smiled. "Mickey Mouse."

She slid her eyes toward him.

Tom explained: "When Hiroko told me that Pender was alone except for Mickey Mouse, I thought it was a joke. It *was* a joke, but she really had seen Mickey in the room with him—the Mickey Mouse telephone on Stewart's computer desk."

"What if he'd held the conference in another room where there was a Mickey?"

"No. Pender told me he was in his conference room at Panda. There are no Mickey phones, or even posters, in the conference room."

"Just foxhunts."

"Right."

Sandy looked past Tom, as though viewing the crime photos in her mind. "Couldn't they see he was in Stewart's room?"

"The camera was pushed in tight on him. . . . He was 'larger than life,' as Hiroko said. He might've filled most of the screen. Also, he could've adjusted the depth of field on his device—pushed the background out of focus." Tom shrugged. "I don't know. . . . It was a risk he took. It would've worked, too, except for Mickey. Mickey was in the foreground."

Sandy closed her eyes, her thumb brushing lightly over Tom's hand. "Pender was attaching a conferencing device to his monitor when I interviewed him."

"Reattaching it, you mean."

She nodded. "Did he hook it up to Stewart's computer?"

"No. If he did that, the conference would have gone through Stewart's phone line. The phone company would have a record of the call. Pender had to bring his own computer—probably a laptop—one with an ISDN line to handle the video. All he had to do was attach a conferencing device to it, run it through a cell phone, and—*Bingo!*—two places at the same time. No one suspected anything. Hiroko certainly didn't."

Sandy opened her eyes. "Any record of the call?"

Tom nodded. "We checked Pender's cell-phone records for last Sunday. There was a long-distance call to Japan, between five and nine."

Sandy grunted. "The whole time Stewart's body is lying on the floor next to him, Pender's cutting deals with Japan?"

"He's a pretty cool customer," Tom said. "He probably held the Beretta to Stewart's head, forced him to erase everything he had on his rabbit pitch, then pulled the trigger."

"Pender had to know you'd drag his computer; you'd find the pitch."

Tom shrugged. "The rabbit pitch was just one document in hundreds that were erased. Who'd know it was important? Besides, Pender could always claim he genuinely thought it was his own idea. With copyright infringement you have to prove intent. Very tricky with intellectual properties."

Sandy gazed at Tom's hand, her thumb still stroking it gently. "What about the powder residue on Stewart's left hand?"

"Simple. Stewart fired the gun."

Sandy frowned.

"Pender knew that without powder residue we'd know it was murder," Tom said. "So he put the gun in Stewart's dead hand and fired it into a container of some kind, filled with sand. That's where the sand in the carpet came from."

"The sand around his pool. All those palm trees."

"Right. My guess is, he brought a briefcase full of it with him. When he fired the second round into it, some of the sand was kicked up by the impact and dusted the carpet. Pender picked up the ejected casing, left the other one for us, then made sure Stewart's prints were all over the gun, magazine, and shells."

"If he's that clever, why would he only use Stewart's right hand to type out the suicide note?" Sandy shifted her position slightly, and Tom felt her fingers tensing.

"Shall I call the nurse?"

She shook her head. "It's nothing. They've got me on a morphine drip. I'm in La-la Land."

Tom was not convinced. "We can talk about this later."

"No. Keep talking; I'm just going to rest my eyes a little bit. I'm listening."

"My guess is, the note was an afterthought," Tom said, watching her closely. "Pender couldn't type the note with Stewart's left hand, since his fingers were now covered with gun shot residue. Residue would've gotten on the keys."

"Couldn't very well have someone who'd just shot himself typing out suicide notes, could we?"

"No. So Pender used his right hand. Maybe he hoped that with all the evidence pointing to suicide, no one would get too ruffled by a one-handed note. Shoot. . . . I figured he typed the note right-handed while holding the gun with his left. That's how it would've gone down, too, except for drawing number five."

Sandy opened her eyes. "I forgot about drawing number five."

"So did Pender. That was a mistake. Leaving a single drawing in the scanner got us to thinking there was more to Stewart's death than a suicide." Tom chuckled humorlessly. "Bit of an irony, isn't it?"

"How so?"

"Pender killed the rabbit's creator, but the rabbit had the last laugh."

Sandy shook her head slowly. "I thought cartoons were supposed to be fun."

"Some are. I'm not so sure about the people who make them, though."

Sandy's fingers went limp, and Tom saw she was asleep. Her mouth parted slightly as she breathed through the oxygen tube. Tom sat watching her, the sun on her face as he held her hand. He realized that he cared very much for this woman, could not think of what his life would be like without her in it. He smoothed her fingers gently with his, thinking, watching her sleep until the Camerons came back from lunch.

Two weeks later. Friday, 9:45 A.M.

Sandy was lying on her sofa at home, her head resting back on a large pillow. The house was quiet except for the ticking of the grandfather clock, the cawing of crows outside. The windows were cracked open, the air cool and breezing through the room with the scent of spring flowers.

As she reached for her journal on the side table, she felt a twinge of pain in her chest and knew that the Percodan was wearing off. The clock told her she had another fifteen minutes before she could take her next dose. She could wait. It felt good to be alive, pain and all.

Dear Paul,

I'm feeling much better today, praise God. The doctor says I'm healing quickly, and should be up and about in a few weeks. A few weeks! I know I'm going to go nuts lying around the house like this, but who's complaining? It'll give me a chance to catch up on my reading—maybe even work on your case without distractions."

The doorbell rang. Sandy looked up. *So much for no distractions.* "Who is it?"

The front door opened and Tom put his head into the house. "It's me, Sandy. Don't get up."

Sandy set her journal down, ignoring another prick of pain, and smiled. Tom was a distraction she looked forward to. "Come on in, Tom."

He walked toward her, holding a light-blue plastic container behind his back, a weird grin on his face. "I brought you something." He looked like a little boy hiding a present.

"What did you do?"

"Here." Tom set the container on the floor beside her. A box with rounded edges, about two feet in length, a foot in height and width. There were holes in the sides, a wire door in front. Something furry moved inside.

"What is it?"

Tom opened the wire door and removed a black-and-white kitten. There was a blue ribbon tied around its neck.

Sandy's eyes widened. "Tom!"

"I thought he could help keep you company." Tom grinned, looking pleased with himself. "I named him Sylvester. You know—*Sylvester and Tweety?* I was going to name him Tom, after *Tom and Jerry,* but I thought it would get confusing."

Sandy felt her eyes watering. "Thank you, Tom." The kitten batted at her face. Sandy put her nose in his fur and nuzzled him, hearing the kitty purr.

"If you'd like, I can come by every day and feed him. Clean up the kitty box, too."

"That would be nice. Isn't he adorable?" Sandy held up the kitty and looked him over, appraisingly. He had long black fur with white paws, a white belly and blaze on his forehead. Green eyes. Sandy frowned.

"What?" Tom's eyes narrowed. "Is there something wrong? If there's something wrong I can take him back."

Sandy shook her head. " 'Him' is a 'her.'"

Tom looked. "No joke? How can you tell with kittens?"

"Some detective you are."

Tom stood looking down at her, a little embarrassed smile tugging at the corners of his mouth. A thought hung suspended between them. Then she saw the change in his eyes, the thought caught in that darkening blue intensity. Feeling it swell in her breast like the movement of tides, she touched his hand, drew him close to her and they kissed.

The End